AN IRISH KISS NOVEL

SIENNA BLAKE

For my FlexHuddlers,

Especially Sinead, Anna, Gerry and the real *Diarmuid.*

Playlist

Damien Rice – The Blower's Daughter
Paramore – All I Wanted
Hinder – Lips of an Angel
Tom Waits – Hope I Don't Fall in Love With You
Edwin McCain – I'll Be
Theory of a Deadman – Angel
Passenger – Let Her Go
3 Doors Down – Here Without You
Paloma Faith – Only Love Can Hurt Like This

Introduction

Someone very special to me once said that we were the "lucky ones". He meant kids like us with no real family.

Because we got to choose ours.

I chose him. Long before he chose me.

He *is* my family. My soul family.

He and I were never going to be a normal kind of love. We were never going to have it easy. And we would break each other's hearts more times than a heart could break.

He also told me, "Those who deserve you, won't judge you."

If you're prepared to set aside your verdict until the final word is written...

Here is our story.

1

Saoirse

Saoirse [SEER-sha]: means freedom and liberty

Then—Dublin, Ireland

I pressed my ear to the slit in the doorway of my bedroom, listening out for any noises that might warn me as to what to expect this morning. My room was no bigger than a closet, really. But it was *mine* and I could lock it from the inside—thank God. In the distance the leaky tap in our grotty bathroom dripped. Car tires slapped wet on the surface of the road, the pitch of their engines getting higher and louder as they neared, then deepening and fading as they passed. That's called the Doppler Effect, did you know?

Underneath all this was the near-constant melody native to this soggy island, the insistent snare-pattern of rain. Other than that, everything was quiet. For the moment.

My stomach growled, urging me to venture out. I took a deep breath, hitched my old, scuffed backpack—one strap left clinging on by a desperate finger—over one shoulder and slipped out of my room.

The door to my mother's bedroom was partly open. I cringed at the yellowing sheets on her bed, pulled out of the corner and scrunched up under a pale skinny calf. Ma's leg. She never remembered to change her sheets. Or to do the laundry. I did it when I could. When she wasn't passed out on top of them.

I passed through our tiny living space: a ratty couch, a dull grey carpet worn to the bones and a low table littered with empty beer bottles, wrappers, papers, a glass pipe and an empty baggie.

Ma had someone over last night.

That's why I locked myself in my room and covered my ears with my hands and hummed every single Damien Rice song I could remember until the noises stopped and I fell asleep.

I crept into our jammed corner kitchen, stained laminate cupboard doors hanging askew, the cooker flaking with bright mandarin rust.

Ah, shite. Someone had left the bread out on the counter again. I could see mold on the crust through the crinkled plastic. It was so moist in this apartment that mold grew in what felt like hours if you weren't careful. That's why I put the bread in our tiny iced-up freezer. But it didn't mean shite if it wasn't put back.

I opened up the bread packet, pulling out the slices left, hoping that I could salvage a piece by scraping the mold off.

No such luck.

I dumped the end of the bread in the bin, my stomach mewling, wished I could shove it into my ma's face as if she were a bad dog. I felt hot with guilt the instant I had thought it.

I pulled open the pantry cupboard, careful not to disturb the broken door that whined like a bitch in heat, praying that there was something in here I had missed, moving aside the bag of flour and container of clumpy salt.

I dropped my empty hand. My chest burned with fury. For once, I'd love it if Ma would go to the damn store before we ran out of food. Just once I'd love to not have to worry. Just fucking once.

Out of the corner of my eye, there was a flash of movement from her room. I froze. Then noises. The creak of bed springs. The rustle of sheets. "Open ye fookin' mouth," in a guttural voice, followed by the sound of slurping and choking.

I screwed up my nose. Her "friend" was still in there. He'd just woken up by the sounds of it. I backed away. I knew better than to disturb them.

I told my ma off the first time she let a man that

wasn't my da use her body like that. I must have been twelve.

Her hand whipped out so fast it was a blur, the sharp crack piercing the thick air in the room. Pain spread through my cheek like a mislaid firework. I'd been too shocked to move. Too shocked to cry or anything.

My ma had fallen to her knees and wrapped her bony arms around my waist, crying into my hair. "I'm so sorry, baby, I'm just so lonely."

I recoiled at first. I couldn't believe this snivelling creature was my ma. I wanted to shout at her, to shake her. To scream at her until she woke up.

But I understood. Every night when I tucked myself into bed I wanted to cry and moan, too. I wanted to forget.

I lifted my arms and patted her back. "It'll be okay, Ma," I said, 'cause that's what you have to say to make people feel better, even if it wasn't true.

"I'll do better, baby, I promise," she sniffed into my hair.

She always made promises. And broke them. I knew better than to believe her.

With the sound of depravity in my ears, I hurried out of our flat, locking the door behind me, sucking in the crisp air outside.

If Dublin had an armpit, we'd be slipped and forgotten into the musty creases of it. We'd been here in this council flat in the north of Dublin since my ma left Limerick on the west coast last year after my da was locked up.

I paused on the railing near the stairs, as I did every time I left the dump I called "home". From the fifth floor of our council flat we were higher than the other buildings, mainly two-level townhouses or four-level buildings. *Closer to the heavens*, I thought with bitterness.

We were surrounded by grey blocks, clumpy patches of mud and clusters of brave grass that were meant to satisfy as a garden.

I dared to look past our neighbourhood to the area nearby. Tree-lined streets, beautiful brick houses with small trim gardens tended to with loving hands, bushes bursting with roses, and dainty rows of lavender. It was only a few streets away but it might have well been the other side of the country to me.

My chest burned. I hated all of those people in those terrace houses, all those self-important fathers with proper jobs, those overbearing helicopter mothers, all those ungrateful brats with full bellies and laughter in their lungs and no idea how lucky they were. They had no idea what life was really like, what it was to burn and ache and hate and struggle. To feel like you had to fight and kick for every breath because life was holding your head underwater, laughing at you all the while.

I'd learned long ago that I was alone. But that didn't bother me. I knew I couldn't count on anyone else except for myself.

"You want a what?" The guy over the counter of the convenience store stared at me.

I know what he saw—a skinny kid with untamed frizzy blonde hair. I straightened up as tall as I could. At just five feet two I was small for my age.

"A job," I said.

He shook his head at me, his lips in a smile. "What are you, twelve?"

Hope sank. "I'm fourteen." Almost. In four months.

He clicked his tongue. "You look no older than twelve."

My insides burned. I hated this. I knew I was smart, smarter than most people twice my age, but I was trapped in a prepubescent body that no one would ever take seriously. Trapped with a ma who had no idea how to care for me. Trapped in this fucking life because I was a nobody.

I gritted my teeth, desperation folding into a bitter ball at the back of my throat. "I swear, give me any two numbers and I'll multiply them in my head."

"I don't—"

"Any two numbers. Go on."

Perhaps he heard the warble in my voice proving that I was close to tears, not that I'd ever let them loose. Or perhaps he just wanted to humour me before he told me to fuck off.

He sighed. "Three and twelve."

I glared at him. "Larger numbers. At least three digits each."

"You didn't even—"

"Thirty-six. Now pick two more numbers."

He looked down to the counter and pecked at his calculator. His eyes widened a little before he looked up.

"Alright," he said slowly. "Nine hundred and thirty-two times four hundred and one."

I inhaled. Everything paused in my world as my mind turned like a planet on its own axis, smashing the numbers together like atoms.

I could sense the man behind the counter staring at me. "Look, kid. You don't have to—"

"Three hundred, seventy-three thousand, seven hundred and thirty-two."

His mouth remained open as it was. After a pause he snapped it shut. He tapped at his calculator again then froze.

His face snapped up, eyes searching my body. "You got a calculator on you?"

I almost rolled my eyes. "Yeah, it's called my brain."

He shook his head. "You can't have… But that's… How did you…?"

"I told you. I'm smart."

He stared at me for a beat before he shook his head. "Sorry, kid. I really want to help. Even if I did want to hire you, I can't. If they caught me hiring someone underage, they'd fine me. Can't afford the fine. Sorry."

Underage.

I cursed under my breath, swallowing back the hot sting. I wouldn't legally be able to get a job until I was fifteen. And even then, in this shitty work climate who was going to hire a fifteen year old with no experience and no skills? I knew this was coming. I knew I wouldn't fucking get anywhere with this dumb idea. I just… I had to try, ya know?

I had just hoped… maybe… someone… anyone…

would fight for me.

Just once.

2

Diarmuid

**Diarmuid [DIER-mid]: an Irish mythological hero
with the power to make women fall instantly in love
with him**

Normally, I wouldn't be caught dead in a suit. But I wasn't going to show up here in anything less.

I even wrote that in my will. Left instructions in black and white to whoever survives me to bury me in my favourite pair of worn leather boots, denim jeans, a plain white tee and my black leather jacket that was like a second skin, leather soft as summer butter.

The collars of these ridiculous button-up shirts were

always too tight around my neck, the material strained around my barrel chest like chains making me feel like I couldn't move my arms properly.

I felt like a fake. The stylish effect of a suit looked at odds with my shoulder-length dark hair currently pulled back into a scruffy bun. The hem of my black pants barely hid the scuffed toes of my favourite boots. Even though I shaved that morning, I couldn't hide the long afternoon shadow across my jaw. The cuffed long sleeves couldn't hide the ink glaring out onto the backs of my hands. Yeah, I wasn't fooling anyone in this penguin outfit.

I stepped through the front door of a large house in the north of Limerick on the Emerald Isle's west coast, ignoring the curious looks from the parents and students huddled around near the door. I didn't look like a parent, not one who would have a seventeen- or eighteen-year-old child. But nobody stopped me. Nobody dared to. Sometimes there were advantages to looking the way I did. People rarely questioned me.

Over their heads, I spotted Timmy's mother waving at me from across the living room. I pushed my bulk through the crowd, knocking into shoulders and nearly knocking over a scowling parent with my elbow.

"Diarmuid, so glad you could make it," Timmy's mother said as I stepped into the space beside her. She held an e-cig in her right hand; in the other she held a pint glass with the dregs of a pale lager at the bottom, the glass wet with condensation around her glaring pink fingernails, her glassy eyes and slight sway telling me that it wasn't her first.

She was wearing a vivid pink and white floral dress, a matching jacket over her fleshy shoulders, her unruly auburn curls tamed into one of those fancy updos.

"Wouldn't have missed it for the world, Mrs O'Leary." I leaned in to dry-kiss her cheek, getting a whiff of her rose-heavy perfume.

"Come on now, call me Mary. You make me feel ancient with all this Mrs O'Leary shite."

I grinned and enquired after the rest of her brood—four boys, Timmy was the eldest. Mrs O'Leary answered happily.

"And where's the lovely Ava?" she asked.

"She was going to meet me here," I said, looking at my watch, trying to keep the annoyance out of my voice. "She's probably just running late."

Again.

I stabbed a curt *where r u?* into my phone and hit send.

"Have you seen Timmy? He'll be wantin' to see ye now. Oh, there he is."

I glanced over to where Mrs O'Leary was pointing with her e-cig. My gaze fixed upon the eighteen-year-old boy-man making his way towards us with a grin slashed across his freckled face.

"Jesus, lad," I said, pulling Timmy in for a quick hug and slapping him on the shoulder. "Look at ye." I pulled back, shaking my head as I eyed him over. His suit was secondhand—I knew because I'd gone with him to buy it just for his Debs Ball—but it fit him well, looking nearly new. "You clean up alright."

"So do you, Mr B."

I snorted. Even after three years, he still insisted on calling me that instead of my first name. "You excited for the Debs Ball, are you? Where's your pretty date?"

Timmy's cheeks flushed pink. He'd liked this girl for almost a year before I convinced him to ask her out. "She's attending another pre-drinks. I'm going to meet her there."

"Right, well, I'll let you get back to your friends now. You probably don't want to spend your graduation celebrations with us oldies." I slung my arm around his neck and pulled him to me for another hug. "I'm so proud of you," I said just for him.

"Thanks to you, Mr B. I wouldn't be here if not for you."

This right here, this was why I fucking loved my job.

"You did it all, kid. I just gave you some direction."

I pulled away. He ducked his head and I knew there were tears rimming his eyes. I cleared my throat, blinking back twin stings, and slapped him on his back just a little too hard. "Oh, go on now."

He grinned, gave his ma a quick cuddle, her tears much less guarded, then strode off to a group of his friends, the world at his feet.

When he'd been assigned to me three years ago, he'd been an angry teen, furious at his father for up and leaving him and his ma, lashing out his only way of dealing with his messy turmoil. He'd was about to get kicked out of school for his behaviour. Now look at him, graduated high school with plans for a furniture-making apprenticeship.

My phone buzzed in my pocket. I pulled it out, my spirit dipping when I read the text.

Ava: Sorry babe can't make it have fun

"What's wrong?" Mrs O'Leary asked.

I slipped my phone back into my pocket and shook my head, forcing the smile back on my face. I wasn't about to let my fucking problems take anything away from what should be an evening all about Timothy.

"Oh, nothing. Ava's had something come up so she can't make it," I lied.

Then I changed the subject.

Later that evening, I pulled up on the street out front of my home, a cosy two-bed brick terrace house with a small patch of garden out front.

I had to mow our small lawn. I had to trim back those rose bushes that threatened to climb over the neighbour's low wooden fence and start a riot. Ava had wanted roses. She'd promised she'd keep them trimmed and take care of them. I'd spent an entire day off breaking my back getting those thorny fuckers in the ground for her. She lost interest only weeks later.

Squinting at the grey drizzle that hung around this city like a bad smell, I could see two figures through the front window—Ava's and another that looked like one of her work friends. I switched off the engine to my truck and climbed out, tempering my annoyance.

The sound of two women giggling hit me as I barged through the front door.

I walked into our small living room to find an utter mess. They'd set up camp, it looked like. Cold lumps of cheese in the bottom of a greasy pizza box along with eight or nine empty bottles of Bulmers cider littering the grey carpet.

Dee, one of Ava's girlfriends from work, sat in my armchair, a ciggie in her hand, her dark hair blown out. I fucking hated it when people smoked in the house and Ava knew it. The smell of cigarette smoke brought back too many bad memories.

Anger swirled around in my gut. "You both been here all evening, have ya?"

"Yeah," Dee slurred, oblivious to the tension snapping in the air like rubber bands, "Ava invited me over after work."

"Did she now?" I turned towards my girlfriend of two years, her throat column bobbing as she avoided my eyes. She knew how much Timmy's graduation meant to me. She promised she would come. She broke her promise.

"Babe," Ava began, her voice climbing into a high-pitched whine, "it's not—"

"Time to go home, Dee," I growled.

Ava gasped. "Don't you talk to her—"

"It's *you* I'm thinking about, Ava. I don't think you want your friend here for this...*discussion*, do you?"

Her normally thick lips thinned to a white slash across her made-up face.

Dee hopped up to her feet, her hands going to smooth down her jeans and grab her bag. "I probably should go anyways, Ava. Paddy will shit bricks if I'm home too late."

I glared at my girlfriend as Dee hugged her goodbye, ignoring Dee when she called goodbye to me.

Ava turned to me the moment the door shut behind Dee. "You are such an asshole, Brennan."

"You knew how much Timmy's Debs celebrations meant to me. You promised you'd come."

"I had a bad day at work, okay? Needed a drink."

Every day for Ava was a bad day it seemed. Every day was some excuse. Some complaint.

"Besides, it was just some kid's graduation. He's not even your kid."

Disbelief stabbed me. She didn't get it. She didn't understand that these kids assigned to me might not be my blood but they were *my* kids.

"You fucking promised me, Ava," I roared.

"Baby…" Ava's bottom lip started quivering. "Why are you yelling at me?"

Fuck. Now I felt like a shit.

The fight sagged out of me as Ava tottered towards me, still in her short skirt and blouse from her part-time work at the beauty salon. I stood like a stone as she collapsed in my arms.

"We just need a holiday," she said into my shirt, her fingers roaming my chest, "you and me, baby.

Somewhere warm. Somewhere nice. Majorca. Or Ibiza."

"I can't take a holiday right now." My arm curled around her small waist and I pulled her closer.

She pouted up at me. "Yes, you can. You have so much leave accrued at your job." She smiled, a twinkle growing in her eyes. "It could be *more* than just a holiday, you know?"

I stiffened. "What does that mean?"

"Just think how everyone will react when we come back all tanned and refreshed…and married."

My arm dropped from around her body and I slid out of her grasp. "Now I need a drink."

"Jesus, Diarmuid," she snapped as she followed me into the kitchen, "we've been together for almost three years."

I rubbed my forehead with my hands, a sudden pressure in my skull giving me a throbbing headache. "And it works, doesn't it?" *Most of the time.*

"I swear to God, Diarmuid, if you're stringing me along—"

"I'm not."

I would do the right thing. It just didn't feel like the right thing right now.

But that would change, right?

3

Saoirse

Last day of summer holidays and the sky was thick grey carpet, threatening to rain. Typical Irish weather. Matching my mood.

I scuffed my way down the street, kicking at loose stones, hands shoved in my pockets, jaw set.

What I wouldn't give to be even two years older. Then I could work. I could leave school if I wanted. I could make it out on my own. I'd been taking care of myself since I was twelve. Since my da was taken from us and my ma stopped being a ma. I ground my teeth. I was smarter than most folks. I was "older" in my head than some people twice my age.

But the stupid government mandated an arbitrary

measure, days on this earth, to account for ability or maturity. Until I could work I was reliant on my ma, a woman who couldn't hold a job to save her life, whose idea of "responsible" was to sometimes remember to grab toilet paper when she went out for smokes.

Fuck that. Fuck them. This wasn't fair. But there was nothing—*nothing*—I could do about it. We didn't have child emancipation laws here in Ireland.

"Saoirse," someone called out my name.

I turned around but I couldn't see anyone on the street. My name came again. This time I was able to pinpoint that it was coming from a dark head peeking round a brick wall down a skinny lane that shot off the main street. He waved me over. "Come here."

It was Kian. He lived in the building over from me, that's how he knew who I was. He was a senior at my school, or at least he would be when the new school year started tomorrow.

It seemed to me his auburn hair always glinted amongst the other guys' duller locks. His confident, easy demeanour meant he was always surrounded by those wishing to bask in it, his boisterous unashamed laugh booming across the school grounds.

Whenever he saw me, he'd slow down and walk with me, talked to me like he would anyone else. I liked him. He was one of the few seniors that didn't make me feel like a kid.

"Kian?" I walked towards him.

"Come 'ere." He ducked back around the corner and I followed.

Another small lane shot off this one, just skinny enough to allow two people or a person with a bike to walk past, two tall wooden fences boarding up the sides. Kian was standing with another one of his friends, a rough-looking lad named Darryl, I think. Darryl stood scowling at me, guarding a partly open black backpack at his feet.

A large birch tree grew over one wall, shading the skinny passageway, making it seem darker than it was. The end of the lane kinked round so I couldn't see where it led. The only way anyone could see into the lane is if they walked past the corner I'd just come from.

I slowed down, edging towards them, frowning at the thing in Darryl's curled hand that I couldn't quite make out.

Darryl glared at me, disdain clear on his face. "Why'd you invite this little squirt back 'ere?"

Fuck you, too, asshole.

"Lay off, Dazza. She's alright." Kian nodded to me. "Come on now. We don't bite."

Dazza looked like he'd bite. I wasn't stupid. I knew not to get too close or to trust someone like Dazza.

I paused and stared at the fence where someone had tagged it with "Fuck yous Gards", catching the sharp whiff of paint. This tag was fresh. Right, Darryl's backpack. Those were the tops of paint cans in there. He'd probably just finished this tag, given the paint was still shiny. Wonder how the stupid knacker would react if I corrected his spelling?

Dazza lifted his hand to his face, catching my

attention. A tiny flare of embers between his fingers told me that was a ciggie in his hand. He blew out a cloud of smoke towards me—I knew a fuck off sign when I saw one—and the smell of pot hit my nose. Not a normal ciggie, then. I forced myself to breathe casually through my mouth, not wanting to cough and make a tit out of myself.

"Good summer?" I asked cautiously.

Dazza snorted and muttered something under his breath that I couldn't hear.

"Don't be a dick." Kian punched his shoulder and snatched the joint from him, taking a drag and blowing out smoke rings.

I watched his lips forming the rings. They were interesting lips. Thicker than most boys'. Not as thick as mine. His jaw, I noticed, was dotted with stubble in straining patches.

He must have caught me looking because he turned to me and held out the joint, the smoke waving towards me, causing more of the strong smell to go up my nose.

"Want some?"

I'd never done drugs. Not even something as benign as pot.

I'd seen plenty of drugs lying around our living room, tight green buds, white powder, small opaque crystals. I'd had more than ample opportunity to nick some if I wanted to.

I'd never wanted to. I'd always steered well clear of it because of how much of a loser it turned my ma into. I knew intellectually that it must be "good" or "fun", otherwise why would she do it so often? Why would she put up with the men she brought home if it wasn't to get the stuff off them? Still, the price looked too steep.

But today, curiosity and desire burned in my belly. Maybe it was the complete despondence I felt. Maybe I had just about given up, relegating my life to the shithole I was unfairly thrown into with no way out in sight.

Maybe today I just wanted to rebel. A giant fuck you to my life.

I stepped closer to Kian and reached out my hand, our fingers brushing as I took the joint from him, copying the way he held it between the tip of his thumb and forefinger.

Kian's beautiful lips formed into a smirk. "You ever smoked before?"

I paused before shaking my head. Despite not wanting to look uncool and inexperienced, I knew lying about it would make me look like an utter eejit if I was found out.

"I'm poppin' your pot cherry, then," he said just low enough for me to hear. "Lucky me."

"Aw, fockin' 'ell. Whyd'ya have to waste it on her?" Dazza whined.

I ignored him. So did Kian. My eyes were locked onto his, two pools of sky-blue encouragement. Two pools of acceptance. I felt warm inside. Despite a tiny warning bell in my head, my desire to please him was louder.

"What'll happen to me?" I asked, in a low voice so Dazza wouldn't hear. I didn't want to give him any more

29

reason to complain. He already thought I was too young to hang out with them.

"You'll get relaxed. S'all."

I looked down to the burning joint between my fingers. Something that looked tiny in Kian's fingers looked too large in mine. It was almost as thick as my little finger, about half as long. If I did this...

"I won't let anything happen to ye," Kian said in a low and liquid voice. "Promise."

That was all I needed.

I held the end of the joint to my face and tentatively placed my lips on the rolled paper, noting the bit of card they'd rolled to keep the end formed. I ignored the clanging hesitation and drew in a breath. The smoke hit the back of my throat and lungs like I'd sucked in hot ash.

"Hold your breath for as long as you can."

I began to cough and splutter.

"Steady now," Kian said. "That was a big breath for such a little girl."

"I'm not a girl," I spat out between the coughs I was trying to suppress.

Kian stepped closer—he smelled like smoke and leather from his jacket—took the joint from me and rubbed his free hand across my back. I was so surprised I didn't think to flinch away. No one had ever touched me like that before. It felt...nice.

He chuckled low. "Sure, you're not a girl now. But a woman, right? You can do things only a woman can do, yeah?"

I wasn't sure what he was saying or what he meant.

But something in his tone made me pause.

He drew in a lungful of pot and held his breath. His hand on my back reached up to grab my neck, so quick I couldn't move, pulling my face towards his, his open mouth coming down on mine, breathing out more smoke into my lungs. I sucked in a breath out of instinct.

His lips were cool, a little dry. But it felt good to be held there like that. Felt good to be paid such attention. To be taken care of like he was doing to me.

He let go of me, a smirk playing at his mouth when he pulled back. "You'll be good and fucked up now."

I swayed where I stood. This time I only coughed a little.

Before I could ask what it was I should be feeling, an odd sensation stole over me. Not there one second, there the next. I felt lightheaded, my thoughts turning sticky and ever so slow. My limbs began to tingle. The heaviness of my life lifted, and I felt like I was hung from a hook on the back of a door, not quite touching the ground.

"Fuck," Dazza yelled, his voice cutting through my fog.

"Shit," hissed Kian. His hand moved quick as a flash. Then he turned and ran after Dazza, who was already pelting down the laneway.

Why were they running?

I watched them run as if I were looking through a telescope from far away. I should move too. Run too.

But I couldn't move.

I realised why when a hand came down on my shoulder. In a delayed second, my body feeling like it was submerged in treacle, I looked up. A tall male Garda officer was standing at my side.

"You smoking pot?"

I just stared at him while my mind struggled to work.

The Garda were here.

They knew I was high.

I bit down my anger. Kian just left me here. He promised he wouldn't let anything happen to me. He lied. They all just lie.

Another Garda, a female officer, walked past us and bent down by the backpack Dazza had left on the ground. With the tip of her pen, she pushed open the top of the backpack, exposing the paint cans I had suspected were in there. She looked up to the "art" Dazza had left behind on the wall and frowned.

The male officer who had me by the shoulder clicked his tongue. "Possession of a controlled substance *and* destruction of property."

I didn't need to be smart to know I was in so much trouble.

"You want to tell me what happened here?" he asked.

It's not mine. I know exactly who it belongs to.

I clamped my mouth shut as my da's words came back to me. *Don't fucking talk to the Gards. Never talk to those fuckers.*

The female officer stood staring at the tag on the fence, then at me. "She's barely five feet. Not tall enough to make this tag. One of the two guys who ran off must have done it."

She turned her face towards me. She looked stern,

thin lips set into a line, her dark blonde hair pulled back into a severe bun at her neck under her cap. But her blue eyes betrayed a kind of softness in them.

"Who were those guys? Is that their pot?" She indicated the partial joint on the ground near my feet. Kian must have thrown it down before he ran.

I pressed my lips even tighter together, a rush of clarity cutting through the sticky high. I was no rat. A rat was the worst thing to be.

"If you don't tell us, you'll be in even more trouble."

I was fucked anyway.

But I was no rat.

The officer at my side sighed. "You're coming with us, then."

4

Diarmuid

I had a new assignment.

"Caught smoking pot," the admin girl yelled at me as she threw me my new assignment's file.

I caught it before folding it into my jacket. Bloody paperwork. Seemed like all they wanted to do was drown me in the shit.

A file wouldn't tell me what I needed to know about my new assignment.

She was waiting for me at my desk, sitting with her skinny arms folded over her chest. Blonde hair brushed straight over her slim shoulders, sweetheart face like a tiny angel.

Something kicked in my chest. She barely looked eleven. What the fuck was she doing experimenting with drugs already?

To her credit she didn't flinch, didn't take her eyes off me once, not even as I neared, my six-foot-five frame towering over her. Instead of rounding my desk to sit in my chair, I folded my frame into the creaky plastic chair next to her.

"Hey." I gave her a nod.

She said nothing. She just watched me with sharp green eyes that seemed to cut through me, that seemed to see everything. For a second, I felt like I was the one who was in trouble.

I cleared my throat. "I'm Diarmuid Brennan. What's your name?"

Still nothing.

I tried another question. "What did you get arrested for?"

She raised a thin eyebrow at me. "I'm sure you've got all that information in my file."

Her voice was a lower pitch than I expected, her tone as cool and sure as any adult. Interesting. If I had to bet, she was older than she looked. She was definitely more mature than her prepubescent body signalled. I bet she got underestimated all the time.

"I don't give a shit what's on your file. I want to hear your story from *you*."

"You're not supposed to swear around kids." A hint of a smile danced on her lips.

I made a show of glancing around us. "I don't see any kids around here. Do you?"

Her eyes widened a tad before she schooled her

features back into place. She straightened in her chair. "No, I don't."

"Good. Then let's talk like adults. I'm Diarmuid. You are?" I held out my right hand.

She blinked at me for a second before she slipped her hand into mine. "Saoirse...Quinn."

Her hand was tiny, like a sparrow, soft and breakable in my palm. We shook. I was careful not to squeeze too hard.

"So, what are you here for, Saoirse?"

She made a face. "Possession and destruction of property. *Supposedly.*"

"You're saying you didn't do it?"

She folded her arms over her chest, a classic defensive move. "I'm not saying anything."

I nodded my head. I expected this. It took time to gain someone's trust. And I sensed with her especially, I'd have to earn it.

"Fair enough."

Once again, she studied me, her eyes pausing on the ink on the backs of my hands peeking out from my long-sleeved shirt. "You don't look like a cop."

That was not the first time I'd heard that.

I shot her a knowing look. "You and I both know not to judge people by how they look, don't we?"

Her eyes widened. Then she nodded, slowly. "Yeah."

"Wanna see?"

She nodded and leaned closer to me. I rolled up my sleeves to my elbows to show her more of my ink. I had full sleeves. More on my back, which of course I wasn't

37

about to show her. She leaned in, eyes wide. To my surprise her soft fingers traced some of the vines and lines.

"So pretty," she near whispered.

Pretty? Well, that was new. I'd never had anyone call my ink "pretty" before.

She slid back into her seat.

"So, what happens from here?" she asked, changing the subject.

I glanced at my watch, then up to the door. "Your ma or da should be here soon."

"My da's not around."

I glanced over to her, her mouth drawn into a tight line, her chin tight. This wasn't surprising. Most juveniles who acted out had at least one absent parent.

"Then your ma. Someone should have already contacted her at home. Once she gets here we can talk about what happens."

The rules were clear. I wasn't allowed to reprimand them officially unless a parent or guardian was with them.

Saoirse looked away, folding her skinny arms across her chest again. "We'll be waiting a long time, then."

"She working today?"

"No," Saoirse scoffed. "She doesn't work. She's probably passed out or too busy under someone."

I blinked back as a wave of anger washed through me. Saoirse had to be exaggerating, I tried to tell myself. But I knew that she wasn't. I'd been confronted with too many kids with nightmare home lives to be naïve about it.

I stood up and grabbed my jacket from the back of

my chair. "Come on. I'll take you home and we can have the chats there."

Something akin to horror flashed in Saoirse's eyes.

"Why can't we stay here? I like it here…" she trailed off.

Jesus. What was her home like if she was more comfortable at a police station?

I bent down so I was eye level with her. "Saoirse, I gotta take you home now. But I swear to you, if you ever need to, you can come here, sit in this chair, hang out, whatever, 'kay? Even if I'm not here."

"Whatever." She shrugged. But her eyes grew shiny.

"Come on, little rebel." I held out my hand and she took it.

As I squeezed her tiny hand, my heart squeezed too.

Saoirse was so small she needed help to get in my truck. I held her elbow to assist her, noting how she snatched her arm away from me the second she was in the seat. I even think she rubbed the spot where I touched her when she thought I wasn't looking.

She was still frowning as I hopped into the driver's seat.

"What?" I asked.

She glanced around the refurbished cab with deep red vintage leather bucket seats. "How old is this thing?"

"It's Bedford J type truck. It's a classic!" I pulled out of the station car park and into the streets.

She snorted. "It looks older than you."

"Hey! I'm not even twenty-five. I'm hardly ancient."

She snorted. "Whatever, Grandpa."

Her address was tucked away in her file, which I threw onto my desk before we left the station. "Direct me to your place, will you?"

Saoirse sat up with a firm nod. She took this responsibility way too seriously; it was adorable. And it gave me hope.

Saoirse was a good kid at heart, I could sense it. A kid with guts and bit of fire in her. She had potential. She just needed someone to direct that potential.

I started the car, the radio coming on automatically over the grizzly rumble of the engine.

"What is this music?" she asked as the radio blasted the pop-y rock of some current chart-topping band.

I shrugged. "It's the radio."

Ava usually left it on this channel. I didn't care enough to change it.

Saoirse screwed up her nose. "That is crap. Here. Let me educate you on good music."

She scooted forward and fiddled with the radio, snatches of music playing in between the crackle of dead air.

"The last man who messed with my radio got his fingers broken," I teased.

She let out a snort, a cute little noise. "Good thing I'm not a *man*."

She settled on a channel playing a lilting Irish folk song, a male singer singing about whiskey in the jar. She sank back into her seat, her legs so short they stuck out straight over the end of the seat, her foot tapping away.

I screwed up my nose, trying to pick the band. "Who is this?"

Her mouth dropped open. "The Dubliners."

Now I recognised the song. The Dubliners were an Irish folk band popular in the sixties, seventies and eighties.

I raised an eyebrow at her. "You actually listen to this shite."

"It's quality music! Not like the pop-trash you were listening to." She shook her head. "And you call yourself an Irishman."

I let out a laugh. It came out so freely and easily, like something about this little girl loosened something inside of me.

"This is the kind of music our parents would listen to. Exactly how old are *you*?" I asked, a hint of teasing in my voice.

"Not old enough, apparently," she muttered almost out of hearing range.

We were silent for the rest of the drive, the folk music filling up the car, a low crackle underneath the melody as if it was being played off a record player. Strangely enough, I found myself tapping to the melody.

I could sense her staring at me out of the corner of my eye. I didn't turn my head. I didn't let her know I knew she was watching, studying me. I let her assess me in peace.

This beginning bit with a new assignment was critical. I had to give her plenty of space, give her time. Let her open up to me.

I pulled the truck into an empty spot on the street in front of her commission housing building. I knew this neighbourhood. It was only a few blocks from mine but a whole other world away. She wasn't the first kid to come across my desk from this address.

I helped her out and she led me to her apartment, her feet slowing as we climbed the stairs.

She paused in front of her door, her tiny teeth worrying her bottom lip.

"I grew up in a place a bit like this. Maybe one of these days I can tell you about it. We can compare war stories," I said with a lightness to my tone.

Her green eyes were on me in a flash.

"You don't have to do that," she said fiercely.

"Do what?"

"Try and make me feel better."

I blinked and said nothing. She was switched on, more switched on than most girls her age. Hell, she was more perceptive than most women twice her age.

Saoirse let out a breath and looked back to the door. "Do you mind if you wait out here for a bit?"

She wanted to tidy up the place, most likely. Make sure her mother was decent. Whatever she needed to make herself feel comfortable.

"Sure. Take your time."

She unlocked her door and slipped inside. While I waited for her I leaned against the balcony overlooking the north of Dublin, a sea of dark grey roofs and dirty brick. So much of our lives was determined with the luck of the dice. Where you were born. Who you were born to. Even if we managed to build an "equal society", these things would still remain unequal.

A few minutes later I heard her door unlatch again. Her sweet face peeked out from the doorway. "You can come in now."

She held the door open for me. I walked into her tiny apartment, bracing myself. To my surprise it was relatively tidy, tiny for sure, but there were no dirty dishes in the sink, no ashtrays overflowing with cigarette butts or empty beer bottles in the living room.

A figure rose from the couch and stepped towards me. She looked to be in her forties, older than I expected Saoirse's mother to be, her hair neat and her simple dress conservative but without creases.

"Mr Brennan? I'm Ms Quinn." She held out her hand.

I frowned as I took it, glancing over to Saoirse who was standing at her side. This was not what I expected. She was not what I expected for an absentee mother who'd forget to come to the police station to pick up her daughter.

"Please," I said, "call me Diarmuid. You didn't come to the station."

Ms Quinn brushed at the front of her dress. "Sorry, I couldn't get away early from my shift, see."

Saoirse told me earlier that her ma didn't work. This woman was lying.

I glanced around and noticed only one bedroom door. Saoirse and her mother would have been allocated a two-bedroom apartment from the housing commission.

"Please, have a seat," Ms Quinn said.

I ignored her, striding to a side table where a pile of unopened mail sat. The top envelope was addressed to a Ms Moina Geraghty, of Flat 36.

As I suspected.

I spun round, glaring at Saoirse. "What kind of game are you trying to play with me?"

Her eyes widened. "I don't know what you're talking about."

"This isn't your flat number and that," I pointed to Moina, "isn't your mother."

"Yes, she—"

"Don't bullshit me; I can smell it from a mile away."

I turned to Moina, whose face had gone pale, fingers worrying the front of her apron.

"Ms Geraghty," her eyes bulged out of her head hearing her real name on my lips, "why did you think it was a good idea to lie to a police officer?"

Saoirse spoke up before Moina could. "It's my fault. I convinced her to lie." Saoirse stepped in front of Moina. "She would do anything for me. If anyone should be in trouble, it's me."

I snorted. "You've got balls, Saoirse, I'll give you that much. Come on. Let's go meet your real mother."

I led Saoirse to the door, nodding to a wide-eyed Moina on my way out. "Nice to meet you, despite the false pretenses."

Outside Ms Geraghty's door, Saoirse paused. "Do we have to—"

"Don't make me knock on every door in this damn building."

"Alright already." She sighed.

She walked up the stairs a level, me at her heels, and stopped outside a faded, chipped door.

She turned to me and her face twisted. "My ma...she's..."

"You don't need to be embarrassed in front of me, Saoirse. I know your ma isn't a reflection on you."

"But say...say you see something that you shouldn't see. Will she get in trouble?"

So that was what she was worried about—her mother getting in trouble with the police.

"I'm here for you, not to get your mother in trouble, okay?"

She stared at me for a beat, her teeth worrying her bottom lip. She still didn't believe me. That was okay. Trust would come with time.

"And no lying to me again," I said. "Friends don't lie to each other."

"You're not my friend," she snapped.

"Not yet. But I will be. You'll see. Now, I need to talk to your ma."

"Do you really—" She shut up when she saw the stern look on my face.

She pulled out a key and unlocked her door. I followed her in.

It was worse than I expected. Dirty dishes piled in the kitchen sink and across the counter, overflowing ashtrays, a glass pipe and an empty baggy beside it, empty

45

beer bottles, pizza boxes. The place looked like it hadn't been cleaned in years, stinking of stale cigarettes and something sour.

Saoirse picked her way through the mess towards an open door, through which I could see a ratty old mattress and yellowing sheets.

"Ma?" Saoirse called as she disappeared into the room.

I wanted to go after her. This whole situation made me want to take Saoirse away from this place, to take her home, keep her there and raise her the way a child should be raised. I always got too close to my kids, but Saoirse... There was something about her that made me feel it even worse than ever.

"I'm busy," I heard a nasally voice croak from inside the room. "Go away."

I bristled. That was no way to speak to anyone, let alone your own flesh and blood. I hadn't even seen her face and already I hated Ms Quinn. I wanted to arrest her and throw her into the cells for a night to teach her a lesson. Or a week.

"Ma," I heard Saoirse's hushed tone as I approached the bedroom, ready to lunge if I so much as sensed a slap or a push coming, "we have company."

"What the fuck did I—?"

"It's the Garda."

There was a pregnant pause. Then a curse. "Fucking hell, Saoirse."

Saoirse appeared at the doorway, her eyes widening to see me so close.

"I'll offer him a cup of tea," she called back to her mother.

Saoirse directed me towards the kitchen table. Of all the surfaces, this one was the least littered. Only a few stacks of magazines and unopened mail.

Saoirse opened her mouth.

"No sugar, splash of milk," I said.

She nodded and walked into the kitchen, turning on the kettle and washing out mugs for the three of us. I thanked her when she slid a mug of tea in front of me and sat down beside me.

Ms Quinn appeared at her doorway, a ratty pink bathrobe wrapped around her gaunt skinny frame.

"Sorry to keep you waiting. Wasn't like I was given any warning that we would have visitors." Ms Quinn shot a glare towards Saoirse, as if the disgusting state of this place was her daughter's fault.

It took every inch of my willpower not to stand up, towering over Ms Quinn as I gave her a piece of my mind.

"The station called you about picking Saoirse up earlier. Seems like I wouldn't have had to come here if you had actually done it," I said, my voice chilly and garnering no argument.

Ms Quinn had the nerve to look fronted, putting her hands on her hips. "Well, I—"

"Sit down, Ms Quinn. Let's get this over with so you can get back to whatever the hell it was that was keeping you so busy from your daughter."

Ms Quinn snapped her mouth shut.

For my work with my kids to run smoothly I usually made sure to charm the parents. I couldn't help the way I was snapping at Ms Quinn. She was failing and failing badly as a mother. I wanted to grab her by her skinny shoulders and shake her until she realised that.

Ms Quinn thrust her chin in the air and strode over to the seat beside me, sitting down and glaring at me, arms folded across her chest. Out of the corner of my eye I could see Saoirse was staring at me, eyes wide.

"Ms Quinn," I began, "my name is Diarmuid Brennan. I'm a juvenile liaison officer with the Dublin North Garda. Have you heard about the juvenile diversion program?"

Ms Quinn shook her head once.

"Instead of arresting and charging minors who have committed criminal offences, we issue them a caution and assign them an officer—in Saoirse's case, me—in the hopes that they won't reoffend."

Ms Quinn glared at Saoirse. "What did you do, you little brat?"

I slammed my fist on the table. Both Ms Quinn and Saoirse jumped in their seats.

"It is in my considerable experience, Ms Quinn, that when a child acts out, it is because there is something wrong *at home*." I didn't bother to hide the accusation in my tone and in my glare.

Ms Quinn's lips pressed together as if she sucked on a lemon. But she didn't say anything.

"I'm here because Saoirse was arrested with possession of marijuana and for destruction of property."

I glanced over to Saoirse. She was sitting back in the chair, her arms tight across her chest, glaring at the wall. "Basically, she was caught with a joint standing in front of a freshly graffitied wall with a backpack containing paint cans."

"It wasn't mine," Saoirse muttered, a look of fury on her face.

"Whose was it?" I asked.

She pressed her lips tightly together.

I thought so. She wasn't going to rat on her friends. Some friends they were though, leaving her behind. I'd heard about the two boys fleeing the scene when the Garda had arrived.

It was acknowledged that the graffiti was too high to have been made by Saoirse. I thought it was unfair that she was being charged with vandalism despite this, just because the backpack filled with cans was in her vicinity.

I knew why the Garda did this. They wanted to use it as leverage to get Saoirse to confess the two boys' names. But she hadn't. This offence was sticking to her even though she didn't deserve it.

Sometimes I hated the way the system worked.

"What happens now?" Ms Quinn asked.

I faced her again. Her demeanour had softened, her eyes skimming over my shoulders and the ink on my forearms, as if she'd only just realised what I looked like. I was used to this kind of reaction from women. Usually my prickly attitude put them off.

"I'll be monitoring Saoirse for the next twelve months that she's assigned to me." I turned to Saoirse.

"Luckily the offence is your first one and it's relatively minor. It'll be wiped from your record when you turn eighteen, *unless* you reoffend another three times, or unless you commit a major felony. Then it's permanent. It'll stay on your adult record. For life. Do you understand what that means? Saoirse, look at me."

She slowly turned her head and our gazes locked, those green fires of defiance boring into me.

"It means you won't be looked at twice for most jobs. There's a stigma, okay. It'll be part of public record. I'm here to make sure this doesn't happen to you."

She snorted and looked away. "Whatever."

"As part of the Young Offenders Program you'll have to check in with me at least once a week for the next year. Got that?" I lied.

The job requirement was that it was a minimum of once a month, but I could tell already that Saoirse needed a more hands-on approach.

Ms Quinn let out a soft laugh. "At least once a week? You'll be around a lot. You'll have to have dinner here with us, you know? You'll practically be family."

"Ms Quinn—"

"Please, call me Patricia." She bent over, squeezing her breasts with her arms and giving me a clear shot down her low top.

Unbelievable.

I wanted to grab Ms Quinn and shake her and scream at her until she understood that her priority should be about raising her kid right.

But I did no such thing.

I caught Saoirse looking at my fisted hands clenched at my sides. I forced them to uncurl. Her eyes shot up and for a moment we just watched each other, a silent song shared between us as thin and haunting as an Irish ballad. She could see my fury at the injustice of her home life, the one place where she should be safe and loved more than anything. No child should go without love. No child should be left behind.

In turn, I saw the flash of surprise in her eyes. She was surprised that I might care enough to be angry at her life. This made me furious, so furious my hands clenched again and my nostrils flared even though I fought not to show the tempest howling through my body. No child should be surprised that someone might care for them. It was their God-given birthright for every child to be loved.

"I won't be coming here for dinner. I'll be coming here to make sure that everything at home is going smoothly." I leaned in to Ms Quinn and heard her gasp under her breath. "This means, *Patricia*, that she needs to be fed properly and this place needs to be clean, is that understood?"

"This place isn't usually like this," she began to defend herself. "If only I'd been given some warning of—"

"Do. You. Understand?" I repeated in a firmer voice.

Patricia nodded and smartly stayed silent.

I turned to the tiny blonde angel, the only bright spot in this filthy apartment. "Do you understand, Saoirse?"

She shrugged her tiny shoulders. "Whatever," she said again.

The helplessness that crashed over me like a merciless wave threatened to drown me. If only I had enough time for every case that came across my desk. If only I *was* enough.

I pushed these thoughts aside. I did what I could. I was one man against an army of darkness. My single efforts were a mere flicker of starlight fighting against the nothingness of the universe. I fought anyway. I gave it my all anyway.

"Where's Saoirse's father?" I asked Patricia, my curiosity getting the better of me. I could read more about it on her file later. But I wanted answers now.

Her mother lifted up a lip. "That no-good bastard. He's in jail, he is."

"I see."

Unfortunately, the statistics for Saoirse reoffending as an adult increased even more with a parent who was already in the system.

I gritted my teeth as I stared at this tiny girl sitting next to me, her tough, mature attitude hiding a vulnerability. Her battle-weary armour guarded a child inside who just wanted to be loved and accepted. For some reason, I wanted to make sure that *she* of all people got that love and affection.

I vowed then and there I'd do whatever I could to make sure she knew that there was a better way of life. I promised myself that she had a bright future ahead of her.

"It's hard, you know, for a single mom. No man around." Patricia laid her hand on my arm, her eyelashes, clumpy with mascara, fluttering.

I saw red. Her daughter was in trouble and all she could think to do was to flirt with the officer that brought her home.

I grabbed Patricia's wrist and pulled her hand off me none too gently. "Make unwanted advances towards me again, *Ms Quinn*, and I will have you arrested for soliciting an officer and for neglecting the dependent in your care."

She spluttered and yanked her hand from me.

I stood, cutting the conversation off there. "We're done here. Walk me out, Saoirse."

The young girl was silent as she led me down the grey concrete stairs to the ground floor. She might have looked like a tiny doll but her soul was old, already hardened and calloused. At thirteen this girl already knew how unfair and cruel life could be. It made me want to rage and scream at the world she'd been born into.

We stopped at my car.

Saoirse turned to me, annoyance clear on her face. "I don't need you to fight my battles for me."

I raised an eyebrow. "Never said you couldn't. I was just making sure that your mother made *my* job easier."

Saoirse snorted and dropped her eyes, toeing a crack on the concrete with her scuffed sneakers, a hole peeling back from one toe.

I couldn't go seven more days without checking in on her.

"You start school tomorrow, yeah?"

She lifted her intelligent eyes to meet mine. "Yeah."

"What time do you start school?"

"Eight fifteen."

"I'll be here tomorrow morning at seven fifteen on the dot to take you to school. Be ready."

Her eyes grew wide for a second before they narrowed, suspicion clearly rolling off her. "Why?"

Why indeed, Diarmuid?

"Part of the program," I lied.

This was *not* part of the program. In fact, there was a line I wasn't supposed to cross in terms of getting too personal with any assignment or their family.

But for some reason, Saoirse blew apart that line for me.

5

Saoirse

Now—Dublin, Ireland

Graduation day. I stood in the row of students from my year. Claire stood at my elbow, giggling and chatting away.

"Jess's parents are letting her have people over at their holiday house in Wexford. They've got, like, eight bedrooms or something. We can all stay the night. It's going to be awesome." She leaned in closer and whispered, "I overheard Luke tell Anna that he could get some gear for the party."

I didn't mind Claire. But I wouldn't call her a friend. She wasn't someone I could tell my secrets to or rely on if

I were in trouble. We just had a lot of classes together.

"Sounds great," I said, no enthusiasm in my voice.

Since my first run-in with pot when I was thirteen I'd not touched the stuff—or anything harder—despite everyone around me experimenting with it. I never felt like I needed to. I'd seen well enough what it did to my ma.

On evenings or weekends I choose instead to work shifts at the corner shop, something I'd been doing since I turned fifteen two years ago, or hide away in Moina's apartment, a blanket around my slim shoulders and curled around a book.

I glanced over the heads of the crowd. I found myself looking for a familiar tall figure, his dark, messy shoulder-length hair tied back in a short ponytail.

Diarmuid Brennan.

Three years and I was still looking for him. Still hoping for him to show up. But like always *he* was never there. He'd broken his promise. He'd left. And he'd never come back.

The principal finished his speech and the parents and siblings cheered for their sons and daughters, brothers and sisters in the rows of graduating students.

But no one cheered for me.

6

Diarmuid

The one good thing about moving back to Limerick from Dublin was getting to see Brian every Sunday for lunch.

I pushed back from the table and patted my belly. "Jesus, B, you really know how to spoil me."

Brian O'Connell had been a JLO, Juvenile Liaison Officer, since the program began in 2001. He'd been a cop even longer.

And he had changed my life for the better.

I would have ended up in jail or dead if not for this man.

Brian snorted, his eyes roaming over the roast chicken carcass and scraps of leftover roast veg on the table. "Still amazes me, boy, how much ye can put away."

I may have been a twenty-eight-year-old man, but he still called me "boy".

"Your fault for making a roast as tasty as that."

His eyes roamed over my muscular figure with a spot of envy in them. "Where the hell do you put it all, is what I want to know."

I shrugged. "I work it off. I don't sit around watching reruns of *Father Ted* all day."

He pointed a fork at me, a piece of potato on the end of it. "Careful, boy. You might be older now but I can still give ye a whopping if need be."

I laughed, snatching the potato off the end and popping it into my mouth.

Damn that was good. Soft and buttery. The only other person who'd ever cooked anything as nice as this for me was...

Saoirse Quinn.

My mind threw up an image of her young face. God, I still regretted the way I'd left things with her. I'd never told her where I'd moved to. I thought it best after...what had happened. It was all my fault.

I thought about her often. Too often, if I was honest with myself. As sad as it may seem, she'd been my best friend at one point. I missed her. I missed that *I* had been the one she came to. I missed the way she used to look at me as if I hung the sun.

I often thought about contacting her again. Then all I'd have to do was to remember what'd happened the last day I saw her and it would squash that urge. She was better off hearing nothing from me. She probably hated me. If she even thought of me.

Regret was a dancer. Day and night, I sighed for her, she spun and twisted for me.

My phone buzzed on the table. Ava's name flashed up on the phone. I gritted my teeth, leaned over to put it on silent, then turned the phone over.

By the look on Brian's face I knew he had seen who had been calling.

He narrowed his eyes at me, glancing to the traitorous phone. "Apparently Ethan kicked her out of his place."

It always amazed me how fast news travelled around here.

"So I'd heard," I said.

"I wondered how long it'd take her to start calling you again."

"I'm not getting back with her."

Not after what she did, hopping into the arms of an old mutual school friend only days after we separated. Ava and I had history. But I'd gotten over the habit of letting her back in. Finally.

I wanted more. I wanted to be…someone's sun. The rising of their day and the centre of their thoughts. I wanted to shine into their life as they moved through mine.

Saoirse and the way she used to look at me flashed into my head. I flicked that away before I could dwell on it or why I had thought of her in this moment.

"I should bloody hope not." Brian threw down his

napkin and crossed his beefy arms. He was always thickset, but after he retired from the force he'd put on a few more pounds. It was all this excellent food he cooked. His *secret wifey skills*, as he liked to joke, even though he was the perennial bachelor. "I never liked her."

Him and everyone else.

"I know," I said, tensing, feeling a lecture coming on.

"You didn't need to marry her, you know? It's not the bloody fifties anymore."

"Brian," I said as a warning.

A warning that he didn't heed. "You stayed too long with her, even after she—"

"Brian!"

"Alright. Alright." He raised his hands. "I'll let it go. For now…"

I let out a breath. "Thank you."

The phone began to ring again. Dear God.

"Don't say anything more," I warned. I stabbed my phone, turning it off this time, praying that Ava would get the hint.

Brian raised his hands, but the look he gave me was a weary warning. *That girl is trouble.*

7

Saoirse

Graduated. I thought I'd feel elated. Excited, maybe. I thought I'd feel *something*. Except I just felt...hollow. Lost.

I sat at our small kitchen table, staring off into nothing, my mind a whirr, my future a blank landscape. What do I do now? What the hell do I do with my life?

If Diarmuid was here, he'd know. My chest squeezed as I allowed myself to miss him more than usual. God, would it ever get any less painful?

A banging on the door jolted me. I whipped my head to the front door. Then to the clock. Ten past nine in the morning on a Sunday.

"Who the fuck is that?" my ma called from her

bedroom.

Who the fuck was it, indeed?

The piece of toast I'd been clutching dropped back onto my plate, and I pushed back from the table with a scrape of the chair legs. I brushed my hands of crumbs as I tiptoed to the door. Debt collectors? One of my ma's boyfriends? Neither prospect felt good to me at all.

The door banged again, this time harder.

"Saoirse? Open up," a male voice called from the other side of the door.

Me? Whoever was on the other side of that door wanted *me*.

For a split second, I thought it might be Diarmuid, finally returned to take me away from this place. As soon as that hope was lit, it was extinguished.

Stupid girl. He doesn't sound anything like Diarmuid. Diarmuid's voice was deep but almost lyrical. This man on the other side of the door, whoever he was, sounded rough and jagged. He sounded older than the few male friends I made in school. Well, not friends really, more guys who occasionally pestered me to "come over".

Who else would it be?

My ma stumbled out of her room, tugging a ratty bathrobe over her underwear. "Don't open it."

I rolled my eyes. They were after me, not her. In an act of defiance, or perhaps I was just so damn bored with life as it was that I'd stopped caring about being cautious, I unlocked the door and flung it open.

Standing there was a man who seemed familiar. Or perhaps he just seemed that way because he looked like almost every other forty-something-year-old Irish man. He had a shaved head, tats peeking up from his leather jacket collar, his fist raised to knock again.

He lowered his fist, his eyes roaming over me, but not in a way that made me uncomfortable. He grinned as his eyes found mine, blue and rimmed with wrinkles when he smiled.

"Saoirse fockin' Quinn, in the fockin' flesh, Jesus Christ, all grown up, like."

I blinked at him. I frowned at this intruder, his face tickling my memory.

My ma gasped from behind me. "What the fuck are you doing here?"

He knew my name. My ma knew him. Which meant… "How do I know you?" I asked.

He held his arm out to the side. "Jase O'Malley. Yer pa's best mate."

The memories slotted into place. I nodded. That's right. My pa and he were as thick as thieves when we lived back in Limerick before my da was locked up and my ma fled with me to Dublin. But he had a thick head of dirty blonde hair back then.

"Uncle Jase," I said.

He grinned wider, revealing a silver-capped canine among crooked teeth. "That's right." His eyes rolled over me again. "Jesus, lass, you've grown up nice, like. I remember when you were crawling around in nappies."

Behind me my ma was hissing. "Go away, Jase." She grabbed at the door, trying to shut it in his face.

Jase stuck out a beefy hand to stop her. He shot her a

glare. "Still being a bitch, I see, Patricia."

"Fuck you."

"No fockin' thanks, love. The years have not been kind to ye." My ma spluttered and howled behind me. Jase ignored her and turned towards me, an affectionate smile stretching across his face. "Get your shit, Saoirse. You're coming with me."

"No, she is not," said my ma. "She's not going anywhere with *you*."

Jase ignored her. "Pack a bag, quick as ye can, girl. We gotta go."

"Where are we going?" I asked, backing up into the house. Already deciding that I'd go with him. Wherever he was going, I didn't care. I'd go anywhere. Anywhere from here. Here was a chance to move forward. To move on. Wherever he was taking me, it'd be better than this fucking hole I was stuck in.

He grinned. "To go pick up your pa. He gets out of prison today."

My ma gasped behind me. "That fucker."

Jase looked up to her and glared at her. "He don't want to see you. Just her."

My da was back.

He promised he'd come get me when he got out.

"Give me ten minutes," I yelled out at Jase and ran into my room.

I grabbed my backpack, the one that Diarmuid bought me, still as sturdy as the day he bought it, and laid it open on the bed. I grabbed the most important thing first. My journal that I hid under the slip of my mattress, tucking it into a pocket carefully before grabbing clothes and throwing them in after it.

My da promised he'd come back. He kept his promise.

My stomach jumbled with nerves. Things would be different now. They'd be better.

My ma grabbed my arm. I hadn't even heard her come in. Her mascara-smudged eyes were wide, anger making her nostrils flare.

"Where the hell do you think you're going?"

I yanked my arm out of her grasp and zipped up my backpack. "You've never cared about me. Don't start pretending you do now."

Her mouth opened. "How dare you speak to me like that."

With the backpack over one shoulder, I shoved past her towards Uncle Jase, who was standing just outside the open front door, smoking a cigarette. He was going to take me to my da. I couldn't wait.

"If you go to that bastard you can never come back 'ere."

"Thank fuck," I yelled back.

I would walk out of here and never look back.

I stopped on the level down and told Jase I'd meet him at his car. I knocked on Moina's apartment door. When she opened the door, her kind, ruddy-cheeked face softened by soft pale curls peering out, I explained that my da had finally come for me and that I was leaving.

"I knew this day would come, girl," Moina said as she gave me a fierce hug. "I just didn't think it'd be so soon."

I squeezed her back just as hard. "I'll miss you. Thank you for everything."

It was about a two-hour drive from Dublin to Limerick. I sat in the passenger seat of Jase's car, my stomach tumbling as the green Irish countryside rolled past once we got out of the outskirts of Dublin.

"So, girl," Jase said, "what are you, twenty, twenty-one now?"

I glanced over to him. His eyes kept flicking to my legs stretched out in front of me, then to my chest, making me want to fold my arms across them. His reaction didn't surprise me.

"I'm *seventeen*," I said clearly.

His eyes widened. "Oh, yeah, right." He looked back to the road. "You don't look seventeen," he mumbled.

Wasn't that the truth. When I was thirteen I would have done anything to look older. Now that I was seventeen, I'd do anything just to look my age.

As we drove closer to Limerick, my guts began to knot up. I'd not seen my da in almost five years. My ma wouldn't let me visit him in prison and we moved to Dublin pretty soon after he was put away. My ma wouldn't even let me go to court with her when he was being tried for drug possession and distribution.

Five years. A lot had changed in five years. I had changed in five years. I imagined five years in prison would have changed him, too.

Limerick hadn't changed, though. I eyed the familiar streets of my childhood as we rolled through town.

When I was younger, I'd lived with my ma in a

council flat in an area south of Limerick. My da had been in and out, living mostly on a property in rural county Limerick, visiting us maybe once every two weeks or so. I'd looked forward to those visits as if they were Christmas. In a way, they had been. My da always brought something home for me, whether it was a new doll or sweets.

We pulled up in front of Limerick prison, an imposing grey stone building. Standing in front of the big green door was my da. Reddish-brown hair, wide jaw and beefy nose. In his mid-forties, he looked so much older than I remembered, wrinkles fanning out from his eyes as he smiled.

Jase pulled up and bounced out of the car, walking right over to him and giving him a quick hug and slaps on the back.

I was slower in unclipping my seatbelt and getting out of my seat, hanging back as the two men eyed each other up.

"Liam," Jase said, calling my da by his first name, "how are ya, ye fucker?"

"Grand, yeah, now that I'm out of that fockin' shithole."

"Jesus, you look good. Been workin' out, yeah?"

"Nothin' much else to do in there."

"Ah, truth."

My da looked up and spied me hanging around the car. He looked like the man of my memories—strong jaw, stubble, and a few more lines around his green eyes, the only physical characteristic I inherited from him. I looked like my ma, but my eyes I got from my da.

The smile from my childhood broke out across his face and my chest warmed. "Jesus Mary Joseph. Is that my little girl?" He took two strides up to me. "Look at ye. All grown up."

"Hi, Da," I said, my voice going all quiet.

"Why you gone all shy, huh? Give yer old man a hug." He closed his arms around me and I was enveloped in familiar smells: tobacco and Old Spice.

I swallowed down the knot in my throat as I held onto him. I didn't realise how much I had missed my da. He was the only man who'd ever kept his promise to me.

I'll come back for ya, baby girl. Promise.

"Jase told me about the state of the place he found you in." My da pulled back to look at me. "I'm sorry I wasn't able to be there for ye while I was in jail. But I'm here now, you hear me?"

He clasped his beefy hand around my neck. I nodded, my throat constricting.

He grinned. "Good. Now let's get the fuck out of here."

Jase drove up to a small two-level terraced house in Dooradoyle, an area of Limerick. It had a grey and white façade, a small patch of garden at the front growing wild and tall with dandelions and weeds.

We pulled up into the short driveway beside a black motorbike. A figure moved out from the alcove of the front entrance. A man, looking to be in his early twenties, ambled over to the car with his hands thrust in his pockets, a grin on his face. He had dirty blonde hair styled in a mess, a lean body in dark skinny jeans and a black leather jacket, a cheeky grin spread across stubble.

My da and Jase got out of the car. I clambered out of the back, grabbing my backpack, all my worldly possessions.

"Malachi, lad," my da said. "Jesus, you've bloody grown, too. How's your old man?"

They clasped hands and did that one-shouldered man-hug. I spotted Malachi whispering something to my da. Da nodded and jerked his head towards Jase. Something unspoken seemed to pass between them.

"Malachi," I heard my da say, "here are the keys. Show my daughter to her room."

"Yes, sir." Malachi looked over to me and our eyes met, interest flaring in them. He grinned as he walked around the car to me.

"Hey." He nodded to me as he came to stand near me, a little too near for someone I just met, in my opinion. "I'm Malachi."

"Saoirse."

His grin widened. "I know."

"Malachi," my da called. He looked over to us and grinned, a stark contrast to the words that next came out of his mouth. "Touch her and I'll fockin' kill ya."

Malachi raised up his hands as if in surrender, but he, too, was smiling.

Men are strange.

Malachi grabbed my backpack off me and nodded

towards the front door. "Follow me, princess."

He took me through the house. It was a little rundown, the old carpet had lost most of its pile and the air was a tad musty from being shut up, but it was cosy: a living room, kitchen and toilet downstairs, three bedrooms and a bathroom upstairs. Malachi showed me to one of the bedrooms, holding the door open for me so that I had to brush past him to get in. He smelled like cigarette smoke and a sharp, spicy cologne.

He handed me my backpack and I unzipped it on the bed, feeling his eyes on me.

"So," Malachi said as he leaned against the doorway all casual like. "You got a boyfriend or something?"

For some stupid reason Diarmuid's face flashed across my mind. "Nope."

"Good."

Good? I raised an eyebrow at him. He grinned back without any self-consciousness.

I folded a jumper in the drawer, making a note to buy some mothballs the next time we were in town. I didn't have a car but would definitely need one if I were to stay here. Dooradoyle was at least a fifteen-minute drive from the city centre. I wondered if my da would let me use his car. If I was going to get work in town, then I'd have to have a car.

A twinge of sadness went through me when I thought of not getting to study this year.

College was technically "free" in Ireland, our fees only three grand per year. But those fees weren't going to pay themselves. Neither would the textbooks and a secondhand computer I'd need to do my coursework. And I still needed to "live". I'd not be able to work and save as much if I was studying. Although maybe now that my da was here, he'd help support me.

I let out a sigh. Anyways it was too late for college this year. The application deadline was well past. I couldn't apply until next year.

"That was a big sigh."

I almost forgot that Malachi was still here, watching me from the doorway.

I shrugged. "Just stuff on my mind."

"Like what? What could such a pretty girl like you have to be worried about?"

"University."

He let out a snort. "Don't think you'll be needing that shite."

"If I want a good job—"

"I thought you were going to work with your da."

I blinked at Malachi. My da wanted me to work with him?

Malachi's mouth dropped open. "Oh shite. He hasn't spoken to ye about it?"

I shook my head.

Malachi gave me a sheepish look. "Well, act surprised when he does."

"Malachi," a voice called up to us from somewhere in the house.

Malachi looked over his shoulder. "I'm going to head down. See what they want. I'll see you soon, yeah? Maybe I can show you round on my bike."

"You have a bike?" That must be his bike out front. Maybe a bike licence would be easier than a car licence. A bike would be cheaper to buy and to run.

He grinned, looking a tad smug. "Yeah."

I nodded. "That'd be grand, yeah, thanks."

He shot me a wink before he left. I turned back to my unpacking in peace, feeling a rush of relief at being alone again.

It took me only a minute to unpack my meager clothes into a chest of drawers. And stick my toiletries into a shared bathroom.

I threw myself across my new double bed. A double bed all to myself. How luxurious. I'd only ever slept on a single bed. And damn this mattress was soft. I couldn't feel the springs in my back.

Maybe this was my new start. My new beginning. I could throw off the young, naïve Saoirse that I'd been and start as a new woman. I could get a job here. Earn some money. Save. Apply to study next year.

Maybe, for once life was giving me a break.

I allowed myself a smile and a small rush of hope and possibilities.

8

Diarmuid

Then—Dublin, Ireland

I let Saoirse into the Sidewalk Café, my favourite local since it opened up a few years ago.

"Hey, Betsy," I called out to the owner/waitress, a short, voluptuous redhead, her curly hair piled into a glorious mess on her head. "Breakfast for two, please."

I directed Saoirse to slide into one of the booths near the window. I slid in opposite her, the hard green leather crackling underneath my bulk.

Betsy strutted up to us with two menus, slipping them in front of Saoirse and me.

"How are you now, Diarmuid?" she asked.

"Grand, yeah, thanks."

Betsy turned her eyes to Saoirse. "Is this your niece or something? You've never bought her in before."

Saoirse scowled. "We're *not* related."

"She's just a friend I'm hanging out with." I shot Betsy a smile. Betsy knew what I did, so I'm sure she suspected that the teens I sometimes brought in here with me were for work, but I never mentioned it out loud. "I'll have a white coffee, please."

"Me, too," Saoirse said.

I turned to her, frowning. "Do you drink coffee, do you?"

Saoirse rolled her eyes. "Don't you tell me I'm *too young* to drink coffee."

I snorted and closed my menu. "Two white coffees and two full Irish breakfasts, thanks, Betsy."

Betsy took the menus and went off to fulfil the order, leaving me alone with Saoirse.

Saoirse leaned back in the booth, head tilted, arms crossed and a defiant glare on her face. She looked so adorable, I almost laughed. I didn't. I didn't think that would go down very well.

"What do you want?" she demanded.

"Well," I said slowly, "breakfast is a start."

She shook her head, her golden hair swishing about her sweetheart face. "I mean, what you want from me? Why you being so damn nice?"

Her words stung with the realisation that this girl had probably never had anyone do anything nice for her without wanting something in return. I clenched my

74

hands into fists under the table so as not to scare her. It was all I could do not to throw the table aside and roar in anger. No child should be this young and this cynical already. So weary of the world.

I tempered my voice when I spoke. "I want for you what I want for all my kids—the possibility of a better life. I want you to get through these next twelve months without reoffending. But right now, I want to get to know you a little over breakfast."

She held my gaze for another second, and I willed for her to see the truth in my face. She glanced away and looked out the window, her chin stubbornly set.

Betsy came with our coffees and breakfast. My mouth watered as I smelled the delicious full Irish breakfast: two eggs, grilled tomato, hash browns, fried mushrooms and blood sausage. For a few minutes, there was nothing but the sound of cutlery scratching on plates and chewing, a Lisa Hannigan song playing in the background.

I started out with a simple question. "Your breakfast good?"

Saoirse nodded before stuffing her mouth full of food. The way she was attacking her plate, you'd think she hadn't eaten in a week. Shit. It was likely she hadn't. Pity coiled on the base of my stomach, making it difficult to swallow my next bite.

"What grade are you in at school?"

"Seven," she mumbled through a mouthful of fried egg.

I repressed the urge to chastise her for talking with

her mouth full. That wasn't my job. My job was to become her friend. Not her substitute parent.

"Do you like your school?"

"S'okay."

"You have a best friend?"

She gave me a one-shouldered shrug, eyes on her blood sausage.

God give me strength, I sent a prayer inward. She wasn't giving me anything.

"You have a favourite subject?"

"Chemistry," she said without hesitation.

I raised an eyebrow at her. I expected... Well, I didn't know what I'd expected her to say, but it definitely wasn't chemistry. I looked at the small, unassuming girl before me. She had practically demolished her entire plate when I thought she would struggle getting through half of it. Shows how much I knew about her.

"Chemistry?" I repeated.

She nodded once solemnly.

"Of all the subjects, why chemistry?"

For the first time during the entire breakfast, Saoirse placed down her cutlery, grabbed a napkin and wiped her mouth. "Are you actually serious?"

"Seriously want to know why you love chemistry so much? Yes."

Her eyes widened and she placed her hands on her chest, inhaling loudly in an overly dramatic fashion.

"Diarmuid Brennan!" She spoke my name with such astonishment and admonishment I almost laughed. She leaned in, resting her fingers on the edge of the table. In a hushed voice, as if she was spilling the secrets of the universe, she said, "Chemistry. Is. Life."

Then, as if she had said nothing of importance, she gathered up her knife and fork and began to tackle her last pieces of food.

I blinked at her. She was pulling my leg. Chemistry? Who the hell loved chemistry?

I cleared my throat. "Tell me more about chemistry, then. Maybe they're teaching it differently from when I went to school."

"You mean a hundred years ago?" she said with a glint in her eye.

"Hey," I protested. "I only graduated five years ago."

"Which makes you around twenty-four." Her eyes did a once-over of me. For some strange reason I felt I was being assessed and somehow came up lacking. "You look older than twenty-four," she finally said, assessment done.

I let out a breath, unaware why I'd been holding it. "You act older than thirteen."

She shrugged. "You and I both know that you can't judge people based on what they look like," she said, using my own words back at me.

I smiled as I thought about how we both looked sitting in this booth to the outside world. Me with the ink covering my arms, the gruff brutish way I appeared, and her with her doll-like stature. We were like oil and water. Like cotton and leather. Light and dark. At least from the outside.

"So, chemistry," I said, putting the subject back on

track. "Tell me why you love it so much."

She popped the last piece of her breakfast into her mouth, chewed and swallowed. She arranged her cutlery across her plate in an angle the way I'd seen people do in fancier restaurants to alert the waiter that they're finished. She wiped her mouth, then leaned back into the booth, one hand resting across her full belly.

"I love math. Numbers just make sense to me. And chemistry is all about numbers and how they relate to life." Her free hand waved as she spoke, her voice growing more passionate. "In chemistry there is no grey, only black and white. It's precise. The outcome is always known. I love the certainty of it. The safety in knowing the outcome beforehand, every time. And I love the idea of combining molecules to create something different, something new, something better."

During her speech, I'd started leaning forward on my elbows, drawn in by the passionate way she spoke, the way she seemed to age almost a decade as she did.

I stared at her. Saoirse's body was that of a girl, but in her head was a mind as sharp and mature as I've ever seen. *You and I both know you can't judge people based on what they look like.* She had a confidence about her that I knew some thirty year olds didn't have.

And yet, there was something so immature, so raw, so naïve about her. Something about her that made me want to nourish her...protect her. More than any kid I'd ever been assigned.

"That's incredible," I said. "I've never heard anyone in my life speak like that about chemistry." *Let alone a thirteen-year-old girl.* "Heck, you make me want to get out all my old high school chemistry textbooks."

She cleared her throat, glancing down into her lap, seemingly uncomfortable with my compliment. "School will be starting soon."

I looked up at the clock on the wall. She was right. It was almost eight o'clock. I didn't want Saoirse to be late on her first day back. I made a motion to Betsy indicating a check.

"The bill should come to 21.32 euro," Saoirse said.

I frowned. "That's a bit of a precise guess."

"It's not a guess. The two breakfasts were 7.87 each plus two coffees at 2.79 each is 21.32 euro."

Betsy slid the bill in front of me before I could say a word. I searched for the total, finding it marked with a blue pen.

Twenty-one euro thirty-two.

My head snapped up. "How did you do that?"

She gave me a look. "Obviously, I looked at the prices before I gave back the menu."

I shook my head. "I mean, how did you add those numbers in your head?"

She shrugged. "It was easy. That's why I like chemistry. I'm good with numbers and stuff."

"You're telling me," I asked slowly, "that you added those numbers up in your head? Do you have like a calculator hidden in your lap or something?"

Saoirse just looked at me.

The gravity of what she just did hit me. I didn't know a single adult who could take those numbers and add them up in their head the way she just did.

"Saoirse, you're really smart."

She let out a long breath as if relieved about something. "I know."

"You could do anything. Whatever you wanted. Go to a good university, get a degree, get a good job. Jesus, you could become a doctor if you bloody wanted to."

She shuffled in her chair, her eyes darting everywhere except for on me. I wondered if anyone had ever given her a compliment before.

"Why the hell do you need to get involved with drugs?" I blurted out.

"I didn't." Her eyes locked onto mine. "None of that weed was mine. It was my first time smoking it."

I nodded, suspecting as much.

"I'm not a rat," she said adamantly.

"I know. I'm not asking you to be one. Jesus," I let out again. "Do your parents know how smart you are? Your teachers?"

Saoirse screwed up her face.

No.

The answer was no. Nobody knew how smart she was. What I wanted to know was, why the hell not?

She had so much potential. She could do something incredible with her life. I vowed on the spot, I'd do everything in my power to make sure her life veered onto the right path. Everything.

9

Saoirse

Stupid girl.

I shouldn't have revealed so much at breakfast. What was the point? Even if Diarmuid knew I was smart, what did it matter?

When Diarmuid dropped me off, he told me that he'd be there after school to pick me up. I merely hitched my backpack over my shoulder and walked away, trying not to let hope rise inside me.

For some reason, I couldn't wait until school finished. I wanted to see him again, I realised. He was the first person who ever treated me like an adult. Like my thoughts and words mattered. Like *I* mattered.

Stupid girl. I should know better than to put my faith

in him. I couldn't rely on anyone. Even my father, who was supposed to be here for me forever, let me down.

"Hey, Saoirse." A familiar male voice broke me out of my thoughts. "Wait up."

Kian ran up to me, his school shirt untucked, the tie around his neck askew and his fancy, probably stolen, Nikkei backpack hanging off one shoulder.

I pressed my lips together, not stopping for him, not even slowing down a little bit. I wanted to tell him to fuck off for leaving me behind and getting me into trouble, but too much of me wanted him to like me still.

He fell into step with me as we walked across the yard towards the front door of the school.

"What's the craic?" he asked.

I shrugged with one shoulder. "Fine, yeah."

"I wasn't sure I'd see you here today."

"Why? You thought I'd be sitting in some cell?" Try as I might, I couldn't help the bitterness that infused my voice.

"Come on, Saoirse. Don't be mad."

I stopped and whirled towards him, making him halt too. I ignored the flow of students who had to break around us like water around rock, staring at us as they passed.

I leaned in, gripping the straps of my backpack so that my nails cut into the material. "*You* left me there."

Remorse broke across his face. "I thought you were right behind me."

"I thought you were my friend."

"I am."

I let out a snort and continued to walk, this time my pace like a march. He jogged up in front of me, opening the front door for me and holding it. I glared at him as I stomped past.

Inside the school building, he continued to follow me down the wide corridor as I walked towards my homeroom on the ground floor, ignoring the guys and girls who called out hello as he passed.

"I'm sorry, Saoirse, really I am."

"Whatever."

He grabbed my arm firmly, swinging me to face him. "Forgive me, please. I couldn't stand it if you stayed mad at me."

He gave me his best puppy-dog look. A look that I'm sure had most girls melting into a puddle at his feet. Despite my best efforts I couldn't help but be affected a little. Kian was cute, popular, well liked and a senior to boot.

I let out a sigh. "Fine, I forgive you. Maybe."

A grin broke out across his face. "You're a doll, Saoirse."

I walked down the corridor and he stayed by my side. I supposed this meant he was walking me to class. I could see the looks of the girls in the corridor as I passed, the envy and jealousy on their faces. Probably a question of why Kian was even giving me the time of day.

I ignored them. I didn't care much for being popular or being seen. Just getting through the school day without event was enough for me. The only reason I was even talking to Kian was because he was genuinely a nice guy.

Well, apart from leaving me behind with a joint that the Garda thought was mine.

"So," he said in a low voice, "did you...did you say anything to them? The Garda? About me and Dazza, I mean."

Un-fucking-believable.

I stopped right in front of my homeroom door. "Is that why you're being so nice to me? You want to know what I said? Whether I spilled my guts about you?"

"Come on, Saoirse. You know that's not true." Kian gave me a pained look.

I almost believed him. "Whatever. I gotta get into class."

Kian grabbed my arm gently before I could turn away. He stepped up to me and leaned in, his lips brushing the corner of my mouth. "See you later?"

"Fine, see you later." I remembered that Diarmuid was picking me up after school. Perhaps he would want to hang out after school like we did this morning at breakfast? A little thrill went through my body before I shoved it away and told myself—*again*—not to be so stupid. "But not tonight."

"Tomorrow night?"

"We'll see."

"I'm taking that as a yes." He backed up, his hands stuffed in his pockets, giving me his famous cocky grin so that I couldn't help the smile that broke through on my face.

The first three lessons of the day went uneventfully. Everything changed when I entered math class. I sat in my regular seat in the far left near the back.

Mr Fletcher was our teacher, a weaselly man with thinning greasy hair that he combed over. Thick black glasses sat on his hooked nose.

Everything he taught us sank in easily to me. Like those algebra equations that he'd written up on the board in chalk.

He pointed to the sums. "Pop quiz today. I want to make sure that you studied during your holidays."

Everyone in the class groaned.

"And it counts towards your final mark."

Groans turned into cries of protest before Mr Fletcher silenced them with a glare.

I did what he instructed silently, ignoring the low chatter of the students around me, asking each other for help, trying to look at each other's work. I always felt separate from them. Always. And not just because I never had to ask for help.

Because I was the one with the backpack falling apart. Who never had spare pens. Who had to write everything crammed into tiny writing on both sides of each note page because I didn't know when I could afford a new notebook.

At the end of our allotted time, Mr Fletcher wrote the answers up on the board so we could mark up our pages. I glanced at his answers and looked down at mine. Frowning. Focusing on question number three.

I knew better than to draw attention to myself. I always made sure to make deliberate mistakes in any assignment or test. There was no point in being noticed.

No point in drawing attention. I didn't want to be seen.

Until today.

Perhaps I felt extra defiant today because I had been arrested for something I didn't do. Perhaps it was Diarmuid's words from breakfast that kept clanging around my head.

"Saoirse, you're really smart. You could go to a good university, get a degree, get a good job, Jesus, you could become a doctor if you bloody wanted to."

I stuck up my hand.

"Ms Quinn," Mr Fletcher said, "have you found your voice today?"

I shuffled in my seat, beginning to think that this was a bad idea. "Question three, sir."

"What do you want to know about question three?"

By this stage the whole class was staring at me. I was known as the quiet loner. The one who came into school in ratty secondhand clothes that never fit. I never spoke up in class. Until today. Today, I was invincible.

"Your answer to question three is wrong…sir."

The class broke out into whispers. Mr Fletcher's face turned purple and his eyes bugged out of his head. I knew then I'd done the wrong thing.

Stupid, stupid girl.

"Excuse me?" Mr Fletcher spluttered.

I hunched my shoulders around my chest trying to make myself disappear. It didn't work. Everybody was still staring at me, eyes wide, mouths open. How dare I question our teacher.

"Well, sir," I stammered, trying to dig myself out of

the hole I had found myself in, "if you look at the sum again you'll see that you forgot to carry the one and so the answer shouldn't be 304, it should be 314."

Mr Fletcher stormed towards my desk. "I am not wrong."

I winced. "If you just look at your sum again—"

"I am *not* wrong," he repeated again, slamming his palms on my desk, towering over me. "How dare you suggest it."

"But sir—"

"Detention this lunchtime for you, Miss Quinn, for being such an obstinate, ignorant a little girl. And you fail today's assignment." He pulled out a red pen and leaned over my desk, marking my entire page with a big fat F. I caught the look of glee on his face before he spun around to walk back to the head of the class.

My cheeks burned, the unfairness of it swelling up inside me. I knew I was right. I was right. He had no right to give me detention or to fail my assignment. Just because he couldn't deal with the fact that he was wrong and shown wrong by a thirteen-year-old girl. Fuck this. Fuck him. I leapt to my feet, almost knocking my chair back behind me.

"That's not fair," I yelled.

Mr Fletcher spun and stared at me with a calm, hateful look, his eyes running across my entire body. "I suggest you learn your place, Miss Quinn. You'll never amount to anything or be anyone. You'll probably end up like your father, in jail. If you're lucky, you'll just end up like your whore mother."

Tears pricked the back of my eyes and my jaw ached from gritting my teeth together. I hated Mr Fletcher. I hated the words that he said. But they buried deep inside me into that soft, tearable place. To that place that knew that he was right.

"Now sit down and shut up, before I add another week to your detention."

Fight, a voice inside me said, sounding eerily like Diarmuid's. *He is wrong. You're right.*

Sit down, another voice said inside me. *Shut up. Don't be seen. Don't be heard. Don't be anyone.*

I can be somebody. I have potential. Diarmuid thinks so.

The other voice inside of me started to laugh, joining in with the giggles that could be heard around the classroom.

My heart sank. Why did I ever think it was a good idea to put my hand up? Why did I think it was a good idea to try to *be* somebody?

Resigned, I bowed my head. And sank silently into my seat.

10

Diarmuid

I sat in my truck, listening to the radio, which was still set on that old rock and folk channel that Saoirse had changed it to yesterday. For some reason I hadn't wanted to change it. To be fair, the grassy beats and melodic flutes were growing on me.

I tapped my fingers on the steering wheel as I stared through the rush of kids pouring out of the front of Dublin North public school, my eyes searching for the golden head that was Saoirse's.

I didn't usually pick up and drop off my kids. But I was still in shock over what I'd discovered about Saoirse this morning at breakfast.

She was the smartest kid I'd ever met. The potential

for her life was outstanding. I vowed I was going to make sure she got out of her horrible home life and made herself a better one.

The stream of kids lessened to a trickle, then finally down to nothing. I glanced at my watch on my wrist, a leather banded vintage watch that had been my father's when he'd been alive. It was ten past four. Where was she? Did I miss her somehow?

Had she gone around me deliberately? Perhaps gone out the side entrance?

I frowned. I thought we'd connected this morning. I thought I was getting through to her, slowly. Why wouldn't she show up when she knew I was here to pick her up?

Finally, she appeared and a warmth spread across my chest at the sight of her.

My stomach dropped when she spotted me and broke into a run. Her face was red, her fists clenched by her sides.

I strode towards her, my senses on alert. "What's happened?" I demanded as soon as she was near enough.

"Epinephrine," she spat out.

"What?"

"A chemical that sends a signal to your frontal lobe to raise your heart rate and increase the rush of blood to your skeletal muscles."

I blinked.

She rolled her eyes at me. "I'm pissed off, Diarmuid."

"I can see that." I squat down in front of her so we were eye level. "Why?"

Tears swam in her eyes, her lip starting to tremble, her anger dissolving into salty water. "He's going to f-f-fail me. Just because he hates me."

"Who?"

"M-Mr Fletcher. My math teacher. We had a pop quiz. I know I got all the answers right. I even corrected him. But he just failed me. He failed me because I told him he was wrong." Her lip began to tremble. "It counts towards our final mark, Diarmuid. It's not fucking fair."

My lungs hardened, my chest filling with resolve. I wasn't supposed to get personally involved with her schooling. That was her parent's job. But I knew her mother wouldn't give two shits about her fail grade. I wasn't about to let this stupid, short-sighted, prejudiced teacher get away with accusing her of cheating.

I picked Saoirse up, spun on my heel and walked to the truck, opening the passenger door with Saoirse still in my arms. Carefully I placed her in the passenger seat. She clung to me for an extra second before letting go.

"Which room is Mr Fletcher in?" I demanded.

She sniffed, her wide pain-glossed eyes on me. "Room 204. Why?"

"Stay here. Lock the doors."

"But—"

"Saoirse," I cut her off, my voice curt, "stay here. Lock the doors. I'll be right back."

11

Saoirse

I wiped my face, curiosity cutting through the swirling anger and unfairness, watching as Diarmuid strode towards the school building. He walked like he was going into battle. Like he could conquer an empire.

As soon as Diarmuid disappeared into the building, I slid out of the truck and followed him, figuring out where he was headed.

Room 204.

I didn't *actually* promise I'd stay in the truck.

The hallways were mostly quiet as I slipped down them, trying to keep my school shoes from clacking against the floor. What was Diarmuid going to say to Mr Fletcher? What would he do?

I neared Room 204 and heard an angry voice coming from the crack in the door. Diarmuid's voice. I glanced around the hallway. Seeing no one paying me any attention, I leaned against the wall near the door.

"Have you even spent five minutes talking to her properly?" That was Diarmuid. I'd know his rough, gravelly voice anywhere. "She's a goddamn genius. You'd know that if you did."

He was talking about me.

"Mr Brennan," Mr Fletcher's nasally voice sounded strained, "you are not her parent. You have no right to come in here and demand I unfail her. Now if you don't leave, I will call campus security."

I heard a bang. I jumped and spun, pressing an eye to the crack of the door, my heart banging away in my chest.

Diarmuid had slammed his fist on Mr Fletcher's desk and was now leaning across it. "I'm giving you a choice, Mr Fletcher. You can give Saoirse the full marks and recognition she deserves. Or I can arrest you."

"You can't threaten me—"

"I can smell alcohol on your breath. If I took you down to the station for a breathalyser, how much do you think you'd blow?"

Mr Fletcher sank back in his seat, stammering incoherently.

Diarmuid cut him off. "What do you think the headmaster would say? The parents, huh? You'd be fired. You'd not get another teaching job. Not anywhere in Ireland."

"Mr Brennan," Mr Fletcher said, his face going red,

his breath coming out in short pants, "let's not be hasty."

"Do the right thing, Mr Fletcher. Give Saoirse the marks she deserves. Quit drinking on the job." He leaned in so close, I thought for a second that Diarmuid was about to kiss Mr Fletcher. "Or I will make you pay."

Diarmuid turned towards the door, conversation over. I gasped and ran back to the truck, only realising when I got there that I couldn't get in by myself.

"I thought I told you to stay in the truck." Diarmuid's voice boomed out behind me.

I spun, my heart in my throat. I disobeyed him. I knew what my ma's boyfriends did to her when she did something they didn't like.

"S-sorry," I managed.

His face was still stormy, but it softened just a touch.

He held out a hand. "Let me help you in."

This time I didn't mind him holding my arm as he helped me into the truck. His touch was warm and firm, but not too firm.

I think I liked that the cab smelled like him. Leather and the hint of his woodsy cologne. I took a deep breath while he was walking around to the driver's side.

Despite that inner voice that told me not to trust him, I wanted to.

Diarmuid got in. He turned on the truck and the familiar folksy music came out of the speakers. I blinked as I stared at the radio buttons. He'd left it on the station I liked. Why would he do that? I glanced over to Diarmuid but his eyes were on the road.

"You shouldn't have any more trouble with Mr

Fletcher." He glanced at me out of the corner of his eye. "But you already know that, don't you?"

He knew I'd snuck into school after him. He knew I'd heard what he said to Mr Fletcher.

A hot ball lodged in my throat. No one had ever done anything like that for me before.

I wanted to tell him thank you. I wanted to let him know how much his sticking up for me meant to me.

But I could not speak.

Diarmuid pulled up in front of my apartment block and I found myself sagging into my seat. The trip seemed like it was over in a second.

I stared at the concrete block through the window. I didn't want to go into that place. In here with Diarmuid, I felt...hope. I felt like my life had potential. When I walked into the hovel I called "home", I remembered that my life was just shit.

Diarmuid turned off the engine and turned his torso to face me. "If that eejit gives you trouble again, you tell me, okay?"

I nodded.

"Right," he said straightening up in his seat. "I'll see you here tomorrow, same time as today."

Was he serious? He had to be lying. Why would he want to take me to school again?

I stumbled out of the truck and walked up the building stairs as if on autopilot. I didn't see the piles of junk on the balconies. I didn't see the cigarette butts littering the dusty, unclean floor or the crusty vomit stain that'd been in the stairwell corner so long it'd dried to cement. I barely noticed these things, my mind was a whirl.

And when I entered my apartment I almost didn't see the dirt and the grime.

I almost didn't hear my ma's new boyfriend yelling at her.

I walked into my room and locked the door behind me.

Diarmuid had been worried about me.

He picked me up and took me home, just as he said he would.

I couldn't help the rush of hope in my heart.

Maybe, just maybe, I had found a friend.

That night, over the sound of my ma and her new boyfriend screaming and plates breaking outside my locked bedroom, I clutched my musty pillow to my chest and whispered Diarmuid's name over and over into the darkness as if he were a prayer, until I had memorized every note of music in every letter.

12

Diarmuid

Now—Limerick, Ireland

"Brennan."

Claddagh, my supervisor's PA, called out to me as soon as I walked into the Limerick Garda station the next morning. She stood at the reception, hand on her bony hip. She reminded me of a school marm, greying hair pulled back tight, slim glasses pinched onto her sharp nose attached to a chain that went around her neck.

"Leary," I replied, using her surname exactly as she used mine.

Claddagh's gaze went disapprovingly to the tats that peeked out from my rolled-up sleeves.

"Would you like a closer look at them?" I snapped.

Her grey eyes flicked to mine, the hint of a smirk on her thin lips. "Coilin wants to see you in his office. Now."

I snorted and pivoted on my foot.

"Hey!" she called out behind me. "Where're you going?"

I didn't bother answering her.

If Coilin wanted to see me, that only meant one thing. He wanted to chew my ass out about something.

This was going to take coffee. Stat.

There was a small coffee shop next door to the station which did a roaring trade delivering decent coffees to the Garda station. We had a coffee machine in our break room, but it only seemed to produce undrinkable sludge.

I pushed through the door into the warm, cosy café that reminded me of a granny's living room, mismatched tea sets and lots of floral pillows. The two girls behind the counter spotted me and I nodded to them in greeting.

By the time I squeezed my way through the chairs and tables to the counter, Marla already had my usual order, a takeaway flat white, ready. She was a sweet-looking girl, long red hair tied back in a ponytail, matching freckles across her pale cheeks. Slender and willowy, she was almost as tall as me.

I handed her cash and she handed the takeaway cup to me, a ritual we'd perfected over the last year or so.

"Marla," I said to the girl behind the counter in thanks.

She flushed and lowered her chin. It seemed the less

I said to her, the more she blushed. She seemed sweet. But I had too many fucking problems to allow her, or anyone, too close.

I nodded to the other girl before striding out of the café.

Coffee in hand, I was ready to face whatever Coilin wanted.

"You're several reports behind," Coilin O'Connell, the Limerick area supervisor barked from behind his huge tidy desk, pens all packed neatly in a holder, papers in perfect stacks, the books on the shelf behind him in alphabetical order by author name, it looked. Made me want to go and put Boland in with the S's and O'Malley up with the A's just to cause some chaos.

I sat opposite Coilin in one of his cushy bucket chairs, long legs stretched out in front of me.

I folded my thick arms across my chest and grunted. "Don't I do a good job with my kids?"

"Yes, but—"

"Don't I have the lowest reoffender rate in this whole goddamn country?"

"Yes—"

"Then what's your fucking problem?"

My supervisor rubbed his forehead, curse words coming out from under his hand. "Diarmuid, you are the best damn Juvenile Liaison Officer that I've ever had, but you can be such a cunt sometimes."

I shrugged. Not denying that.

"The reports will get done *if* I have the time. The kids come first. They're *all* I care about."

"Yes, but in order to continue to care about those kids, you need to submit your reports for each one. Each one, Diarmuid. Or the committee will come down on my ass and I'll have to fire you. I don't want to have to fire you. Got that?"

I glared at Coilin. He wasn't a bad guy. Just a pencil-pushing suit who never spent a night on the street and cared more for dotting i's and crossing t's than anything else. I suppose that's why they gave him the supervisor job.

"Are you done?"

Coilin let out an exasperated sigh. "Jesus, just go. Get out of my fucking sight."

Finally.

I raised my bulk out of the chair and strode to the door.

"Your newest assignment is at your desk," Coilin called out as I opened his door. "Her father should be here by now. I want your reports on her submitted on time."

I gave him the Hitler salute just to piss him off, then slammed the door between us before he could yell at me some more.

Claddagh gave me a wary eye as I strode past her desk. The walls weren't soundproof. She probably heard everything. Not that I gave a shit.

Officers leapt out of my way as I barreled down the hall. I knew I had a reputation as an asshole. I preferred it this way. Adults were fucking stupid. Prejudiced, set in their ways, pride-driven eejits most of the time.

I preferred kids, even the lost ones. Kids were easy, open, respectful if you just listened to them, if you first gave them the respect that they deserved as young adults. They were so willing to do better, be better. They just needed the right direction. They just needed someone to care.

Adults could learn a lot from kids.

I entered the "bullpen", as I liked to call the main open office area.

"You got a reoffender," Nina, the office girl, said. She threw a file at me as I passed her desk.

I caught it and let out a snort. "You give me all the good ones."

Nina gave me a smirk. "I put her in room seven. Enjoy."

I dismissed her with a wave and strode down the hallway to room seven, a cosy living room-style space where we put witnesses and families of victims to make them feel more comfortable. I pushed my way in and halted at the doorway.

Standing at the window was a tall woman, her back to me, fluffing her long waist-length blonde hair with her hands. Her small waist on display in her tight white jumper and her denim shorts hugging the curve of her rounded ass. My reoffender.

She must have heard me enter, because she spun to face me.

The blood drained from my limbs as our eyes locked.

The familiar steel glint like the edge of a blade, a blade I felt tangled in my guts. Her pink lips parted and I could hear her gasp even from here.

Oh dear God.

That was no woman.

That was Saoirse Quinn. The girl I left behind three years ago.

But she was no girl anymore. She was a woman. A seventeen-year-old woman.

And my latest assignment.

13

Diarmuid

Of all the police stations in all the country, she had to walk into mine.

We stood there for what felt like an eternity, our pasts weaving around us, between us, pulling up from the soil of buried memories. A rush of affection washed over me so hard that it almost hurt.

Even now when I got a new assignment, especially a girl, I always compared them to Saoirse. They were never as smart as her. They were never as sharp as her. They were never able to pull out the playful side in me like she did. I cared for them but I never *cared* for them like I did her. Like I still did.

My body vibrated with the familiarity of being in her

presence again. Three years. Had it really been that long? And look at her now—pride drew over me like a curtain—she was a woman.

She'd lost the baby fat around her cheeks, her mouth was full and wide, a natural deep pink. Her blonde hair had developed honey tones and hung down to her waist. Her eyes were chips of jade, sharp enough to cut.

"Diarmuid." Her voice breathed around my name. The way her lips caressed around each syllable tickled something in my solar plexus. An unfamiliar feeling.

I watched as emotions flickered across her angelic face. Surprise, that one was obvious. For whatever reason that the universe decided to throw her my way again, she didn't orchestrate it, that much was clear. Her shock mirrored mine.

But it was drowned quickly with a longing that I now recognised. The look I had ignored when she was thirteen, never imagining that she could ever look at me that way.

I closed the door behind me so that no one walking down the hall might witness our reunion. Everything seemed to quiet and still as the door shut.

I realised the instant that the door was shut that it had been a mistake. It felt like we were too closed in. This cosy room, set up like a living room with comfortable worn armchairs circled intimately around each other, felt like our very own labyrinth, our personal home, just her, me and the lifetime that had stretched out between us.

I found my voice, finally. Her name, a name I hadn't spoken out loud in three years —just in the deep recesses of my head—fell from my thick tongue.

"Saoirse."

I could have avoided this ambush if I had just looked at her file. But I never looked at their file, preferring as always to talk to my kids, to get all my information from their mouths rather than from a typed-up report.

"What…what are you doing here?" I asked. Perhaps she was a figment of my imagination. A fairy from the netherworld.

"Waiting for my JLO."

Her eyes flicked down then up my body. I found myself standing up taller, holding my shoulders out wider.

"Which looks like, through some strange twist of fate, is you." Her eyes felt like they reached into me and peeled back my armour as easily as if it were foil.

"I thought I'd never see you again." The way her voice quieted, so fragile with pain, hit me in the chest.

I thought I'd never see you again. Hot, sticky air sucked into my lungs, coating the inside of my chest.

I hadn't wanted to leave her. But I'd had no choice. It had been the best thing for her.

The memories of the last time I saw her hit me as fresh as if they had happened yesterday. The pain twisting up her mouth. Her voice, begging me, *begging me…*

My legs felt weakened. I held out an arm indicating that she take a seat, but it was more for me. I needed to sit down before I fell over.

She strode towards me. Jesus, when had she gotten so tall? When had her legs gotten so long?

She stopped right in front of me. Three years ago,

107

she wouldn't have been even up to my shoulder. Now her head came up just past my chin.

She looked as if she was going to say something. To hit me. Strike me. I almost hoped she would.

Instead she sat in the chair beside me, crossing her long legs.

I practically dropped into my chair, my legs giving out rather than a deliberate movement.

Her eyes were still on me, still feeling like they were peeling strips off me.

I cleared my throat, reminding myself that I had a job to do. That I should stay professional. But there was so much I wanted to say.

"Congratulations," I began. "For graduating."

Her mouth parted. "How did you know…?" she trailed off.

I gave her a sad smile. "Just because I couldn't stay, doesn't mean I stopped…"

I licked my lips, which had gone dry. Since when had talking to Saoirse become so difficult? When she was thirteen, she and I would never run out of things to say. I never got tongue-tied or unsure of myself.

She wasn't thirteen anymore.

"You kept tabs on me," she said, not a question. Just a statement of something she realised.

I had been keeping track of her. Of course I had. I had local Garda friends of mine checking up on her every so often, making sure she was ok. They hadn't mentioned that she'd moved. It must have been recently.

I checked up on her even though I knew I couldn't

contact her. Especially after the way things had ended…

"What are you doing in Limerick?" I asked, changing the subject.

"I live here now."

"With your ma?" I frowned.

The memory of Ms Quinn still made me tighten my hands into fists. That woman had no business being a mother. If Saoirse had any other living relative who could have cared for her, I'd have called Social Services in a second and had her relocated. But the foster system was not perfect—I knew that dirty fact from the inside—and chances of her being even worse off in the system were too high for me to risk. I would have taken her in if I could have. But it was clear three years ago why I couldn't.

She shook her head. "My da."

He must have been let out of jail. Shit, something I'd failed to keep tabs on. And she was living with *him* now?

My stomach tensed. "You're living with your da?"

"Yeah. He came back for me. *He* never forgot me."

Guilt stabbed me with her words. She still blamed me for leaving three years ago.

I let out a sigh. "Saoirse—"

"And what about you?" Her lips pressed together. "Was it a boy or a girl?"

I looked up. "What?"

"Did you replace me with a boy or a girl?"

I gritted my teeth. "I didn't replace you."

She snorted. "Whatever."

I cleared my throat and flipped open her file,

straining to focus on the written words. I could see her creamy slender leg flicking in my periphery. Shit on a brick, what was she wearing? A pair of denim cut-off shorts and a cropped top, revealing a line of toned creamy stomach.

I fought the urge to go and grab a police blanket and cover her up. It was already the beginning of September, didn't she know? Didn't she understand that she'd attract all the wrong sort of attention wearing that? She didn't look a day younger than twenty now.

She was *seventeen*. That might not mean something to other men, but it meant something to me.

File. Work. Right.

I scanned her file, looking for the important bits of information, hungry for every single piece of info about her. Where was she living exactly? She'd given an address as a house in Dooradoyle. Hmm…that wasn't the best location. Why was she arrested?

Driving without a licence and drug possession. Fuck. Drugs again. Tell me she wasn't using. I wiped my face before looking back up to her, my eyes scanning the whites of her eyes, her skin, the creases of her elbows. Her whites were white. Her skin wasn't sallow. No track marks. She looked healthy. Thank fuck.

"You were picked up driving on a provisional licence without another driver in the car," I said, my tone asking for an explanation.

She rolled her eyes. "I can drive."

"You can only legally drive with another driver in the car."

"Please. Everyone my age drives by themselves."

I stamped down my frustration. "And this drug possession charge…"

"The pot wasn't mine," her eyes flashed, her voice growing hard.

The Garda who'd written the arrest report had stated that they'd spied a small baggie of weed on the floor of the unregistered car after they'd pulled her over.

I stared at Saoirse. This was beginning to sound too much like déjà vu. "And let me guess, you won't say who it belonged to either. Or whose car that was."

She glared at me, defiance clear on her face. "I wasn't a rat then, I'm not a rat now."

I placed the file aside. "Saoirse, off the record—"

The door banged open, cutting me off.

In walked a heavy-set man, looking like a boxer, with reddish-brown hair and piercing green eyes the same colour as Saoirse's. This must be her father.

Liam Byrne.

He'd never married Saoirse's mother, which is why she'd been given her ma's surname and not his. Saoirse had no idea how much of a small mercy that was. Byrne was not a well-regarded name around here. Or anywhere in Ireland.

"Da." Saoirse leapt to her feet and ran to Liam's side. He enveloped her in a one-armed hug at his side.

A stab of jealousy went through me. I used to be the one who she ran to. I used to be the one who she clung to.

I stood, my hands fisting at my sides, and tried not to

scowl. Every single cell in my body was on high alert.

Liam Byrne was as bad as they came. He ran one of the largest drug operations in Ireland, a string of suspected murders in his wake.

Did Saoirse know? I doubted it, otherwise she wouldn't be looking at him that way.

Liam kissed the top of her head. "Are you alright, love?"

She smiled up at him as if he'd hung the stars for her. Another stab went through me. That smile belonged to *me*.

"So good of you to join us, Mr Byrne," I said.

Liam's eyes darted to me. "Who are you?"

I stood up to my full height, making full use of my six-foot-five frame. "Diarmuid Brennan. I'm the Juvenile Liaison Officer assigned to your daughter."

Liam eyed me up and down and then shot me a searing look. "She doesn't need no JLO." He turned to leave, pulling Saoirse with him.

"In that case we will charge her and she can go to court."

Liam stopped and turned back to me, studying me.

I kept going. "Saoirse was charged with driving without a licence and drug possession. Drug possession is a crime that could land her jail time if it goes to court, especially as it's not her first offence. You can risk your daughter going to jail. *Or* you agree to letting her into the Young Offenders Program for minors who have offended. You can let me be her JLO."

His eyes narrowed and he shrugged, but I knew I had

his attention. "What does this program mean exactly?"

"We'd have to have weekly contact." My eyes flicked to Saoirse. She was avoiding my eyes, looking like she just wanted to get the hell out of there. I thought I saw a flicker of anger underneath her apathy.

Once upon a time I could have read all her emotions on her face as if they were words on a page. But now...

"I'll be supervising her until she turns eighteen," I continued. "Making sure she knows what she's done and keeping her from reoffending."

Liam watched me for a pause, then nodded. "Fine."

He turned and this time he dragged Saoirse away with him, his arm slung around her shoulders.

Before the door shut on them, Saoirse glanced back. Our eyes met. My stomach tightened.

It was six months before her birthday.

I had six months during which she was forced to spend time with me. Six months to positively influence her.

I was already running out of time.

14

Saoirse

It had been a stupid infringement. Stupid. Jase had lent me a car to use so I could drive to my new job at a café and the tail light was busted. I hadn't noticed. But the two Garda in the cop car did. They pulled me over.

I should have known that the car was dodgy because, well, Jase was dodgy, and then one of them spotted the baggie of weed that had slipped on the floor. I doubted that Jase would have left it there on purpose.

The minute the cops ran my name they realised I already had a mark on my name for drugs and they took me in.

It was a bullshit charge.

This was what was on my lips when I'd heard the

door of the interrogation room open behind me as I waited in room seven.

I turned.

And froze.

Caught in the net of his chocolate eyes, the ones that seemed to cut right through me. The ones that used to look at me as if I were the most important creature in the world.

A pair of eyes I didn't think I'd ever see again. That I looked for every time I went anywhere.

Diarmuid Brennan.

It couldn't be him.

I was dreaming. Or hallucinating. I must be.

I blinked. Diarmuid was still there, staring back at me from the doorway. Same shoulder-length hair tied back, trimmed beard darkening his strong jaw. Same wide frame, thick muscular arms that used to contain my whole world. Looking just as I had dreamed of him every night for three years.

Old feelings flooded back, slamming into my chest and winding around my body. I remembered feeling like the only one that mattered. Like he was my fortress, my shield, my castle. I was safe as long as I was with him.

I wanted to run to him, fling my arms around his neck and nuzzle my nose into his leather jacket, which no doubt smelled like his woodsy cologne and leather.

He had been my world. My hope. My guiding light. He had been safety. Security. Unconditional love.

Unconditional...until it wasn't.

Until he left, taking it all away.

That old wound tore open again, never having healed. The love I felt for him drowned in anger.

But I refused to let it out. I refused to give him the satisfaction of knowing that he still affected me. I was no longer a stupid fourteen-year-old girl.

I was a different Saoirse. An older Saoirse. I would not make the mistake of throwing myself at him again.

"You alright, pet?"

I shook myself out of my thoughts. My da kept glancing over to me from the driver's seat of the car.

"Fine," I lied.

I hadn't told my da that I'd known Diarmuid from before. I doubted somehow that Diarmuid would tell him either.

"You didn't say anything to them about who owned the car, did you?" my da asked.

I shook my head. "Of course not. You taught me never to trust the Garda."

My heart squeezed. Once upon a time I had trusted Diarmuid with my life, with my heart. Then he had broken it. Dashed it into a thousand tiny pieces.

My da smiled and patted my knee. "That's my girl."

I was right to keep silent at the station. I was Daddy's girl.

Not Diarmuid's.

15

Diarmuid

I did not like Liam Byrne.

After Saoirse had left with him I'd looked him up on our criminal database.

Imprisoned twice, both times on drug charges. He'd been caught running a small cannabis plantation in rural Limerick. Rumour was that his operations had continued on via his partner even while he was still in prison. Now that he was out, it was only a matter of time...

And Saoirse was living with him, dear God.

Six months. I had to keep her clean for six months. Then she'd be eighteen and free to go live on her own. To choose her own path.

How the fuck was I supposed to keep her on the

straight and narrow when her father was one of Limerick's most notorious drug pushers?

How the fuck was I supposed to do that when I shouldn't even be going anywhere near her?

Saoirse Quinn.

Jesus Christ. How the hell was I going to deal with her?

I wound a set of wraps over my hands as I stood before a bag in O'Malley's gym. My two friends, Declan and Danny, and I had started boxing together when we were teens. We started training together in this very gym.

I used it as a form of meditation. As a form of stress relief. As therapy. As penance.

Danny did it to keep fit. To distract himself while his subconscious worked on a song or melody that was giving him grief.

But Declan…he took to it like a duck to water. There was a darkness in Declan that was deeper than any in Danny and me. Now he'd gone on to become a pro MMA fighter, Mr World Title himself.

Fuck, I missed those guys.

Danny was based in Dublin now and Declan in the US.

I made a mental note to call them both when I got a chance. It'd been a long time since I'd spoken to either of them. Too long. And I needed a non-judgemental ear right about now.

I began to rhythmically hit my fists against the bag, remembering the shock that had gripped my body when I'd realised it was Saoirse in that room, the girl who had coaxed out all the gentle pieces of my heart all those years ago. Shock had given way to the foreign rush of heat in my veins at the sight of her all grown up.

Shit.

I would not think of her that way. *I would not,* I repeated to myself with each smack of my fists. She had been like a little sister to me then. But now...

"Mr B," a familiar male voice called.

I dropped my guard and spun, grinning at the sight of the lad walking up to me. "Tadhg, how are ya?"

Tadhg, pronounced Tiger but without the r at the end, was an up-and-coming Gaelic football player who did boxing training at the gym to keep fit during off-season. He'd just come back from a week away with his mates. His dirty blonde hair was streaked with the sun and his skin a golden colour; he was one of the lucky ones whose skin actually tanned.

"Grand, yeah," he replied.

"I hear the Dubs team manager was wining and dining you last night?" Nothing—and I mean *nothing*—was kept secret here.

His cheeks reddened. "It was just dinner."

I nodded. "Oh, yeah, I see. You bloody turncoat."

He grinned, ducking under my arm when I tried to hug him.

I let out a snort. "Throw on a set of wraps and let me hold a couple of pads up for you. We'll see how unfit you got sunning your lazy arse in Las Palmas."

I worked him out hard until he collapsed to the bench with a moan.

I did not think of Saoirse once. I swear.

16

Saoirse

Then—Dublin, Ireland

It was my birthday.

Usually I didn't care about my birthday. It was just like every other day of the year. But this year... This year, I had Diarmuid.

I practically ran to the truck to meet Diarmuid that morning, a spring in my step. I knew he was watching me closely as he helped me into the truck.

"You look happy," he commented as he pulled away from the sidewalk.

"Of course," I said, and waited for the penny to drop for him. He had my file. He knew it was my birthday. I even kinda maybe dropped a hint about it, a week ago, so as not to be obvious.

He wouldn't forget, would he?

It wasn't like I was expecting anything big. I didn't even expect a present. Or a card. Just a *happy birthday* from his beautiful lips.

But he said nothing about it.

Not even that afternoon when he came to pick me up from school and drop me off at home.

"Saoirse," he called out at me through the open window of his truck.

My hopes soared into my cheeks, lifting them up. I spun on my heel to face him, grinning at me with that devastating grin.

He remembered. He remembered.

"Yes?" I asked, my heart beating like a hummingbird as I stood on the sidewalk outside my building.

"See ya tomorrow," he called out before he drove off.

I watched the back of his truck disappear around the corner, the dust he was kicking up feeling like it was coating my lungs, making it hard to breathe.

He forgot.

He totally forgot.

No one ever remembered my birthday. Well, except for Moina. But I'd thought that Diarmuid might. I just wanted him to remember. Something to indicate that he cared.

I trudged up the grey concrete steps to my apartment, cursing myself for being so upset over this. I knew

Diarmuid cared. He already took me to school and shouted me breakfast.

That's his job. You're just a job, Saoirse. Remembering your birthday is not part of his job.

"Hey, Saoirse," Moina called out from the stairwell as I stuck my key into the apartment door. "You wanna drop your stuff, change and come down in about twenty minutes?"

I nodded, forcing a smile to my face. At least Moina remembered. She probably had a small cupcake there for me. Moina didn't have much money either but she always had something small for me every year on my birthday since she moved in a few years ago.

See, someone did remember. Moina did. So why was I still sad?

'Cause I wanted Diarmuid to remember. I didn't want to be just part of his job.

In the apartment, my ma was sitting on the couch in a vest and her underwear, ratty grey slippers on her feet. She was only in her mid-thirties but she looked ten years older, the skin on her thighs already sagging, crinkles all around her thin lips and yellowed eyes.

"Hey, ma."

"I feel like fockin' shite. Like a truck ran over me."

Maybe if you stopped inviting assholes who beat you into your bed and stopped doing drugs you'd feel better. But I said nothing. I knew better. The times I'd actually said something I just ended up with her hand across my face.

I walked into my room and changed into my best pair of jeans. I only had two. This pair was denim washed,

125

with diamanté on the hip. My ma had bought them for me from a secondhand store on a mother-daughter shopping day. It had been during one of the rare times my mother was sober. She'd just gotten paid her benefits so she was feeling flush and generous. Usually the jeans hung off me but lately, I'd been filling them out more.

I pulled on a shirt and cringed as I accidentally knocked my chest. My breasts were tender. My chest had been flat but now my boobs had started growing and fast. I'd need a bra soon. Hopefully Moina would take me. I couldn't rely on Ma to do it.

I left my room and walked past my ma, still moaning on the couch.

"Saoirse, honey."

I turned around to look at her. Would it be too much to ask that she remembered that she gave birth to me fourteen years ago?

My ma looked at me with dead eyes and held out a hand, a folded twenty-euro bill between her fingers. My heart flipped. She actually remembered. Twenty euro! Was this my birthday present?

"Be a doll and grab me a pack of smokes, will ya?" She waved the note at me.

Not my birthday present, then. I snatched the money off her and backed up to the door.

"Smoking will kill ya. How 'bout I get some *food* with this money instead?"

She gave me a sour look. "You little shite, you have no idea what I've been through. That's me last bit of money 'til next Tuesday."

Of course she'd buy stupid cigarettes with her last slip of cash. I slipped out of the apartment before she could throw an ashtray or something at me.

"I'll be back later," I called.

"Ungrateful little shite," she yelled as I locked the door on her, muting her yells. "You come back here."

I ran down the stairs to the level below us. I listened out for her footsteps but heard nothing. She didn't follow. I took a deep breath outside Moina's door to calm myself, tucking the twenty into my back pocket. I'd buy her stupid smokes later. *If* there was any money left, I'd get some basic groceries.

I knocked on Moina's door. Moina's head appeared through the crack. I was about to unleash my frustration over my ma to her—she'd heard it all before but she always let me rant—when she flung open the door and stepped aside.

"Surprise!"

I blinked. Her tiny apartment was decorated with colourful streamers and balloons, bowls of chips, bottles of soda and boxes of pizza stacked on her dining table. And standing in her living room was Diarmuid, a huge grin on his face, holding a cake in his hands, fourteen candles circling the thick icing on top.

He bought a cake for me. With actual birthday candles.

He remembered my birthday.

He was just pretending not to.

He cared.

Tears pricked the backs of my eyes. My throat closed,

trapping the happiness swelling in my chest, like a tiny sun had bloomed. I thought I might burst from it.

"Are you gonna just stand there with your mouth open? Come in, girl." Moina grabbed my arm and tugged me inside the apartment, closing the door behind me.

"You…you did this for me?" I asked, blinking, still unable to believe it.

"It was all Diarmuid's idea," Moina said, beaming.

I looked up at Diarmuid, grinning at me in a way that made me want to reach out and touch his face.

"I thought you'd forgotten," I said quietly.

He winked at me. "All the better to surprise you."

It was my first real birthday cake. The biggest chocolate cake I'd ever seen. It must have been at least a foot wide with *Happy Birthday* written across it in thick white icing and edible stars creating a universe across the top, candy roses brushed with silver dust decorating the base. He didn't buy this from the bakery section at Aldi. No way. This cake was too special. He must have bought it from an actual bakery. Jesus, how much did he spend?

Diarmuid and Moina closed around me as they burst into a rendition of "Happy Birthday". Moina could sing, she had a voice of an angel. But Diarmuid couldn't, his voice slightly off-key, but it didn't dampen his enthusiasm or his smile. It was beautiful. He was beautiful. I couldn't take my eyes off him as the candlelight brushed a warm glow on his cheeks.

Their voices trailed off as they finished their song. I found myself clapping and laughing even though I felt like I was going to cry.

"Go on, Saoirse," Diarmuid said, holding the cake underneath my nose. "Blow out your candles."

"Don't forget to make a wish," Moina added.

I glanced once more at Diarmuid. Even when I squeezed my eyes shut, I could still see Diarmuid's face in front of me. I smiled, inhaled and blew.

I wish you were mine, Diarmuid.

I heard clapping and opened my eyes in time to catch the wisps of smoke rising from my candles, caressing Diarmuid's neck and face.

He set the cake down on the dining table and grabbed something with his left hand. Before I could see what it was, he picked me up around my waist and lifted me over his shoulder to spin me like a helicopter. Diarmuid was so strong.

I let out a squeal as the apartment and all the colourful decorations blurred around me in a vibrant whirl, Moina laughing in the background. He put me down and presented me with a gift wrapped in purple and gold.

I blinked. "For…me?"

He nodded and kissed the top of my head. "Happy birthday." My scalp tingled where his lips touched me.

I took the present and lowered it to the dining table, Diarmuid and Moina crowding around me. It had been properly wrapped, with a bow and everything.

I pulled the ribbon open first and unwound it from the rectangular gift and studied it in my fingers. It was like a silky strip of gold that shone as the light caught it.

"I chose gold because it matches your hair,"

Diarmuid said.

My throat felt thick, like I'd swallowed part of a ribbon. I folded the gold ribbon and slipped it carefully into my back pocket. Using my fingers, I worked the tabs of sticky tape on the ends of the present.

"Oh, go on, just tear it," Moina said.

"Nah, let her open it however she wants," Diarmuid said.

I ignored them, my sole focus on the present he gave me and making sure I didn't tear the beautiful purple paper with gold stars on it. I wanted to stick it on my wall later like a painting, to cover up a little of the grimy walls opposite my bed so I could wake up and it'd be the first thing I saw, reminding me of this amazing day.

Finally, I peeled the last sticky tape off and the wrapping paper fell open to reveal a black journal decorated with formulas in what looked like white chalk. Chemistry formulas. I ran my fingers over the thick cover.

It was beautiful.

"Everyone needs someone to tell their secrets to," Diarmuid said quietly. "You can write them down in here. Don't miss my note inside."

I opened the journal. A hundred-euro bill fell out and flittered to the floor. I picked it up and frowned. Was this meant to be in the journal? He must have accidentally dropped it into the gift. I held it out to Diarmuid.

He shook his head and pushed my hand back towards me. "I thought you could use the money to buy yourself something…nice." He looked sheepish. "I admit

I don't have the first clue what women like to buy."

He gave me a hundred euro. That's more money than I'd ever seen in my life.

I could get a bra.

A new backpack.

I could save the rest and put it towards my dream of moving out of my ma's place on my own one day.

I clutched the note to my chest. "Why…?"

He shrugged. "I wanted to."

Written on the first page, on thick, luxurious cream paper, was this in his scratchy bold handwriting:

Dear Saoirse,
Never forget how special you are.
Love, Diarmuid

My throat closed up.

He said "love". He signed "*Love, Diarmuid*".

No one had ever said that word to me. No one had ever claimed to. That single word jumbled around inside me. I felt like I might scream or burst or cry. Or all of the above.

I slammed against Diarmuid, wrapping my arms around his waist, my body shaking as I tried to control my tears.

"Best present ever," I mumbled into his shirt, which smelled like his grown-up cologne. He was the best-smelling man in the world. He never smelled of stale beer or cigarettes.

His arms closed around me. "You deserve it, little

rebel. You deserve it."

It was late by the time I'd left Moina's, drunk on cola and high on the best chocolate cake I'd ever tasted. I'd only remembered about the twenty euro and my ma's smokes when I reached my door. The local shop would be closed by now. It was too late to go buy them. Fuck. She'd be fuming.

I worried my lip with my teeth, glancing down the stairs. I could go back to Moina's and beg to sleep on her couch. She'd let me. She'd let me before when my ma brought home a very bad man who stared at me with a glossy sickness in his eyes, who made me feel dirty even before he touched me under my shirt. Luckily my ma woke up then and came looking for him. He snatched his hand off me and I was able to run out of the apartment.

I could stay with Moina tonight. But I didn't have any clothes with me for school tomorrow. No toothbrush. Nothing. I pressed my ear to the door and listened. Maybe Ma was passed out. Maybe I'd get lucky.

I couldn't hear anyone moving in there. At least, I didn't think I could hear anything...

I unlocked the door as quietly as I could and slipped inside and kept the light off, letting the moon filtering in from the window be my guide. Thank God. Ma wasn't home, the living room silent and soggy with the scent of stale beer and unwashed bodies. I slipped into my room and locked my door using the latch inside.

I got ready for bed and took my hundred euro present and slipped it between the pages of my old math textbook in my tiny bookcase. By the dim light of my old bedside lamp, I wrote my first journal entry before I fell asleep clutching my journal and thinking of a certain gentle, dark-haired giant.

17

Diarmuid

I pushed open the door to my home late that night after Saoirse's birthday party. I could barely wipe the smile off my face. She'd been genuinely surprised and ecstatic with the cake, the little party, and the journal.

God, that young girl should be utterly jaded, miserable and sullen from the shitty hand that life had dealt her. Instead she was like a ball of sunshine, taking happiness from the smallest things.

It made me want to please her. Keep pleasing her.

It made me want to build a wall around her delicate rays of light. To protect her from people who I knew could be inherently cruel.

I flinched when I saw Ava waiting for me in the

living room, her arms crossed over her chest, her painted mouth pursed into an ugly pout. Her wild red hair was all about her head, her blue eyes glittering at me with fury.

The smile dropped from my face and I almost let out a groan. What the fuck did I do wrong now?

"It's almost midnight. Where the hell were you?"

"Work."

"I know you weren't at work. I called. You weren't there."

I fought not to roll my eyes. "Most of my work doesn't happen at the station, you know that. I gotta go out and see my kids. I was at a birthday party for one of them tonight."

I slung my jacket onto the hook and walked past her to the kitchen. Funny how all my joy had shattered the second I got home. I needed a fucking beer.

Ava followed me into the kitchen. "Who's this kid, then?"

For some reason I was hesitant to tell her about Saoirse. I popped the lid on a Guinness can and took a long pull, leaning against the counter before I answered.

Ava stood in front of me with a glare on her face. "Lately you shoot off so early every morning that I don't get to see ya. Most evenings you disappear too. What the hell is going on?"

I sighed. "I have a new girl, she's only turned fourteen today. Her home life would break your heart."

Ava frowned. "So what? You're going over there every day?"

"I'm taking her to school to make sure she goes.

Buying her breakfast on the way." I left out the fact that I was picking her up after school as well.

Ava's mouth dropped open. "You're buying her breakfast every day?"

"It's the only way I can guarantee that she's getting at least one decent meal a day."

"Diarmuid, that's a lot of money," she yelled. "She's not *your* kid."

"I *know* that." But she was worth it.

"I don't believe this," Ava yelled. "You won't take me on fucking holiday but you're spending your money on feeding someone else's pimply-faced kid?"

"Don't talk about her like that."

Ava's eyes bugged out of her head. "Ex-fucking-cuse me?" she shrieked.

This fight was giving me a fucking headache. I let out a huff, rubbing my forehead with my fingers.

Ava never seemed to understand why I did what I did, why I got so involved. Didn't stop me from trying to explain it to her.

"You should meet her, Ava. This kid, she's a friggin' genius or something. She's so smart. So switched on. She has all this potential. But she has no one looking out for her. I need to make sure she doesn't mess up her life."

"She's not *your* responsibility."

"If not me, then who?" I stood up, jaw twitching from clenching my teeth together. "If there's one thing Brian taught me, if you see something wrong, it's your responsibility to fix it. That's what I'm trying to do. That's what I'm going to keep doing."

Ava didn't understand, and she never would. I stormed into the bathroom just to get away from Ava and slammed the door shut, locking it after me.

I wouldn't give up on Saoirse. No fucking way. I didn't care what Ava said.

18

Saoirse

When I woke up the morning after my birthday, there was no one else in the apartment. My ma was still out.

I tucked my journal under the mattress and slipped the twenty euro into my pocket. I told myself to remember to ask Diarmuid to drop me off at the shops after school.

As always, he was there waiting to pick me up.

"Write in your journal yet?" he asked me at breakfast.

I swallowed my eggs, almost choking.

"Told it any secrets?" He winked at me.

I wish you were mine, Diarmuid.

I felt my cheeks heat up. I shrugged. "Not yet," I lied.

I eyed the shadows under his eyes. "You look kinda tired today," I said, glad to change the topic.

His lips pressed together momentarily before he shrugged. "Didn't sleep very well." That was all he'd say before he changed the subject.

Looked like we were both keeping secrets.

After school Diarmuid stopped at the local shop when I asked him to. He wanted to come in and help me carry my stuff. I had to argue with him not to help. He wouldn't be happy if he knew that I was buying smokes for my ma.

I know, stupid to protect a woman who cared nothing for me. But she was still my ma. I think I was also a little embarrassed for her.

I convinced Diarmuid to stay in the car by telling him that I had to buy "woman's stuff". He took the hint and his face went a little pink before he muttered, "I'll wait here, then" under his breath.

In the store, I grabbed a loaf of bread, some cereal and a carton of milk, calculating the total in my head. With the pack of tobacco I knew she liked costing fifteen euro, I'd just have enough. I set my items on the counter and asked for a pack of rollies, too. The man behind the counter didn't blink as he grabbed the tobacco and rang up the total. They knew me here. They knew I was always sent here to buy for my ma.

I glanced out the glass shop window. Diarmuid was on his phone, so he wasn't looking. I grabbed the smokes and shoved them into my jacket pocket so they wouldn't be seen through the thin plastic bag. I hated hiding things from him.

After Diarmuid dropped me off with calls for me to have a good weekend, I watched him go from the sidewalk. Weekends were the worst. Two whole days without seeing him.

At least I could go shopping this weekend. Maybe Moina would come and help me buy my first bra.

I opened the door to my apartment to find my ma, sitting on the couch in her matching a ratty velour sweatpants and jacket, sucking on a glass pipe, her eyes as wide as a doe's.

"Oh, ye fucking decided to come home, did ya now, you little thief." Her words came out of her mouth in puffs of white smoke that gave the air a sharp medicinal scent. "Where ya been?"

Ugh, I hated when she got speedy. She got so chatty and followed me round the apartment asking stupid questions, picking at her arms or pulling at her eyebrows.

"At school." Duh. I rolled my eyes and threw her pack of tobacco and rollies at her. They landed on the table in front of her, right next to the tiny plastic bag of crystals. "I got your stupid smokes."

"Looks like you got more than that, selfish girl," she said, indicating the plastic bag in my other hand. The lighter clicked as she took another hit of her stupid drug. "I didn't say you could buy yourself shite with my fucking money."

Buy myself *shite?* I gritted my teeth, shoving down the anger swirling hot in my stomach. I'd learned that the best thing to do was not to argue with her when she was in this mood. Just stay out of her way.

I walked to the kitchen and put away the scant groceries I'd bought with the five euro change from her smokes, shutting out her jabbering about how I was disrespectful and had notions that I was better than her.

I walked past her, smacking down the twenty-four cents change that was jangling around in my pocket. "Here."

Then I aimed straight for my room, her still nattering away about nothing in between clicks of the lighter. All I wanted to do was to grab my shit and go to Moina's. I couldn't stay here while she had a fresh bag of meth. A fresh bag...

Something niggled in my head.

It had been her last twenty euro that she gave me. Where did she get the money to buy drugs?

My stomach dropped into my toes as I opened the door to my room. The bed that I had made this morning was tossed about, my mattress askew, my journal fallen onto the floor.

No.

I glanced to my bookcase. All my books had been pulled out and were scattered like fallen doves across my floor. My eyes narrowed on my old math textbook, landed on its side.

No no no.

I fell on my knees before it, reaching for the book with shaking hands. I grabbed the book and shook it out. Nothing fell out.

Gone.

My hundred euro was gone.

Fury unleashed inside me. I leapt to my feet before I knew what I was doing and ran into the living room where my ma was now on her feet.

"You took it, you fucking bitch," I yelled. "Give it back."

She pointed an accusing finger at me. "You took my last twenty euro. I *needed* a smoke."

"I got you your stupid smokes. Give me back *my* money."

"*Your* money? You are a little criminal just like your father." The decrepit woman masquerading as my mother laughed. "Tell ye ma the truth. Who'd you steal it from?"

Tears stung my eyes. I was never getting my present back. No new bra. No new backpack. She'd stolen it and spent all of it on her stupid fucking drugs.

"That was my birthday present," I roared and threw myself at her, hitting out at her.

She just gathered my wrists and held me. She was surprisingly strong, despite how gaunt she'd become. Meth will do that to a person.

"You little liar. Nobody gives a hundred fucking euro as a present."

"Diarmuid did," I said, my voice cracking into a sob.

I wanted to hurt her. But it was useless, the anger draining out of my body, replaced with utter despair. Hurting her wouldn't get my present back. Hurting her wouldn't turn her into someone who cared.

My ma let go of my wrists and grabbed my shoulders, shaking me until my teeth rattled. "You dirty slut. Are you sucking his dick?"

"What?" I screamed, my cheeks flaming red. "No!"

"No man gives a woman nothing unless she's giving him a bit of something."

I tore myself out of her grasp. "Diarmuid's not like that. He *cares* about me."

The dumb bitch began to laugh, her cackle echoing through the room. "You stupid girl. Nobody cares about you."

The tears I'd been holding back broke free. I turned and ran for the door, her words echoing in my head as I fled.

Nobody cares about you.
Nobody cares.
Nobody.

19

Diarmuid

I pulled up to the sidewalk in front of Saoirse's apartment that Monday morning with a smile on my face, despite the fact that Ava and I had had yet another fight.

I didn't like to play favourites with my kids but Saoirse was, although I'd never tell her. Her company gave me a sense of lightness. A sense of rightness. Of peace.

Saoirse trudged towards me with her head down against the light drizzle.

"Well, hey, sunshine," I said.

She said nothing.

I helped her into the truck, but she slammed the door shut. Strange. She was in a right mood this morning.

I slid into the driver's seat as she dropped her backpack into the space at her feet, her old crappy school bag with one arm strap broken and the other one frayed to hell.

"Weren't you going to get a new backpack this weekend?" I asked.

She had told me at her party that's the first thing she was going to buy with the birthday money I gave her.

She slumped in her seat and stared out of the window, saying nothing.

"How was your weekend?" I tried again.

Still nothing.

She was silent at breakfast, only eating half of her usual amount, pushing the rest of it around her plate. I studied her as discreetly as I could. She was pissed off about something, that much I could tell. Whatever was eating her, I was not going to pull it out of her. I had to give her space to open up to me.

She was in an even worse mood when I helped her into the truck that afternoon after school. Her brows furrowed into a V over her pale green eyes. She slammed the door behind her so it rattled in its frame.

"Careful there," I teased lightly when I'd gotten in the driver's seat. I rubbed my hand along the dashboard of the truck. "She's a fragile old girl, and you don't know your own strength."

Saoirse burst into tears, covering her face with her hands and pulling her knobby knees to her chest.

Oh fuck.

"What's wrong?" I tried, my heart tearing into pieces

146

with every sob.

She just kept crying, her tears a language I had no chance of reading, slipping through her fingers like braille.

What was wrong? What was wrong, for fuck's sake? If she would just *tell me*. Whatever it was. I could fix it. She just had to tell me what was wrong. It was all I could do not to shake the problem out of her.

"Saoirse. Tell me, goddammit," I growled. I didn't mean to sound so gruff, so harsh. But a brute such as me was never made to soothe gentle creatures.

She just sobbed harder, her body shaking in the seat.

Fuck.

I felt utterly helpless. Useless. A failure.

What the hell was I supposed to do now? I had no experience with crying girls. None. I tore at my hair.

"Please," I begged, desperation clouding my voice, coating my voice box, "tell me what to do. How do I make it better?"

To my surprise she turned her body towards me and reached out to me with her arms. She hardly ever instigated touch between us.

My chest constricted. She was reaching for me now.

I slid my arms around her gently, picked her up and placed her, still curled in a ball, on my lap. She wrapped her arms around my neck and cried into my shirt, her tears soaking the fabric, her body shaking in my arms like a broken bird.

I would kill the person who hurt her. So help me God.

I reached out and gingerly stroked her hair, which

147

was as soft as down.

I was grasping at straws now, desperate for a way to calm her. I suddenly remembered how my mother used to calm me when I was very, very young.

Eveline Brennan.

I never let myself think of her. It was always too painful, the wind still echoing across the gaping hole that she left in my heart when she died. But the pain was worth it now.

I did what my ma did, copying the ghost of her in my memories. I ran my hand across Saoirse's hair and over her back, her tiny body like a doll made of twigs.

I began to speak in a low voice, barely a whisper, just for her.

"Once upon a time, on the Aran Islands off the west coast of Ireland, there lived a fisherman by the name of Kagan. He had good friends and a nice little house. He always brought back just enough catch to sell at the markets. But at night when the wind howled its ancient song over the dark sea, he was lonely, for he had no family, his parents having died suddenly many years earlier."

Perhaps it was me, but I could swear that Saoirse's sobs were growing farther and farther apart. I kept going, bolstered by this tiny sign that perhaps she was calming.

"One day when Kagan was out fishing, he spotted what looked like a woman's head bobbing up and down upon the waves. He ran to the front of the boat to get a better look, but the creature was already swimming away. He could only catch glimpses of the silvery tail of what looked like a seal. He followed it until he lost sight of it, ending up in a part of the ocean he'd not been before.

"Before he could turn back, his lines began to tug frantically. When he pulled back his net, he found the largest, fattest fish he'd ever caught, enough that he'd earn what'd usually take him a week! He turned back to the ocean, searching for the seal-creature to thank her, for he knew she had led him there. But he could not see her."

Saoirse's breathing had slowed, her sobs fading. I could feel her listening intently to me, her body alert.

It was working.

Thank you, Ma, I sent up to her.

I continued, "When Kagan returned to his small bay near his hut and pulled his boat onto the shore, he found a woman, naked, lying on the beach. He ran to her, praying she was alive. He flung himself at her side and pressed his fingers to her slender neck and to her lips. Thank God. There was a pulse. She was breathing.

"She opened her eyes and he was caught in her stare, a stare so hypnotising that he knew he'd never be let go. She was the most beautiful woman he'd ever seen. Long blonde hair, eyes like the greeny-blue waters off Galway Bay. And her name…was Saoirse."

Saoirse lifted her chin to peer at me through her wet lashes. There she was.

I smiled. "He fell in love with her radiant smile and her tender heart. He married her in a small ceremony by the sea. Little did he know that he had married a selkie."

She sniffed. "What's a selkie?"

"You've never heard of a selkie?"

She shook her head.

"It's an old Irish legend. A selkie is a seal who can take off their seal skin to become a man or woman. They can live as a human for many happy years but will stare longingly to the sea. Once they return to their seal form, they can never become human again. They say," I leaned in closer as if to share a secret with her, "that if a man takes a female selkie's skin, then she is in his power and is forced to become his wife."

Her fingers curled into my shirt. "You've got my skin," she whispered.

My heart melted. I felt her slipping deep into the recesses of the iceberg that had been my heart. I knew I'd never get her out.

"And you've got mine, my little selkie," I promised.

The last of her frown dissolved. Even edged in tears, her tiny smile reached into my chest and squeezed. This little girl held my battered heart in her tiny hands. I wondered if she knew how much power she had over me in that moment.

"Then what happened?" she asked, nudging me.

"Kagan and Saoirse lived happily and in love for many years…until…" I trailed off.

I remembered my mother's smile fading when she told me the ending.

"Until?"

I shook myself. "It's a sad ending. Maybe for another day."

Saoirse snorted. "I can take it, Diarmuid. Tell me."

I looked down at this fragile girl-woman. She didn't

150

deserve to be patronised, which is what I'd done. She deserved to hear this ending, no matter how sad it was.

I nodded. "One day, when it was almost winter, when it was too late in the year, Kagan set out to fish despite his wife's pleading with him not to go. He was trapped out at sea in a fierce storm, unable to find his way home. His wife shifted into her seal form and swam out to find him.

"Kagan, huddled and freezing in his boat, was clutching on for dear life and praying. He spotted the familiar silvery form in the water, and he knew it was the seal-woman from before. The seal-woman kept waving at him but Kagan couldn't understand what she was trying to say. Did she want him to rescue her? Was he to jump into the ocean to her?

"Finally, overcome with desperation, Kagan threw over a rope to the seal, hoping she would catch it so he could pull her in. The seal-woman grabbed the rope and began to tug his boat. On and on she swam, through the violent waves and the howling winds and the whipping rain. On and on, until the boat reached the safety of a cove. Kagan tumbled out of the boat, scrambling for the shore. He spotted the seal-woman out in the waves and waved his thanks, before running home, thanking God that he'd been saved.

"But when he burst into his hut, Saoirse was gone. That's when he knew what she was and what she'd done. She'd sacrificed her happy life as his wife to save his life."

Silence descended in the cab of my truck. I tucked Saoirse in tighter against me. She rubbed her tiny fingers across my chest as if she was consoling me, not the other way around.

The end of this story had always made me sad. I wasn't sure why I even liked it so much.

Perhaps this was what I'd always been looking for: a love worth sacrificing for.

Saoirse mumbled something, snapping me out of my morose thoughts.

"What was that, honey?" I asked softly.

Saoirse pulled her face back, her eyes rimmed with red, her nose wet. Her lip trembled and I knew she was on the verge of crying again. "S-she took my money. Y-your present."

What? Fury rose in me and crystallised into an arrow. It just needed a target. Who the fuck would dare steal a birthday present from a fourteen-year-old girl?

I would get to the bottom of this. I would make it right. But first...

I leaned over, being careful not to jostle her, and pulled a tissue out of the glove box. I handed it to her and she wiped her face and blew her nose.

"Who took it?" I asked, trying hard not to let the venom into my voice, unsure if I succeeded. I didn't want Saoirse to think I was angry at her.

"My ma. She went through my things and took my money."

Her own fucking mother stole from her?

Saoirse continued to ramble, "She gave me her last twenty to buy her smokes—"

My eyes widened. Her mother did *what?*

"—and I was gonna do it the next day, I was, but not that night because it was my party. But she thought I'd taken it for myself. I only take money from her to buy food, I swear, because she forgets all the time. So she went looking for it and found my money and she went and spent *all* of it on dr—" Saoirse cut off, her eyes going wide as if she was about to say something that she wasn't supposed to.

I saw the state of their apartment. I could see Saoirse's mother's eyes were dilated when I'd met her. It didn't take a genius to figure out what Saoirse was *about* to say. But as she'd said before, *I ain't no rat.* She wouldn't rat out her mother even if the bitch deserved it.

How the fuck could a mother steal money from her own fucking daughter?

"We'll just get it back from her," I said through gritted teeth. If I had to shake each and every euro from her…

Saoirse's eyes widened. "No! You can't tell her I told you."

I understood. To tell the cops anything was the worst sin in a household where one parent was already in jail. I was a cop. I was the enemy. Saoirse's home life was already shit but it could get much worse if she crossed her mother.

Dear God, did I want to confront her mother.

But not at the risk of making Saoirse's life at home even more of a hell.

I let out a sigh. "Okay, we won't confront her."

Saoirse looked me straight in the eye, giving me a

stern look. This close I could see the flecks of gold in her irises. "You can't tell anyone."

"I won't."

"Promise."

"I promise."

Her lips pressed together, studying me as if she was trying to decide whether I was trustworthy. I didn't say anything. I lowered my defenses so that I was as naked as a babe. I just let her see *me*.

She gave me a small nod. Relief and a swirl of warmth went through my chest.

I had finally earned her trust.

Saoirse climbed back into her seat, letting out a long breath. "You can take me home now," she said in a small voice.

She thought I was going to just let this go with just that? No friggin' way.

I pulled away from the curb, turning the truck around opposite from the usual way that we went. "I'm not taking you straight home just yet if that's okay with ya?"

She sat up in her seat, wiping the last of the moisture from her cheeks. "Where are we going?"

"You'll see."

I drove us to Charleston shopping centre where I knew there was a specialty store that just sold bags, all kinds of bags. I told her that she could pick out a backpack, any backpack she wanted. I watched her discreetly pulling out the tags and glancing at the prices.

When she did it again, I covered her hand and the price tag with mine. She glanced up at me, her mouth slightly parted.

"Don't worry about the prices," I told her. "Just pick out one you like. One that will last you the rest of your schooling."

"But some of them are over—"

"It's your birthday present, Saoirse. Let me worry about the money, ok?"

Her eyes got wet and glossy. I thought she might start crying again. I could see she was fighting against it.

I pulled my hand away from hers and cleared my throat, taking a step back. "You, um, you just tell me when you've picked one."

She picked out a cherry-red backpack. It was well made, with reinforced stitching and waterproof, a must for living in Ireland. I approved.

Saoirse strode out of the shop with the backpack slung proudly over her shoulders, the widest smile on her face.

I had put it there.

I did.

I couldn't remember the last time I'd been happier.

20

Diarmuid

There was a figure hunched over on my porch and a flashy Audi parked in my driveway when I got home from the boxing gym. I got out of the car and the figure rose into an imposing six-foot frame of one of Ireland's most violent fighters.

I slammed the door of my truck behind me. "Look what the bloody cat dragged in."

Declan grinned at me as I strode up to him. "Nice to see you too, fucker."

He was a brutal-looking man, his handsomeness hardened by the steely planes of his face. He was also one of my oldest and best friends.

"You should have rung me," I said.

"And have you pretend to be too busy to see me?"

I snorted. It was always Declan that was too busy for us. We hugged and he slapped my back.

"I was just at O'Malley's," I said, pulling back.

"Jesus, is that old shed still running?" he said, but his tone was full of affection.

"If I knew you were here I'd have gotten you to meet me there."

"And risk having you show me up in the ring? Not a chance, mate."

I laughed. As if I would have a chance in hell at showing him up. Declan was only the world's current number one MMA fighter.

I let us both into my house, a small terraced home in Limerick's west side. He dropped into the couch while I went to grab us a couple of beers. I returned and handed one to him.

"What did I do to deserve your presence?" I dropped onto my armchair and took a swig of my beer. "I'm surprised you didn't bring the damn paps to my door."

"Still grumpy as fuck, I see." He grinned and knocked back his beer, downing half in one go. Declan's metabolism was like a racehorse, I swear. He could drink more and train more than either Danny or me. "I'm just back in Ireland for the next few days."

"Lucky us. Have you been over to Dublin to see Danny yet?"

"Not yet."

"News flash, the bastard's the same old moody prick as always."

He let out a snort. "That's musicians for ya. So, what's the craic?"

Before I could answer, my phone began to buzz across the table.

"Who's calling ye?" Declan swiped it before I could grab it. "She better be hot."

"Hey, asshole. Give me my phone."

Declan's face screwed up when he saw the screen. "Why the fuck is Ava calling you?" He turned an accusing look to me. "I thought you were moving on?"

The phone continued to blare.

"I have moved on. I'm separated from her."

"So why is she calling you?"

"I don't bloody know."

"Are you going to answer it?"

"No."

"I'll answer it."

"No, don't—"

Too late. Declan had swiped the screen. "Hello, wench, it's Diarmuid's answering service...nah, he doesn't want to speak to you..."

I tried to grab the phone off him but Declan hopped off the sofa, skipping out of my reach. The fit fucker. I was never getting my phone off him now.

Declan let out a snort. "Ava, honey, I suggest you go fuck yourself."

He hung up and threw the phone at me, plopping back onto the couch.

"Nothing's going on between Ava and me," I said before he could ask.

He raised a thick eyebrow at me. "Are you seeing anyone else?"

I shuffled in my chair. "No."

"Have you even fucked anyone else since her?"

I winced. Sometimes Declan could be so crude. "No."

"Jesus, brother, it's been almost three years since you kicked her out."

I let out a groan. "I'm still *married*."

Declan let out a snort. "Technically."

"Not technically, *literally*."

"That's because the Irish marriage law is fucked and they won't let you get divorced unless you've been separated for four years."

I rubbed my face. "So you can ask me again in a year when I'm a single man."

"Jesus Christ, Diarmuid, are you actually going to go four fucking years without getting laid?"

"You sound like it's the end of the world."

"It would fucking be for me. Jesus Christ, my dick would fall off."

"What would all your ringside bitches do then?" I muttered under my breath. Louder I said, "That's the difference between you and me. I don't *need* to get laid."

"Bull-fucking-shit. You're a grumpy fucking shite 'cause you're *not* getting laid. It's practically a medical condition what you've got."

Trust Declan to view sex as a pill he had to take daily.

160

Or hourly…if the rumours in all the papers were true.

"Come on, mate," he said. "I have a fight here in a few weeks, I'll get ye a ticket, introduce you to a few fine gals."

I rolled my eyes. "Thought you were happily married, brother."

He grinned and held up his left hand where the huge platinum ring glinted off his ring finger. He'd recently gotten hitched to an American model in Las Vegas, of all places. How very cliché of him.

"Still am. That's why I need to throw the groupies your way. That's the kind of friend I am."

"No, thanks. I don't need your scraps."

That's what I'd been accepting for those years that I'd been with Ava. Scraps. Scraps of her love. Scraps of her attention. I was done playing second best. If I was ever going to get married again, it'd be for the right reasons. With a woman who made me feel like a lifetime wouldn't be enough. With a woman who looked at me like I was the centre of her world. And she would be mine.

Declan shook his head. "Brennan, you've been with the same damn woman for the last six fucking years. Don't you think it's time you got out there and had a bit of fun? Let a few more women get a ride on the Diarmuid train before you shackle yourself up to a station again."

I snorted. "I am not a train."

Declan shook his head. "That bitch has fucked with your head. Made you feel unworthy. Dude, you know I'd do ye, if I were a chick."

"Dex!"

"What?" he gulped down the rest of his beer. "I am comfortable with my masculinity. I can say shit like that and not feel like my manhood is threatened."

Declan had very different ideas about fidelity and sex. I knew that his new wife and he have invited other parties into their bedroom, including other men. Not my cup of tea, but whatever floated his boat.

I shook my head. "Thanks, but no thanks."

A phone buzzed with a message and this time it was Declan's. He looked at it and grinned. "I gotta run. The missus calls."

"Go. You've worn out your welcome anyways."

He laughed. "Good to see you too, asshole."

We both stood and hugged, slapping each other's backs.

He sent a soft punch to my shoulder. "You're coming to my fight. I'm not taking no for an answer. You couldn't come for years 'cause that bitch wouldn't let ye. Now you're not with her, you've got no bloody excuse."

He was right. I needed to be a supportive friend. Declan had done so well for himself in the last few years. He'd reached his potential. *Unlike me.*

I nodded, forcing a smile. "Alright. I'll come, then."

He grinned as if he'd won. "I'll send ye two tickets. Bring a date. A *woman*, Diarmuid. One you'd like to fuck."

For some reason Saoirse popped into my head. I shoved that inappropriate thought away and wouldn't allow myself to dwell on it.

162

21

Saoirse

I was not nervous about meeting Diarmuid again.

I repeat, I was *not* nervous about meeting Diarmuid again.

And just to be clear, I didn't put on a touch of makeup for him. I didn't just spend two friggin' hours trying to pick out what to wear because I wanted to look good for him. I didn't give two shits what he thought of me.

Yeah, right.

I sat in the waiting room chair at the reception of the Limerick Garda station, playing with the hem of my shirt. My hands were clammy so I had to keep rubbing them on my skinny jeans. I was supposed to be here for my four o'clock weekly "catch-up" with him. But it was already ten past four and he still hadn't come down. The bastard was late. He had never been late for me before.

Things change.

"Saoirse?" I jolted as his deep, so masculine voice saying my name sent a shiver down my spine.

Stupid body. Stupid reaction.

I turned to him—damn him, he looked so good in a black leather jacket over a white t-shirt stretched across his pecs—and stood, forcing the most bored, uncaring look I could on my face. I wouldn't even mention his tardiness. I wouldn't let him know that I cared.

"You're late." It just slipped out, I swear.

His beautiful face cracked. "Sorry, Saoirse, my previous assignment went overtime."

His previous assignment. One of his other kids.

When I was a thirteen it felt like I had been his only one. Guess that was a lie.

I guess I was no longer his favourite.

I shoved aside the stab in my gut and shrugged to cover up my hurt. I didn't care. I didn't, okay?

"Whatever. Let's get this over with."

He directed me to another one of those living room-style rooms. They had glass mirrors looking out into the station, but you could close the blinds completely to get privacy. I plopped into the farthest armchair from the cluster, thinking it would force some distance between us. It didn't help. He grabbed another chair and pulled it to sit facing me, our knees less than a metre apart. I let out the breath I didn't realise I'd been holding.

He said nothing. He just looked at me, concern edging his chocolate eyes.

My heart had swollen to Diarmuid-size. And it had never recovered. He seemed to slide right in, right back into the spot he occupied all those years ago.

Fuck him.

I did *not* care.

"Are we just going to sit here for the next hour or what?" I blurted out.

Diarmuid blinked, the only sign that he heard me. "How are you?"

"Fine. Except I'm being forced to spend every Friday afternoon with *you*."

His face cracked. I'd hurt him. A crack mirrored in me and guilt seeped in.

Back then it took more to hurt him.

Damn him. I didn't want to care if I hurt him. He hurt me. I folded my arms across my chest and glanced away.

"Saoirse."

"What?"

"Look at me."

I didn't want to give him the satisfaction of having me follow his orders just like I used to when I was a kid.

Still, as if he'd placed invisible fingers on my chin, I turned to face him anyway. Damn him. My chest felt like a weight was pressing on it as soon as I saw his face. So long I had wanted to see it one more time. Now that he was here in front of me, I just wanted to run. Or to fall into him.

"Have you decided what you're doing now that you've graduated?" he asked.

Something tightened in my stomach. I shrugged.

"What courses did you apply for?"

"What does it matter?"

"I always thought you'd apply for a science degree. You did, didn't you? You used to love chemistry."

He remembered.

"I still do," I admitted.

"So, which university?"

I looked away. "I don't have to tell you that."

He sighed. "This isn't going to go very well if you don't want to talk to me. Perhaps we might have to stay here an extra hour. Or two."

I let out a rasp of frustration. "I didn't apply for university, okay?"

His mouth parted. Disappointment flashed clear in his eyes and hit me right in the guts.

"Saoirse, why—?"

"I don't need to hear it."

"You have so much potential."

"Yeah, well potential means fucking nothing when all you're trying to do is keep your head above water."

He opened his mouth as if to argue. Then snapped it shut again. He rubbed his face in his hands.

"Okay," he said, even though it sounded more like a sigh than an acceptance. "But you have a plan...right?"

My plan. My plan?

Damn him.

I hated that he refused to let me live in the shadows.

I hated that he shone a light into my life, into every crack and corner, exposing them for what they really were.

I didn't have a fucking plan. I didn't have any idea.

22

Diarmuid

She didn't apply to university?

My head spun with this new information. She was a friggin' genius, for God's sake. She couldn't throw away her potential. She couldn't just work in a café and live with her drug dealer father all her life.

I wanted to grab her and shake her.

Or just grab her.

But I could hold her no more easily than I could scoop the moon off the surface of the lake with my hands. She was forbidden to me.

"It's fine," I repeated. "It's fine. You can apply next year."

She let out a sigh. "I don't think I will."

"What? Saoirse, you have to."

"Why?"

"You have a gift. You can't just throw it away."

She stood up, kicking my chair out from behind me. "What does it fucking matter to you?"

"Because I care about you," I said. "I care about your future."

I cared. God, did I care. The problem three years ago was that I cared too much. I crossed the line in my job getting as close to her as I did, in letting her get as close to me as she did.

Here we were again. On the other side of Ireland. Jesus, life was funny sometimes.

"You didn't three years ago," she said.

I gritted my teeth, her words stabbing me like needles. "Saoirse. I did what I had to do."

She still hated me for what I did. What I had to do. I did the right thing for her back then even if she didn't see it that way. I'd do the right thing by her now. Even if it meant she'd hate me forever.

She whipped her head around to glare at me. "You *left* me."

"I had responsibilities."

"I was supposed to be your *soul family*," she hissed, leaning forward towards me. "Or did you forget what you promised me?"

For a second we just stared at each other. I could see the young girl in her face, hidden by the woman she was now. The girl who clung to me when life had gotten unfair, the girl who had looked at me as if I was her whole world. The girl who had relied on me to fix things for her.

I could have gone on forever being her hero.

I could have.

But it wasn't to be.

I let out a long breath. "I'm so sorry, Saoirse."

Saoirse blinked as pain flashed behind her eyes. She slammed back into her seat and crossed her arms over her chest, hugging herself. "Yeah, well, it doesn't fucking matter now, does it."

"Yes, it does."

"Whatever."

"I missed you," I admitted quietly.

She squeezed her eyes shut and let out a shaky breath. "Don't."

"I thought of you every day." I pushed again even though I knew I shouldn't.

Her eyes flew open, the sadness replaced with pure anger.

"Screw you!" Her eyes flicked up to the clock. "Oh, look at that. Time's up."

I let out my own sigh. This meeting had not gone to plan. I didn't mean to admit those things. I didn't mean to lose my cool. My plans seemed to go out the window around her.

She stood and grabbed her bag from beside her. "Guess your stimulating little lecture will have to wait until next week."

"Same bat time," I said without thinking.

"Same bat channel," she said, then froze.

171

Our eyes locked.

There was a softness in her sea-green eyes. The old Saoirse looked back out at me. The one who I hadn't hurt beyond repair. My heart tugged. Maybe I still had a chance...

A chance for what, *Diarmuid?*

Her wall came crashing down again and that sweet girl disappeared behind a sneer.

I walked behind her as she strode to the door.

I had to change things up. Shake things around. Get her doing something so that she'd forget how angry she was with me.

"Come to O'Malley's gym next Friday," I said. "We'll meet there instead."

She shrugged, one hand already on the door handle. "Doesn't matter to me."

Then she left.

As I watched her walk away, something knotted in my stomach. Three years I hadn't seen her. But she still had my skin. I still had hers.

23

Saoirse

My da was twenty minutes late picking me up from the Garda station. I tried not to let my annoyance show as I slammed the passenger door shut behind me.

"How did it go?" he asked as we drove off.

Flashes of Diarmuid and our fight went through my head and I flushed, anger burning under my skin. If I was honest with myself, lust too.

Damn him.

Why did Diarmuid have to be so damn…damn beautiful.

I almost snorted. Even if he wasn't built like an Irish giant, as handsome as a high king, he'd still get under my skin.

You have my skin.

And you have mine.

I shrugged and stared out of the window into the dreary autumn. Leaves of the trees that lined the sidewalks were all turning. Autumn used to be my favourite season. *Used* to be. "Fine."

"That JLO of yours is trouble."

I snapped my face towards my da and blinked, studying his face. Did he know that Diarmuid and I had a history?

"Why do you say that?" I asked as casually as possible.

My da grunted, his eyes flicking between me and the road. "Just a feeling…"

My da was lying.

I shoved that thought away. Why would my da lie to me? He wouldn't. I was being paranoid. Diarmuid was making me paranoid.

"Well," I said, crossing my arms over my chest, "you don't have to worry about me. I'll be careful what I say around him."

My da nodded, his shoulders relaxing a touch.

"Hey," he said, a smile lifting the corner of his mouth. "Why don't we order a takeout pizza for dinner and watch a movie tonight?"

My heart flipped. Diarmuid and I used to do that.

Stop comparing anything everyone does to Diarmuid.

I forced a smile. A father-daughter night.

"That sounds great."

We got back to the house and Da ordered pizza while

I went up to have a shower and change into more comfortable clothes for hanging out.

It'd been almost four weeks since I first arrived. It was true that my da had been out of the house a lot since I'd come to live with him, hardly ever coming home for dinner. I woke up and he was asleep. I'd go off to my café job before he woke. At night he was never around and I made dinner and ate by myself in a lonely house, the TV on in the background for the noise.

Strangely, I missed Dublin. I knew people there even if I didn't really call them friends. Here I was all alone. Knowing only my da.

Well, and now Diarmuid.

God…

Diarmuid Brennan.

My stomach flipped. Of all the twists of fate in the world…

Somehow, he seemed more rugged, more masculine to me. Or perhaps I was now looking at him through the eyes of a woman. When I was thirteen, all I wanted to do was to curl up next to him. But now…

As the water ran down my body in the shower I couldn't help but think of how Diarmuid's hands might feel on me. Even though the water was hot enough to make tea, a shiver ran down my spine.

I came downstairs after my shower in sweatpants and a long-sleeved t-shirt. It was early October and the nights were getting cool.

My da was hanging up the house phone. "Hey, pet. I didn't know what you liked so I just ordered two supremes. Malachi's going to pick it up on the way here."

It wasn't going to be a father-daughter night, then.

Malachi was the cute boy who'd been here on the day I arrived. He'd been around here a bit since I moved in. But always when my da was around. We still hadn't gone for that bike ride yet.

"Oh, okay. What's on a supreme?"

"Beef, onions, mushrooms, peppers, olives…"

Diarmuid always ordered pizza without olives for me. "Um, I don't like olives but it's fine. I can pick them off."

My da fell into the couch, grabbing the remote. "What shall we watch?"

The doorbell rang before I could answer. "I'll grab it."

I opened the door and found Malachi at the threshold, holding two large pizza boxes in his hands. He grinned when he saw me, his eyes giving me a once-over. "Hello, beautiful."

He held the boxes to one side as he leaned in to give me a kiss on the cheek, his mouth lingering on my skin, his breath smelling faintly of cigarettes underneath the rush of sweet mint.

In the living room, with my da taking up the armchair, Malachi sat next to me on the couch, closer than he needed to. I noticed my da giving us both the eye but he didn't say anything.

"What do you want to watch?" he asked, flicking through the movie subscription channel.

"What about the latest Batman one?" I suggested.

My da wrinkled up his nose. "Aren't you a little old

for superheroes?"

I didn't think you could ever get too old for superheroes. I sank into the couch and said nothing more.

My da stuck on some shitty war movie. I was hardly paying attention to the film. I was too engrossed with remembering how I used to watch movies with someone else.

And when Malachi's arm went around me, a thread of disappointment went through me because I wished he was someone else.

24

Diarmuid

Then—Dublin, Ireland

I fell into the couch and laid back, resting my eyes shut and enjoying the silence in having the whole house to myself. Ava had gone back to Ballyannagh, the west coast village just outside of Limerick, where we both grew up.

She'd been pissed off at me for not going back with her, but I was too damn tired from this week. I needed a bit of space from her. We'd been bickering more than usual lately and it was driving me up the wall.

I'd organised with Danny to go to the football match tomorrow at Crowe Park, Mayo versus the Dubs, but

179

tonight was all mine.

A banging on my front door made me groan. "That'd be fucking right," I muttered to myself. I strode to the door and swung it open, a curse on my tip of my tongue. I halted when I saw it was Saoirse, shivering in the rain. I'd given her my address just in case she ever needed it.

Now she needed it, I could see from the furrow of her brow.

She needed me.

"Saoirse?" I gently pulled her inside out of the rain. "Jesus, you're soaked. Stay here. I'll get you a towel."

She stood in my hallway, shivering, as I ran to the hot press to grab the biggest, fluffiest towel we had. I hurried back and wrapped her in it, drying off the worst of the rain. We left her soaked sneakers drying in the hallway and I led her to the living room where I turned on the fireplace and sat her in front of it.

I pulled up the footstool and sat beside her, leaning forward, my elbows on my knees. "Talk to me, Saoirse."

"My ma brought home a guy..." she swallowed. "He's not a nice man."

My blood boiled at the fear in her voice.

"Did he hurt you? Did he touch you?"

I will fucking kill him if he did. I swear to God I will murder him and bury his body where no one can find it.

She shook her head and my veins flooded with cool relief.

"He just scares me. I didn't know where to go."

"You did the right thing coming here. You can come here any time, you know that, right?"

She nodded, her eyes round and full of hope. "Can I stay here tonight?"

I hesitated for a second before I spoke. "Of course. But I gotta ring your ma to let her—"

"No." Saoirse's eyes widened so I could see the whites all around her irises. "Please don't ring her."

"I have to." There was no question in my mind, regardless of how poorly Ms Quinn behaved as a parent. Saoirse was still under her legal care.

Saoirse grabbed my arm before I could rise up. "She won't care where I am, I promise."

It hurt me to think that could be the case.

"I'm not arguing with you, Saoirse," I said firmly. "Either I ring her and let her know where you are or I take you home."

She let go of me, sinking back into the chair and glaring at the wall.

I let out a soft sigh. Saoirse was pissed at me, but she could never stay mad at me. Letting her mother know that Saoirse was here was the right thing to do. I'd get that out of the way, then I could focus on cheering her up.

I walked into the kitchen, grabbing my phone along the way, and rang Ms Quinn's home number.

A woman answered the phone with a crackly voice as if she'd just woken up. "Hello?"

"Ms Quinn?"

"Who's this?" Suspicion clouded her tone.

"It's Diarmuid Brennan. The Juvenile Liaison Officer assigned to Saoirse."

"What she done now?"

I gritted my teeth. "Nothing. I'm calling to let you know that Saoirse's here and she's safe."

There was a pause. "Well, I'm not picking her up in this bloody weather. Don't have a car, do I?"

I swallowed the fierce retort that was begging to unleash from my tongue. "If it's alright with you, she can stay here the night and I'll drop her off in the morning."

"Oh, yeah, sure, whatever. But don't come too early." Then she hung up on me.

I rubbed my forehead. Un-fucking-believable. Saoirse's mother was a real piece of work. I walked slowly back into the living room.

"I told you she wouldn't care," came the quiet voice of the broken girl huddled in the towel.

The truth in Saoirse's words sliced me open. What could I say? That her mother did really care for her deep down? That the woman who was supposed to love her above all others was just going through a selfish phase? That this world would stop being cruel when she grew up?

All things I knew—and she knew—were lies.

25

Saoirse

Diarmuid cleared his throat. "Come on, selkie. Let's get you into some dry clothes."

And just like that, we agreed without speaking not to talk about my mother and her apathetic attitude towards me for the rest of the evening.

I followed him into the bathroom.

"You can have a hot shower here. Be back in a sec." He left and returned with a pile of clothes. "You can wear these."

I unfolded the shirt on top—a black faded Led Zeppelin shirt that I would swim in.

"I hope it's okay," he said. "It's the smallest one I have."

It was still huge.

"It's great," I replied, a small thrill going through me at the thought of wearing his shirt.

I unfolded the other item. It was a pair of gym shorts with a tie in the front. I eyed the slim size, then glanced at Diarmuid. There was no way that these were his.

"They're Ava's," he said. He could always seem to read my mind. "She won't mind if you wear them."

I frowned. "Who's Ava? Your housemate?"

Diarmuid blinked. "My...girlfriend."

Girlfriend.

The word hit me like a blow to the chest. "You...have a girlfriend?"

"Yeah," he said casually as if he didn't just rip my heart into two pieces.

My chest felt heavy and sore, swollen like my thumb did when I'd accidentally caught in between the door and the doorframe. "You never told me you had a girlfriend. You've never talked about her."

He rubbed his beard. "I must have."

I shook my head adamantly. "I would have remembered if you did. You haven't. Not one peep about her in the whole time we've known each other."

"Oh. Well...I can tell you about her once you've showered and dressed."

I didn't want to hear about her. I didn't want her to exist.

A girlfriend...

Diarmuid left, closing the door behind him, leaving me standing alone and shivering in the middle of the bathroom.

I undressed and stepped under the hot water, my head whirring. Diarmuid had a girlfriend.

A girlfriend.

He wasn't allowed to have a girlfriend.

He was supposed to be mine.

And I, his.

After my shower, I stood naked in front of the mirror, wiping the steam off the glass with my hand. I stared at my body. It had been changing this last year. My breasts were budding, my hips widening and my thighs developing shape. But I was still stuck somewhere between a girl and a woman.

Did Diarmuid's girlfriend, this *Ava*, have big breasts? Did she have hips and hair between her legs?

Does she do for him all the things that my ma does for those men she brings home? Is that why he's with her?

Is that what I have to do for him to make him like me?

My gaze fell upon the two toothbrushes in the holder, one blue one, the other was red. A stab went through me.

That was *her* toothbrush.

Suddenly all the evidence became like glaring beacons. The pink, sugary-smelling body wash in the shower, the two razors, the tropical shampoo and conditioner, the second towel hanging off the rack and a pale blue lace bra hanging behind the door.

Until now, I could have almost imagined that she

didn't exist.

But she was here. Even if she wasn't *here*. She lived with him. She got to live here with him instead of me. I had to live with a mother who didn't care if I didn't come home. My belly churned, the back of my throat going bitter, tasting the foulness of my jealousy.

I grabbed her bra off the back of the door and held it up against my chest. There was so much space between the material and my tender flesh. She had big boobs. Much bigger than mine. Is that why Diarmuid liked her?

A thought went through my mind almost causing me to drop the bra. What if he more than liked her...what if he loved her? What if he was going to marry her?

There was only one way to find out.

I tossed the bra back on the hook, trying not to throw up, and turned my attention to the clothes Diarmuid had left me. I pulled on the shirt. I finished dressing and stepped out of the bathroom.

Diarmuid wasn't in the living room. I wandered back into the corridor. Where was he?

I walked past the bathroom to the only other door at the end of this short corridor, partly open. I froze at what I saw inside. Diarmuid was naked from the waist up, unfolding a plain white shirt.

He was the most glorious man I'd ever seen. Thick torso, powerful arms, beautiful intricate ink tattooed across his back and shoulders. I wanted to run my hand across his skin, across the ridges of his abs. A buzzing grew in my lower belly. I was getting drunk off the sight of him.

I'd seen men with their shirts off; the men that Ma brought home. But none of them looked like this.

Maybe I gasped. Or maybe I let out a groan at the sight.

He looked up and his eyes locked onto mine. For a second he looked shocked, embarrassed, even. He pulled down the shirt over his beautiful body and tugged down the hem.

"Hey, I just ordered pizza to be—" He cut off as his eyes lowered to my body.

My undies were dry enough to put on again but I hadn't put my bra back on.

"What?" I looked down at myself. His shirt swam on me but I didn't think it looked so bad.

Diarmuid grinned as he walked towards me. "You look cute in my shirt."

I wrinkled my nose. Cute? I wanted to look beautiful. Or sexy. But not cute.

He ruffled my hair as he passed and I grimaced.

"Just you and me tonight, selkie," he called over his shoulder as I followed him to the living room. "Pizza will be here soon. I ordered your favourite."

Pepperoni and jalapenos. Extra cheese. He always remembered. Did he remember Ava's favourite pizza?

"So…" I said as I walked into the living room, arms folded. *Ava. Ask him straight out if he loves her.*

"So…" Diarmuid plopped onto the corner of the L-shaped couch.

"What do your tattoos mean?" I was such a coward.

He raised an eyebrow. Even he didn't believe that

187

was what I was planning to ask.

"Well…" he began slowly, turning one colourful arm. It looked like a jungle crammed with animals and leaves and flowers and stars. "I've been collecting tattoos since I was sixteen. Each one has a meaning."

I perked up, watching him as he spoke, mesmerised by every single piece of information about him, as if each piece was another panel in a quilt I was building. Once I wove together all the pieces, he would be mine.

I came closer, drawn in by the thickness of his bicep, by the power shifting underneath his skin-like silk. Drawn in by just…him.

I reached out my hand, then drew it back

"You can touch them if you want," he said.

I traced my fingers on a cluster of beautiful pink roses. They looked so real that I almost thought I could lean in closer and smell them.

"These roses are for my ma."

"You don't talk much about her," I said.

His lip twitched. "She died when I was younger."

A feeling lodged into my throat. I hated my ma sometimes but she was still my ma. She was one of the only people I had in this world. I don't know what I would do or where I would go if she died.

"How much younger?" I asked him, my voice small enough that he could just pretend not to have heard it if he wanted to.

"When I was five."

My heart ached for a five-year-old Diarmuid who had just lost his ma. It hurt when I lost my da but he didn't die. I knew he would come back one day. "Do you remember much about her?"

He shook his head. "Just that she had the most beautiful singing voice, and she smelled like powder and roses."

Hence, the roses. I smiled. I thought she sounded beautiful.

"So you lived with your da?"

Diarmuid's jaw clenched as he shook his head, just once. "My ma had me when she was young. Only seventeen. We lived with my grandma, so when my ma died I just stayed with my granny until she passed away nine years later."

He would have been fourteen. My age now.

"After that I went into foster care. Bounced around a few homes because no one could control me. I was angry at the world for taking everyone away from me. So angry." He flexed his hands in and out of fists, and I could see the pools of anger still there, soaking around him like a bog, appearing to be solid until you tested the ground. "The world isn't fair, selkie. You and I know it the most."

I don't know why I did it, but I reached out with my hand and slipped it into his. He flinched. For a second I thought that he might pull away from me. Instead his fingers closed around mine, causing my heart to warm.

"I could have ended up a criminal instead of a cop," he said quietly. "But I didn't."

So could you, his unsaid words were clear in my mind.

"Why didn't you?" I asked.

Diarmuid let out a long breath. "For a while it looked like I was headed in that direction. Until I was arrested and was assigned my very own JLO. He mentored me, gave me direction, taught me how to channel my aggression into fighting in a ring instead of on the street."

"That's why you're a JLO now," I realised.

He smiled. "I guess so."

"Why did we get so unlucky?" I asked, not really expecting an answer.

"You and me," he said, "are the lucky ones."

Lucky? I snorted. "How d'ya figure that?"

"Some people are born into family. We get to choose ours. We make our own, forged out of our hearts and weaved together by our souls. And *that* is stronger than blood."

"So, you and me…" I said, "we're soul family?"

He smiled. "Yeah. We are."

Feeling brave, I crawled onto his lap. He let me sit there.

I pushed up the sleeve of his shirt, thrilled with the feeling of pushing cloth across skin, and traced my fingers down his arm to another tattoo, loving the feeling of smooth, warm skin under my finger.

He told me the story of each tattoo on his arms, some of them his "kids" as he liked to call them, all the people he'd come across in his life who'd made an impact, no matter how small.

"I have more on my back," he said.

I hoped he might take his shirt off again and I'd get to touch him there, but he didn't.

"You don't have one on your chest, though." I remembered thinking that space looked empty when I saw him without his shirt on.

"You noticed, huh?"

I blushed. Perhaps I shouldn't have revealed that I'd been looking so closely.

"I haven't found anything I care about enough to place it there." He placed a hand on his heart. "Over my heart. It's a special place, you know? I can't put any old tattoo there."

"You don't want to put a tattoo there for your girlfriend?" I probed.

He let out a laugh. "Who, Ava? No."

I nibbled on my bottom lip. God, I wanted to know about her. At the same time, I didn't want to know.

"Why not?" I asked, as casually as I could. "She's your girlfriend, right?"

"Yeah, and she might get a tattoo…I guess."

"But not over your heart."

He shrugged.

My hope floated. If he wouldn't put Ava on his heart there was still room for someone else…for me.

"And what about a tattoo for me?" I dared to ask.

His eyes flicked to me, his gaze catching me in its intensity. His lip tweaked up in a half-smile. "You want a tattoo?"

I shrugged, holding back a smile. "Maybe. If I did, where would I go?"

I held my breath. The air between us feeling like it went taut. He opened his mouth to say something.

The doorbell rang. I cursed who I guessed must be the pizza delivery guy. Diarmuid gave me an apologetic look, saved from answering, and shifted me off his lap so he could go and answer the door.

Diarmuid paid the pizza guy and came back into the living room holding the box, the smell of baked dough and melted cheese making my mouth water.

"What movie do you want to watch?" he asked.

Our eyes met. We both cracked into a grin and spoke at the same time.

"Batman!"

We ate the pizza in his living room and Diarmuid stuck on *The Dark Knight*, a Batman reinvention directed by Christopher Nolan. I'd not watched it but Diarmuid had promised that it was the best Batman movie he'd ever seen.

As the closing credits rolled up, I let out a sigh. "Batman is the best superhero."

"Absolutely," Diarmuid agreed. He glanced at me. "Why do you like him best?"

Because he reminds me of you.

I let out a shrug. "Batman doesn't have superpowers, he's just an ordinary man who sees all the wrong in the world and makes it his business to make things better. He doesn't just sit back like most people and let it happen."

Diarmuid cracked a smile. "Yeah, that's why I like him too. He's braver than any other superhero because he doesn't have super strength or a superpower to fall back on."

I nodded. "It would be easy to be brave if you had

Superman's powers."

He nodded. "Batman's a real hero."

"Like you," I said quietly.

The smile on his face could have kept me warm for the rest of the Irish winter.

Soon the pizza box was empty before us and we laid back among the cushions. The movie was good. I found myself getting lost in it, almost forgetting all about Ava and the fact that *she* was Diarmuid's girlfriend.

I shuffled closer to Diarmuid, testing the boundaries. When he glanced down at me with a smile, I took that as a good sign and leaned my head on his arm. After a beat he pulled his arm out and wound it around my shoulder, tugging me into his side. A warmth glowed through me. It felt so good.

It felt right.

I decided then I didn't care if he had a girlfriend. Diarmuid belonged to me. And I belonged to him.

You have my skin.

And you have mine.

26

Diarmuid

Now—Limerick, Ireland

Twenty-three minutes past five next Friday afternoon and Saoirse wasn't here at O'Malley's gym like she should have been.

I gritted my teeth. My insides had been bouncing around like a can full of worms all week. I'd been dreading this session with her.

And looking forward to it at the same time.

Go fucking figure.

I grabbed my phone from my bag just as it started ringing. I answered without looking at the screen. "Where are ye?"

"Diarmuid?"

Fuck.

It wasn't Saoirse's voice. It was Ava's.

I rubbed my fingers across my closed lids. I'd managed to avoid Ava's calls until now. "Oh, hey."

"I've been trying to reach you." I hated when she got her whingy voice on and boy, was it on in layers today.

"Yeah, I know. Sorry." *Fuck, Brennan, get off the phone.* "I've been busy. With work."

She snorted. "You're always busy, Diarmuid. But it's about making time for the things that are important. We need to talk."

Fuck, no.

"About what?" I said, stalling.

"That's what I want to talk to you about. I thought we could get together sometime this weekend. Have dinner, maybe."

"I don't know, Ava." I silently slapped my forehead. Why couldn't I just tell her to fuck off like I should. I was perfectly capable of telling everyone else who pissed me off to fuck off.

"Like it or not, Diarmuid, I am still your wife. You owe me this."

I looked up in that moment. Perhaps I had been drawn to look up because I heard a noise. Or perhaps I just sensed *her.*

Saoirse was standing in the doorway of the gym in sweatpants and an oversized hoodie, fresh-faced, her long blonde locks pulled into a high ponytail. My heart tugged. Would I ever get used to seeing her all grown up? She looked effortlessly sexy even in baggy clothes.

Shit. Not sexy. *Not* sexy. I could not be calling my *seventeen-year-old* juvenile assignment sexy, for fuck's sake.

"Diarmuid? Are you even listening to me?"

Shit on a stick. Ava was still on the line.

"Sorry. The person I've been waiting for just arrived. I'll call you later." I hung up and turned off my phone before Ava could yell at me.

Saoirse walked towards me like a panther, watching me. I felt an unreasonable flush on my neck, as if I'd been caught doing something wrong.

She strode right up to me until we were toe to toe, her rose perfume curling around me in wisps. The scent sent a stab through my gut. My mother used to wear rose perfume. Saoirse used to favor vanilla scents when she'd been younger.

Saoirse had changed. Matured.

"You didn't have to hang up on Ava," Saoirse said. "She *is* your wife."

I took a step back, trying to get some space. My mind seemed to go fuzzy at her proximity.

"You're late," I said, trying to avoid the subject of Ava.

She tilted her head, her hands fisted on her hips, an aggressive stance if I ever saw one. "And you're married. So what?"

I almost let out a groan of frustration. This session was not going how I planned it to go. I wanted to drop my face into my hands. But I would not. I'd had difficult assignments before. Saoirse was just another difficult

197

case.

Except…she wasn't, was she?

"How 'bout we just get started," I said, wanting desperately to stop talking and start doing. "I wanted to go through some fighting basics."

She smirked at me. "You wanna fight me, Diarmuid?"

"I want to teach you how to defend yourself."

Her voice lowered. "I could have used that three years ago. To defend myself from you."

Through the cracks of her snippy façade was a deep well of pain. It shone as clear as a full moon on a lake.

I had done that to her. Even in trying to do what was right for her, I had failed her.

"Saoirse," I breathed. "Please…"

"Whatever." She walked past me, flicked her ponytail over her shoulder, her smell hitting me right in the chest.

I squeezed my eyes shut and prayed to whatever deity was listening to give me strength.

"I'll just get into my workout gear," I heard from behind me.

I frowned. Her workout gear? Wasn't she wearing that?

I spun round just in time to watch her pushing down the tracksuit bottoms to her ankles as she stood at one of the benches that lined the wall, her back to me, legs straight, round ass in the air, covered only by a pair of tiny running shorts.

I choked.

Holy shit.

Something tugged in me, something unfamiliar. Something hot and foreign like a blade. Lust. Want. Desire.

Oh fuck.

She straightened and grabbed the hem of her hoodie and pulled it up over her head, revealing her slender waist, those curves, in a tiny fitted workout singlet. She dropped her hoodie on the bench and spun to look straight at me.

I was too shocked to hide my emotions. She caught me, my raw, openly lusty stare.

I was going to burn in hell.

I slammed down my mask as quickly as I could. *What the fuck, Diarmuid?*

Thank God we were the only ones in the gym and I had no witnesses to my blatant drooling. That's why I picked Friday afternoon to work out with her. I knew no one would bother us. She and I were alone.

Oh shit.

She and I were *alone*.

Maybe this wasn't such a good idea.

27

Saoirse

The way he was looking at me…

Like I was a woman, not a girl.

Like I was the most gorgeous creature he'd ever seen.

Like I was dessert and he was starving.

I'd waited years to have him look at me that way. Dreamed about it. Yearned for it.

His stare hit me right in my lower belly, tumbling and twisting into hot knots.

Damn him.

I was just getting over him. I was just learning not to care.

Yeah, right.

I shoved these feelings aside, locking my arms across

my chest as if they were armour and could protect me.

Nothing had ever been able to protect me from him.

"Lead the way, oh venerable master," I said. Yes, sarcasm would totally work as a defense.

Diarmuid cleared his throat and indicated for me to come with him.

I followed him as he strode towards the other side of the gym. My eyes couldn't help wandering over his hard, fit body, dressed simply in a pair of light grey sweatpants and a tight black sleeveless shirt. His shoulder-length hair was tied back into a small bun at the nape of his thick neck. His muscular arms and rounded shoulders were on display, colourful ink across smooth skin like a piece of art.

He was a piece of art. This sight should be fucking illegal.

He stopped in front of a battered, faded red bag hanging from one of the beams. I stopped beside him.

"I'm, er, going to show you the basics today." He sounded nervous. Unsure of himself, even. Why would he be nervous? He wouldn't even meet my eyes. "Neutral stance should be feet hip-width apart, your left foot forward because you're right-handed."

I stood how he instructed. My body heating as he gazed over my exposed legs. Why the hell did I think wearing running shorts was a good idea?

"That's good. Now make a fist."

"Are you going to let me hit you?"

His eyes snapped to mine, a twitch pulling at his top lip. "Just do it."

I held up my right hand in front of my face, gave him the finger, *then* made a fist.

He let out a snort. "Tuck your thumb in."

I frowned at my hand. Then pushed my thumb, which was sticking out, under my fingers.

"Not like that... Here."

He grabbed my hand in both of his. His hands were huge, dwarfing mine, rough and warm and calloused, just like I remembered. He gently pulled out my thumb and tucked it under so it was out of the way, totally unaware of how wobbly my knees had just gotten. Or how my heartbeat had quickened.

"Like this. Or you'll break your thumb when you hit something." His glanced up and his eyes locked with mine. His thumb brushing lightly across the back of my hand.

Damn him.

I yanked my hand out of his. I wanted to rub it against my clothing to get rid of the residue feeling ghosting the back of my hand.

He turned and faced the bag as if nothing had happened.

"You want to extend your right hand forward, leading with your hips as you go. Start slow." He moved as he spoke, extending his arm, his muscles shifting underneath his smooth inked skin, his slim hips turning. He returned back to his neutral stance. "We want you to get your technique right before you start adding speed."

He punched again, this time striking out so hard and fast that his arm was a blur, the bag smacking back as his fist impacted it. The bag never had a chance.

Holy shit.

He was fast. And strong as fuck. I snapped my mouth closed as he grabbed the bag to steady it, then turned towards me.

"Your turn."

I let out a scoffing noise. "Watch and learn, Brennan."

I had no idea what I was doing. But it was better than him realising just how impressed I was. I stepped up to the bag, wearing my false bravado around me like an oversized coat, and gave it what I thought was a decent punch.

My fist tapped the bag and it hardly moved. I made a face.

Diarmuid's face hadn't changed. "Try again."

I glared at the bag, pretending it was Diarmuid's balls. I lashed out.

Diarmuid let out a small sigh. "You have to lead with your hips, selkie."

"*Don't* call me that." I hit again.

"Lead with your hips."

I smashed the bag with my fist, frustration pouring out of my hand. "You keep fucking saying that but I have no idea what you mean by it."

"Here." He moved around me, coming to stand right behind me, the warmth of him soaking into my back. His right hand grabbed my right wrist and his left hand closed over my hip.

Oh, God.

I froze. "What are you doing?" I asked, my voice a mere squeak.

My body was betraying me. I wanted to lean back into him. To roll my ass against his hard body.

"Just relax."

Relax? *Relax?* How the fuck was I supposed to relax when he was crowding me like this.

"Release your arm from your shoulder," his voice rumbled into my ear as he extended our arms out. "And *lead* from your hips."

At the same time his hand pulled at my left hip, twisting us, his warmth flooding into my body.

I might have whimpered. I'm not sure.

I realised we were just standing there, his arms round me, my fist against the bag. I swear I heard him inhale against my hair.

Shit. Fuck. I shoved his hands off me. It pained me to have his hands on me. It pained me to be without them.

I stumbled away from him. "Why are we doing this, anyway?"

"Self-defense. You need to know what to do just in case you ever need to defend yourself."

I bristled. "You're the only one I've ever had to defend myself from."

His face crumpled. "That is not true."

I knew we were both thinking of the last time we'd seen each other three years ago, of the *reason* he left me.

I shook my head, my insides warring. I wanted to hate him for leaving all those years ago. I did hate him.

And yet, I wanted nothing more than to fling myself into his arms and sob with relief that we'd found our way back to each other. I wanted to give him every hurt and fear I'd saved so he could fold them away, the way only he could. I wanted to make him laugh and laugh to make up for all the happiness we'd missed. The thought of letting him back in made the armour around my heart harden. It made the girl inside of me recoil and hiss with fear. Which led me back to anger.

My emotions tumbled so hard inside me I almost felt dizzy.

There was so much I wanted to let out.

But I couldn't.

I couldn't let him hurt me again.

I wouldn't.

"Time's up," I said.

He opened his mouth as if to speak. I didn't want to hear it. I was running out of energy to keep him at a safe distance. If I let him back in, it'd be the end of me.

I strode past him to the bench where I'd left my bag, giving him no chance to continue the conversation.

I pulled my sweats and hoodie back on. I almost jumped when I heard Diarmuid's voice behind me.

"I'll wait with you outside."

Either he had the lightest footsteps in all of history or I was too worked up to be paying much attention to my surroundings.

"I don't need you to wait with me. I'm not a child anymore." I slung my duffle bag over one shoulder and strode towards the exit.

Damn him. He kept up with me easily, his long legs cutting across the polished wooden floors.

He raced ahead so he could open the door for me. I scowled as I stormed past, refusing to say thanks, then feeling like a bitch. I didn't want him to be sweet to me. I wanted to hate him. It was easier to hate him.

Then he was beside me as I stopped on the sidewalk, watching me with concern on his face.

Screw him and his concern. Where was his concern for the last three years?

I crossed my arms over my chest. "Leave me alone."

He frowned, his stance widening as if to make a point that he was not leaving my side.

"Saoirse, this is an industrial neighbourhood and it's dusk. I wouldn't let anyone wait out here by themselves."

"Whatever." I made a point to roll my eyes, trying to tamp down the little voice inside me that whispered that he still cared about me.

He stood too close to me. Too damn close, it made my hairs stand on end as if he were magnetized and I was metal.

I sidestepped away from him. Not discreetly enough, because I caught the side glance he gave me and the press of his lips.

The air was crisp and the sun was streaking like blood across the underside of clouds in the darkening sky. As much as I hated to admit it, Diarmuid was right. There was no one around at this time of the evening. The warehouse next door that had been open when I had arrived was now shut up.

We stood in silence for what felt like hours, the sky darkening, the temperature dropping, making me shove my hands in the front pocket of my hoodie.

I had to fight the urge to glance over. As my anger subsided, I was left with burning curiosity. What had he done in the last three years? Did he have a boy or a girl? Was he happy with his new family? Did he ever wish he was with me instead?

Diarmuid glanced at his watch, my eyes latching onto that movement. He pressed his full lips together.

"My da *is* coming to pick me up," I said in defense of an accusation unspoken.

He said nothing. His eyes scanned the empty road as if to say, *oh yeah? Where is he, then?*

I couldn't even hear any oncoming cars.

I worried my lip. Then looked at my own watch.

"He should be here…" I trailed off. My da was almost fifteen minutes late.

"Let me drive ye home."

"He wouldn't forget," I snapped. I took out my phone and dialed my da's number. He answered after five rings. "Da, yeah. Where are you?"

"Out at the farm, pet."

"Oh…were you going to pick me up?"

"Oh shite, sorry, I got caught up with work, you know how it goes. I can be there in an hour."

My face fell. I caught Diarmuid's eye, concern clear on his face. I frowned and turned away, walking a few steps away from him.

"…Oh. Right. No bother, then. I can find my own

way home. K…bye." I tucked my phone in my pocket and let out a long huff. I'd have to call a cab or something.

"Let me drive you home." Diarmuid's voice came from behind.

"I'll just catch a—"

"Saoirse." I felt his firm hand on my shoulder. He turned me to face him. "I'm driving you home."

I felt his hand all throughout my body.

He grabbed the rest of his things from inside the building and he closed up. I followed him wordlessly, watching his strong hands deftly move across the equipment as he put it away. He was as sure of his movements as always.

He locked up and I loitered at his side, wondering how it was that he had a key to this place. Did he work here part-time? Did he…own the place?

"I used to train here as a teenager," he started to say, as if he'd heard the question in my head. "My two best friends and I learned to fight here. It kept us out of trouble as teens. Well…mostly," he admitted.

I knew all about the trouble that he'd gotten into as a teen. The drugs, the alcohol. The street fights.

I kept a casual face on like I didn't care. Even as every cell in my body was waiting to hear more.

As if he knew it would annoy me, he stopped talking.

Damn him. Well, I wasn't about to ask him any questions. It wasn't like I was desperately curious to know. Every. Little. Thing. About. Him.

Diarmuid locked the back door and led me to the

tiny parking lot out back. There was a single old maroon truck parked near the door.

I frowned. Was that...? No way.

"Is that the same truck as you used to have?" I blurted out before I could remind myself that I didn't care.

"The very one." He strode ahead and opened the passenger door for me.

I scowled.

He smirked.

"You don't have to help me up into the truck anymore, you know?" I grumbled as I got into the passenger's seat, ignoring his outstretched hand, the hand that used to lift me up every time I fell.

He laughed as he leaned against the top of my open door. The sound plucked several memories inside of me, like a haunting melody, loaded with sweetness and layered with my sorrow.

I remembered the first time I'd ridden in this very truck with him, the first time I'd made him laugh. The pleasant, rich sound had seemed so foreign coming out of such a broody brute. But it only made it more beautiful. Because I came to learn that I was one of the few who could pluck laughter from him.

"Your legs are a lot longer than they used to be," he said.

I'm sure he meant it to be casual, but his eyes flicked down for a moment before coming up to meet my gaze. That single movement drew a trace of wildfire across me.

"Some things change," I said, my voice squeezing out

of my throat, which had gone tight.

"Some things haven't," he said quietly, his eyes latching onto mine.

Damn him.

Damn him for not changing. Damn *us* for not changing.

Damn him for looking at me the way he did when I was a kid. Like I meant the world to him. Like he'd do anything to protect me.

He shut the door and walked round to his side.

I swallowed back the knot in my throat as I glanced around the cab. It still smelled like him, leather and Diarmuid's woodsy cologne.

"I can't believe you still have this truck," I blurted out as he slid into the driver's seat. So many memories, just him and me, inside this truck.

"She's a classic, I told you." He petted the dashboard. "She hasn't let me down yet."

He turned on the engine, the familiar rumble travelling through my body. The radio turned on automatically. The radio blared and it took a second for me to place the familiar tune.

The Dubliners.

I swallowed.

"Since when do you listen to The Dubliners?"

He shrugged. He pulled out of the parking lot into the street.

"I thought you said this music was shite," I pushed.

The lower half of his face shifted as he worked his jaw around unspoken words. "I guess it grew on me. It reminds me of…you."

"Oh," I said, my voice almost a whisper.

Oh.

We were silent all the way home. I tried to relax in the truck, but I was too aware of him next to me. Too aware of every movement he made, of every breath he took, every sound he made.

We pulled up in front of my house. I shifted in my seat, knowing I should get out but stupidly not wanting to. My cheeks flamed when the silence had gone on too long.

"Well, thanks," I blurted out and hopped out the truck.

"Saoirse," Diarmuid called out before I could shut the door.

My heart skipped a beat when my eyes met his.

"Whatever happens between us, I want you to know you can always call me if you get stuck without a ride. No matter what time. Even if I'm not your JLO anymore."

I nodded because I couldn't speak, my heart having crawled up into my throat.

28

Diarmuid

What the fuck was wrong with me?

I slammed my fists into the boxing bag, my arm and shoulder muscles screaming for relief. I kept pounding, ignoring the cry of my muscles. I deserved the pain. Every single ounce of it.

Finally my arms gave up, dropping to my sides, as my muscles shut off in order to protect themselves from too much damage.

I bent over, chest heaving, trying to suck in air.

Images of Saoirse Quinn as a thirteen-year-old girl and her now—body like a wet dream, ass in the air, bent over as she pushed her sweats down her long, shapely legs—flickered like strobe lights in my mind.

I winced. My head ached. I rubbed my forehead as if I could wipe the images from my mind and staunch the rush of heat that shot through my veins.

But I couldn't.

It was burned into my brain.

I had to stop this. I couldn't be thinking about Saoirse this way. She was only seventeen, for Christ's sake. And I was supposed to be her Juvenile Liaison Officer, her protector, her mentor.

Not thinking of her in such a salacious way. *Not* imagining her as a woman, naked, writhing under me as I—

I hissed, recoiling from my own thoughts.

I had to stop this.

Before I was tempted to do something stupid.

What was I talking about? I was already tempted.

No, dammit, I *wasn't* tempted. It was just a momentary lapse in judgement.

Maybe Declan was right. This was because I'd been almost three years without being laid. I needed to go out on a date. With an *overaged* woman. Someone who wasn't *her*.

I tugged the wraps off my fists and flexed my aching fingers before I grabbed my phone and texted Declan.

Me: Can you still spare two tickets to your fight?

My phone beeped back almost instantly.

Declan: Only if you're bringing someone you're

looking to fuck.

I let out a snort. Crude as always.

Me: Yeah, I'll bring a date.

Declan: About fucking time. Your dick has cobwebs.

I made a mental note to ask Marla, the sweet girl from the coffee shop, if she'd go with me. Yes, this was what I needed to keep my mind off...things that I shouldn't be thinking about. I should be focusing on getting to know a woman *my age*. A woman who wouldn't land me in jail if I touched her.

A woman who looked nothing like the curvaceous, effortlessly sexy blonde angel from my past who had stolen a piece of my heart a long time ago.

Thinking this way about Saoirse should feel wrong.

It *was* wrong.

Right?

I was so fucked.

216

29

Diarmuid

Then—Dublin, Ireland

"Are you cheating on me, you son of a bitch?" Ava demanded as soon as I walked in the door.

I'd only stopped home to drop off a bag before I had to pick up Saoirse. Now I regretted this decision.

I halted, halfway in the living room, halfway in the entry way. "What are you talking about, woman?"

Ava grabbed something from the living room table and swung to face me, accusation on her face. She strode up to me and shoved an item of clothing into my chest. "You think I don't know if another woman has been wearing *my fucking clothes?*"

It was the shorts I'd loaned Saoirse over the weekend.

The ones I'd pushed down to the bottom of the washing basket, figuring Ava wouldn't notice. It wasn't like I was hiding anything. I just knew Ava would make a bigger deal out of Saoirse staying over than she should. I'd just wanted to avoid an argument. Like the one we were having now.

I let out a tired sigh. "Jesus Christ, Ava."

"Who is she? Who the fuck is she?" Her voice shook with anger.

"I'm not cheating on you, okay? One of my kids got into a bad situation at home over the weekend and needed to stay the night. I gave her your shorts to wear."

"*Her?* You let *another woman* stay over?" Ava yelled. "*Where* did she sleep, Diarmuid?"

"The couch."

I wasn't lying. Saoirse had fallen asleep in my arms on the couch that night. I hadn't wanted to wake her so I stayed watching over her until I, too, had fallen asleep.

Ava's eyes narrowed. "And where did *you* sleep?"

I let out a growl. "Don't turn something innocent into something sordid."

"Me? *Me?*"

"I don't have time for this right now, Ava. I'm late to pick up…" *Saoirse,* "one of my kids."

"It's *her* again, isn't it?" Ava's face screwed up. "You spend more time with that fucking *girl* than me."

I turned and strode towards the front door, patting my keys which were still in my pocket. "You can yell at me later. I have to go."

"Diarmuid, if you walk out of here, I swear to God—"

I closed the front door in her face, knowing I was in deep shit when I returned home. I didn't care, though. I *was not* going to let Saoirse down.

30

Saoirse

Kian and I were both standing on the sidewalk in front of school.

"Come on, Saoirse. Come over," Kian whined, giving me his puppy-dog eyes, the ones that every girl seemed to be affected by, except me.

Funny how I used to think he was hot. I used to care what he thought of me. It used to make me happy when he'd speak to me.

Then I met Diarmuid. Strong, handsome, rugged Diarmuid.

Now Kian didn't seem so special.

I shook my head. "Can't. I'm getting picked up."

I glanced at the street, eyes peeled for the familiar

truck. What if he wasn't coming this time?

Diarmuid had been picking me up from school for months, and still, a part of me deep down was waiting for the day he didn't show up. It was better to expect the worst. Then when it happened, I wouldn't be surprised.

"Later tonight, then," Kian said, pulling my attention back on him. "My parents are never home till late. It'd just be you and me."

There was a glint in his eye. I was not so juvenile to not understand what that meant. I suppose losing my virginity to someone like Kian wouldn't be the worst decision I'd ever made.

For some reason, Diarmuid's face flashed before my eyes.

"Maybe."

"Maybe?"

"Maybe," I confirmed.

He stepped in closer. "What can I do to turn that maybe into a yes?"

I shrugged. Maybe I should say yes. He was a good-looking boy. And popular. And he seemed to like me...

"Not sure if I've told you yet, but you look real sweet today." He reached out to tuck a lock of hair behind my ear.

Sweet? Diarmuid never called me sweet. He called me beautiful. That's what he said and that's how I felt around him.

"Thanks," I muttered.

"Saoirse." A familiar gruff voice barked out my name, sending a rush down my spine.

Kian jumped back from me. I spun towards the voice, a smile spreading across my face. He was here.

Diarmuid slammed the door to his truck, parked haphazardly on the sidewalk, and stormed towards us.

"Holy shit," Kian muttered, "is that your brother?"

I almost rolled my eyes. Diarmuid and I looked nothing alike. I was fresh-faced and pale and blonde while he was tall, dark and made up of hard planes and sharp lines.

"No. He's my best friend."

My best friend.

He was my best friend, I realised. I'd never had a best friend before.

Diarmuid halted before us. His face looked murderous but his eyes softened when he glanced at me. I grinned up at him. Somehow the world was better when he was here. I could almost believe that it could be *good*.

"Hello, sir," Kian mumbled as Diarmuid towered over him.

Kian didn't look half as good-looking or half as tall and strong standing next to Diarmuid. Diarmuid gave Kian a glaring once-over in which I swear, Kian shrank even further into himself.

Diarmuid grunted. *Grunted.* Then turned to me. "You ready to go?"

I nodded, beaming at him. The fading sunset flared behind his messy hair, let loose from his usual ponytail, making him look like he had a halo.

I waved back at Kian, who looked about ready to piss himself, and Diarmuid helped me into the truck as always.

"Who was that boy?" Diarmuid demanded as soon as he was inside the truck. He was still glaring at Kian, who was still standing shell-shocked on the grass.

I sat up in my seat. Was Diarmuid...jealous?

"He's a friend from school," I said slowly, watching Diarmuid's face.

Diarmuid still didn't start the engine. He was still staring at Kian, his jaw twitching. "I don't like him."

My heart did a flip. He *was* jealous.

"He's popular," I said casually. "Lots of girl at school think he's good-looking."

Diarmuid narrowed his eyes at me. "Do you think he's good-looking?"

I hid a smile and gave him a one-shouldered shrug. "He's alright."

He's not as beautiful as you. No one is as beautiful as you.

"He was standing too close to you."

"He's just a boy. Harmless, really."

Diarmuid snorted. "He might just be a boy but you're too young for him." He started up the engine with a rumble as if to emphasize his point, then pulled out onto the road.

You're too young for him.

Diarmuid's words stabbed my gut. Kian was younger than *Diarmuid*. Did Diarmuid think *I* was too young for *him*?

"That's stupid." I crossed my arms over my chest, the familiar streets flashing by my window.

"What's stupid?"

"That I'm too young for him."

"Saoirse, you're only fourteen. You've got the rest of your life to grow up and like boys."

"But say if I did. Say…" I said, testing the waters, "if I wanted to date someone older. So what?"

Diarmuid slammed on the brakes, holding his arm out to keep me back in the seat.

"What the hell?" I asked, sucking in a breath.

His turned his entire torso towards me, eyes like slits. "You want to date *him*?"

"I was just asking theor—"

"And I'm asking you," he leaned in close, so close I could smell the mint on his breath, "do you want to date *him*?"

I was pinned to the seat by his stare. So intense. So full of fire.

I shook my head because I didn't trust myself to speak.

"Good," he said simply.

Good? Why was that good?

A horn blared from behind us and I jumped. We were still stationary in the truck in the middle of the road.

Diarmuid straightened in his seat as another blare sounded long and harder this time.

"You can fucking wait," he yelled out of his open truck window. He looked back at me, his eyes like hardened onyx. "Promise me you'll wait."

"Wait? For what?"

"Wait to date. Wait to *be* with someone. Wait…for someone special. You deserve to be with someone special, selkie."

You. I'll wait for you.

"Selkie?"

"I promise," I said.

31

Diarmuid

I expected World War III when I got home. But Ava wasn't there.

I let out a sigh of relief. She must have gone over to one of her friends' place to bitch about me, no doubt. Hopefully she'd be gone all evening. I had no fucking energy for her bullshit right now.

I was still fuming over that fucking kid who'd been standing so close to Saoirse when I'd picked her up. That boy was trouble. I could see it a mile away.

The front door opened behind me. I spun to see Ava walking in the front door, murder written all over her face.

My shoulders dropped. Luck wasn't on my side this

evening.

"Asshole," she hissed, her voice as bitter as poison.

"Ava—"

"I jumped in a cab and followed you."

"You *what?*"

Ava strode towards me, her long legs cutting across the carpet, her arms flying out wildly, stabbing me in the chest. "I saw your precious Saoirse. I saw the way you glared at that boy she was with at school. You were jealous. *Jealous!*"

"You are fucking delusional," I ground out.

"No, *you* are delusional. I saw the way she looked at you."

"Because I'm the only one who cares about her, Ava," I exploded. "She sees me as a big brother."

"That is *not* the way she looks at you. And the way you looked at her—"

"Don't you dare finish that sentence." Anger boiled inside me. "How dare you try to make something innocent and precious into something sick and twisted."

"Is it all just innocent?"

"Of course it fucking is. She's four-fucking-teen," I bellowed.

Ava shook her head, her hair falling around her face. I used to love her long, thick, dark hair extensions. Her long wing-like eyelashes. Her glossy acrylic nails. Now she just looked...fake. The words we spoke to each other sounded...hollow.

I rubbed my face. I knew couples went through rough patches. I couldn't remember when this one had started. I wasn't sure I could see the end in sight.

"Sometimes I think you *want* to fight," I said, my voice sounding worn out.

"Sometimes I think you'd rather be with *someone else*." Her accusing look fisted into my chest, pulling back the layers, getting too close to uncovering the truth I didn't want to see.

I shoved this thought aside.

"I am not talking about this anymore," I said firmly.

I turned and stormed out of the house, slamming the door behind me.

This time as I drove away, I watched my rearview mirror in case she decided to follow me again. Thankfully she didn't.

I drove for what felt like ages.

Until I found myself outside the building of the only person who made me happy these days. The only person who never judged me. The only one who never questioned my intentions or accused me. The only one who accepted me. Who understood me. Even though she was almost a decade younger than me.

What did age between friends matter anyway?

I knocked on Saoirse's door and shoved my hands into my pockets.

Moments later it opened and a familiar sweet face peeked out from the crack of the doorway. My favourite face. The mere sight of it made my spirits lift.

"Diarmuid?"

I shuffled my feet and gave Saoirse a bashful grin. I almost felt like a teenager again, asking if his friend could come out and play.

"My evening just freed up," I said. "Wanna do something with me?"

The smile that beamed from her face made all my troubles melt away.

32

Diarmuid

Now—Limerick, Ireland

Twenty bloody past four on the next Friday and Saoirse was late. Again.

I'd even texted her yesterday to confirm she was attending our Friday appointment. I didn't hear back from her.

I found Saoirse's mobile number in my phone contacts and stabbed the call button.

The phone rang. And rang. Until it went to her message bank.

"It's Saoirse. You know what to do after the beep..."

Something twinged in my chest at the sound of her

mature voice. Jesus, where had my little selkie gone?

I hung up just as I heard a roar outside. That better be her.

I marched out the door, only to find Saoirse hopping off the back of a motorbike parked on the side of the road—a *fucking* motorbike—dressed in a pair of tight black workout pants that showed off every curve and muscle in her lean thighs. On top she wore a slimline grey Everlast hoodie that clung to her waist, a tiny backpack on her back.

The driver of the bike was a skinny dickwad in a fake leather jacket, not more than twenty-two, I bet. The fucker was leering at her, taking no pains to hide it. He wasn't wearing a helmet. She hadn't been wearing one either.

Un-fucking-believable.

"Saoirse!" I yelled and stormed over to them, ready to beat the living crap out of that fucking idiot who let her ride without a helmet. If anything had happened, she would have been seriously injured…or worse.

I was going to put this fucker in the ground.

Saoirse glanced over her shoulder and our eyes met. Her eyes widened. She turned back to dickwad and said something I couldn't hear. She stepped away from the bike and he gunned the engine.

"Hey," I yelled out at him. "Stop right there, fucker." I grabbed his collar and practically ripped him back off his bike.

"What the hell are you doing?" Saoirse cried out.

"What the hell is wrong with you that you put

someone on the back of your bike without a goddamn helmet?" I screamed at the guy.

He stared at me as if I was about to chew him up and spit him out. "I-I didn't have one?"

I was going to kill the boy.

"You fucking get one or else you don't ever give her a ride again. Give me your fucking wallet."

The kid did what I demanded, handing over his brown leather wallet. I frowned. This was an expensive brand. What was this kid doing with a nice wallet like this? A nice bike like this, too?

I pulled out his driver's licence and glared at the photo of him, a sneer on his face, hair unkempt around his head. I supposed some girls might find him attractive.

"Malachi Walsh," I read out. "Now I know your name. I know where you live. Has she told you I'm a cop?"

He shook his head, the whites of his eye showing.

"Are you fucking her?" I blurted out without thinking.

"Jesus Christ, Diarmuid," Saoirse cried. "That's none of your fucking business."

I glared at the shaking kid, my rage causing me to ignore Saoirse's probably reasonable ranting at me. "Are you?" I growled into Malachi's face.

"N-no."

I glanced over to Saoirse. She was glaring back at me, her arms crossed over her chest. "Fucking hell, Diarmuid," she said, "I'm over the age of consent."

Except not for me.

He was legally allowed to be with her.

I wasn't.

Short of killing this prick and burying his body, there was no way I was going to stop the un-fucking-thinkable from happening between him and Saoirse. She was now a beautiful woman. Why wouldn't he want to sleep with her?

The thought made me so fucking mad I wanted to put my fist through to the back of his head.

I couldn't protect her from him if she *chose* him.

But I could *try*.

I gripped Malachi's shirt tighter and yanked him right up to me so that I could see the whites all around his dark brown eyes.

"If I hear that you even breathe on her, I will hunt down your unworthy ass and rip your fucking dick off with my bare hands. You got that?"

He nodded, looking like he was about to piss himself.

"Now get the fuck out of here." I let go of his shirt.

He drove off in a roar, gravel spitting out from his back tire.

"What's wrong with you?" Saoirse cried, frustration pouring out of her voice.

"What the fuck were you doing on the back of his bike?" I pointed a shaking finger at the rider disappearing into the distance.

She frowned at me. "He was nice enough to give me a lift."

"You will not see him again."

She slammed her fists onto her hips. "Fuck off."

I was about to lose my fucking mind, my control unravelling like the fibres of a frayed rope.

"Saoirse Quinn…" I spat out, a warning through gritted teeth.

She rolled her eyes. "Diarmuid Brennan," she said in a mocking tone.

"What fucking eejit doesn't wear a helmet while riding a motorbike? You could have been killed."

"Relax. He drove safely."

"It doesn't fucking matter, Saoirse, there are other drivers on the road."

She rolled her eyes again and I wanted to strangle her. She was fucking lucky that they weren't in an accident.

I made a vow. If I ever saw this boy again, I would make him regret he ever got her on the back of his bike without a helmet.

"Whatever," Saoirse said, dismissing me.

My vision bled red.

I raised a finger. "You are not to see him again. You are not to get on the back of his bike again."

"You're not my father, stop trying to act like one."

"If your fucking father acted like one I wouldn't have to worry about you falling off the back of a bike."

Her cheeks flushed red. I knew I had crossed the line.

"Screw you, Diarmuid. I'm out of here." She spun as if to leave.

I caught her arm before I knew what I was doing.

"You walk away from me—from these weekly sessions—and I will advise the court that you are a disobedient juvenile and unfit for the program. Your case will go to court. You will go to jail."

Jesus fucking Christ, Brennan. Blackmail? I was resorting to blackmail to keep her close. I'd sunk to a new low.

Her eyes widened, her nostrils flaring. "You wouldn't."

I leaned in close, so close I could see the flecks of gold in her green eyes. "Test me."

Underneath my palm, she burned like embers. I felt the heat all the way into my gut.

My eyes dropped to her mouth. Her lips parted and her tiny pink tongue darted out to lick at her bottom lip. I bit down on the groan before it could leave my throat.

"Fine," she said, tugging her arm from me. "You win. For now."

I let go of her and she backed up. Backed all the way up so that my body felt cold, drained of her heat.

Jesus, she had more sense than me. Here I was getting closer to her, exactly what I promised myself I *wouldn't* do. She was the one who was trying to run away. I tried to pretend that it didn't hurt.

33

Saoirse

Diarmuid fucking Brennan.

I wanted to hit him. I wanted to hurt him. To slam my hand into his chest and smash his heart like he was doing mine.

Instead I pounded the bag, pretending it was his face, as he watched.

"Come on, selkie. You can hit harder than that."

Damn him.

"Don't call me that."

Slam.

Slam.

Diarmuid moved around me, disappearing from my

line of vision. I could feel his eyes on me. They dragged across me, burning me, marking me.

"Maintain your guard, selkie." His voice came from behind me.

God, I wanted to kill him.

I hit the bag again. I felt a slap on my left elbow, lifting my arm up.

"Guard up."

Infuriated, I grabbed the bag and flung it at him. He sidestepped without any effort.

I slammed my fists onto my hips and sucked in a breath. "What are we doing this for?"

Diarmuid stood, stoic, like an unmovable mountain. "Martial arts will teach you discipline, persistence, grit."

I gritted my teeth. "Are you saying I have none of those things?"

He studied me for a pause. "I'm saying that martial arts will teach you these things."

"Because I have none."

He blinked, his eyes going hard. "You tell me."

Fuck him.

"You're punishing me."

He let out a snort. "What for?"

"*Discipline, persistence, grit,*" I quoted him. "You think I made a mistake not applying for college."

His face grew hard, like it had been chiseled out of marble. "You have a gift, Saoirse. You're wasting it if you don't do something with it."

"Fuck you," I yelled. "You have no right to tell me what I should or shouldn't do."

"You—"

"You *left* me, Diarmuid. You left me alone with no one."

His face broke into a mask of pain. "You had your ma…" he trailed off.

"My drug-addicted, incompetent, uncaring mother," I scoffed. "Really?"

"I had no choice, Saoirse."

"You had a choice. You had a fucking choice and you chose *her* over me."

"She was pregnant…"

"So you give up your soul family for a real one? I hope they were worth it."

His mask cracked open. I saw it; the deep well of pain underneath, of guilt, of regret. I realised it hurt him to leave just as much as it hurt me. I always thought that his decision to go had been easy for him. I didn't think that leaving might have torn strips off him, too.

Diarmuid tore his eyes away from mine, as if he couldn't take letting me *see* him anymore.

I didn't want to *see* him. I didn't want to understand him. If he left once, he'll leave again.

He let out a sigh. "Maybe that's enough for one day."

"Fine," I let out.

My head was spinning. I had to get out of here. I turned and strode to the bench against the wall to grab my things.

He followed me. "I am not letting that *boy* take you home."

I rolled my eyes. "He's twenty-one."

"Because twenty-one is *so* mature."

I narrowed my eyes at him. "So much more mature than twenty-eight, apparently."

I zipped up my hoodie and slung my bag over my shoulder.

He stepped in my way, his wide chest and rounded shoulders taking up my vision.

"You are not leaving with him."

"Try and stop me."

He took a step closer so we were toe to toe. He crowded me. His presence. His heat. His smell. All around me like chains.

I couldn't stand to meet his gaze, so I followed a drop of sweat that ran from his hairline, over his sharp cheekbone, down to his granite jaw. What would he do if I leaned up and licked it off him? I almost shivered at the thought.

"Saoirse Quinn," his voice snapped me out of my reverie. "Here, now...*I* am responsible for you. I can't do anything about the rest of the week, but for this hour. You. Are. Mine."

You are mine.

His words lodged into my chest. If only that were true. I swallowed down a whimper.

Diarmuid straightened, clearing his throat.

"Truck. Now," he mumbled.

Diarmuid switched off the music—The Dubliners again—as soon as he turned on the engine of his truck. It

240

seemed even that was too painful a reminder of who we used to be and where we were now.

We rode in his truck again, the silence swelling like a painful abscess, filled with heartache, regrets and everything unsaid.

"So…" I blurted out when the silence got too much. "You never did answer…did you have a girl or a boy?"

His jaw flinched, his eyebrows coming down over his eyes, staring firmly on the road. "I, er… She lost the baby. Not long after we moved."

Oh. Shit.

Guilt flooded the back of my throat. I'd been such a bitch to him about it. "I'm sorry. I didn't know."

He shrugged. But his lips paled as he pressed them together. It was his tell back then when he was feeling too much. Some things never changed.

"These things happen," he said.

We stopped at a set of red lights, the tension in the truck like hot pressurised air.

"I'm still sorry. I…" I played with my bottom lip with my teeth. "Even if I didn't want you to have a family without me, I never would have wished that on you."

"I know, Saoirse. But thanks for saying so."

He glanced over to me, our eyes locked. I felt like I was thirteen again. And he was my world.

I looked away first.

"The light's green," I said quietly. I could still feel his eyes on me.

He drove on, entering the area where I lived. In less than five minutes, we'd be at my house. This moment would be gone. The quiet connection of a shared past and an unwanted grief, broken. I had to say something.

I just wasn't sure what.

When he pulled up in front of my house, the lights were all off, meaning my father wasn't home yet. I guess it was another dinner where I'd be eating at the table in the cold kitchen. Alone.

"We're here," Diarmuid said, indicating that it was time for me to get out.

I didn't want to get out of his warm truck.

I didn't want to go into my house.

I didn't want to be alone.

"Can we...can we go for a drive?" I asked, my voice small. I didn't look at him. I couldn't stand to see his face if he said no.

In the silence, I felt his surprise.

He didn't say anything. He reached for the indicator and pulled us back onto the road. I sagged into the seat, a sigh loosening from my too-tight chest.

He just drove. I didn't ask where he was going. I didn't care. I just wanted to sit in his truck with him and feel...*this* for a while. Warm. Safe.

Like maybe the world was *good* for once.

Soon the houses of Limerick grew farther and farther apart. He kept driving until we were clear beyond the city limits, down skinny country roads, the trees lining the side creating a canopy over our heads.

He turned down a skinny one-lane dirt road, two trenches showing where tires had worn into the earth like parallel snakes. The trees turned to thick bushes lining a wooden fence.

Finally he pulled up on the side. There were no cars before or behind us. It felt like he and I were the only ones in the world.

Beyond the fence was green fields, a few cows dotting the grass, an ancient-looking wooden farmhouse on a hill.

"Haven't been here in a while," he said after a pause, his eyes fixed on the farmhouse. He shuffled in his seat. "I…I don't know why I brought you here."

I stared at the farmhouse. Now that we were nearer, I could see that part of the roof had collapsed in. Obviously no one had lived here in a while.

I knew without him having to tell me that this was the farmhouse he grew up in, where he watched his mother, then his grandmother, die. Before he was finally taken away.

My heart squeezed as I imagined a young Diarmuid standing on the aging porch.

I realised something. "What happened to your dad? You've never spoken about him."

Diarmuid's jaw tightened and his fingers flexed on the gear stick so that his knuckles turned white.

"He walked out on my mum and me when I was very little. Haven't heard from him since. Don't really care to."

Oh shit.

Now I understood why he married Ava when she fell pregnant. He didn't want to be like his father.

"Everyone I've ever cared about has gone away," he said. He lifted his eyes to me. The truck filled up with the resonance of pain. It reverberated like a low solemn bass note, rumbly and aching. "Except you. You came back."

This part of Diarmuid pushed me away all those years ago because he didn't think he would get to keep me. If everyone you loved left, why would you love at all?

He let out a long breath, a weighted breath, sweet and bitter all at once. "I'm glad our paths crossed again, selkie." This time I didn't tell him not to use my nickname. This time the familiar moniker settled around me like a favourite coat. "No matter how short this time will be."

His words pierced my lungs, making it hard to breathe. I didn't want us to end. I just got him back.

I won't leave, I wanted to yell, *if you promise never to leave me.*

"Diarmuid…" I turned towards him and found he was already looking at me. I swallowed, my pride like a too-large morsel in my throat. "Can we call a truce?"

"A truce?"

"Yeah. A do-over. Put the past in the past. Draw a line between then and now." I didn't want to waste any more time. I just got him back and I didn't want to waste any more time.

Slowly a smile dawned across his mouth. I used to live for his smiles. They used to light up my whole world.

"I'd like that," he said.

I stuck out my hand. He took it. I was enveloped in the warmth of his calloused hands. Such strong hands. Strong, honest hands. Hands that I wanted to pull onto my body. *All* over my body.

I tugged my hand back, my palm radiating heat all up my arm and to my cheeks. "We should go. My da might be worrying where I am."

Diarmuid started up the truck and turned it around. This time the air was peppered with questions about the years we'd been apart.

"So, how is Ava?" I almost choked on her name.

Diarmuid shrugged. "I don't know."

I frowned. "She's your wife. How do you *not* know?"

Diarmuid inhaled, then exhaled before he spoke. "She and I separated not long after she lost the baby."

Oh. Shit.

"I'm…sorry." Not that they had separated, but that she had caused him pain.

"You were right, selkie. I should have listened to you back then."

I was?

"Right about what?"

His eyes locked onto mine. "I never loved her."

I turned my face to the window and squeezed my eyes shut as my heart cramped in my chest. It had killed me when he chose Ava over me. It ripped pieces off me—still ripped pieces off me—to think that he might have loved her. For years I had dreamed of hearing him say those words to me. Dreamed about it. And here he was saying exactly that. I must be dreaming.

"And so…" I began, when I thought I had recovered enough to keep my voice steady, "you have a new girlfriend or something?"

"No." He let out a bitter laugh. "Some catch I'd

make. I'm a twenty-eight-year-old ex-juvi cursed with a dead family and a failed marriage already under my belt."

God, it hurt to think he thought of himself that way. But it made sense now, why he tried so hard with Ava, why he thought marrying her when she was pregnant was the "right thing" to do. Diarmuid Brennan did not love himself.

I slid my hand over his that was sitting on the gear stick. "I think you're a catch."

You're the *catch*.

He smiled at me and my stomach did a flip. "Thanks, selkie. That means a lot to me."

I slid my hand off his before I said anything even more stupid.

He pulled up outside of my house again. Still no lights on inside. No da. I let out a silent sigh and hopped out of the truck.

"I'm coming to pick you up next Friday," Diarmuid said before I could shut the door. "You don't need to be getting on any motorbikes."

I rolled my eyes, but there was a smile threatening to break through. "Whatever, Brennan," I said, but my voice was soft, teasing.

He let out a snort. "Get out of here. Stay out of trouble."

"Trouble finds me."

He shook his head. "Don't I know it," he mumbled.

I shut the door between us. He pulled away from the curb. I stood there on my sidewalk, watching the truck until it disappeared, a piece of my soul feeling like it was leaving with him.

I had been so in love with Diarmuid when I was younger. I never got over him. Because he *was* mine.

You have my skin.

And you have mine.

34

Saoirse

Then—Dublin, Ireland

It was my last day assigned to Diarmuid. He wanted to celebrate my not reoffending in the year. I said yes, of course, and visions of us out at our favourite pizza place spun in my head. Maybe he'd even take me to a movie afterwards.

When he told me that Ava was cooking dinner at their house, I felt a stab go through me.

Ava.

His girlfriend.

I'd still not met Ava. I'd never cared to. Diarmuid had never asked me to meet her before now. I wasn't looking forward to it.

When Diarmuid and I were together she didn't exist. He never spoke about her. His eyes were only on me.

I was happy enough for Diarmuid and I to drift around each other, the axis of our own world.

When I met her, would she then become real? Or would she re-emerge into the waters like a myth.

That evening I dressed in an emerald-green and black polka-dot dress that used to be my ma's. Moina took up the hem and pulled in the waist for me so that it fit my blossoming body. I had boobs now, mere tender buds. Not nearly as big as Ava's. My hips were widening too, my thighs losing the concave scallop of youth.

Moina helped me put a touch of mascara on my lashes to darken them. It brought out the green in my eyes. I would have to learn how to do this. Finally, a touch of gloss on my lips.

When I walked down to meet Diarmuid, my shitty commission housing building had transformed in my mind into a grand ballroom staircase. Diarmuid's truck was a carriage and he was my prince.

He stood as regal as ever, even in grey dress slacks and a black shirt, waiting for me in the glow of the bleeding sunlight.

His eyes widened when he saw me. In them I saw stars and light, and for the first time, I saw myself as beautiful. Something to be cherished.

"Wow." He walked towards me and we met part way on the path. "Saoirse, you look amazing."

I brushed down my dress, my cheeks blooming with

heat. "Thank you."

He made no movement. He just stood there looking at me. I could almost detect a hint of pride in his eyes.

He held out his hand. "My lady."

My flush heightened. I outstretched my hand and placed it in his. He escorted me to the truck, lifting me into the passenger seat at usual. All the while, I dared to lean into his touch.

Everything was perfect.

Until he mentioned her name.

"So, er...Ava's excited to meet you." He wound the car deftly through the streets.

Ava. His girlfriend.

My chest stung like I'd fallen into nettle. I pushed aside the brambles, for what fairy tale heroine *didn't* have to fight an evil queen or push through a forest of thorns.

"I'm excited to meet her. Finally. After all this time I almost thought she mightn't be real," I said, proud that only a hint of sarcasm slid out between my words.

He let out a short laugh, the curt laugh of someone unsure how to react.

His phone beeped, saving us from this awkward moment. He snatched the phone up at the next set of red lights and frowned at it as he read the message. The lines deepened between his brows, and for a second he looked murderous. That look melted as he sagged into his seat, resignation replacing it.

He pulled up on the side of the road and I knew it was bad.

Shit.

Ava was going to make him cancel dinner. She was going to make him take me home instead. I could already feel tears welling up inside me.

"So…" he rubbed the back of his neck, something he did when he was pissed, "Ava," he practically spat out her name, "isn't going to be home in time to cook dinner like she promised. Do you want pizza instead? We can pick it up from Mizzoni's."

Yes. I felt a thrill go through me. It would just be Diarmuid and me, the way it was meant to be.

"Why don't we cook?" I suggested, visions of a romantic candlelight dinner flashing in my head.

He made a face.

"What?" I asked.

"I don't really know how to cook." He gave me a sheepish look.

I blinked at Diarmuid. "What? But you're like thirty—"

"Twenty-five!"

"Whatever," I waved my hand to shut him up. "You're old enough to know how to cook."

He shrugged. "I guess I never learned. I always had someone to cook for me. Or relied on takeout."

I let out an exaggerated sigh. "I will teach you, then."

Diarmuid looked at me out of the corner of his eye. "Yeah?"

I rolled my eyes. "You've seen how useless my ma is, Diarmuid. Do you think I'd not have starved to death if I didn't know how to cook?"

"Well, alright then. But I'm buying groceries."

I grinned. "Deal."

We drove to the nearest Tesco grocery shop. I picked up ingredients for Dublin Coddle: potatoes, onions, sausages, bacon, pearl barley, bay leaf, chicken stock. Diarmuid walked beside me, placing the items I handed to him into the trolley.

I also picked up a frozen apple pie to heat up in the oven while we were eating, and vanilla ice cream.

"I think that's all we need."

"Hey, Saoirse," Diarmuid whispered to me like a conspirator.

"Yeah?"

He nudged his head towards the back of the trolley. "Hop on."

I grinned. He moved aside while I stepped one foot each on the tiny ledges over the back wheels. He moved his body in right behind mine, his strong arm wrapping around me to grab the handle. I'd never felt so warm, so protected. I never wanted him to unravel himself from around me.

"Hang on, selkie," he whispered in my ear, his beard tickling against my cheek making my belly flip.

He pushed us along, dodging other shoppers and their baskets, making engine noises in my ear and making me giggle.

I let out a squeal as he turned, then ran us down an aisle, garnering stern disapproving looks from the fellow shoppers. We skidded to a stop in front of a cashier, earning us a scowl from the lady behind the till.

"Sorry," Diarmuid mumbled, but the grin on his face

said that he wasn't at all.

I hopped off the ledges, pressing my lips together to stop from laughing. Diarmuid loaded the food onto the conveyor belt, then packed the shopping bags and paid.

"Bloody children," the cashier muttered as we walked away, Diarmuid carrying the groceries. He and I took one look at each other and burst out into laughter.

Back at Diarmuid's place, he unpacked the groceries onto the kitchen bench while I searched the cupboards for the utensils I'd need: frying pan, casserole pot, cutting board, peeler and knife.

Diarmuid won the rock, paper, scissors for music choice. He turned on Two Door Cinema Club, a contemporary Irish indie rock band, and we danced and sang along as he peeled and chopped the potatoes and onions, while I fried the bacon and sausages.

I'd never cooked with anyone before. It made my chest flutter like a caged bird when I glanced over to him to find him smiling at me as he mimed the words to the songs.

It was perfect.

Diarmuid placed the final casserole in the oven and I set the timer for fifteen minutes. Diarmuid grabbed me, holding me up against his chest, my legs dangling, and we danced around the living room. Turning and giggling. I felt lightheaded. Dizzy. The best kind of dizzy. It felt so good to be tucked into him like his. I only wished I was taller so that we'd fit like this all the time.

It felt like only minutes before the timer went off. Diarmuid lowered me to the ground, and I felt a sense of loss when I unwrapped my arms from around his neck. I set the table while he pulled the hot dish out.

Diarmuid walked into the living room and stopped. I'd turned the main light off, leaving just a side lamp on and lit a bunch of candles I'd found in a drawer. I stood to the side with my hands clasped behind my back.

"Saoirse, what's this?" Diarmuid asked, walking slowly to the table and placing the pot down on a placemat.

I shrugged, hoping the dim light hid the warming of my cheeks.

"Figured I'd add some atmosphere," I said as casually as I could. "If you don't like it I can blow them out and—"

"No, no," he said, "leave it be." He smiled. "Let's eat."

We sat across from each other at the small two-person table. His legs were so long that his knees brushed mine under the table.

"This is perfect, thank you. Better than my pizza idea." He reached out across the table and placed his hand over mine.

He placed his hand over mine. As if we were a real couple on a real date. My breathing got all short and tight.

He took his hand away all too quickly, grabbing his cutlery with his strong hands and cutting up his food. He did what I liked to do, cutting up all the elements of the dish to create a perfect bite.

God, he looked so beautiful in the candlelight, the warm light glowing off his handsome face. His lovely lips pursing as he blew on the food on his fork.

His eyes caught mine. "You're not eating."

Right. Idiot. Stop staring. Start eating.

I cleared my throat and picked up my knife and fork, cutting up a portion of sausage and potato.

I almost stopped breathing as he placed his food in his mouth, waiting for the verdict. The Dublin Cobble I'd made with his help came from a recipe that my gran had saved and kept in a scrapbook of recipes. I don't really remember her clearly, I just have warm feelings every time I handle her cookbook. This recipe I knew by heart because it was one of my favourites.

Diarmuid let out a groan and sank back into his chair. "Saoirse, Jesus, this is so delicious."

A rush went through me and I couldn't help my smile. He cut up his next piece and continued to eat with gusto. My heart warmed. There was something so satisfying about watching him eat something I'd cooked.

I shook my head and let out an exaggerated sigh. "How have you survived without me, Diarmuid Brennan?"

I popped my bite into my mouth. Oh yeah, it was good.

I looked up from my dish to find him staring at me. "I don't know, Saoirse."

His voice was so full of gravity, so intense and serious were his dark eyes that it sucked the air out of my lungs.

Now I understood what it meant when someone took your breath away.

After dinner, I helped him clear the table. He filled up the sink so he could wash up.

There was some Cobble left over, which I spooned into a plastic container and popped in his fridge.

"You can take this to work tomorrow and have it for lunch," I said, a small thrill going through me at the thought that he'd be eating this tomorrow and thinking of me.

I grabbed a tea towel and stepped up to him, drying the dishes after he handed them to me. He left the radio on and we sang as we worked.

It started off as an innocent hip bump. Then turned into a hip bump war which he was winning, of course, because he was so much bigger than me.

Then he blew a piece of white soapy bubbles my way. I giggled and waved it out of my face.

"You're such a child, Diarmuid."

"Am not."

He blew a larger piece. And another. I swatted him with my tea towel.

He plopped a large bit of foam on my head. I let out a scream and flicked out my towel at him as he flicked water at me. He grabbed me with his wet hands and curled me against him, rubbing foam and water into my hair. I giggled and kicked out, dropping the tea towel in the process. "Let go of me."

"Never," he growled in my ear. That single word lodged in my chest and began to throb as if it had its own heartbeat.

"What the hell is going on?" a stern female voice rang

through the kitchen.

Diarmuid let go of me and straightened. I whirled around to find a woman standing in the doorway to the kitchen, a disapproving scowl on her face.

Ava.

Diarmuid's girlfriend.

I got my first look at my competition.

She was taller than me, about Diarmuid's age, I guessed. Dressed in a pair of skinny jeans and a thin jumper that clung to her boobs. Dammit, she did have great boobs. Her long dark hair was straight and hung over her shoulders.

"Ava, you're home," Diarmuid said.

He hesitated for a second before walking to her and leaning in for a quick kiss. It felt like he'd stabbed my chest with a hot blade.

I fisted my hands at my side as Diarmuid stepped aside.

"Ava, this is Saoirse, the young lady I've been telling you about. Saoirse, Ava."

I noticed he didn't introduce her as his girlfriend.

Ava gave me a thin smile. "She's a pretty little girl."

She, as if I wasn't standing right fucking here.

I hated Ava.

I hated her so much.

"I'm not a girl," I said, my hands tightening so that I could feel crescents of pain in my palms from my fingernails.

Ava ignored me, her eyes casting around the kitchen, which was now splashed with water. She shot him a sulky look. "Look at this mess. What's gotten into you?"

"We'll clean it up," Diarmuid said, his voice sounding tired.

"Yeah, you will." Her eyes flicked back to me. She spun on her heel and strode out of the kitchen. Moments later I heard the slam of what I assumed to be her bedroom door.

Diarmuid turned to me, a scowl on his face. "Wait here."

He disappeared after her.

I stood in the kitchen with my ears pricked, listening to the raised voices coming out of the bedroom. I tried not to listen, but I couldn't help it.

"...making a mess... in our house... the way you were..."

And I heard his voice. "...one of my kids... didn't even bother to come home for..."

I felt bad that he was getting yelled at because of me, but my heart warmed to know that he was sticking up for me.

Ava was a bitch. She didn't deserve him. Why couldn't he see that?

I heard the opening of a door. I grabbed the tea towel and pretended I'd been drying here all this time, just minding my own business.

Diarmuid came out, rubbing the back of his neck, and gave me a mournful look.

"She's been under some stress lately," he said, but even he didn't sound so sure. "She's not usually so..." he trailed off.

Bitchy? I finished for him in my head.

"So…curt," he said.

That was one way of describing her.

"Sorry, Saoirse. Let me take you home. I'll deal with the cleanup later."

"But we still have that apple pie." I tried not to sound so disappointed. It had been warming in the oven while we'd been cleaning the dishes from dinner.

Diarmuid rubbed the back of his head. "I think maybe we should save the pie and ice cream for another night."

"Oh." I forced a shrug, like my heart wasn't cracking. "Sure. Whatever."

Diarmuid turned the oven off, the light and my hope switching off as he did.

My heart sank. Stupid Ava, coming in and ruining the best night of my life.

She didn't deserve him.

If he didn't see it on his own, then I would show him.

It was silent in the car on the way back. Everything tumbled around inside of me, swelling until I couldn't hold it back.

"Why are you with her?" I blurted out, my jealousy spilling out over the rim of my voice.

He glanced back and forth between the road and me. "What are you talking about, selkie?"

I crossed my arms over my chest, furious with her for existing in his life, furious at him for letting her. "It's a simple question. Why are you with her."

He shuffled in his seat, obviously uncomfortable. "We've been together a long time."

"Do you hear yourself?"

"It's complicated."

"Do you love her?"

His jaw worked back and forth. "Like I said, it's complicated."

"You don't even love her."

"I never said that."

"But you never said you did. *Wait for someone special*, isn't that what you told me? *Wait for love.*"

"That's not the same," he growled.

"It is the same." I shook my head. "If you don't love her, then why are you with her?"

"It's not that simple."

"Yes," I said, firmly, "it fucking is."

He let out a half-sigh, half-groan. "Please just let this go."

I sagged into my seat, leaning against the door. This wasn't fair. This wasn't right.

Diarmuid didn't love her. She didn't love him.

How much simpler could it be?

We pulled up to the sidewalk in front of my apartment, my stomach twisted into knots.

This was it. As of midnight tonight, I was no longer officially his responsibility. Would he still pick me up for school? Would we spend as much time together? Would he still be my best friend? My thoughts of Ava dissolved under these thoughts.

"Are we...are we still going to be able to hang out?"

My question slid out like a desperate plea. God, I could barely look at him when I asked, too terrified that he might say no, that our time was done.

He turned towards me, a shocked look on his face. "Of course. But only…only if *you* want to." Why did *he* sound unsure?

"Of course I want to." What a stupid question.

He grinned at me. "Just thought I might not be cool enough for you anymore. Now that you're only months away from being fifteen and all."

I flung my arms around his neck. He wrapped a strong arm around me, closing me into his chest.

"I love you, Diarmuid," I said, the secret I'd written into every corner of my journal loosing from my lips.

His response rumbled into my ear in that deep, gravelly voice of his. "I love you, too, selkie."

My heart filled to near bursting.

He loved me.

He loved me.

He loved *me*.

35

Diarmuid

I sat in my truck watching Saoirse walk away as I always did. Upstairs on her floor, she appeared on the balcony. For a few moments we just watched each other. She lifted her hand in a slight wave and disappeared inside her shithole of an apartment.

Something twisted in my gut. What did it say about you when your best friend was a fourteen-year-old girl? What did it say when she was the one I was most comfortable with?

I hated grocery shopping. Saoirse had made it fun. I hated washing up, but with her beside me it felt like a game, not a chore.

She had such a tough life, but she was still so brave

and hopeful. She gave me hope.

I didn't go straight home after I dropped Saoirse off. I drove around, my mind whirring over Saoirse's words from earlier. I ended up at the pizza joint we always went to. I ordered a Club Orange, a fizzy orange soft drink, and sat at Saoirse's and my usual booth, sipping my drink and staring at the spot where she usually sat.

You don't love her.

Why are you with her?

I took Ava here once. She didn't like the place. Too casual. She liked places where she got to dress up. I used to as well because she looked great when she was dressed up. But now…when was the last time we even went out on a date? When was the last time that Ava and I even laughed together or had fun?

I thought over the night that Saoirse and I had. I couldn't remember the last time I'd laughed so hard or felt so at ease. Had Ava and I ever laughed like that?

I tried to imagine Ava jumping on the trolley and letting me push her through the aisle. I tried to imagine her dancing with me in the kitchen. But I couldn't. She just didn't fit.

She didn't fit.

Dear God. And it took a fourteen-year-old girl to make me realise it. Saoirse was so wise and yet so innocent. A fourteen year old going on thirty.

You don't love her. Why are you with her?

Did I love Ava? Had I ever loved her? We had wanted each other. That much was clear.

I squeezed my eyes shut.

I remembered how I'd felt when Ava had smiled at me.

She was dressed to the nines and with her stylish girlfriends. I had never imagined that a girl like that could ever look twice at an ex-juvi foster kid like me. I saw the way she looked at me, a large brute of a man from the wrong side of the tracks, my tattoos and my shoulder-length hair. The lust had been obvious. I thought that lust had turned into love.

Had it?

I remembered Saoirse telling me about the frog. That if you throw a frog in boiling water, it will hop out. But let it sit in cold water and turn up the heat slowly, it will sit there and boil.

Was I the frog? Had Ava and I stopped being right for each other so slowly that we couldn't see it? Were we boiling alive together?

Ava and I didn't connect. I mean, Christ, a fourteen-year-old girl understood me more than Ava did. And when was the last time Ava and I had sex?

Weeks ago. A quickie in the morning which I felt was almost an obligation rather than the fact that either of us wanted it.

Was this what long-term relationships turned into? Ava had been hinting at a wedding. Actually, more than hinting.

If Ava was the right woman, shouldn't I be thrilled at the idea of marrying her?

I knew I was in trouble the second I pushed open the door. Ava was waiting for me in the living room, her manicured hands fisted right where I used to love grabbing her.

"Where the hell have you been?"

"Just driving around, Ava. Calm down." I hooked my jacket on the stand, kicked off my boots.

"Driving around, huh?" Ava followed me into the bedroom where I dropped my keys on the dresser.

"Yeah."

"With that *girl*?"

I spun around to face Ava. Her eyes glittered with hatred. How could she hate Saoirse? She hadn't even given Saoirse a chance. *She* was the one who cancelled on our dinner where she was supposed to meet Saoirse, a concession I'd allowed her when she'd complained that I was spending too much time with the girl.

"Her name is Saoirse," I said through gritted teeth.

"I tried to call you but you left your phone at home."

What was she trying to accuse me of?

"I hadn't even noticed I'd left it."

"How fucking convenient."

I let out a groan and sank onto the edge of the bed. Fuck. Did we have to fight again?

We'd always fought. In the beginning it was kind of thrilling; the drama of it, the excitement, the hot make-up sex afterwards. Now it was just exhausting and pointless. I had no energy for this anymore.

"Jesus, Ava, do we have to do this now?"

"You son of a bitch." Ava crossed her arms over her

chest. "Are you fucking her?"

My head snapped up. "*What?*"

"Are you fucking that...that Saoirse girl?"

"Jesus fucking Christ, Ava. She's four-fucking-teen," I exploded, leaping to my feet. "Do you really think I'd be attracted to a *girl?*"

"I saw you two together. I was watching you both before you realised I was even home."

My body burned with rage at the thought. How could she accuse me of something so vile? Saoirse was a *girl*. A child. I cared about her more than I'd cared for any of my other kids, but I never, not once, looked at her in *that* way.

"I am going to pretend that you didn't just accuse me of *fucking* a fourteen-year-old girl."

"She doesn't act like a girl. And you don't act like she's a girl. You don't talk about her like she's a girl."

That's because she's not *a girl in her head*, I thought angrily before I shoved that thought aside. "For fuck's sake, she's like a little niece to me. Like a little sister."

"She has a crush on you, you know?"

"She does not. I'm like a big brother to her."

Ava snorted, and it was an ugly sound. "You really are fucking clueless." She grabbed something from her back pocket and shoved it in my face, the familiar symbols like rubberbands snapping at my skin.

Saoirse's journal.

"This is hers," Ava said as she waved it in front of my face.

"Where did you get that?" I growled, snatching it off

267

her.

"I took it out of her bag."

"You went through her bag?" I said, disbelief coating my voice.

Saoirse carried that journal almost everywhere. She must have brought it with her tonight. Ava must have snatched it out of the bag before I took Saoirse home.

"Read it," Ava said. "It's a fucking love shrine to *you*."

I lowered the journal to my side, my fingers digging into the leather cover, the contents calling to me like a siren.

I *would not* read it.

It was private.

I respected Saoirse enough to let her keep her privacy.

Ava did not.

I stared at the woman I'd shared a bed with for over three years, disappointment filling my body. Funny how the person lying next to you can turn out to be a stranger. But then again, perhaps Ava and I had been strangers for some time. I'd only just let myself see it now.

I shook my head. "I can't believe you'd *steal* a young girl's journal, that you'd read it, invading her privacy like that."

"I had to, Diarmuid. I had to find proof. She wants you and she won't stop until you are hers. You can't deny it anymore." She sounded almost deranged.

I wiped my face as Saoirse's words from earlier came back to me.

You don't love her. Why are you with her?

I couldn't keep lying to myself anymore. I couldn't keep lying to Ava.

"Ava," I said slowly, weighing up my words, "I can't do this anymore."

She froze. "What are you talking about?"

"I can't do this," I pointed my finger between us, "*us* anymore."

She shook her head. "No."

"Yes."

"No. *You* are not leaving me for a fourteen year old."

I sighed, tired of being accused of a crime I had no intention of committing. "I am *not* leaving you for a fourteen year old. I'm just leaving *you.*"

"I was going to wait for another night," she looked up, her eyes flashing, "but this can't wait."

"Ava, just let it go. It's over."

"No, it's not. I have something to tell you…"

36

Saoirse

Now—Limerick, Ireland

The week dragged. I found myself counting down the days until the next Friday in between replaying every single glance, every single word from our last encounter.

A truce with Diarmuid Brennan.

Truthfully, I wasn't sure whether this had been a good idea.

He'd gotten under my skin.

Who was I kidding? He'd never gotten out.

I was lying on my bed early Thursday morning. My father had already headed out to his farmhouse. I didn't have work today so the whole day stretched out in front of me.

My phone beeped with a text. I reached out to grab it, my stomach doing a flip when I saw who it was.

Diarmuid: Slight change of plans tonight. Wear something nice rather than gym gear.

I sat up, my head spinning from the sudden movement. *Wear something nice.* Was he…taking me out? My stomach flipped. On a date?

Jesus, don't be stupid, Saoirse. It'll probably be as innocuous as your old breakfasts together.

Still, I couldn't help my fingers trembling as I typed out a response.

Me: Where are we going?

His response came back almost instantly.

Diarmuid: Dinner at my old JLO's house.

See, *not* a date. His old JLO's house? Was this like a double-team intervention effort?

Me: Why?

Diarmuid: Because.

Me: Diarmuid…

Diarmuid: Because Brian wants to meet you.

He's been talking about me to his old JLO?

He's been talking about me. To his friend. His old mentor. I knew how much Brian meant to Diarmuid. Brian was the reason that Diarmuid is the man he is today.

And Brian wanted to meet *me*.

Another text came in.

Diarmuid: Brian is a stubborn bastard and won't take no for an answer.

Me: Okay…

Diarmuid: He likes to meet my kids.

His kids. His assignments. This wasn't a special invitation to dinner. This was something he did with everyone. As my stomach coiled with bitterness, I shot him another text.

Me: Whatever.

The bastard didn't reply.

If I was going to this dinner, I was going armed. In the best armour I knew. I slid on a tight pair of skinny jeans, my favourite brown ankle boots and a fitted pale-green jumper that always made my eyes stand out even more. I wore my waist-length hair in loose curls that fell over my shoulder and finished off the look with grey eyeliner and mascara, gloss on my lips.

At two minutes to go until he was due, I stood in front of the mirror.

I looked damn good. And *at least* twenty-one. So there.

I grabbed my jacket and bag and was out the door in seconds, locking up behind me because my da was still out doing God-knows-what at his farmhouse.

Diarmuid was already waiting for me, leaning against the passenger door of his truck parked slightly farther down the road, looking down at his phone.

Damn, he looked good. In his usual denim jeans, showcasing his strong thighs, and grey long-sleeved jumper that clung to his wide torso, rounded shoulders and those achingly perfect arms. His shoulder-length hair was tied back into a low man bun at the nape of his neck.

"Hey," I said.

He looked up and froze. The heat that flashed in his eyes caused a flush to go up the back of my neck.

Then he blinked and the cool mask was back on.

"Hey." He opened the passenger door for me and smiled.

God, this felt too much like a date. The edges of my nerves started to jangle as I walked the final steps towards him. He stepped aside so I could get into the car.

I flinched when he placed his hand on my elbow, just like he used to when I was younger, and helped me into the seat. I was too surprised to say anything.

It was only when he'd gotten into his own seat and we were driving down the road that I spoke up. "You didn't have to help me into the cab. I'm not fourteen anymore."

Diarmuid let out a low breath. "No, you're definitely not."

His voice, all breathless and hushed, made the hairs on my arm stand on end. I rubbed my arms and instructed myself to calm the hell down.

"So, your old JLO—"

"Brian."

"Brian. Right. What does he know about me?"

Diarmuid glanced over, his look piercing me, before he focused back on the road.

"I mean, does he know that we used to know each other from before?"

"No."

"Oh."

Diarmuid let out a long huff. "Look, I wouldn't have brought you but he insisted. And he would have thought something was weird if I didn't bring you."

"Well, sorry you were put out so much. It's not like I want to sit through an entire dinner with you either." I scowled and crossed my arms over my chest. God, that stung.

"Ah shit, I didn't mean it like that, selkie."

"Don't call me that."

Diarmuid let out a sigh as we pulled up in front of a small terraced house. He put the truck into park.

"I'm sorry, I just…" He ran his hand through his hair, mussing up his bun and causing pieces of it to fall out over his forehead.

I wanted to reach out and push those locks back behind his ear. Instead I clamped my arms to my body.

He ran his hand through his hair again.

Oh my God. That was his tell when he was nervous.

Diarmuid was nervous.

Why?

He turned to me, a small crease between his brows. "Can we start over? Pretend that the night just started?"

How many times could he and I start over?

"Sure. Whatever," I said and pushed my way out of his truck without waiting for him to respond.

Diarmuid scrambled out of the truck behind me as I walked up the skinny brick path, lined with bushes of purple flowers I didn't know the name of. I hung back just before the front door to let him through first. His arm brushed past mine and I hated the way my body reacted, a shiver of heat, a rush of fire.

The door opened. There stood a man I guessed to be in his mid-sixties, white hair, a broad nose and deeper smile lines than frown lines. A glorious smile spread over his face, shaking his jowls slightly. This must be Brian.

"Diarmuid, about bloody time."

Diarmuid and he clasped each other in a hug. I noticed how delicately Diarmuid patted him on his back, how he towered over Brian.

"Now move out of the way so I can get a good look at her."

Diarmuid stepped aside.

Brian gave me a once-over that had me straightening my spine. There was something about him that made me want his approval. To like me, even.

He grinned. "She'll do."

"I'm Saoirse, sir." I stuck out my hand.

Brian let out a snort. "That won't do."

Before I knew what was happening he was pulling me into a hug. A warm, firm hug that smelled like powder and fresh laundry.

It was lovely.

"We're friends now, Saoirse," Brian said into my ear. "Friends hug hello."

Brian stepped back, patted me on the arm and disappeared into the house.

"You folks wait in the living room while I get set up," he called back to us.

Diarmuid motioned for me to enter first.

My heart did a flip. Until I remembered that I didn't want him to act like a gentleman.

I walked into Brian's living room, cosy and warm with lots of wood, dark grey and green plaid. Through an archway I saw Brian moving around in the kitchen. I could smell roasting meat and garlic, making my stomach rumble.

The front door clicked shut and Diarmuid's presence appeared at my back. I sucked in a breath and practically ran for the mantle covered in photos on the opposite side of the room.

I grabbed the closest photo and found myself staring

at one of Brian and…oh my God, was that a younger Diarmuid standing next to him? I peered closer. He must have been seventeen, perhaps. He had shorter hair sticking up about his head like a flame. His jaw was softer as were his cheekbones. He was still towering over Brian, his shoulders wide but his body wasn't as built as it was now.

He had a scowl on his face. Some things hadn't changed.

The real-life Diarmuid's presence warmed my side, his cologne filling my nose. Speak of the devil.

I set down the photo, not wanting to seem like I was drooling, and stepped away from him, picking up another photo. Diarmuid followed me.

I frowned. This photo was another one of Diarmuid; this time he was flanked by two other guys, both good-looking as hell. Holy wow. It was like a wall of hotness.

"Is this you as well?" I asked.

He peered over my shoulder and I felt his breath on my cheek. Half of me wanted to yell at him to go away. The other half wanted him to move closer.

"I lived here with Brian for a few years after I turned eighteen. He took me in." Diarmuid swallowed. "Was more of a father to me than my own ever was. More of a family to me until…"

Until you.

No, he couldn't have been about to say that. Right?

"That's Danny." Diarmuid pointed to the dark-haired, dark-eyed, broody-looking male on the right. "He moved to London chasing stardom soon after that photo was taken, though he's back in Dublin now."

"Any relation to Dillan O'Donaghue?" I said on a whim. Dillan O'Donaghue was the lead singer in one of Ireland's most famous rock bands.

Diarmuid hesitated. "Dillan's his father, actually."

Damn. Really?

"That'd be cool to have a rock star dad."

Diarmuid shrugged. "Danny and his father don't have much of a relationship. Not even when they were living in the same house…"

Ah. Right. Daddy issues came a dime a dozen, it seemed.

"Who's the other guy?"

"That's Declan on the left."

I pulled the photo closer to me. "He looks familiar."

"He should. His last name's Gallagher."

My mouth dropped open. "As in, Declan Gallagher the MMA fighter, Declan Gallagher?" I squeaked.

"Yeah." Diarmuid looked almost miffed. "You like to watch fights?"

"No, but my da does. He used to watch the fights all the time when I was younger… He'd let me sit next to him."

"He let you watch MMA?" he sounded incredulous.

"At least he keeps his promises," I said, my defenses automatically rising.

Diarmuid's face fell and I knew I'd struck a nerve. "Saoirse—"

I let out a huff. "I know, I know. We have a truce."

But Diarmuid wouldn't let it go. He held my chin in

his fingers, forcing me to face him. His eyes probed me, his voice was as soft as I'd ever heard it.

"It hurts me to think that you'd believe the worst of me. I stayed away because I thought it was the best thing for *you*. You have to know that, I only wanted what was best for *you*."

"What if what was best for me *was* you?" I whispered.

His eyes looked pained. "Saoirse—"

"I was only fourteen then. But..." I chewed my bottom lip. "I'm not fourteen now."

His gaze dropped to my mouth. Instinctively I wet my lips with the tip of my tongue. I swear I heard him groan.

His eyes lifted to mine. In them I saw wonder and awe. I saw *me* as he saw me. I saw myself as beautiful.

He was the only man who'd ever made me feel beautiful. Worthy. Then and now.

He leaned in, perhaps not because he wanted to— lord knows he'd been fighting against me from day one— but because he and I had too much power over each other. Like two atoms colliding.

I leaned in, not because I purposefully leaned in, but because I was drawn to him, the way a sunflower reaches for her sun. I needed him to blossom. To grow. To shine.

Until there was only breath between us.

"Diarmuid!"

We jumped apart. Brian was standing in the edge of the kitchen, his eyes flicking between me and the man by my side. "Set the table, lad."

Diarmuid recovered faster than I did. He straightened

and strode to the kitchen, brushing past Brian. Leaving Brian's eyes on me.

Diarmuid and my lips hadn't met, but mine were tingling. I swear Brian could see the *want* still clinging to my mouth like too bright red lipstick. His eyes narrowed and I forced what I hoped was an innocent smile. He looked like he wanted to say something. Instead he said nothing, disappearing back into the kitchen.

I turned aside and rubbed my mouth, trying to make the aching go away. I studied each framed photo on the mantle. Most of them were of Brian and people I didn't recognise. But there was one more of Diarmuid, with Danny and Declan in it too.

"We were so young then," I heard Diarmuid's voice say by my side. I hadn't even heard him reappear next to me. "We had all been Brian's kids. We met at O'Malley's boxing gym where Brian insisted on bringing us."

That's why he was insisting I do the same.

Diarmuid took the photo from me and looked at it, his eyes going misty. "We recognised something in each other. We found something in each other. Even though the three of us don't live in the same city anymore, I could call them right now with a problem and they'd be there for me, no doubt. And I for them."

My stomach squeezed. Was that…jealousy that I felt?

I pointed at the tower in the background. "Where is this? Is this in Ireland?"

He shook his head. "No, that's Tower Bridge in London. It was Danny's eighteenth. He's the youngest of the three of us by a whole three months. His father had pulled a dickhead move, as per bloody usual. He wanted to get out of Ireland for his birthday. He said it was so we could really go wild. But Dex and I knew it was to make a point to his dear old dad."

Go wild. I could imagine.

Diarmuid was already so good-looking, but more boyish in this photo. Not like the brutish man standing beside me today. Standing too close beside me. So close his presence seemed to radiate heat to me.

"And did you? Go wild, I mean."

He grinned. "What happens in London…"

I let out a snort. "That good, huh?"

Something clouded his eyes. "I almost didn't make it back," he said, setting the frame back on the mantle.

What? A shiver of anxiousness went through me at his words. *What did he mean by that?*

"Why not?"

He shrugged. "Almost didn't get on the plane."

I frowned. "You were late?"

"Something like that." He shuffled his feet, unable to meet my eyes.

"You don't want to tell me the real reason," I said. "Why?"

His eyes darted to mine, catching me in their dark net before he looked away again.

"I can't hide anything from you, can I, selkie?"

I wish. There was plenty about him that I wished I could uncover.

"Tell me," I pleaded.

"You'll laugh."

I felt a giggle bubbling up already.

"I promise I won't."

He scrunched up his mouth to one side, his thinking face.

"Come on, Diarmuid. You used to tell me everything."

He let out a breath. Then nodded. He pointed a finger at me. "But *no* laughing."

I crossed my fingers over my heart.

"I'm scared of flying."

A weighted silence fell over us as I let this revelation come over me.

He was scared of...flying?

Diarmuid Brennan, tall and strong as an Irish giant. Scared. Of *anything*.

It was almost unbelievable.

"Are you serious?" I asked hesitantly.

"Would I lie about something like this?"

No, he wouldn't. He wouldn't even joke about it.

Diarmuid...scared of flying. I looked over to him, realising he suddenly looked...different.

When I was younger I'd placed Diarmuid far up on a pedestal. No one could live forever on a pedestal. It was only a matter of time before he fell from the heavens. And when he fell, the crash almost destroyed me.

Part of growing up was placing aside fairy tales, curtains and myths born of mist.

He might still have been an Irish giant in my heart, but for the first time, I saw Diarmuid Brennan as a *man*.

A man who bled. Who made mistakes. With fears

and flaws. A man who did his best, even when his best wasn't enough.

He became real.

This…*this* was the moment I *truly* fell in love with him.

"I'm scared of being forgotten," I whispered. "Of falling into the cracks of life and disappearing."

He stepped closer to me and I felt his fingers twisting into mine, the warmth of his palm like a balm against my naked soul.

"I won't ever forget you," he promised. "I *never* forgot you."

It wasn't true. But I let him think that I believed him.

If Brian suspected anything between Diarmuid and me, he certainly didn't let on through dinner. The three of us sat around and talked and laughed, me, Brian and Diarmuid sitting across from me. My heart warmed as Brian affectionately teased Diarmuid and vice versa. And the food was delicious, Irish stew with steamed green beans and cheesy cauliflower.

Diarmuid clasped Brian on the shoulder as he tried to get up off his seat.

"Stay in your chair, old man. Saoirse and I shall do the dishes." He winked at me.

Brian swatted at his arm, Diarmuid jumping out of arm's reach before he could get to him. "Cheeky boy. I'm not too old to give you a thrashing."

"Ahhh, you'd have to catch me first."

Diarmuid sprinted into the kitchen. I followed him, laughing with a pile of plates in my hands.

He stood at the sink and washed up while I stood next to him drying the things he handed to me. In the background Brian turned on his stereo, and the familiar sound of The Dubliners floated out through the house.

Diarmuid snorted, glancing into the living room where Brian had taken up residence in an armchair. "You two are meant for each other," he said to me. "You both have the same shite taste in music."

I nudged him with my hip.

That was all it took.

His hip bumped me. I hip bumped back. Suddenly white foam was being flung at my head. I squealed and lashed out with my dish towel, trying to snap it on his ass.

Three years apart reduced to nothing. Like those years never separated us.

He grabbed me around the neck with his arm and dumped a large glob of bubbles on my hair. I let out a squeal.

"Doesn't look like much cleaning going on in here," Brian's gruff voice came from the doorway.

Once again, Diarmuid and I jumped apart, like two school kids caught by the teacher.

"Sorry, Brian," I mumbled, picking up the dishcloth I'd dropped on the floor and getting back to my drying up, my cheeks still feeling the heat from being so close to Diarmuid.

"Yeah, sorry, old man," Diarmuid said, catching my eye and shooting me a conspiratorial look. "We'll clean it up."

Brian grunted, but thankfully he left us to it.

Later that evening, Diarmuid drove me home. Neither of us spoke during the drive home. It was a comfortable silence, the kind that wrapped over you with warmth and comfort.

I kicked off my shoes and pulled my knees up to my chest and just sat in the soothing calm of his presence, tapping my toe along to the soft quirky voice of Lisa Hannigan crooning out of the radio.

"I thought you didn't like this modern indie rock shite?" Diarmuid asked, a hint of teasing in his voice.

I shrugged. "Maybe it grew on me," I said, using his words.

He pulled up outside my house and it was all dark.

Diarmuid frowned. "Your da's not home yet?" He glanced at the dashboard. It was almost eleven at night.

I shrugged, hoping he didn't see how much it stung that my da wasn't really around. "He's busy."

I climbed out of the truck, not really in the mood to talk about it.

"Selkie," Diarmuid called through the open door.

I spun, expecting a lecture from him or something.

Diarmuid flashed me a grin. "I'm glad you came tonight."

Even though we were metres away, I could feel the warmth of him and his fingers on my chin from earlier. I could have sworn that he'd been about to kiss me in that living room.

But three years ago, I could have sworn the same. So what did I know. Except that I was good at deluding myself, twisting my want into warped reality.

"Me too."

I spun on my heel, feeling some relief now that I had my back to him so that I could stop hiding the longing bubbling around in my chest. I strode up the path to the front door, my keys jangling in my bag as I grasped for them.

I could feel his eyes on me, watching me. Even now I knew he wouldn't drive away until I was safely inside. Just like he used to do.

An ache went through me. It hurt that he watched over me because I couldn't let him see how much it meant. It pained that he cared because he would never care enough. Not how I wanted him to care.

I found my keys and reached for the door.

It swung wide open. A dark figure barrelled out of the house, knocking me over. I fell aside, my keys lost from my grasp, crying out in pain as the palms of my hands scraped across gravel as I held them out to break my fall.

"Saoirse!" Diarmuid's panicked voice broke through the calm of the night.

I winced as I sat up, brushing my hands gingerly to get rid of loose gravel.

Diarmuid appeared at my side, cursing. His arms wound around me, pulling me up to my feet. He didn't let go of me and I leaned into his warmth.

"Are you ok?"

"I'm fine. Just a scrape."

He pulled back and searched my body. His eyes were almost pained with concern. "Where?"

I lifted my palms to show him. He took my hands carefully in his, his thumb brushing at loose dirt. The lightest of touches, but it seared me deep in my soul. His bottom lip curled up and his eyes turned murderous.

"Son of a bitch," he muttered. "Did you see who it was?"

I shook my head. "I didn't get a good look at him."

He turned to look at the house, dark and still. "I'm going in to check it out. Someone might still be in there."

My blood chilled. I hadn't even thought of that. The perpetrator might not have been working alone.

"Get in the truck, Saoirse, lock the doors."

The thought of sitting alone in that cold truck made me shiver. I wanted to feel safe. To feel safe was to be with Diarmuid.

"I want to go in with you."

"No. It's not safe. He might have a weapon or have grabbed a kitchen knife."

A shiver ran down my spine. "Then what about you? It's not safe for you either."

"I know how to take care of myself."

I shook my head. "I'm coming in with—"

"Goddammit, selkie," he exploded, "don't fucking argue with me, just this once." He sagged and his palms came up to cup my face. I wanted to lean into his warmth, into the safety of his hands. "Sorry," he muttered, "I just need you safe. I just need you safe, selkie."

I just need you safe.

He cared. He cared about me. Just not the way I

wanted him to care.

I pulled away from him because it hurt too much to have him so close, to have him touching me, to have him looking at me like that and for it to mean less than what I ached for.

"I'll stay in the truck," I whispered and walked on wobbly legs down the path. Diarmuid stood there watching me—why did he always have to watch me?—until I was locked safely inside the truck.

This safety was a lie. I would never be safe unless he was here.

I tucked my arms around my body and shivered, even as I had the heat blasting. My heart rate kicked up a notch when Diarmuid disappeared inside.

Oh God. What if there was another burglar in there? What if Diarmuid was hurt? Or worse?

I forced myself to calm down as the lights inside turned on. I watched the windows and door for any sign of movement. I spotted Diarmuid's shadow moving through the house.

Then my bedroom light flicked on.

Diarmuid Brennan was in my bedroom.

Oh God. I squeezed my eyes shut. I hadn't considered the state of my room. Had I left anything embarrassing out? Dirty underwear, old photos of him, my journal...?

I had left my journal on my bed.

With all the secrets of my heart splashed across the pages in ink. Oh God. He wouldn't go through it, would he?

I stared at my bedroom window, wondering if I should run inside, wondering if I'd be too late to stop from embarrassing myself when he read every single thing I felt for *him*.

I unlocked the truck and hurried to the front door.

Diarmuid was climbing down the stairs as I pushed open the door. As soon as I neared him, everything in my body sighed.

"I told you to stay in the truck," he said, but there was no bite to his voice.

"What did you find?"

"There's no one in here. It doesn't look like anything's been disturbed. We've got to call the police."

"No!" I yelled.

Shit. My da would lose his shit if he came home to find cops came crawling around the place.

Diarmuid frowned. "Saoirse—"

"You said so yourself that nothing's been disturbed. We don't even have a description of the guy. It'll achieve nothing."

"Selkie—"

"Don't make me do this, please." I pleaded at him with my eyes, willing him to understand.

He let out a sigh. "Okay, fine."

Thank God.

Diarmuid turned back to the house. "None of the windows have been jimmied so he didn't get in that way." He reached out and jangled the lock. "It's busted." He spun to me, his eyes a hard jade. "You're not staying here while the lock is busted. You're coming home with me."

You're coming home with me.

Those words. The way he said them, so full of raw, take-no-arguments hardness, it sent a shiver up my spine. And a rush of longing through my veins. I scowled internally at myself, because I know he was not saying it in the way I wanted him to.

I nodded, because when a man like Diarmuid Brennan makes a demand like that, you can't say no.

His entire body relaxed, as if he expected me to fight him and was relieved that I didn't. He reached up and cupped the back of my neck, the warmth of his palm in contrast to the chilly night air.

"Call your da. Tell him you won't be home tonight."

I nodded again, because I knew arguing with him was pointless. But mostly, with his hands on me he could ask me for anything and I'd give it to him.

I pulled out my phone and rang my da's mobile. He picked up on the third ring. I explained about the house having being broken into, that the perpetrator had knocked me over on the way out and that the lock was broken.

My da responded with a series of curse words. "Are you okay?"

"I'm fine. Just a scrape or two on my hands. I'm…going to stay at a friend's house, okay?"

I glanced up to find Diarmuid watching me. He didn't make any motion to argue that I should give my da his name and address. At least we agreed on one thing. No way in hell was I telling my da that the "friend" was a cop, my JLO officer and not so much a "friend" as a…Jesus, I didn't know what the hell we were. God, I hoped my da didn't ask where I was staying because I didn't want to lie to him.

"Okay, baby girl. Shit, I'm sorry I wasn't there. I'll get it fixed, okay? I'll get an alarm system installed. I want you to feel safe there, yeah?"

We hung up. Thank God. He didn't ask who I was staying with. A thread of disappointment weaved through my relief. Shouldn't a parent ask where their underage daughter was staying?

Diarmuid followed me through the house, saying nothing even as I turned all the lights on as I went, so I could grab a few things and shove them into an overnight bag such as toiletries, toothbrush, clothes. He looked respectfully aside when I went through my underwear drawer. I might have been dreaming, but I swear his cheeks coloured.

I grabbed my journal too, resting on my crumpled bedspread, before he could see it, and shoved it into the bottom of my bag. It was my turn to flush.

We walked back out, turning lights off as we went. When I reached the front door, the lock practically hanging off the frame, I felt the adrenaline wearing off. My legs were becoming shaky. As if he knew what I needed, Diarmuid slipped an arm around my waist and helped me to the truck. He always knew what I needed, even without my having to ask.

Damn him.

Damn him and his caring. Damn him and his warmth and his smell and the tousled dark hair that fell across those magnetic eyes.

We were silent in the truck, even the music had been turned off. Until Diarmuid broke the silence.

"You kept the journal I gave you," he said quietly.

I sucked in a breath. He *had* seen it. Had he read any of it while he'd been in my room alone?

I shrugged, trying to downplay the significance. Not that it'd matter if he'd read it. "It's useful to write things down sometimes."

"What do you write in it?"

Thank fuck. He hadn't read any of it. Or was he bluffing?

"Don't tell me you didn't sneak a peek."

"That's private. I'd never." He shot me a glare as if he was insulted that I'd questioned his morals.

Because that was Diarmuid Brennan, the guy who always did the right thing. Too moral to read through someone else's journal. Too moral to go after a seventeen year old, even if he wanted her.

Perhaps it was the adrenaline, the shock of having been burgled, but it didn't hit me that I was going to stay over at Diarmuid's house until he pulled up in his short driveway.

My nerves wound around each other, tightening like a coil.

Me. And Diarmuid. In his house. Alone.

How the fuck was I ever going to survive this?

37

Diarmuid

Jesus Christ.

When Saoirse had pulled open her underwear drawer earlier, I'd spotted all those lacy, skimpy *adult* panties. Saoirse Quinn should not be wearing underwear like *that*. My blood burned at the sight of them. I had to turn my head away before I said something I shouldn't.

What got me even hotter was the idea that there might be a *boy* who was getting to see all those sexy lace panties *on her*.

Now she was in my house—my house—in my room getting changed. Naked.

I yanked open my fridge with a little too much strength, the bottles rattling in the shelves. I needed a drink. Something to cool me off because I still felt like I was feverish.

I grabbed a bottle of a pale IPA lager and ran it across the back of my neck before I cracked the bottle and skulled half of it down.

An image of Saoirse in my bedroom changing flashed through my mind, making my veins simmer.

Dear God, I was going straight to hell.

"Hey," her sweet voice came from behind me like a siren's call.

I jolted out of my reverie and spun, the beer bottle almost slipping from my hand.

She was standing there in a pair of sleep shorts, showing off her slim legs, and a thin t-shirt that clung to her chest. Dear God, I don't think she was wearing a bra.

I tore my eyes away from her and gripped onto my beer bottle. "I'll sleep on the couch. You can take my bed."

She shook her head. "Diarmuid, you're a giant. You won't fit on the couch."

I grunted. "I've slept in worse places before." Including on a park bench and in a doorway when I was a teenager.

Saoirse crossed her arms over her chest, a cute little crease between her brows. "I will not kick you out of your bed. You've been good enough to let me stay."

"Saoirse, this isn't up for discussion." I pointed to my bedroom. "Go to bed. I'll see you in the morning."

I glowered at her, a clear signal that I would win this argument no matter what.

She shut her mouth. And her face softened. "You're a true gentleman underneath all that gruffness."

I grunted.

She walked over to me, her steps cautious as if she were approaching a dangerous animal. She was, in a way. I froze as she slipped her arms around my waist and leaned her head against my chest.

I caught the honey scent of what I imagined was her body wash. She must have brought her own. I certainly never smelled this damn good after a shower.

It was just a hug. An innocent hug.

I closed my arms around her, holding her gently to me. Everything in my body felt like it sighed with relief. Just a hug. This was fine. Fine.

"Thank you," she whispered, her breath tracing the skin of my collarbone.

"Anything for you," I said, knowing in my heart that it was one of the truest things I'd ever said.

The couch was the most uncomfortable piece of shit I'd ever slept on. It was one of those horrid black pleather two seaters that seemed to exist in every property in Ireland, with arms that were board-straight and too high for my neck. It was so short I could barely get my torso on it when I lay lengthways, my legs hanging over the other arm and going numb.

"Fucking couch," I grumbled, and shifted yet again, trying to get comfortable and failing.

I heard a patter of footsteps, then smelled honey and

roses around me, a soft hand brushing hair off of my forehead. I squinted and saw a figure with a golden halo. An angel.

I must be dreaming.

"Stubborn man," a sweet voice muttered. "You look so uncomfortable."

I tried to open my eyes properly, but they were too heavy and stinging from being awake this late. My angel slipped her tiny hands into mine and tugged.

"Come on."

I rose to my feet, drawn towards the angel, following her through the darkness, trusting her completely. Then I tumbled onto a soft mattress and I let out a groan of relief, stretching out my legs. I felt a blanket being pulled over me. Then my angel climbed into bed next to me.

So soft.

So warm.

And she smelled so sweet.

I loved my angel. I may have even told her that, my words coming out as a mumble.

Then I fell completely to sleep.

38

Saoirse

I watched him sleeping for the longest time, his thick chest rising and falling like the ebb and flow of a tide, mesmerising me, soothing me, at the same time causing something warm inside me to ebb and flow. The way the silvery moon filtered through the window dusted his sharp cheekbones. He looked younger sleeping, at peace.

Before I had pulled the blanket over him, I saw that he was only wearing a light t-shirt and a pair of briefs. They hid nothing. Round ass, strong thighs, wide muscular torso. Knowing all of this was less than a foot away from me was making my head spin like I was on one of those hurly whirly rides.

God, I wanted him.

But it was more than just his body, it was *him*.

His mind, his heart, his flaws. Him.

I reached out for his hair spread across the pillow and touched the ends of it. It was softer than I'd imagined it would be. And it smelled like the masculine shampoo he had in his shower.

He grunted in his sleep. I yanked my hand back, squeezing my eyes shut, my cheeks flaming at the thought of being caught.

There was no more movement. No more noise from him. He must still be asleep. Slowly I opened my eyes again and gazed upon this beautiful sight.

What I wouldn't give to lie here with him every night. To be his.

His.

My wishes crumbled and blew away into an impossible wind. Diarmuid would never care for me the way I wished he would. I just needed to accept that fact.

Tomorrow. I'll accept the fact tomorrow.

Tonight, I was going to get as close to him as I could. I would take warmth from him without him knowing so he didn't have to feel guilty. I didn't know when I'd ever get to lie next to him again. If ever.

I shuffled closer to him until my arm pressed lightly against his. I didn't dare get any closer. Although I wanted to.

Feeling brave and giddy from his proximity, I ran the tip of one finger along his arm, memorising the dip and curve of each hard muscle, remembering how I'd done this three years ago when he'd shown me his ink. Back then I thought I'd known what it was to be a woman who wanted a man. I didn't. I'd been too young.

I knew now. Now this simple touch was all it took to set off a twisting, burning need inside me, a yearning in my lower belly that felt so wild. So primal. So...adult.

I wanted Diarmuid to sink into where it ached for him. I wanted him to live there. To own me.

He moved suddenly, his arm flinging out to grab me, yanking me against his chest. My entire front pressed against his hard body. My soft flesh moulding around steely muscle. He mumbled in my hair and then let out a soft sigh, sinking back into sleep, his eyes never opening.

I sucked in a breath.

This.

Here.

He was my harbour. This was my home.

It felt so damn right I could have cried. I could have begged him to never let me go.

Instead I curled my fingers into his shirt. I held on for as long as I could. Stealing his seal-skin under the cover of darkness, with the non-judgemental moon as my only witness.

Because come morning, when he woke, he would cease to be mine.

39

Diarmuid

I dreamed I was in the arms of an angel.

She kept me warm and she brought me peace. The kind of peace I'd never known. The ghosts from my past stopped rattling their chains. The heaviness that lay across my shoulders fell away. And the uncertainty, the feeling of being untethered, a single cork bobbing in an ocean, fell away.

She was an anchor. My anchor. My safe harbour.

As I woke, I felt every outline of her soft body, her breasts pressed against my side, her softness tangled around my limbs. My blood began to heat. I reached for her and found her slim waist under her shirt, my hand moving across her smooth skin as I shifted towards her.

She let out a soft moan and her leg slid across my thigh, pressing against my growing hardness. I rocked against her, every movement like a tide pulling me closer to awake.

I opened my eyes and found the blonde angel curled in my arms, her sweetheart face—the most beautiful face I'd ever seen—lay on my chest, her long lashes almost touching her high cheekbones.

It felt like cold water had splashed over me, snapping me out of my near-dream state.

Oh shit.

Saoirse.

In my bed. Up against *my erection.*

I jumped out of bed. She stirred, blinking. "What's going on?" she mumbled, her voice heavy with sleep.

"What the fuck? How the…? Wha?" I wasn't making any sense, my mind still trying to put together the pieces.

I had been on the couch. I swear I had gone to bed on the couch.

Saoirse sat up in bed, the sheets falling around her. Dear God, I wanted to get back in there with her.

"You looked so uncomfortable last night," she said, "I dragged you here."

And in my half-asleep state I had gone with it. Even though I shouldn't have.

"Jesus Christ." I rubbed my face. I was going to prison. Even worse, I was going straight to hell.

Saoirse rolled her eyes. "Don't worry. Nothing *happened.*"

Except something *did* happen. It happened inside of

me.

My erection was evidence of it. I had *pressed it* against her. *Rubbed it* against her. God help me.

I had to get out of here. I spun and practically ran out of the bedroom.

"Where are you going?" she called after me.

"You shower. I'll coffee," I grunted back, just needing some distance from her. From *me* around her.

In the kitchen, I cupped my hands around a mug, letting the heat from the freshly brewed coffee within burn my skin. If only it could burn away my sins.

I'd woken up in bed with Saoirse. I'd pressed my filthy erection against her clean body. Heaven help me.

"Why is there a box with my name on it in your closet?" Saoirse's voice broke through my reverie.

Ah, shit.

I looked up to find her standing before me, dampness at her hairline, wearing a pair of skinny jeans and a fitted jumper that showed off all her curves. Curves that I instantly remembered being pressed up against me in bed.

Double shit.

"You went through my closet?" My voice came out like a growl. The best defense is an offence, or so they say.

"No." She shifted her feet. "Maybe. I was just looking for a hand towel, I swear. You didn't have one in your bathroom." She screwed up her face. "Or your closet, for that matter."

Now that I was living on my own there were a lot of

things I realised I missed about living with a woman. Feminine things. Like candles, flowers and hand towels.

I didn't miss them enough to take Ava back, though.

"So the box…" Saoirse said.

Right. The Box.

"It doesn't have your name on it," I said, stalling.

She rolled her eyes. "Fine. Why is there a box with *Selkie* written across the top?"

I let out a sigh. I hadn't meant for her to ever see that box; it had been for me. Especially now that things were more…complicated between us.

No, I scowled to myself, *things were not complicated*. I *did not* have a complicated attraction to a woman who was over a decade younger than me.

It was simple.

Keep my hands *off* Saoirse.

Make myself stop thinking these illicit things. *Right now*.

Her jade eyes met mine, her tiny teeth chewing on her lip. "I didn't open it. I wanted to, though."

"You've seen it now," I said. "You might as well have it."

She blinked several times at me. "The box is *for* me?"

"No. Yes. Sort of."

She frowned. "Clear as mud, Brennan."

I downed the rest of my coffee as if it were a shot, the bitter burning searing the back of my throat—I needed something stronger, but this was all I had to hand—before dropping the empty mug in the sink. I wiped my mouth with the back of my hand.

Saoirse was still staring at me, the stern look on her face telling me that there was no way she was letting this go.

I let out a sigh. "Come on. It'll make more sense when you see it."

I felt her eyes on me all the way to the bedroom. And when I heard her dainty footsteps enter the bedroom behind me, my skin became electrified.

Saoirse and I were in my bedroom.

Alone.

I shoved this thought aside, yanking the closet door open just a tad too hard. The box was sitting plain as day in the back corner on top of the set of inbuilt drawers, Saoirse's nickname, *selkie*, written across the top in my tiny script.

I pulled it out and placed it on the bedspread, sliding it in front of the lady in question.

Saoirse glanced at me, a request for permission.

I nodded, permission granted.

Even after being apart for three years, we could still have a whole conversion without uttering a single word.

She slid the top of the box off and peered inside, my stomach flipping in my belly.

Ah, shit.

I was nervous.

40

Saoirse

It was an old shoebox. *Selkie* written in black scrawl across the top. I brushed my nickname written in Diarmuid's hand before I slid off the lid.

I pulled out the couple of papers on top first, my eyes scanning the pages, greedy for the contents.

My gasp caught in my throat.

It was my report card, the one where I'd gotten my first A+ in science. The one I'd given him.

And my short story, "Diarmuid and His Selkie", the story I'd written for him.

"You…you kept these?" I glanced up to Diarmuid.

He swallowed, his eyes not meeting mine, then nodded.

My heart swelled up, all tender and warm. He kept them. All this time.

I pressed the papers to my chest before setting them aside.

All that was left in the shoebox was another box, light blue and small enough to sit in one hand.

"What's this?" I asked.

"For—" Diarmuid cleared his throat. "For you."

For me?

My heart began to pound as I slid the lid off the blue box.

Inside was a charm bracelet with three charms on it. I pulled it out, dropped the box aside, and held the bracelet in the palm of my hand.

The first charm was a tiny Irish harp. I recognised the second as the serotonin molecule, the happiness molecule. And the third was a woman with a seal's tail, a tiny selkie.

I collapsed, sitting on the bed, my knees failing me.

Diarmuid lowered himself to kneel in front of me, so we were eye to eye, face to face.

"I bought the bracelet and a single charm for you for each of your birthdays. I just didn't send it to you because…" he trailed off, his stare going soft.

He didn't have to finish that sentence. I knew him well enough to do it for him.

He didn't send it to me because he thought it was better for me not to hear from him. To forget him. To get over him.

This whole time I thought he didn't care. I thought

310

he forgot about me, too busy with his new life and his new family to even spare me a thought.

Turns out I was wrong.

He thought of me every year that we'd been apart.

He bought me a gift every year even though he didn't think I'd ever receive it.

"Saoirse, no…"

I only realised I was crying when his warm palm slid over my cheek and he brushed aside my tears with the rough pad of his thumb.

"Not sad," I mumbled. "I'm…serotonin." In my hand I fingered the tiny metal molecule.

His lips lifted into a soft smile. "Me, too."

This was what I had always dreamed about since the day I met him five years ago, that he'd look at me this way, just once.

I lost myself in his eyes, his intense stare. Or perhaps I had only just found myself.

Before I could think about it, I leaned forward...*we* leaned forward. Or perhaps we fell.

And fell.

Until our lips connected.

His mouth was soft, firm. His lips fit perfectly against mine as if they belonged there. His palm, still cupping my cheek, went from warm to searing against my skin.

But he didn't move.

He didn't kiss me back.

Oh shit. Once again, I'd misjudged things. Shit shit shit.

I pulled back, our mouths separating, my lashes

fluttering open, desperate to see his reaction to my kissing him for a second time, even though I was just as terrified to see the rejection waiting for me, his pained refusal for a second time.

His eyes were open, wide and shocked. Just like last time.

I pulled farther away, excuses tangled on my tongue.

I didn't get a chance to voice any of them.

His hand on my cheek slid back, grabbing me by the back of my neck and yanking me towards him.

This time I really did fall.

I dropped the bracelet. My hands, open to catch my fall, landed on his shoulders, so firm and hard.

This time our mouths crashed together on purpose, a deliberate accident. A beautiful wreck.

His lips parted and I felt his tongue stroke against my lips. I gasped at the sensation, my own lips parting, letting him in.

My head spun. My thoughts silenced as he kissed me with enough ferocity to bruise, with a hunger that felt violent and insatiable. And yet, I couldn't get enough.

I had always been his. But now he had laid claim to me. His kiss branding me deep into my soul.

When he groaned into my mouth, the noise rumbling through my very centre, his soft beard brushing my skin, his fingers tightening around the back of my neck, I knew I'd forever be wrecked. Ruined. Broken into a thousand pieces that would only fit *him*.

My fingers slid across his shoulder, his neck, gripping into his shoulder-length hair, tangling into the soft curls at the base of his neck. I was making a mess of his ponytail, but I didn't care.

All I could feel was him. All that existed was us.

And it was beautiful.

And wrong.

And bliss.

Until it wasn't.

His hands shoved me and I went flying onto my back across his bed.

41

Diarmuid

I blamed the softness of her mouth.

I blamed fate that had twisted our lives back together again, even after I had cut all ties.

I blamed the part of me deep down, the part of me that had been waiting for her to grow up.

And now she was grown.

Unfortunately, none of these excuses would be a suitable defense in a courtroom.

Because I was kissing my seventeen-year-old assignment as if she was the very air that I needed to breathe.

Reality doused me like icy water. Before I knew what I was doing, I pushed her from me and she fell on her back across my bed, sprawling over my bedspread, her hair flying around her sweetheart face like a halo. She looked so beautiful just like that, her parted lips red and slightly puffy from where mine had been, eyes heavy with lust, her breasts heaving, legs askew.

It would take nothing for me to crawl over her, covering her with my body, tearing every last teasing shred of clothing from her and claiming her body, the last thing I'd yet to claim of her.

Fuck, Diarmuid, what are you thinking? my logical mind screamed at me.

"Diarmuid?" Her voice, so sweet and innocent, cut through my desire like a knife.

I stumbled back, bile rising up my throat. Oh God. I was sick. I was demented. What kind of man thought these things about a seventeen-year-old girl?

She's almost eighteen. She's a woman. So much a woman now.

No. I shook my head. That kind of thinking would ruin me.

I turned and bolted from the room, no idea where I was going, I just knew I had to get out of there. I stumbled into my living room and felt her hand on my arm. When I spun towards her, she was staring at me with concern.

"Diarmuid, what's wrong?"

Oh God, her voice was so sweet and concerned. I did not deserve it.

"*That* didn't just happen."

Shock spread across her face. "You don't mean that."

"I do."

She grabbed my arms, forcing my attention only on her. "Look at me and tell me that wasn't the most incredible kiss you've ever had in your life."

"Saoirse—"

"Look at me and tell me so," she practically screamed at me.

I pulled her hands off me, everywhere burning that was under her skin, shaking the foundations of my willpower.

"It doesn't matter what I feel, we can't ever do that again." I practically had to spit the words out, each one tasting like lies.

Her face screwed up. "Why?"

"You're too young."

"I'm seventeen, over the age of consent in Ireland. It's not wrong."

Shit. Fuck. Shit.

"Not for me. I'm a person of authority. You have to be eighteen…"

"But…but I turn eighteen in less than five months. We could wait—I'd wait."

My face softened. My sweet girl. My selkie. "Saoirse…"

"I'm not thirteen anymore. I'm a woman. I've seen the way you look at me, at my body. It's okay to want me now."

"No, it's not okay. It's sick and it's wrong."

Her eyes rimmed with tears. "You don't mean that."

"I do, I—"

Fuck. I realised too late that I'd made her cry, tears flowing freely down her cheeks.

The fight sagged out of me. I reached for her, just wanting to make her sadness go away, wanting to make it all better just like I used to do.

"Saoirse—"

She sidestepped out of my grasp, spinning and running from the living room. I heard my bedroom door slam.

Shit.

I've made a right mess of this.

What the hell was I thinking kissing her?

I wasn't thinking. I was reacting. Giving in to what my body wanted, what my heart yearned for.

The bedroom door banged open and Saoirse stormed past me, her overnight bag over her shoulder.

I chased after her. "Where are you going?"

"Leave me alone!" She slammed my front door in my face.

I sagged against my front door, resting my forehead against the wood, desperate to go after her.

Leave her alone. Let her go.

The truth was, that was all I could do.

Her lips still lingered on mine. The way her skin felt, so soft and smooth, still ghosted my palms. I was terrified that if I went after her, I'd lose complete control.

And ruin us both.

42

Saoirse

Then—Dublin, Ireland

On the Monday after the disastrous dinner that Ava ruined, Diarmuid picked me up from school.

He was silent. But that was okay. He and I were often silent, no need to talk.

I sat up when he took the turn that led to his area instead of my apartment. "Where are we going?"

"I thought we could have afternoon tea at my place. Is that okay?"

I nodded. This was perfect. Our stars were aligning. Only one possible flaw in the plan.

"Is..." I began, "is Ava going to be there?"

"Oh. No."

It *was* perfect.

Just Diarmuid and me, alone. Just like it was meant to be.

At his house, Diarmuid held open the door for me as if this were a date. I blushed as I stepped past him.

I felt like I was exiting my old life as a girl and stepping into my new life as a woman. His townhouse enveloped me with warmth and security as I walked into his living room. His place had always felt more like home than my own.

He felt like home.

I scanned the mantle where the framed photographs of him and Ava had sat. They were gone. All gone. The places they'd once sat was marked only by the absence of dust.

Oh my God.

He'd done it. He'd broken up with her. And now he was acting like there was something he wanted to tell me, the air around him heavy with gravity. This was it. He was free to be mine.

You have my skin.

I heard him drop onto the couch. I spun, our eyes locked and my breath caught in my throat.

He shot me a shy smile. "Whatcha doing all the way over there, selkie?"

I shrugged because I couldn't speak. He and I were alone in his house and Ava was gone.

He let out a smile. "Come sit with me."

I don't know how but I managed to get my feet

moving, my breathing quickening as I neared him. My knees gave out and I dropped onto the other end of the couch.

"Why've you gone all shy for? Come here." He patted the spot next to him.

A ball lodged in my throat. I shuffled closer until my knee was touching his strong thigh muscle covered in his usual denim. A warmth spread through my leg, making it tremble. I wondered if he noticed. He always noticed everything with me.

Diarmuid eyed me for a few moments.

"Jesus," he let out, "everything is changing so fast. I don't know how to say it."

Then don't say anything.

I shifted up onto my knees and leaned in. He enveloped me in a hug, his warmth, his presence, his everything blanketing me in safety, my heart banging against my ribs so hard I thought I was having a heart attack.

"Oh, Saoirse," he spoke into my hair, his voice reverberating around my name. "It'll all be okay."

Of course it would. He'd left the one he wasn't supposed to be with. Now he could be with me. I pulled back to look at him and he let me.

I brushed his shoulder-length hair back from his face. He'd let it out loose today. I'd rarely seen him with his hair out. He was my scruffy prince. My long-haired knight.

I leaned in and pressed my lips to his warm firm ones, my eyelashes flicking shut so all I could feel was him.

Then he was gone, his mouth tearing off mine.

My eyes flew open. Diarmuid's dark eyes were wide and on me, surprise on his face. How could he be surprised?

"I love you, Diarmuid," I explained.

I didn't care that he'd only just broken up with her. They were never meant to be together. But he and I were.

He blinked at me. He didn't say it back. But we had all this time for him to say it back. I leaned in to kiss him again.

"Saoirse, Jesus." His hands wrapped around my upper arms, holding me there. His mouth parted but no sound came out.

It was time to offer him my gift.

"Diarmuid, I want you to have my virginity."

43

Diarmuid

Saoirse kissed me.

She *kissed* me.

Right on the mouth. I was so shocked that it took me a second to tear my lips away.

"Saoirse, Jesus," I muttered.

This was so wrong. So fucking wrong. My stomach filled with sickness. She was fourteen. Just a child. With a crush. Why didn't I see this coming?

Ava had. Why didn't I listen?

Saoirse spoke and her words were like knives in my gut. "Diarmuid, I want you to have my virginity."

Fuck.

Oh fuck, oh fuck.

She reached for me and my stomach turned. I leapt to my feet, pushing her aside so that she fell back on the couch. "Saoirse, no! Oh God."

I should have never let her in so close. I should have never treated her like an adult, even if she was more mature than her physical years. My mind weaved back through the last year with her—every hug, every innocent touch was now tarnished. How could I let this happen?

"What's wrong?" she asked, standing up and reaching for me again to soothe me. *To soothe me.*

I backed away from her, my hands out, trying to keep her from getting any closer.

"Jesus, Saoirse, you're only fourteen."

"I know what sex is. I've seen my mother do it with the men she brings home. I can make it good for you."

Oh my God.

I snatched my arms away from her hands like her fingers were poisonous. My fingers ripped at my hair.

"No, Jesus, fuck, no." I choked. "I'm not touching you like that."

I saw the instant something broke inside her, the tears swelling in her eyes. Her bottom lip trembling.

Fuck. I've hurt her.

Her tears cracked something in me. My self-preservation flew out the window and all I cared about was softening the blow. I sank to my knees in front of her.

"Saoirse," I said, my voice calmer than my ragged heartbeat. "I don't want to hurt you. But that can't happen between us."

"Why not?" she wailed, the first tears flowing down her cheeks, leaving burn marks across my heart.

I cursed under my breath. "You're *four-fucking-teen*, Saoirse."

"I'm almost fifteen."

I shook my head. "It's still wrong."

"Why?" Her voice started to rise. "Because of my age? Age means shit, you said so yourself."

"I meant age doesn't mean shit when it comes to mental maturity."

"So it means something when it comes to sexual maturity?"

"...yes."

"A hundred years ago women were being married off at thirteen and fourteen. Wasn't anything wrong with it then. Why now?"

I spluttered, my reasonings feeling like butterflies I was trying to catch.

"Selkie, you've got years ahead of you to be a woman. Enjoy being a kid for now."

"I'm *not* a kid!" she yelled in my face. "It's because I don't have big boobs like Ava, isn't it? I'm not sexy enough."

Her words killed me. I hated that I lived in a world where a fourteen-year-old girl could think these things. What happened to being a child?

"Jesus, selkie, it's got nothing to do with that."

"Then why?"

"It's illegal." I swallowed down bile. "You're only fourteen. It is wrong for *any* adult to touch you in that way. You need to save it for when you're older. For when you've found someone you love."

"But I love *you*, Diarmuid. I want my first time to be with *you*."

Dear God, help me.

The thought of a man touching her made me want to commit murder. If it had been any other man who she was offering herself to, I'd fucking kill him. But it was *me* she was offering her immature body to. Right now, I wanted to hurt myself.

A small kernel of me *wanted* to be that special one. Because I knew I'd be gentler with her than any pimple-faced, selfish teenage boy. I'd be gentler with her than any other man on this fucking planet. I'd take my time, show her how to make love. I'd be the most generous, kindest lover. It would be a fucking honour to accept the gift of her virginity.

Except not now.

She was *fourteen,* for fuck's sake.

Her face twisted, her nose and her cheeks red. "You told me you love me."

"I do. Like…like a best friend."

She let out a wail that cut through my heart. "But you brought me here so we could be alone. You broke up with Ava."

"What? Why do you say that?"

"Y-your pictures. They're gone."

I glanced over to the mantle. Of course she noticed. Dear, sweet perceptive Saoirse. I let out a sigh. I had to tell her. Even though it would break her little heart. I had to tell her now.

44

Saoirse

"Saoirse, there's been a big misunderstanding."

I heard Diarmuid's words but I barely registered them. My body was shattering, my heart bleeding into my chest cavity with every beat, making it hard to breathe.

Diarmuid's eyes were filled with pain. "The photos are gone because Ava packed them. We're... We're leaving."

Leaving.

That single word cracked through my liquid pain like a knife of ice. My lungs froze over that cold knife so that I couldn't breathe.

"She's pregnant," he continued, his voice growing softer. "We're going to move near her family. And...get married."

No.

No no no.

This was not supposed to happen this way. He couldn't marry *her*. Not her. He was mine. The only one that was mine.

"No." My arms flailed, beating out at him, the source of my pain. "You can't marry her."

He grabbed my arms in a light hold. "Saoirse, stop."

"You don't love her," I screamed.

"I'm going to have a baby with her. I have to do the right thing."

Of course he did. He wouldn't be Diarmuid otherwise.

My heart ached. Despite myself, a part of me understood why he was doing this. He was a good man. He was too good. He had morals that held stronger than the walls of Charles Fort. That was why I'd fallen in love with him. Now his very morals were taking him away from me.

"You promised you'd always be here," I cried, trying to release myself from his grasp. I wanted to run away. Far away where his words couldn't hurt me. "You promised me."

"I'm sorry, Saoirse," he said, his words cracking with pain. "I'm so sorry. My family comes first."

"I thought *I was* your family."

He said nothing.

"Some people are born into family. We get to choose ours. We make our own, forged out of our hearts and weaved together by the

strings of our souls. And that is stronger than blood."

"So, you and me…" I sniffed, *"we're soul family?"*

He smiled. "Yeah. We are."

He lied.

He lied about everything.

I ripped my arms out of his grasp. He let go of me.

I turned and ran, banging out the door.

Diarmuid didn't follow me.

He just let me leave.

He didn't care at all.

I trudged home, my heart filled with pain, the backs of my eyes stinging.

Diarmuid didn't want me.

I was just a *girl* to him.

A kid.

That's all he thought of me as.

That's all I'd ever be to him.

It didn't matter that I understood him like no one else did. It didn't matter that he got me. That's all I was to him.

Not a woman.

Not an adult.

A fucking *girl*.

I didn't want to be a girl anymore. I wanted to be a woman. A woman who could make her own decisions and who had power over her own life. I wanted to shed my childish body, to rip away every last piece of ignorance and innocence. It was these things that gave other people the power to hurt me.

"Hey, Saoirse," a male voice called out, too young

sounding to be Diarmuid's.

I glanced up from the footpath I was staring at as I walked. It was Kian, waving at me, jogging up to me.

He frowned as he neared. "You crying or somethin'?"

He would do.

Mind made up, I faced him. "You wanna fuck me?"

His mouth dropped open. "I—w-wha?"

He'd been hinting at it for months, asking me if I'd come over to his house when his parents were away. Now that I was offering it to him on a plate, he was acting like a dumbstruck idiot.

I almost rolled my eyes. "You wanna or what?"

"I, er, yeah."

"Let's go, then."

I grabbed Kian's arm and pulled him along behind me until we got to my apartment, ignoring him as he gabbed away behind me.

"Oh, shut up, will ya?" I said.

I let go of his hand and unlocked the door, praying my ma wasn't home. Even if she was, she wouldn't care if I went into my room with Kian.

I opened the door, listening for the sounds of life inside. Great, she wasn't home.

I tugged Kian in behind me and made a beeline for my room, my nerves jangling away in my belly.

There wasn't much space to stand in my bedroom. When he closed the door behind him, we were only less than a metre apart. Kian just stared at me, his eyes wide.

I let out a sigh, then pulled my school uniform off so

I was just standing there in my bra and cotton panties. Still, he just blinked at me.

Diarmuid wouldn't be standing there like a lump if he was the one I was undressing for. He would know what to do, what to say, how to touch me. A slice of pain went through me as I thought of him, which I ignored.

"So? You gonna undress?" I asked.

Kian sprang into action, pulling his shirt off his head and dropping it on the floor beside him. His pale, skinny torso, ribs visible, was so different from Diarmuid's thick, muscled body decorated with ink. While Diarmuid had curls of hair on his chest, Kian had none.

Hesitation coiled inside me. I slammed that down and stepped up to Kian.

"Er, not to sound ungrateful or anything," he said, as I fumbled with his pants and briefs and pushed them down his skinny milk-white thighs, "but, like, what's made you want to…to, er…you know?"

I stared at his dick, a slender protrusion, erect and waving slightly at me. Was I really doing this?

Yes, I was fucking doing this. No more being an ignorant girl. I would become a woman. Then maybe Diarmuid would want me.

"I'm tired of being a virgin."

His eyes widened. "Oh, shit, and you want *me* to pop your cherry?"

I swallowed down a sob as I pushed down my panties, revealing the light patch of hair between my slim hips. Perhaps, once I was a woman, my hips would grow.

"Wait to date. Wait to be with someone. Wait…for someone

special. You deserve to be with someone special, selkie."

My heart cracked further. The voice that screamed *don't do this* grew louder, sounding so much like Diarmuid's.

I slammed a mental door on that voice. Diarmuid lied to me. He was leaving me. He had no right to tell me what I should or shouldn't do.

"It's not a big deal," I lied.

Kian reached out for my bra and I slapped his hand away.

"But I wanna see your tits."

"No."

If only I had big boobs like Ava. Then maybe Diarmuid would have said yes.

I lay a towel down on the bed and climbed on top of it. Kian climbed over me, our knees knocking as he tumbled in between my legs.

"Shit," he said, "I don't have a condom."

Fuck. I was wavering. If I made him go get one I'd change my mind once he was gone. I grabbed his arm to stop him from leaving.

"It's fine, just…don't come in me."

He nodded and stuck his hand down between my legs, fumbling with himself. I felt him nudging at me down there.

I squeezed my eyes shut. It would all be over soon. I'd be a woman.

He pushed in and pain ripped me in half. I let out a cry, muffled by the fact that I was biting down hard on my bottom lip. I tasted the copper of blood and felt the sting of tears.

"Oh, fuck yeah," he breathed against my hair.

My hands fisted the sheets as he thrust between my legs, his breath panting over me, smelling of cigarettes. Pain tore through me. Tears stung the backs of my eyes.

This was not how this was supposed to happen.

It was supposed to be Diarmuid above me, with his sweet mint breath and his gentle hands. With his woodsy clean-smelling body, so warm and so safe.

"Kian, stop."

He didn't.

I pushed at his chest.

His eyes opened and he looked down at me. "What?"

"You're hurting me." I shoved his chest again.

"Hang on, I'm almost finished."

He pumped into me harder, the stinging pain feeling like it was tearing me open. This time I hit him.

"Stop, Kian."

Then he was gone. Slamming against the wall, disappearing behind a wide back I'd recognise anywhere.

"Motherfucker, she said *stop*." Diarmuid's voice boomed through the tiny room.

Breath whooshed out of me.

Diarmuid came for me.

He came for me.

Diarmuid drew back his fist and swung. I heard the crack as it collided with Kian's face. Kian let out a long wail.

I sat up. "Diarmuid, stop."

Diarmuid let go of Kian, his hand yawing open like

335

rusty hinges.

"I'll tell. I'll tell on you." Kian whimpered as he snatched his clothes and tumbled back out the open door, naked, the lower half of his face covered in blood.

"Sure, tell the Garda I punched you. I'll tell them you were *raping a minor*," Diarmuid bellowed.

"She wanted it."

"She said *stop,* you fucking asshole," Diarmuid yelled. "Now get the fuck out and don't you *ever* come near her again."

Kian ran out, the front door slamming behind him.

Diarmuid turned and cursed under his breath. "Jesus Christ, Saoirse."

I wrapped my arms around my body, pulling my knees to my chest, my heart and that place between my legs throbbing.

Oh God. What had I done?

I burned. From shame. From gut-tearing regret. From the place I'd been ripped open by the *wrong* man.

I started to cry, heart-wrenching sobs that tore through me. I thought I was all cried out. Apparently not.

I felt Diarmuid's presence beside me, the bed shifting under his weight as he sat beside me, his warm hands pulling the sheets around my shoulder. "Shh. The bastard. Did he hurt you? I'll fucking kill him."

Diarmuid wrapped his arms around, and everything grew still again. My globe was the space between his arms, the wind was his sweet voice whispering that it was all going to be okay.

I loved him.

I hated him.

But he was here now. And that was all that mattered.

Diarmuid's mouth brushed against my forehead. "Jesus, why did you let him do that to you?"

"It should have been you," I mumbled. "I should have given my virginity to you."

He froze. His hands slid off me. I scrambled for him, reaching for him, desperate for him. He pushed my hands off him.

"Saoirse, no. It shouldn't have been me, do you understand?" His beautiful face was etched in pain. "This is wrong, you and me."

His words stabbed me in my heart. I felt every sharp point of each letter, every cut of each syllable.

"But you came back," I cried. "You came back for me, which means you do love me. Somewhere deep inside you, you do."

Diarmuid pulled out a small notebook from his back pocket.

My journal.

"I wanted to return this to you before I left. I found it in my bedroom. It must have fallen out of your bag. I didn't read it. I would never breech your privacy that way."

Before he left.

He was still leaving.

He didn't love me. I was such an idiot.

I spun in my bed, gathering all the blankets around me. I wanted to bury myself into a deep, dark hole and never come out.

"Saoirse."

I felt his hand on my shoulder. I hated the touch even as I wanted to lean into it. Because when he touched me, he was touching me like a child, a friend. Not a woman. Not as *his*.

"Don't touch me." I snatched my shoulder away, glaring at him from my huddle of blankets. "I *hate* you."

Genuine pain tore across his beautiful face. "You don't mean that."

"I do. I hate you. I never want to see you again."

His fingers reaching out for me dropped, making my guts wrench. "I don't want to leave us like this."

Leave.

He was still leaving. He didn't come here to tell me he'd changed his mind. He came to return my journal and to say goodbye.

Fuck him.

"Leave. Go. See if I fucking care."

I grabbed the closest thing—a pillow—and threw it at him. He batted it away as he backed out of my room.

"I'm sorry," he repeated over and over, his voice cracking as he closed my bedroom door, severing the connection that we'd weaved together over the last year.

My heart was turned to a sack filled with sand. When Diarmuid came into my life he struck me like lightning, turning my heart to glass. And now he'd dropped it, shattering it all over the floor.

He was my home.

My world.

My safety.

338

And now he was gone.

Just like that, our unbreakable bond—and my hope in something *good*—snapped.

45

Diarmuid

My heart felt like it took on the weight of the world after I walked away from Saoirse that day.

I could still see the image of that weedy pale boy on top of her. Could hear the echoes of her crying *stop*. Could feel her fragile, girlish body shaking in the sheets as I held her afterwards.

They would haunt me until my dying breath.

So would her last words to me, *"I hate you. I never want to see you again."*

Knowing she hated me, *crushed* me.

But another part of me welcomed it. Because I deserved her hate.

I'd failed her by not seeing her crush developing. By

not being able to stop the consequences. By causing her to throw her virginity away.

It should have been with someone special.

With someone who deserved her.

Most of all, I failed her because I was leaving.

My arms felt like lead as I packed up our place in Dublin, Ava laughing on the phone to her ma in the background like the crackle of an out-of-tune radio.

I came across the leftover wrapping paper from Saoirse's birthday and smiled at the memory of her face as she'd opened her gift. I thumbed the shirt that she'd worn that night she stayed over, still unwashed, still smelling faintly of her soap.

I found Saoirse's end-of-year report card, an A+ in Science, which she'd given to me.

"This is thanks to you," she'd said, pride shining in those emerald eyes.

I found the story she'd written in English class, entitled "Diarmuid and His Selkie", inspired by the story I told her.

"This is for you," she'd said shyly, her cheeks tinging pink.

I ran my fingers over her neat, slanted writing.

Ava would want me to throw all these reminders of Saoirse away. But how could I when Saoirse was weaved into my life.

I glanced up. Ava was too busy on the phone to pay me any attention. I folded the slips of paper and slid them into the bottom of the suitcase, hiding them among my things.

Finally, we were all packed and ready to go. The moving van had been loaded and was already on its way to Limerick.

I locked up the house for the last time and pushed the keys through the mailbox, turning slowly, expecting a certain blonde-haired figure to appear behind me.

But she didn't.

My heart felt gouged out. My mind clawed onto scraps of the last time Saoirse and I had been happy together. Her squealing as I raced us down the aisle on the trolley. Her tiny hip bumping up against mine. Her laughter as I dumped foam on top of her sweet head.

I'd never see her again.

God, was I really doing this?

Was I really leaving without a trace?

"What the hell are you just standing there for?" Ava yelled from my truck. All my responsibilities slammed into me.

I had to leave.

I had a family to take care of.

I'd only keep hurting Saoirse if I stayed.

"It should have been you. I should have given my virginity to you."

I winced at the memory before shoving it away. The best thing I could do for her was to leave her alone. To let her get over me. To let her grow up.

I forced myself into the truck, slamming the door behind me, trying to ignore the fact that the wrong woman was sitting in my passenger seat. I turned the truck on and the radio blared to life, the familiar twangs

343

of The Dubliners filling the cab.

Saoirse's favourite band.

Her favourite song.

She was everywhere. Even when she was gone.

"What is this shit?" Ava turned the radio knob, cutting off the music, changing it to that pop channel she liked. I almost yelled at her for it. I stopped myself before a word left my mouth.

I had to get used to pop now. Pop was my life.

On the way out of town, we passed the café where Saoirse and I had breakfast every morning. I saw us in that booth near the window, laughing, talking, teasing each other. I saw her sitting there as clear as the road in front of me.

Then I blinked and the image was gone, replaced by an elderly couple sitting in the booth.

I forced myself to focus back on the road. With every beat of my heart the sinking feeling grew.

Turn back.

Turn back.

You're making a mistake.

But I couldn't.

There was an even smaller soul growing inside of Ava's stomach who needed me even more than Saoirse did. At least, that's what I kept telling myself. It didn't make it any easier. Or any less painful.

I could not be like my father.

I *would not* be like my father.

I had a responsibility. I had to do what was right, even if it killed me.

Perhaps there was a part of me that was terrified of what might happen if I stayed. If I chose Saoirse over Ava.

"I love you, Diarmuid."

I swallowed hard.

I could never love her like that. Not now. She was a child.

But she wouldn't always be.

And what *could be* in the future for Saoirse and me...it loomed so fierce and large that it threatened to consume me.

Snatches of my mother's voice and the scent of roses washed over me. Before the black hole of her loss sucked any happiness away.

I didn't know if I could survive loving someone that much again.

So I drove away from my soul family for the sake of another.

46

Saoirse

Now—Limerick, Ireland

For the first time, I was thankful for my da's absence when I arrived home. He wasn't around to ask me what was wrong. I didn't have to lie to him.

I slammed the door behind me, a new lock magically having been installed. He must have been home at some point. I ran up to my room and flung myself onto my bed, kicking off my shoes and burying my face into the pillow.

You're too young.

Diarmuid's words echoed in my head.

Damn him.

347

Damn him for kissing me like that, then pushing me away.

He rejected me again.

No, I saw how he looked at me.

I felt the way he kissed me, like he was drowning and I was air.

He felt what I felt, I know he did.

I wouldn't let him push me away again.

I rolled over and grabbed my mobile out of my bag. There were already three missed calls from Diarmuid and a message.

Diarmuid: Just tell me you got home safely. Please.

My heart tugged. I wrote out several texts, deleting them all until I settled on something simple. Noncommittal.

Me: I'm fine.

Diarmuid: I'm sorry for what happened earlier.

Anger surged through me. He was still beating himself up about a sin that was all in his head. I stabbed out my reply.

Me: I'm not.

Diarmuid: It was wrong of me.

Me: The only thing wrong is you denying how you feel. I want you, Diarmuid. And you want me.

Diarmuid: You're just a child. It would be wrong of me.

Screw him. I'd show him *child*.

Me: I get wet thinking about you. I'm wet now.

Diarmuid: Jesus. Selkie.

Me: I'm playing with my pussy, running my finger through my wetness, imagining it's you.

Diarmuid: Stop. Please.

Me: Tell me I can cum and I will. Just for you.

Diarmuid: Fuck.

Me: Tell me, are these the words of a child?

I gripped my phone with my left hand, waiting for his response, my other working furiously in my panties. Frustration tumbled around, sharpening the need coursing through my body. I wanted to hate him. I wanted to fuck him. I wanted to kiss him until we both ran out of air.

349

I came, my body jerking as the orgasm crashed through me.

But he never replied.

47

Diarmuid

I get wet thinking about you. I'm wet now.

Dear God.

I lay on my back staring at the ceiling of my bedroom, my sheets twisted around my legs, Saoirse's messages burning a hole in my brain.

After she'd sent them to me, I'd oscillated between wanting to tear over to her house and throwing my phone out the window.

My skin itched. My joints ached, my muscles burned as if I had a fever.

Tell me I can come, Diarmuid, and I will.

I couldn't sleep, lying in my bed, smelling her scent of roses on my sheets and her tropical shampoo on my pillow, remembering waking up beside her, feeling that this king-sized bed was too big without her warmth.

I groaned and flung my arm over my eyes, praying for unconsciousness. But all I saw on the backs of my eyes was *her*.

I'm playing with my pussy, running my finger through my wetness, imagining it's you.

Need surged through my body. I needed her. Wanted her with a fury that terrified me. My willpower was ebbing with every breath I took, and it became easier and easier to justify giving in.

I'd be *good* for her. I *cared* about her, unlike that fucker who put her on the back of his bike without a helmet, who just wanted to get into her pants. My heart was already tangled with hers, our souls already family.

She's seventeen, Diarmuid. You've known her since she was thirteen.

She was going to ruin me. And in turn, I would ruin her.

What the hell was I supposed to do?

Two a.m. Two a.m. and I couldn't sleep.

I rang the only person I knew who'd be up at this ungodly hour.

Danny picked up and his familiar brogue sounded over the phone, the strains of a melancholy guitar instrumental in the background. And…was that a violin, too?

"What the fuck's wrong?"

I snorted. "Hello to you too, fucker."

"It's two in the morning."

"And you're wide awake." I cleared my throat. "What's that you've got playing in the background?" That was me, Mr Avoidance.

Danny let out a snort. "Alright, asshole. We'll do it your way. It's something I've been working on lately."

"It that a violin as well?"

"Well done, D, it *is* a violin."

"That's new. I thought you said, and I quote 'violins are for pansies'."

"Shite, you actually listen to me when I talk about music."

"Only sometimes."

"Yeah, well…maybe I changed my mind about violins." I wasn't sure what *that* was supposed to mean.

I hummed under my breath as I listened to the song end, the strains ebbing away until they were gone. "It sounds almost cheerful. Well, compared to the suicide earporn you usually listen to."

"Yeah, sure." I heard shuffling from his end, like he was moving around on his bed. "So, what's the craic?"

Nope, still avoiding. "You heard from Dex?"

Danny paused. Then he spoke, seemingly okay to let me keep talking shit. "Not since his shotgun wedding to Miss Thang. You?"

A few chords of a guitar strummed in the background. That was Danny. Half his mind was always on his music, even when he was talking to you.

"Saw him the other day. Popped into town the other week. He's invited me to his next match here in Limerick. I got a spare ticket. You should come."

Danny was not the "date" that Declan had in mind for me when he gave me the spare ticket. He'd probably rib me about being gay for a decade at least. Still, it'd be good to get the boys back together. Fuck, I hadn't realised I missed these two assholes as much as I did until right now.

"When is it?"

"Friday night in two weeks."

Danny let out a sigh. "Can't. Sorry. I'm teaching."

"Yeah, of course. Right. Semester's back on, yeah?" Danny had been working part-time at the music college in Dublin for the past few months. "Any student prodigies this year?"

I heard a twang, an off-key note, and frowned. Danny never missed a note.

"That was a shitty chord. You losing your musical touch or what?" I teased.

"When was the last fight of Dex's you went to?" Danny said, ignoring my question.

Looked like I wasn't the only one in avoidance mode.

I shifted on my bed, thinking. "Shit, not since he won his first title ages ago."

God, we were all kids back then. I used to go to almost all his fights. I'd been so proud of Dex, making something of himself, channelling all that rage into something positive. Then life seemed to get in the way. Actually, Ava got in the way. She hated the fights and I stopped going just to avoid fighting with *her*.

I promised myself then and there I'd make more of an effort with these two guys. They meant so much to

354

me.

Danny was silent on the other end of the phone. "I wish I had been at that fight with you guys."

My throat closed up when I remembered what had happened to him that year. "You had other things to deal with, Danny," I said softly. "Don't beat yourself up about it."

Danny cleared his throat. "Yeah, well, you didn't fucking ring me at two in the morning to talk about my sob story. Spill it, bro. What's got your knickers in a twist?"

Avoidance time was over now.

I rubbed my face, wondering how damned I would become if I said it out loud. I wanted to bury this secret so deep inside of me that no one would ever find out, not even God. I bet He Himself had some things to say to me about it.

Truth was, I wanted to scream Saoirse's name out loud while I pounded into her, claiming her, consuming her, making her mine, her body as well as her heart and soul.

Jesus, I was a dirty fucker. She was *seventeen*. Over a decade younger than me.

It was so wrong.

How could something so wrong feel so *right*?

"Diarmuid, did your dick fall asleep? Spit it out."

"There's a girl…" *Fuck, not a girl.* "A woman."

Danny snorted. "About fucking time. That Ava was a waste of fucking space if there ever was one."

I shut my eyes and breathed through my teeth to

keep from yelling. "You're telling me you *don't* like Ava."

"Wouldn't piss on her if she was on fire."

"Jesus Christ. And you didn't think to tell me this when I told you I was *marrying* her?"

"Mate, you only married her because she was *supposedly* having your baby."

"What the fuck is that supposed to mean?"

"I'm just saying, did you ever *see* this pregnancy test?"

I did. She showed me the doctor's pregnancy test result. "Ava wouldn't lie about a baby."

Danny snorted. "That's your problem, you think everyone else is as moral as you."

Ava was not an argument I wanted to get into.

I let out a noise of frustration. "Motherfucker. I thought we were friends."

"We are, asshole."

"Then don't keep shit like that from me again."

"As if you'd have listened to me if I'd told you I didn't like the bitch, you stubborn bastard."

"I would have listened," I grumbled. I would have done what I was going to do anyway, but I would have at least listened.

Danny let out a snort. "So, this girl…?"

Saoirse Quinn, I wanted to scream.

And she wasn't a girl.

"Do you remember about three years ago I had this genius kid assigned to me?"

"Saoirse Quinn."

Hearing her name coming easily off my best friend's lips made me want to punch him. Jesus, I was getting possessive over her fucking *name*.

"How could I forget her?" Danny let out a laugh. "You spoke about her all the time, like she was your own flesh and blood."

I gritted my teeth against that "flesh and blood" reference. She may not have *been* my flesh and blood, but she was *in* it now.

"She's been reassigned to me again. She's seventeen but God, she doesn't look it..."

There was a long pause on the other end. I could practically hear the light flicking on in Danny's head.

"Oh shit," he spat out.

Oh shit, indeed.

"Diarmuid, that's—"

"I know.

"She's—"

"I fucking know," I growled.

Danny let out a string of curses. "Jesus, Diarmuid. Seventeen-year-old pussy might be tight as fuck, but it ain't worth jail time."

"Don't you fucking talk about her like that, man, or I'll rip your fucking head off."

"Oh...shit."

I squeezed my eyes shut, letting my breath out between my teeth. I had called Danny wanting to talk, wanting his help. He did not deserve me yelling obscenities at him.

"You're in love with her."

My eyes snapped open. What the hell did he just say?

"I am *not* in—"

"Man, you're so far gone you don't even realise it."

"I. Am—"

"You asked me not to keep shit from you anymore. You said you'd *listen* when I talked."

Danny's words hit me like a slap to my face. I sat there stunned, my skin tingling with pins and needles.

"You're in love with her. You're so far gone you don't even realise it."

Jesus, fuck. Was he right? Was I *in love* with Saoirse?

We're soul family.

I love you, too.

No. I shook my head even though Danny couldn't see me. I couldn't be in love with Saoirse Quinn. I was supposed to be her mentor, her guiding light. I had watched her grow up. I saw her going through puberty. I had looked after her when she'd been thirteen.

You have my skin. And I have yours.

What if I'd just been waiting for her to grow up?

"I want someone I shouldn't want, too." Danny's voice was so quiet, I almost missed it.

I sat up. "You what?"

"You heard me."

I had. I just couldn't believe it. For as long as I'd known Danny, he'd been a slave to his music, married to his guitar. He rarely spoke about a woman that he was interested in.

Scratch that. He *never* spoke about women. Never.

Sure, he fucked women, but only ever strangers. No strings attached. Never anyone he knew. Especially not from the music scene, which could complicate his life.

Women were "distractions from my art", he said. All they did was want to take up all his time, demanding his energy and efforts.

This woman must be something special if he was admitting he wanted her.

"Who?" I asked.

"Don't judge."

I snorted. "Do I ever?"

"No." He let out a sigh. "One of my students."

I let his words sink into my skin. "Jesus Christ."

"I know."

"You could be fired."

"So could you, you fucker."

I squeezed my eyes shut. Danny was right. Even after Saoirse turned eighteen, she'd still be one of my assignments, and we'd still be almost a decade apart in age.

I wasn't allowed to touch her.

My skin burned at the thought. How unfair was life. How cruel. The only woman I'd wanted in years and she was the one woman I was not allowed to have.

"So…" I said into the phone.

"So," Danny replied, because what else could he say?

"What are you going to do about it?" I asked him. Maybe he'd have a plan I could follow.

He let out a snort. "Not what I want to, obviously." Then he sighed, and his voice turned bitter and hard. "The only thing I can think to do is to be cruel to her so she never knows that I want her."

I could never be intentionally cruel to Saoirse.

But I guess that was the difference between Danny and me.

But perhaps my being kind to Saoirse was just another form of cruelty. A more painful one.

48

Saoirse

I didn't hear from Diarmuid all week.

I didn't message him again, instinctively feeling like he needed space. He still had half a mind that I was still fourteen.

I was *not* fourteen anymore.

I was a grown woman, legally able to give my consent at seventeen. Legally able to give *him* my consent. He just needed time to get used to the idea of us.

I went to my café job, taking every shift that I could. I ate dinner alone and called Moina most nights, just enjoying the sound of her voice and the feeling that I wasn't alone.

By the time Friday came around, my body itched with

the need to be near Diarmuid again, my head spinning at the thought of hearing his deep voice cascading over my skin. I twitched like a drug addict knowing that her next hit was just around the corner.

He didn't come and pick me up like I thought he might. I caught a cab to O'Malley's.

I entered the boxing gym, early for once, my eyes seeking out his familiar figure.

He was in a corner, beating his wrapped fists into a boxing bag. His shirt stuck to every muscle, his ink like art down his muscular arms, shifting and ebbing with each movement.

God, he was beautiful. Moving like brutal lightning, somehow managing to be both graceful and fierce at the same time. A shiver went down my spine.

He spotted me and my breath caught in my throat at the click that seemed to fall in place when our eyes met. He straightened, brushing sweat from his forehead before dropping his fists to his side.

He nodded to someone across the room and strode towards me, unwrapping his black boxing wraps from his fists.

He stopped before me and I had to lift my chin to maintain eye contact with him. Once again, I had to admire how tall and broad he was.

"You're early," he said, his deep voice sounding even better than in my memories.

"Would you rather I be late?" The low seductive voice that came out of me didn't sound like me at all.

"This is Tadhg," Diarmuid said, pronouncing his

name like Tiger without the r. "He's one of the regulars here."

Only then did I pay attention to the man standing next to him. He was handsome in more of a pretty way, clean-shaven, strong jaw and a cheeky twinkle in his hazel eyes.

"Tadhg's going to be taking you through a boxing session."

I flinched, my gaze snapping back to Diarmuid. "What about you?"

"I have…some other stuff I have to take care of," Diarmuid said before he left me alone with the pretty boy.

"Okay, Saoirse…" Tadhg began, a half-grin on his face, one I was sure made most girls weak at the knees.

I almost rolled my eyes. *Most* girls. But not me. I was immune to all things except for Diarmuid. "Just shut up and train me."

Tadhg shrugged and led us over to a corner of the gym. He walked me through some basic self-defense and ways to get out of various holds.

He was a good teacher, his touch firm but never painful. He was patient even when it was clear I wasn't giving him my full attention. I kept glancing over to Diarmuid, every cell of my body aware of his exact location.

"He's a good guy."

I snapped my attention back to Tadhg. "What?"

Tadhg nodded towards where Diarmuid was standing, chatting to an older man, a weather-beaten, thick-set bloke with a full head of hair, the owner of this gym, I presumed. "You keep looking at him."

I flushed. "I do not."

"Sure you don't."

I frowned and turned my back on Diarmuid. Tadhg chuckled but he said nothing further. Good, I wouldn't have wanted to break his pretty straight nose.

At the end of the hour I was thoroughly worn out. Tadhg nodded at me, approaching me with a small towel. "You look sweaty. Let me."

I flinched as he got near. "What are you doing?"

Tadhg did not back off, the grin on his face widening. "You want his attention?" Tadhg asked in a low voice.

I didn't have to ask who. I didn't even have to respond, I could feel the eagerness pouring out from my features.

I let Tadhg stand right near me, his breath cool against the dampness on my forehead.

"You look wet," he said, loud enough to carry across the gym. He used the small towel to wipe at my face first, then my neck, then dipping lower—

It was snatched out of his hand.

"Get out of here, Tadhg."

I spun at the presence at my side, the familiar rumble of a voice.

Diarmuid glared at Tadhg like he was seconds away from punching him.

Oh shit. I hadn't wanted to start anything.

Tadhg wasn't fazed. In fact, his grin widened.

"She's all yours." He patted Diarmuid on his arm as he strode away, winking at me over his shoulder.

Diarmuid and I were left alone.

His eyes darted to me, and he wrung the small towel in his hands, as if he just realised what he'd done and was embarrassed at his behaviour.

He cleared his throat. "Good session?"

I nodded, my body flushed, half from the workout, half from having him close to me again. I kept watching his mouth moving as he spoke and remembering how it felt on my lips. His body radiated warmth that rolled over me, calling me like a siren to get closer.

"Tadhg behave himself?"

I nodded again.

Jesus, what was wrong with me? I'd never had any problem talking around Diarmuid. Until he kissed me. And now I felt like a giddy little girl.

The irony.

"Good," he said.

There was a pause.

"Well, okay then." He turned to walk away.

"Diarmuid," I called after him, finally finding my voice.

"See ye next week, Saoirse."

Goddammit. He'd ignored me this whole session and now he was just going to walk away from me? I chased after him.

"Diarmuid."

He didn't stop.

"Goddammit, Diarmuid, stop." I grabbed his upper

arm, trying to get him to look at me. His bicep was hard and warm and smooth under my palm. "Are you just going to ignore me from now on? Is that it?"

"I'm not ignoring you." He tugged his arm free of me and my insides wailed at the loss of him.

"Yes, you are."

"I'm talking right to you."

I let out a noise of frustration. "You're avoiding me."

"I'm…not." But he didn't sound so sure.

"You're just going to pretend that the kiss didn't happen?" I hissed, lowering my voice.

He rubbed his face, a curse slipping out between his fingers. When he removed his hands, strain left creases around the corners of his beautiful eyes.

"I don't know what more you want from me, Saoirse." He sounded tired. So damn tired.

I was such an idiot. Rejection tore through the old wound, exposing the raw nerve ends.

"Nothing," I cried, hating that I sounded close to tears. "I don't want anything more from you."

I turned and practically ran out of the gym.

I never wanted to see him again.

It was only after I tumbled out of the gym into the dying light that I realised I had no way home.

"Saoirse," Diarmuid called after me. "Wait."

Damn him. I did not want to see his face anymore.

I strode down the street as fast as I could. Maybe I'd be lucky and stumble across a cab. Dammit, I'd walk home if I had to.

I heard my name being called again from behind me.

Shit. He sounded closer, his footsteps coming up fast behind me. Damn him and his long legs.

"Saoirse, stop."

"Go away."

"Where are you going?"

"Away from you."

"Dammit, you can't just walk home."

"Watch me."

"Stop right now."

"No."

"Selkie," he warned.

My nickname cut through my anger like hot water through ice. "Don't call me that," I near shrieked, "you don't get to call me that anymore."

I pumped my arms and legs faster. It didn't help, though. He was upon me in a second, tackling me around the waist and throwing me across the shoulder.

I let out a shriek that echoed into the night.

"You stubborn woman," he muttered. "If you just stopped when I bloody asked you to, you would have made it easier on yourself."

"Put me down," I demanded as I beat at his back, which felt like granite under my fists.

"If I put you down, will you behave yourself?"

"No."

He let out a snort and kept walking, jostling me on his shoulder with each step. The sound of his heels on the smooth sidewalk changed to the crunch of the parking lot gravel under his feet.

"Stop treating me like a child."

"Stop acting like one."

"Screw you, Diarmuid."

I yelped as he hauled me back down his shoulder. I slid down on my front until my feet touched the ground and I was standing between him and the passenger door of his truck.

We were so close I could feel the heat radiating off him, the anger vibrating off him, causing all sorts of breath-clenching, knee-shaking sensations throughout my body. Mutinous, traitorous body.

His dark eyes were dilated, looking almost black. His nostrils flared as he leaned right in. I took a step back but went nowhere, my back banging up against the passenger door. I was trapped. And yet, there was nowhere else I'd rather be.

"Get in the car. I'm taking you home."

I crossed my arms over my chest, trying to act tough even though my knees were shaking. "So, you ignore me, then you demand that I sit in a confined space with you. No thanks."

He leaned in even closer, the width of him feeling like it was closing around me. I swear I heard a low growl coming from his throat.

"I'm not asking you. Get in the truck."

"And if I refuse?" So stubborn. And yet my pride wouldn't let me be any other way.

"I will tie you onto the roof of my truck and take you home that way."

I gasped. "You wouldn't dare."

He tilted his head, a challenge. *Try me*, his eyes

seemed to dare.

I swallowed. I knew when I was beat. I patted the door behind me, searching for the door handle. I found it and pulled it open into my back, forcing me forward until my front was pressed up against his chest. I might have died right then and gone to heaven. The softness of me and the hardness of him. I may have even mewled.

The sternness in his face dissolved and the creases on his forehead softened. The sweet tenderness that had always been there underneath rose up to the surface. I decided right then that this look of his, this one right here, was his most dangerous. This look could have me losing everything to him. My body, my soul, even the pieces of my heart he'd shattered.

"You need to move so I can open the door," I said, my voice coming out a mere whisper. I licked at my lips, as dry as desert sands.

His gaze dropped to my mouth, watching that tiny movement. He licked his own lips, mirroring me. For a second I thought he was going to kiss me again.

Kiss me. Please, kiss me.

Instead he backed up, a single step, cold air rushing between us. I felt unsteady, as if he'd kicked the ground out from underneath me.

His eyes burned into me as I turned and fell clumsily into the passenger seat. He, the bastard, was as graceful as ever when he slid into the driver's seat.

"Just because I'm letting you take me home, doesn't mean I'm not still angry with you."

Diarmuid let out a snort. "I wouldn't have expected

369

anything less."

The tension in the truck was thick and ropey. We drove for maybe ten minutes before Diarmuid leaned over and turned on the radio. The chords of a guitar wafted out from the speakers, some generic rock band. The low music did little to cover up everything unsaid.

I stared out the window at the passing houses, a distinct feeling of being stuck, of déjà vu, gripping my body. I felt like all I was doing was beating up against a wall, a wall that Diarmuid had put up between us. I didn't know how to get through to him. I didn't know how to get over the wall. Only he could tear it down.

I wasn't sure he wanted to. Even if he wanted to, I wasn't sure he could.

The music changed and I recognised instantly the sound of The Dubliners.

I loved the song.

I reached for the volume dial to turn it up. His fingers brushed mine as he reached for it too.

I snatched my hand away, the feeling of his touch burning up my arm like a fever.

Diarmuid cleared his throat. "I seem to remember that this was your favourite."

He turned up the volume. I hated that he knew me this well.

I clenched my jaw shut and stared out the window. I couldn't even seem to bring myself to enjoy the song right now.

Diarmuid pulled up in front of my house. As usual, all the lights were off, indicating my da wasn't home. Big surprise there.

"Where's your da?"

Of course, Diarmuid noticed. Why did he have to notice everything I wanted to hide?

"It's late," Diarmuid said, "when's he coming home?"

"I'll be fine."

"I don't want to leave you on your own."

"You didn't seem to have a problem with that three years ago."

I felt Diarmuid tense beside me. I almost regretted saying that. Almost.

He let out a sigh. "I don't want to fight."

"Who's fighting?" I said through gritted teeth.

"Fine. See you next Friday."

Inside, I fought the growing swell of inevitability. Diarmuid and I could never be anything. The longer I tried, the harder I tried, the harder my heart would smash when he finally broke it again.

I didn't think my heart could take being shattered twice.

"I can't do this anymore," I said, fighting back tears. "I can't be around you when everything screams at me that we are meant to be *something*. And you...you with your fucking cool logic and detached emotion. You're like a zombie. You don't feel anything."

"I feel." He grabbed my arm, causing my gaze to snap to his. "God dammit, Saoirse, I feel. Too much."

"Then why don't you—"

"Feeling something and choosing not to act on it for

the greater good, that's what being an adult is about. Being an adult is not about age, it's about how you act."

"Are you're saying I'm not an adult?"

"No, I'm saying what we want and what we should do are two different things."

"That's shit."

"That's life."

I shoved his hand off me, all the old cracks in my heart reappearing. "Leave me alone. You hurt me too much, Diarmuid. You hurt too fucking much."

I shoved open his door and tumbled out onto the sidewalk. Running for the house, fumbling for my keys, I tried to get some distance from him. I heard him behind me, calling for me to stop.

Why did he have to keep chasing me? Why couldn't he just leave me alone?

This time I couldn't let him catch me. I would break if he did.

I tumbled in through the front door.

"Saoirse, stop."

I did not. He followed me into the house, his footsteps crashing across the old wooden floors. If I could just get to my room, it had a lock inside the door. He grabbed me right as I turned the corner into the short corridor before the stairs.

His hands gripped me around my waist as he slammed me against the wall. His other hand gripped my chin, forcing me to look right into his tortured, burning eyes.

"You think I don't *feel?* Dear God, Saoirse," he

sounded furiously, "the things I want to do to you... It kills me that I'm not allowed to touch you the way I want. It fucking tears me apart to hold myself back from stripping you naked and worshipping every single fucking inch of you with my tongue. It's like I've become a savage inside. A beast."

I felt every single one of his words in every single one of my cells, ringing out like bells.

His fingers on my chin became soft, tracing my cheek, his eyes growing tender. "This is what you do to me. No one else. No one. Ever."

I sucked in a breath and let out a moan. His words were like hands all over my body.

"Please," I breathed," touch me."

"I...can't." He was fighting himself. I could see it. The moral man trying to hold back the beast inside with feeble chains. Chains that were cracking.

He couldn't touch me. But I *needed* to be touched.

"Let me show you," I whispered, my breath sucking in and out of me, "how I want you."

I moved my hands up my stomach, towards my heavy breasts, across my diamond-hard nipples. I let out a moan, shocked at my own boldness. My other hand found my waistband and dipped inside, his eyes widening as he followed my hand with his eyes.

He swallowed hard. "What are you doing?"

"I ache for you. Right here." I let out a cry as my fingers found my wet sex and slid inside easily.

He let out a groan too.

His fingers tightened around my waist, his other hand

now gripping at the back of my neck as if he'd be blown away if he let go.

I stared right at him, my need for him, for release, overriding any embarrassment.

"Tell me what you want to do to me," I whispered.

He warred with himself. How he warred. Conflicting emotions flashed in his eyes.

"Selkie, please," he begged.

"You're not touching me, I am," I panted, as my fingers worked against my body, dragging me closer and closer to the edge. "They're just words."

His gaze hardened. "You don't know what you're asking for."

"I do."

"Damn you." He yanked his hand from around my waist and slammed his fist into the wall above my head. I jolted from surprise, not fear. I could never be afraid of him.

He leaned in, his body pressing against mine, his mouth going above my ear. "I can feel your nipples like two little pebbles nestled in the softness of your breasts."

I swear they got harder, painfully hard as he spoke.

"I want to suck on them, take them into my mouth."

I sucked in a breath, my fingers moving faster. His hand slid down the wall, down my arm and gripped my wrist, forcing me to stop moving my fingers, my pussy aching at the sudden cruel halt.

"Slow," he said. "It'd take it slow with you."

He held my wrist for a second longer as if to make a point.

Slow. Okay. I nodded. He released me.

It was painful and frustrating to move slowly, but I did just as he asked, my head going lightheaded.

"I'd kiss every inch of your body. Every inch, Saoirse. Twice. Then I'd go back over you with my tongue." Goosebumps rose along my arms. This was slow, sweet torture.

I heard him sucking in breath through his nose, inhaling me, smelling me. "I bet you smell this good every-fucking-where."

His lips brushed against my neck. "I've dreamed about how your sweet pussy would taste. Wondered how hard your back would bow the first time I dipped inside you. What noises you'd make when I sucked that pretty little clit in between my lips."

Dear. Fucking. God.

I was going to lose my mind. He was around me—his scent, his heat, his voice—everywhere except where I truly wanted him. Inside me.

"More," I whispered.

"Not yet. Even as wet as you are right now, it'd still hurt when I pushed inside you. When I slowly stretched you around me. Add another finger."

I whimpered. Did what he asked of me. But it was not enough. Still wasn't enough.

"Fuck me," I begged.

"What was that?"

"I've had enough with slow, Diarmuid. Fuck me."

His fingers twisted into my hair, yanking my head back, exposing my neck to him, and I was pinned between him and the wall. It hurt but it felt deliciously good.

"Then take it hard," he growled, "let it hurt a little."

With his permission, I slammed my fingers into my body, wishing it were him, letting his hard voice spur me on.

"That fucking kid who took your virginity, I'd pound him out of your memory so that *I'd* be your first. Your only."

Oh God, I wanted that too.

"I'd angle your hips so I'd hit your g-spot. Over and over, no mercy."

His fingers gripped at my hip, cutting into my flesh. Pain blurred with pleasure.

"Curl your fingers for me. Feel what it'd be like."

I did as he commanded, finding that sensitive spot inside me. "Oh God," I hissed, as my body reacted, as I began to tumble. I squeezed my eyes shut.

"Eyes open, selkie."

I pried them open. He had pulled back so he could see me.

The second our eyes locked, my orgasm tore through me, waves of powerful pleasure slamming through my body, making my head knock back against the wall, while the edges of my vision turned to stars.

It went on forever. I felt lost in the two pools of his midnight eyes. If he wasn't leaned up against me, I'd have collapsed.

When I settled back into my body I felt like warm liquid, sated and sleepy. He was still watching me, his eyes glossy.

"That was so fucking beautiful," he whispered, his throat tight. "Thank you."

He leaned in, his sweet breath swirling around my cheeks. His lips brushed mine, soft, tender. His fingers cupped my head tenderly like I was precious, adored. Loved.

This was more than just lust.

This wasn't dirty or wrong.

It was love.

How could love be wrong?

Before I could deepen the kiss, he tore himself away from me, a cry of anguish leaving his mouth. Flinging himself around the corner, he disappeared from my sight.

I heard the front door slam, followed by the distant roar of his engine and the squeal of tires as he drove away.

I slid down the wall, my legs too shaky to keep me up.

49

Diarmuid

What the fuck had I done?

Even after I'd fled Saoirse's place, I had to take three goddamn cold showers to calm myself down.

Still, like the savage I was, I hardened to stone every time her face flashed in my mind, her mouth open, the sound of her coming against my thigh, her fingers making wet sounds as she pumped them inside her, watching her experience such an intimate, adult act.

She'd never looked so much a woman as in that moment.

It was wrong.

But it *felt* right.

And now I hated myself for it.

Technically, I hadn't touched her. But in my words, in both our minds, I'd committed such depraved acts on her innocent body.

I could not be trusted around her.

I strode up the hallway to Coilin's office, my footsteps not as sure as they usually were.

How the fuck was I supposed to explain myself? I couldn't very well tell him that I lusted—*lusted*, dear God, what the fuck was wrong with me?—after a seventeen year old who I'd *kissed*. Who sent me dirty text messages that made my blood burn and my body ache.

She doesn't look *seventeen. She doesn't* act *seventeen.*

I shoved that voice of justification away. There was no justification for it. It was wrong. And I had to put some distance between us.

Getting her reassigned to another JLO was the first step.

First, I just had to get Coilin, my supervisor, to agree to it.

"Why?" he demanded when I asked him.

I couldn't give the real reason without exposing myself. And Saoirse.

I shifted in my seat. "I just think maybe she'd be better off with…" with someone who wasn't falling for her, "with a female JLO."

Saoirse would hate me. She'd take it personally. She'd see it as another rejection. But if I spent any more time with her, it was only a matter of time before I did something stupid. Something irreparable. I *had* to get her reassigned.

Coilin let out a snort, looking a little too amused for my liking. "Why? She giving *you*, the infallible Diarmuid Brennan, trouble?"

"No," I said, just a little too quickly. Ah, shit, I fucking put my foot in it using the gender card, I just knew it. "I just think maybe she'd loosen up with a female officer."

Coilin folded his fingers together, his gaze going past my head. The asshole wasn't even taking me seriously. "You and she just need time together. Maybe you should spend more time with her?"

Fuck, that's what we should *not* be doing.

"Will you just do it, Coilin?" I let out.

He raised an eyebrow.

I regretted all those times I told him to fuck off when I was late with my paperwork. He was getting me back. He wasn't going to pull any strings for me because I'd always been an asshole to him. Served me fucking right.

"I'll get all my paperwork in on time from now on, I swear it," I promised. Begged.

"Jesus, you really must be desperate to get rid of the girl if you're offering me that."

Shit on a stick.

"She's not bad. It's not like I can't handle her." Lies, the lot of them. I didn't know how to handle *myself* around her. "It's more for her that I think she should be reassigned."

Coilin studied me for the longest time. "You know Kate's on mat leave. She's my only female JLO."

I felt my hope sinking. "I thought Livvy was stepping

up into a JLO role."

He shook his head. "She decided to move into burglary."

I let out a grunt, frustration building in me. "So what you're saying is…?"

"I'm not going to reassign her."

Fuck.

Despite my disappointment, I felt a trickle of relief. Then I wanted to slap myself.

"Besides," Coilin continued, "there's another reason why I want you on Saoirse Quinn's case."

What?

Before I could ask why, the door behind me banged open. In strode someone I'd rather not have seen again.

Niall fucking Lynch.

A royal pain in my backside.

A thick-set man with a stern forehead who waved his arms too much when he spoke. He was also the most persistent fucker I'd ever met when he got an idea in his head, like a bulldog with a bone.

Niall Lynch also just happened to be the top dog on the Limerick "drug squad". He'd been on my case for the last twelve months about joining his team. I don't know how many times I could say "fuck off" to this guy without punching him in the face to make sure the message was clear.

He'd been going around my back to my supervisor and our captain as well, trying to manoeuvre a transfer for me without my knowing. If there was one thing I hated, it was manipulative little bitches like this dickwad who always had their own agenda to push.

What was worse was that no one seemed to want to call him out on his game-playing bullshit. I guess that was why I'd always be a soldier in the trenches instead of calling the shots. I was no good at politics.

Niall grinned at me, then nodded at Coilin. "Boys."

That, I fucking hated. He called us all his "boys". As if we were his little minions, little kids instead of grown-ass men.

I growled under my breath. If I had fangs I would have bared them. "Can't you see we're in a meeting here?"

I didn't like the fucking twinkle in Niall's eye. "Then I'm just in time."

Ah shite.

I suddenly realised what this was.

An ambush.

"What the fuck is going on?" I shot a glare at Coilin. He didn't even have the decency to look guilty.

Niall pulled out the chair beside me and sat down with a flourish. It took everything in me not to kick out his chair legs. He placed his ankle over one knee, his leather shoes spit-shined and his dress pants perfectly pressed, then leaned back, arm slung over the back of the chair, the arrogant asshole, sitting as casually as if this office was his.

"You may or may not know," Niall started, as if *he* was the one leading the meeting, "but Liam Byrne, one of west Ireland's most notorious drug kingpins, was *just* released."

I grunted but didn't say anything. I knew this and I had a feeling I knew where Niall was going with this. I didn't like it one fucking bit.

Niall leaned forward as if he was about to reveal some great big secret. "Saoirse Quinn is his daughter."

"What a revelation," I spat out.

Niall's eyes narrowed just a touch. "I know you were previously assigned to her when she was thirteen. You have a relationship with her. She trusts you."

What *relationship* we had was complicated. And her trust in me, shaky. All these things I did not say.

"We've been trying to get something on Liam. So far we have next to nothing. I want him back behind bars before the year is out. Saoirse is our way *in*."

Fuck.

No way.

"I am *not* using Saoirse to get to her father," I snarled. "She doesn't have anything to do with his business. She's just a *girl!*"

Niall snorted. "Apples don't fall far from the tree, Brennan."

I bristled. "Your father must have been a right prick."

"Brennan," Coilin barked out in a warning tone. I knew I was toeing the line.

Niall just threw back his head and laughed, long and loud. He wiped under his eyes and wagged a finger at me. "You're a riot, Brennan."

"Glad to have entertained you." I pushed up to my feet. "But I've gotta go. Got shit to do."

I strode out of Coilin's office, fuming. I'd come in

here hoping to get Saoirse reassigned. Instead I had been ambushed and asked to get even closer to Saoirse in order to pin something on her father. All the while my supervisor, who was supposed to have my fucking back, watched on silently.

I was so lost in my own thoughts I didn't hear him coming up behind me until he grabbed my arm.

I spun to face Niall once more.

The politician's mask he'd had on in Coilin's office was gone. In its place was the real, ruthless Niall, who only cared about his own goals, even at the expense of a child.

"You'll help me, Brennan," he said, his voice too low for anyone else to hear.

I yanked my arm out of his grasp. "Not a fucking chance."

"You will. Every man has his weak spot." A smile crawled over his face, terrifying me more than his scowl. "I *will* find yours."

50

Saoirse

I woke up to a warm hand shaking my shoulder and a low voice saying my name. For a split second I thought that it might have been Diarmuid; it'd been days since The Wall Incident, as I was calling it to myself.

I realised the voice was too croaky to be his.

I opened my eyes, squinting at the light filtering through my curtains.

"Da?"

My father was sitting beside me on the bed, his eyes wide open, cigarette smoke clinging to his clothes.

"Morning, girl. How did you sleep?"

Terribly. I tossed and turned for hours, Diarmuid's mouth ghosting my lips, his voice echoing through the caverns of my soul, my body burning like a fever. When I had gotten to sleep, I'd dreamed of him.

"Okay," I lied.

"I got the door fixed. I've installed an alarm system. I need my girl to feel safe here."

I shoved the hair off my forehead and sat up. "That's okay."

"Who was the friend you stayed with?"

The reminder of the night I'd spent in Diarmuid's bed hit me like a slap in the face. I shrugged, trying to play it cool, even as my stomach tumbled. "Just a friend."

My da's forehead creased. "I've been neglecting you lately. How about we go for breakfast?"

I smiled. "Sure. Just give me ten minutes to change and wash my face."

He drove us out to a local café where we sat at a table by the window and ate eggs and bacon. I almost ordered the full Irish breakfast but stopped myself when Diarmuid's face flashed in my head, sitting opposite from me in our breakfast booth in Dublin.

Why did everything have to remind me of him?

"I've heard you won the chemistry award back in your old high school," my da said. "Took the gold at the science fair for the last three years running."

I almost dropped my fork. "Oh, yeah. You heard that?"

My da smiled at me, the creases deepening around his eyes. "Of course, baby girl. I made sure someone was keeping tabs on you."

I frowned. "You were keeping track of me?"

"Yeah, honey, of you and your ma." He shook his head. "She was always a difficult woman. A lost soul. I sent her money sometimes for you but I know it never made it to you. I'm sorry I had to leave you with her."

He reached out and placed his hand over mine.

I swallowed down a large piece of toast, my throat suddenly so dry that it scraped down the sides. My da cared.

"It's fine," I said in a near whisper.

"Well, I'm here now, and I promise you, baby girl, I'm not going anywhere. Okay?" He squeezed my hand.

"Okay, Da." I smiled.

He promised he'd come for me and he did. My da kept his promises. He'd keep this one.

After breakfast we drank coffee—me a cappuccino, him a long black—and he asked me more about school, specifically about chemistry. I rambled on about my science projects and my math results, my head spinning a little at the fact that I actually seemed to have a captive audience.

My da beamed at me. "I knew my girl was smart."

My heart warmed at his praise, his words unlatching a hunger in me for more.

I sat up. "I'm more than smart, Da. Numbers make sense to me. That's why I love chemistry. It's all about numbers and equations. Give me any complex equation and I can do it in my head, just like that."

He raised an eyebrow. "Oh, yeah?"

I nodded fiercely, ready to show off my brain to him. "Give me two numbers."

He called out a series of numbers and I multiplied them in my head. He checked my answers on his phone calculator, his eyes growing wider and wider with each sum that I got right.

Finally he sank back into his chair, a look of awe on his face. "Holy shit. My daughter's a goddamn genius!"

He was proud of me. I wanted to make sure he stayed proud of me.

"I think I want to apply for university next year," I blurted out. "Something in science. Maybe become a chemist or something."

There was a strange look in my da's eyes. "What do you need university for?"

Miffed, I paused. I thought that he would have understood. "I can't get a job in a lab or anything without it. I don't want to work at the café forever."

My da grunted. "No daughter of mine needs to work in a shitty café."

He pulled out his wallet and threw down a bunch of bills. I spotted the thick wad of cash in his wallet. Where the hell did he get all that money? I didn't ask. I didn't even make out that I'd seen it.

He stood, scraping his chair. "Come on, girl. Let's go for a drive, yeah?"

We got into his car and he locked the doors, but he didn't start the engine.

A thread of unease weaved through me as he turned to face me, a serious look on his face. "I want to take you to see where I go during the day."

"Okay." I had always been curious about his job. I

knew it had something to do with farming, agriculture and distribution. I'd heard snippets of things said between him and the colleagues that showed up at the house occasionally.

"But I need to know I can trust you."

I blinked. "Of course you can, Da."

"I mean it, girl. No letting anything slip. Not to your ma, not to your friends, especially not to that JLO cunt."

I flinched at his derision for Diarmuid. An instinct to defend Diarmuid rose up in me and I almost said something. I quickly caught myself, snapping my mouth shut.

I mimed locking up my mouth and handing my da the key.

He grinned. "That's my baby girl."

I loved it when he called me his baby girl. It made me feel all warm inside.

My da drove us to a remote farm about twenty-five minutes southwest of Limerick. The first sign that something wasn't right were the two guards at the gate, long black guns strapped to their backs.

They spotted my da and waved him through. We drove through an overgrown field first, then the dirt road weaved through a stretch of forestland, the trees blocking out the sky completely and the air feeling colder, even though we were in a car.

Finally we drove out into another field. The road widened and rows of sheds lined it.

There were more guards with guns walking in pairs around the buildings, people darting in and out of sheds and trucks parked nearby. The side of the closest truck read "Jim's Butchers".

I frowned. It didn't look like livestock were being reared here. Why the sign, then?

My da slowed his car down as we passed a shed, the doors partly open. Inside were rows and rows of glass cases, some kind of plants growing underneath glowing lamps.

"What is this place?" I asked in a whisper.

"We grow pot here," my da said.

"Pot? Like, weed?"

"That's it, girl. You ever tried it?" He peered at me.

This felt like a strange thing to ever be admitting to my da. I nodded, but I didn't give away any specifics.

"We're one of Ireland's biggest growers," he said proudly.

"Isn't that...wrong?"

My da snorted. "Alcohol is legal. And it can fuck you up more than pot. Pot is natural. It's a plant. Used for medicine and shit. D'ya wanna know why alcohol is legal and pot isn't?"

I nodded my head, holding my breath.

"Taxes. Control. The greedy fucking government wants the taxes earned on alcohol, so they keep it legal. They can't regulate pot so they keep it illegal. Same thing with meth."

"Meth?"

My da nodded. "Here."

He pulled up to a final shed, smaller than the others. Through the open door I could see that the inside was bright and white, sterile looking. A laboratory.

"Pot is a steady earner," my da said. "But I want to expand. We're setting up a new operation. Most of the meth sold in the country right now is imported." He shook his head. "That shit is getting too dangerous to do. Ports are being overrun with cops. The waters around Ireland are being patrolled too much. I want to setup a local lab right here."

I was silent as the tension in the car grew.

Part of me wanted to run screaming. The other part wanted to be okay with this, because my da was okay with this. Surely if *he* thought this was okay, then it was. Right? I mean, that whole thing with the government and being greedy and stuff.

Another smaller part of me screamed that it would be dangerous to have my da think that I was against this. I knew too much. I'd seen too much now.

He'd never hurt me. He's my da.

"Cat's got your tongue, girl?"

"There's not any labs here already?" I blurted out, a safe neutral question.

"Smaller ones, yeah. Run by fucking amateurs out of their mother's basement." He sneered. "Idiots. They don't know what they're doing. And their product is substandard. I'm going to change all that. I'm going to give Ireland the best fucking meth they've ever seen."

His face and voice vibrated with excitement, with passion. He could have been talking about a new device that would cure cancer or a new seat belt that would save lives.

I remained silent, unsure of what to say, my stomach twisting with uncertainty. I knew my father had been jailed for drugs the last time. But after he was released I thought that he had changed his ways. I mean, why would he keep doing something that could get him thrown in jail again? He promised me he wouldn't leave me again. What if he got arrested for a second time?

"The setup is almost complete. My distribution lines organised." My da placed a hand on my shoulder, forcing me to look right at him. "I just need a head chemist. One that I can trust."

It took me a second to realise he was talking about... "*Me?*"

My da nodded. "You'd make more money in your first year than a decade in any other fucking lab."

Shit. What did I say to that?

"What if...what if we get caught?"

"We won't."

You can't promise that, a voice inside me said.

"I'll...I'll have to think about it."

"Baby girl, what's there to think about? I'll make you rich."

I shifted in my seat, staring into the bright white lab. That could be mine. My office. My lab. I wouldn't have to study for years, work as a shit-kicker intern and then a shit-kicker assistant for years. I could have my own lab right now.

Meth was just chemistry.

I loved chemistry. I was good at it.

"You could do anything. Whatever you wanted."

Cooking meth for my father was definitely not what Diarmuid had in mind when he spoke those words to me.

I imagined the horror on Diarmuid's face if he ever discovered I was cooking meth. I was struck with a deep sadness. He'd be disappointed. I don't know if I could stand to disappoint him.

"And...if I say no?" I asked.

For a moment, I might have sworn that I saw a flash of irritation across my da's face. But it was gone so quickly I couldn't be sure.

Fuck. I didn't want to disappoint my da, either.

He smiled. "If you don't want to work in the family business, then that's okay. If you'd rather struggle through university and get a shitty lab job somewhere else, that's fine."

He said it was fine. Somehow it didn't sound fine.

"How about this, baby girl?" he continued. "You work for me for one year, and I'll set you up with more money than you need to support yourself while you study."

"One year?"

He nodded. "Just one year. Although I suspect, once you see how much money is in it for ye, ye won't want to leave." He raised his hands in a surrender-style motion. "But if you do, no harm, no foul."

"You'll just let me go."

"I'll just let you go," he promised.

My mother's weathered face flashed in my mind, her eyes glassy from the white smoke that came from the crystals in her little glass pipe.

Somehow, I felt like this white crystal was the kind of thing that never let go.

51

Diarmuid

"Diarmuid," a familiar male voice called from behind me as I strode through the hallways of the station.

Niall fucking Lynch.

"The answer's no," I called back over my shoulder without even stopping to look at him.

"You don't even know what I'm about to say."

"It's still no."

"For fuck's sake, Diarmuid. Stop for a sec."

"Can't. Places to be." I pushed out the front door of the station, tumbling out into a rare fine, bright evening. I wasn't lying. I had a cold beer in the fridge and a hurling match on TV waiting for me.

Another evening alone.

Another evening trying to stop myself from thinking about a certain blonde-haired woman who I should not be thinking about.

Another evening tossing between remembering how her lips felt against mine and beating myself up for wanting more of her. So much more of her.

I heard the door catch behind me. Fucking Niall followed me. I sped up, aiming straight for my truck. Dammit, why did I have to park so friggin' far away today?

Niall caught up and jogged beside me. "When was the last time you met up with Saoirse?"

"I've dreamed about how your sweet pussy would taste. Wondered how hard your back would bow the first time I dipped inside you. What noises you'd make when I sucked that pretty little clit in between my lips."

I halted. And turned on him, bristling. "None of your business."

Niall narrowed his eyes. "It is actually my business. What do you guys talk about?"

"More," she whispered.

"Not yet. Even as wet as you are right now it'd still hurt when I pushed inside you. When I slowly stretched you around me. Add another finger."

I winced at the memory assaulting my mind. I forced these thoughts from my head, focusing on Niall's ugly face, feeling the stirrings of my erection relax.

"She's not involved with her father."

"You don't know—"

I grabbed his shirt collar and yanked him towards me.

"I do fucking know. I *know* her."

"Settle down, Brennan." Niall pushed at my hands.

I regretfully let him go. Technically I was assaulting another officer right outside the fucking Garda station. It was a stupid move to even put my hands on him. He could have my badge for this. But fuck, did he make me want to hurt him, bad.

Niall brushed down his shirt front. "Even if she's not involved in his operations, she knows something."

"Even if she did, which she doesn't, I am *not* making her turn against her father." I turned on my heel and kept walking.

Niall, of course, followed. "Do you know how long we've been trying to pin down Liam's full operations? We only managed to find one small field five years ago. Only one. The fucker didn't spill at all."

I let out a snort. "And you thought he would? Eejit. Even threatened with jail time, these guys don't rat out."

Niall's face reddened. "It was a good strategy."

"It was an impatient strategy. You got tired of having to wait him out. Nabbed him before he could lead you to the golden goose."

"See," said Niall, "that's why I need you on my team."

I rolled my eyes. "Never happening."

"I still don't understand why. Your career could go places if you just moved into the drug squad."

I wanted to work with my kids. I *needed* to. With them, I made a difference. Niall would never understand. That's why I'd stopped trying to explain it to him.

I unlocked my truck, swung the door open and slid into the driver's seat. I tried to slam my door shut, but Niall moved his body in the way.

"Move," I growled.

"I tried the carrot, but I think you'd respond much better with the stick." Suddenly the look on Niall's face made me uneasy, like he'd been holding his best hand until now.

"What the fuck are you talking about?"

"You know the captain and I are good mates. We play golf together every Sunday."

"Why do I give a shit about whose asshole you lick?"

Niall smiled and it reminded me of a snake. "I have you figured out, Brennan. I used to think that the promise of promotion would get you on board. But now I know you only give a shit about one thing…"

He slung his arm along the top of my truck door and leaned in, the gleam in his eye worrying me. "You get me something on Saoirse Quinn, something I can use against her father. Or I will get you kicked out of the JLO program."

My blood froze. My whole purpose for living disintegrating before my eyes.

"You wouldn't," I said.

Niall shrugged. "You're a difficult man to work with, everybody knows that. You never hand in your reports, never attend team meetings or work functions."

My hands turned to fists in my lap.

"Maybe if you'd played nice it'd be more difficult to convince the captain to get rid of you."

It took everything in my willpower not to crack my fist into his face. I had never hated a man as much as I hated Niall fucking Lynch right now.

I hated myself more because he was right.

I *was* a difficult person to work with. A difficult man. An asshole.

I knew that. But thus far, it'd done its job, keeping people away from me. It'd not harmed me too much.

Until now.

Niall buttoned up the breast of his suit jacket. "This is your last chance to prove that you're a team player. I don't give a shit about the girl. Get me something to pin down Liam or you're gone."

He shut my door for me, shot me a wink, then strolled back into the station as if he didn't just curse Saoirse and me both.

I sank back into my seat and rubbed my eyes, reeling from what had just happened.

This wasn't just a job to me, it was my life, my calling. What would I even do if I wasn't a JLO?

But could I betray Saoirse? Could I use her to keep my job? My stomach twisted at the thought, making me feel sick.

Whatever I did, I would lose.

Fuck. I was screwed.

52

Saoirse

It had been days since my da revealed to me the extent of his "work" and made me a job offer. Inside me, all the parts of me warred. Confusion pulled me this way and that. The only person I wanted to talk to was the *last* person I should be talking to about this.

Still, I messaged Diarmuid asking to meet. Perhaps I did it because I knew what he would tell me. I knew the faith he had in my future, and it had nothing to do with cooking drugs. I just needed a little bit of his belief that I was something more than a criminal's daughter. I needed him.

Diarmuid's message came back hours later. It was not what I wanted to hear.

Diarmuid: I'm not sure meeting is a good idea.

Strings of annoyance twanged in me again. I stabbed back a reply.

Me: I just want to talk, nothing else.

What does that say about me that the only one who truly understood me was a man over a decade older than me, who just thought of me as a girl. There was a long pause before his reply came back.

Diarmuid: I can't be trusted around you.

Me: What the hell?

Diarmuid: I think it's best if you ask to be reassigned.

Reassigned.

That was it. Diarmuid wanted me out of his life. Rejection flooded through my veins like boiling water over glass.

Not again. Dear God, not this again.

I shouldn't have touched myself in front of him. I shouldn't have been easy.

Did he think I was a slut? Like my mother? Is that why he was rejecting me now? I knew he wanted me. That much was clear when he pressed up against me. Did

I disgust him? Was that why he was telling me to leave him alone?

And by text message. He didn't even have the balls to say this my face. Anger made my fingers shake.

Me: You are a coward.

Diarmuid: I'm sorry. It's for the best.

Me: Fuck you.

I threw my phone across the room and flung myself on my pillow, my tears already soaking the cotton. That's where I lay for a long, long time.

I only dragged myself out of bed when I had to go to work the next morning. I stepped into the café and knew instantly something was wrong. Lisa and Claddagh, two other waitresses who were friendly enough, stopped talking and stared at me from behind the counter.

I frowned as I passed them, heading towards the staff room at the back.

"What's the craic?" I asked.

They exchanged a look, then Lisa came jogging over to me. "Saoirse, you never told us your da was Liam Byrne."

I hadn't lied to anyone here, I'd just been evasive when they asked about my family. Thank God that my ma and da never married and that I was given my ma's last name. I'd had enough of the bullying and teasing at school when people eventually found out I shared DNA with an infamous criminal.

"What does it matter who my father is?"

"Not to me, but—"

"Saoirse," my boss, Ed, called from the staff room entrance. "Come have a chat with me, will ye?"

Lisa gave me an apologetic look, patted my arm, and mouthed, *sorry.*

My stomach sank. I knew already what he was going to say.

Sure enough, Ed went on a rant about how I'd lied, how he couldn't be associated with a criminal family, how he spoke to a friend of his at the Garda and they'd told him that I'd already been arrested twice.

I burned at his judgement. Not just his but *everyone* who had come before him. Before I knew what I was doing I was shoving him back, raising my voice, cussing at him as I got in his face. I heard the footsteps of the other staff coming through the door to their boss's rescue. I felt their hands on me, pulling me off him, telling me to calm down. My anger sizzled like water on coals.

Ed straightened and pointed a shaky finger towards the exit, his face slightly pale. "Get out before I call the Gards. Don't ever come back."

I yanked my arms out of their grasp. I felt their accusing eyes on me, worry, fear, vindication. *See, she's just like her father.*

I wanted to scream at them all. *I'm not like him. I'm*

better than that.

What good would it have done? They already thought they knew me. They'd already laid down their judgement. And I'd already done the damage by attacking Ed.

So I said nothing. I ate up all my anger, turned and walked out of the café, tears blurring my sight and numbness swallowing me.

Because at the end of the day Ed was right—they were all right. I was a criminal's daughter. I had bad blood flowing through my veins. I guess I couldn't run from what I was.

They'd already made up their minds about me. Why bother fighting the box they'd put me in? Why not just embrace it?

I wiped my eyes and my vision cleared a little. Rebellious resolution turned my blood to granite.

I grabbed my phone out of my pocket and dialed Diarmuid's number. I just needed him to tell me that everything would be okay. I just needed to know that there was one person—*one person*—on this planet who thought more of me.

He didn't answer. I stabbed out a text.

Me: Please. I need to talk to you.

Please Diarmuid. Just one word from you and my faith would be restored.

I waited for a response.

And waited.

He never replied. The silence cut me like the sharpest

knife. The shackles of my parents' sins closed around me, making it hard to breathe. When nobody believes in you, why keep fighting against it? Why keep trying to prove them wrong?

I called the one person who I could truly count on, the only person I should have trusted from the beginning.

"Yeah?" he answered when he picked up the phone.

"You remember the job offer you made me?" I said in a low whisper.

"Yeah…?"

"I'm in."

I could almost hear the grin widening across my da's face. "That's my girl."

My da took me back to his farmhouse. This time we went inside the lab.

Its setup was surprisingly professional. Rows of stainless steel tables, cupboards of beakers and trays, all brand new. And shiny machines.

It was unlike the school lab where I'd spent so much time, cheap laminated tables with burn marks and graffiti on them, chipped or broken equipment, low inventory of chemicals and ingredients.

A small rush filled my insides, even as it was tainted with this feeling of…*wrongness*.

I was getting my very own lab.

My own lab.

"Well, baby girl, this is where you'll be working. You like it?"

I nodded. I did like it, the space at least.

Chemistry was like cooking. You just needed a recipe and to understand the process of change that the molecules went through when you combined them or treated them in a particular way in a particular order. It was precise. It was still science.

I could ignore *what* I was making. Right?

"I'll need some things," I said. "Ingredients…"

Acetone, anhydrous ammonia, ether, red phosphorus, lithium… There were thirty-two ingredients needed. I'd looked up the process earlier.

I glanced up to the ceiling. "And I'll need better ventilation installed. Industrial-sized exhaust fans. The fumes can be toxic."

My da grinned, pride glowing on his face and warming up my skin like the summer sun. "Whatever you need, baby girl."

53

Diarmuid

After I told Saoirse to get herself reassigned, I ignored her texts.

I hated myself for it.

But it was my only hope of getting out of this rock and a hard place with Niall. If she demanded to be reassigned, Niall had no leverage on me.

I waited every day for the announcement from my supervisor that Saoirse had been taken off my case.

That announcement never came.

Saoirse didn't show up to our usual Friday meeting. She didn't answer my text message asking if she was okay when I caved and messaged her.

I fucked up.

I know I had.

But what else could I do? I implore you, what else could I do?

The days dragged, each one feeling empty and brittle, each one without sunshine or magic. I went to work, I went to the gym, I went home. And I saw the ghost of Saoirse everywhere: in my truck, at O'Malley's, in my bed.

Another week came and went and another Friday approached. I only remembered that I was meant to go to Declan's fight that night when Marla had reminded me at the coffee shop that morning.

"Are you still taking me out tonight?" she'd asked with a flush to her cheeks. "I bought a new dress."

Right. The fight. The date I was supposed to be having with an adult woman.

I had asked Marla to come with me weeks ago and forgotten all about it.

The last thing I wanted to do was to sit through a date and pretend to be involved in the conversation. I was being more of a prick than usual lately, my temper short, my replies at work even blunter than normal. Marla didn't deserve to hang around my grumpy ass this evening.

But I couldn't back out now. Firstly, it wouldn't be fair to Marla. She'd bought a new dress, for fuck's sake. Secondly, I'd never hear the end of it from Declan.

I forced a smile. "Of course. Pick you up at seven thirty. Fight starts at eight."

Seven thirty came and I arrived at Marla's apartment to pick her up. She appeared at her door wearing a pastel green floral dress that fit her perfectly and fell to just above her knees. A grey jacket over the top of it, makeup on and her red hair piled up on top of her head.

She looked sweet, ladylike. Exactly the kind of grown woman I should be interested in.

Except, I frowned… This was not the kind of outfit a woman going to a watch a fight should be wearing. She looked like we were going to go out for tea.

I felt completely monstrous next to her in my distressed denim, boots and leather jacket. At least I'd run a comb through my hair and tied it back. And I'd trimmed my short beard yesterday.

"You look…nice," I said to her. Apparently, I'd left my thesaurus at home. I still managed to coax a blush out of her.

As I leaned in to kiss her cheek I caught the scent of her fruity perfume and I found myself wishing for the smell of roses and honey.

We drove to the theatre where the fight was being held, and I parked in the VIP parking lot, a smaller section next to the public one. I got out and faltered for a second before realising that Marla was waiting for me to open her door.

Jesus. I was such a dick. What was I thinking going out with *any* woman? I had to be reminded to even open doors for them.

Except Saoirse. You never forgot to open the door for her.

I shoved that thought away and ran over to help

413

Marla out of the truck.

A roar of a motorbike screeching to a halt in the public parking lot caught my attention. What held my focus was the flash of long blonde hair coming out of a helmet.

Jesus fucking Christ. That was Saoirse.

She was getting off the back of a motorbike, wearing distressed jeans and black combat boots teamed with a black leather jacket.

The guy who'd been riding in front of her took his helmet off. It was the same douchebag with a motorbike who dropped her off at the boxing gym: Malachi fucking Walsh.

At least this time he'd gotten her a helmet.

My blood boiled at the thought of Saoirse sitting on the back of his bike, her arms wrapped around his waist. Her place was beside me in my truck, not on the back of some asshole's bike.

I don't know how long I was staring, the noise of engines and slamming car doors fading into the background.

I swear she felt me watching her. Actually, I *know* she felt the tug, the same one I did whenever she was near. Because she turned right then and her eyes locked onto mine from across the parking lot.

Her eyes widened. Then her features hardened. She turned to her date, flicking her long blonde hair over her shoulder. She laughed and placed her hand on his chest.

It took every inch of willpower not to go over there, rip her arm off him and beat the living shit out of him.

"What's wrong?" Marla asked from my side, her hand slipping to my tense forearm.

I forced my eyes away from Saoirse, uncurling my fists from my side. I tried for a smile but was sure it came out like a grimace. "Nothing. Let's go find our seats."

I told myself not to look back at her as Marla and I entered the VIP door to the theatre.

But I failed.

Every time I looked at Saoirse, she was looking back at me.

54

Saoirse

I knew that Declan Gallagher was Diarmuid's close friend. I'd suspected that I might see Diarmuid here—not that it had anything to do with the fact that I wanted to come—but it was still a shock to see him *with* someone.

Damn him.

He had a date with him.

A fucking date.

A woman, full grown, with a sophisticated dress sense and a pretty ladylike smile.

Unlike me.

Suddenly I hated that Malachi had his arm round my shoulders, leading me into the theatre. He'd been pressuring me for weeks to go out with him. I'd said no because I thought that Diarmuid and I were going to become something. How stupid I had been.

I was coerced, partly by my own father, into coming with Malachi. I was originally supposed to go with my da to the fight; he'd told me about the tickets he'd bought days ago. But at the last minute, something had happened out at the farm, which meant my da had to go and sort it out. He sent Malachi in his place to pick me up.

I hadn't wanted to get on the back of the bike. Not until he produced a second helmet. Even then, I heard Diarmuid's warning in my head. I made Malachi drive like a grandma, pinching him on his side every time he went too fast or took a corner too hard.

The theatre was round, velvet red seating rising up from the fighting ring positioned in the centre, ornate boxes hanging around the walls. It was a strange juxtaposition between the elegant eighteenth-century theatre, more used for Shakespeare and opera, and the modern gladiator show that was on tonight.

Malachi and my seats were near the front, close enough to smell the sweat, to see the frown lines on the referee's face. My da must have paid a lot of money for these tickets.

I spotted Diarmuid and his date sitting in the section to my right just as the light dimmed. He was smiling at something she said, his attention on her.

Bitch.

I hated her already.

The announcer's voice came on introducing the two fighters that would start the match. Declan Gallagher and his opponent were the main match and would come out later. I barely heard the announcer calling the warmup fighters' names or when the first round bell clanged. All I could see was Diarmuid.

I swear his eyes were on me.

I couldn't tell you when it started.

Like most brawls, all it took was one flare, one strike of a match. Add that to testosterone-filled air soaked in tension and booze, and whoosh. It all went up at once.

A push became a punch and then all of a sudden the crowd around us had turned into savage beasts.

"Oh fuck," Malachi said, his hand gripping my arm.

"We have to get out of here," I said.

Someone slammed into me from the side and I fell into Malachi, letting out a scream. We tumbled, almost falling on the floor between the seats. Holy shit. Getting hit wasn't the only risk; getting trampled was a possible reality too.

I shoved at Malachi as we stayed crouched down low. "Go, keep moving, towards the exits."

He remained frozen at my side.

I almost rolled my eyes. Malachi talked tough, dressed like a tough guy. But it was all show.

A figure grabbed me, yanking me to my feet. There was a male, some rage-drunk spectator, his eyes wild, his arm raised back to hit.

I braced for the hit, throwing my arms up to shield my face.

It never came.

He was yanked back off me, causing me to wobble at his disappearance.

Diarmuid's face and wide shoulders took up my entire vision. "Are you okay?"

My breath whooshed out of me. Diarmuid was here. He'd saved me from being hurt.

Even as the sounds of violence, the screams and crack of breaking glass echoed around us, I was safe. Because he was here.

I nodded. "I'm fine."

Diarmuid pulled me against him, his arm wrapping around my shoulder. "Thank God."

His lips brushed my forehead, and I closed my eyes as I leaned into him, sucking in his scent of leather and his woodsy cologne.

"Hey," Malachi's voice pierced through my peace, "Get your hands off my... *You*."

I opened my eyes in time to watch Malachi's face drain white, having obviously recognised Diarmuid.

"Fuck off, kid," Diarmuid growled. "I'm taking her home."

Malachi didn't even protest. He just scrambled through the seats.

Diarmuid kept me close as we made our way out of the theatre, his strong arms shoving brawlers away from me so that they never got close. He was my walking bodyguard. My shield. My protector.

At the entrance, when we made it out into the night air, the chaos behind us, he let go of me, having no need to keep me close anymore.

My stomach dropped. Did he regret coming for me? Did he remember that he didn't want me around?

Then he grabbed my hand, our fingers lacing together, his eyes soft as he eyed me over as if to assure himself again that I was okay.

"Stay close," he said, and for once, it sounded like a request.

55

Diarmuid

When the brawl started I just reacted without thinking, leaping from my seat and running towards it.

Saoirse was stuck in that mob.

I wasn't leaving without her.

I used my weight and strength to push my way through the crowd, thankful that my height allowed me to spot the flashes of her blonde hair.

When I'd found her, her fucking asswipe date cowering behind her, I'd almost lost it. I could see the fear in her eyes. I hated that she had to feel such fear. If she had been hurt...?

I should have just decked that Malachi like I'd wanted to.

But Saoirse's safety came first. Getting her out of there was more important.

I led Saoirse through the parking lot towards my truck, tugging her behind me, her tiny hand in mine making my chest swell with purpose.

I was shaking from the adrenaline. High from the fight. From being near *her*.

I wanted to get her somewhere quiet so I could strip her of her clothes and check every single inch of her to make sure she wasn't hurt. Until I neared my truck.

There was Marla standing by my driver's door, her arms wrapped around her waist.

Oh fuck.

I'd forgotten about my date. The second the danger erupted around Saoirse I could think of no one and nothing else except for finding Saoirse and getting her to safety.

Now I was walking towards my date holding another woman's hand. I was an asshole, but this was even beyond me.

I let go of Saoirse's hand as if it were on fire.

Only realising afterwards what that might look like to Saoirse. I'd been holding her hand until we got in sight of another woman.

Double fuck.

I was fucking up left, right and centre tonight.

"I lost you in the crowd," Marla said as I approached.

"Shit. Yeah, sorry about that." Guilt weaved through me. I had lost Marla because I'd been too focused on finding Saoirse. "I'm glad you got out."

Marla shrugged. "I wasn't anywhere near the fight. But you looked like you ran straight into it."

Straight to the arms of another woman.

God, I was an asshole.

Marla's eyes went past my shoulder and widened. Shit. Here we go.

"Hi," Saoirse said from behind me, unease in her voice.

"Hi." Marla's voice sounded unsure, too. Marla's eyes went back to mine. "Who's this?"

"This Saoirse. She's…a friend. One of my kids."

I felt Saoirse stiffen beside me

"She's lost her ride home," I explained to Marla.

Saoirse snorted. "Diarmuid scared off my ride home."

I whirled around to her. "The only thing that dickwad wanted to ride was you."

Saoirse slammed her fists onto her hips and glared at me. "What's wrong with that, Diarmuid? I'm *single* and I'm *legal*."

"May I remind you that *your date* was using you as a shield before I arrived. He is not worthy of you."

"That's none of your concern."

I rolled my eyes, unlocking the truck with my keys. "Get in the truck."

"I'm not sure *your date* would appreciate you taking her and another woman home."

I could strangle her.

I stormed around to the passenger door and yanked it open, pointing into the empty seat. "Get. In. The. Truck."

Saoirse shot a look to Marla. "I'm sorry he's such an asshole. It's probably best you learn this upfront."

"Saoirse," I warned through gritted teeth.

She rolled her eyes and stomped her way over to me, sliding into the passenger seat with an ungrateful huff. I shut the door on her, then turned to my date, who was staring at me with wide eyes.

I forced a bashful smile. "Some night, huh?"

She didn't answer.

I helped Marla into the back seat of my truck before I got into the driver's seat.

It was more convenient to drop Saoirse off first, but... "I'll...er, drop you off first, Marla."

From the passenger seat, Saoirse shot me a look from the corner of her eye. She didn't say anything. Dropping Marla off first meant that Saoirse and I would be alone for part of the drive.

I'd be *alone* with her.

Something I'd been trying to avoid doing. And yet, like the masochist that I obviously was, I barrelled straight into trouble.

56

Saoirse

I was sitting in Diarmuid's truck with *his date.*

How the fuck did I get here?

I'd forgotten about his date the instant that Diarmuid had appeared before me, throwing that spectator aside like he had been a doll. I forgot all about her when he held me close, pushing our way to the exit. I'd forgotten everything except for him, especially when he laced his fingers into mine and tugged me across the parking lot to his truck as if I was *his.*

Then the bastard let go of my hand the moment her saw *her.* His *real* date.

Even now in the passenger seat of his truck, his date in the back, my stomach stung with jealousy.

It didn't matter that he had come for me when the fight had started. He had arrived at the fight with *her*.

She was a grown woman, closer to his age, someone that he *should* be with. And she seemed sweet, too. That's who Diarmuid needed. Someone sweet. Someone not like me.

We pulled up in front of what I assumed to be his date's house.

"Well," she said from the back seat, "it's been interesting. Nice to meet you, Saoirse."

"Oh, uh, you too."

I realised I didn't know her name.

She got out of the truck.

Diarmuid opened his door. "I'll be back in a sec."

I watched with a heavy heart as Diarmuid chased his date to the front steps of the porch. If he kissed her, I would throw up. When he leaned in I had to turn my head.

How could he do that with me watching? Did he want to torture me?

The driver's side door opened quicker than I expected, making me flinch.

"That was quick," I said sarcastically. "Didn't you wanna take her in for a quickie? I could have sat here for a few minutes."

"Don't be childish, selkie."

Childish? Fuck him.

I sank back in my seat, arms jammed across my chest, hating him with every second that went past, with every glare that he shot me.

He was angry at *me*? How dare *he* be angry at *me* after what he'd done.

Diarmuid pulled up onto the sidewalk of a deserted suburban street, his tires screeching, probably taking out part of that poor person's tiny lawn. He leapt out of the truck. I pushed the door open and jumped out too, meeting him halfway around the front bumper.

"What the hell were you thinking going to a fight with that douchebag?" Diarmuid yelled, his voice echoing into the night. The neighbours were probably already calling the cops on our fight, not that I cared right now.

"Me? What about *you* acting one way then dropping my hand like a hot potato as soon as we get near *your date.*"

His cheeks flushed and I knew I'd hit on a point.

"If I wasn't there to get you out of the brawl, who the fuck knows what could have happened? That kid is a fucking loser. You don't go out with him again."

"How dare you think you can tell me who to see. You don't want me, remember?" I choked on this bitter truth. "You have no fucking right."

"*Don't* want you?" He grabbed my upper arms. "Do you know what it does to me to think that he might be touching you? That he is allowed to touch you while I can't?"

He was so angry he was practically vibrating with it, shaking me in his hands.

"It kills me, selkie, it *fucking kills me.*"

I sucked in a breath. His eyes, dark and intense, had never been so damn beautiful.

"I want *you* so much I'm choking with it," he said. "I want to *be yours* so hard it hurts. I can't be yours. I *shouldn't* be yours. But I'm too fucking selfish. I need you—only you. The rest of the world can go to hell."

I don't know who moved first. It didn't matter. Because we both lunged for each other, his hands yanking me to him.

Our lips collided. They parted, our tongues warring as we had been warring, fierce and passionate, with love and tenderness underneath it.

We were kissing like the world was ending right here in the middle of a public street, and I didn't care.

I just wanted him. The rest of the world could go to hell.

If only the lawmakers could *feel* what we were feeling right now. Then they'd turn a blind eye to my age and his.

His hands grabbed my ass and pulled me up against his hardness. We groaned into each other's mouths at the illicit contact as he settled me on the bonnet of his truck. I wrapped my legs around him, pressing my hips against the very thing I ached for.

Our kiss went from flame to raging wildfire in a second. I twisted my fingers in his hair, tilting my head so I could get closer. God, I couldn't get close enough.

His hand ran up my side and cupped my left breast. I moaned at the forbidden touch, a touch I'd been dreaming about for years.

When he pinched my nipple through my clothing with his thumb and forefinger, I almost died.

I would let him have me right here in the street if he

wanted it.

Dear God, did I want it.

He pulled back, snatching his hand off my breast. "Wait…" he breathed.

I moaned at the loss of him. He rubbed his nose against mine in placation, then leaned his forehead against mine, his breath coming out in hard pants.

I saw the second reality hit him. He winced.

"Fuck," he hissed. "That wasn't meant—"

I shoved him back off me. I wasn't that strong compared to him, but he stumbled back, probably out of surprise rather than my brute strength.

I pointed a stern finger at him. "Don't you dare say that wasn't meant to happen."

Before he could say anything, I jumped off the bonnet and stormed into the passenger side, slamming the door shut behind me. I sat in the seat, glaring out the front window, arms crossed.

Diarmuid remained standing where he was for what felt like hours. Then he walked slowly to his side and got in.

It was deathly silent as he drove the final way to my house.

Even as my nerves kept jumping around all over the place. My lips still raw from his kiss, my core throbbing in time with my anger.

Fuck him. Seriously. Fuck him.

I was sick to death of this *want you, shouldn't have you,* push-pull bullshit.

Diarmuid pulled up in front of my house, turning the

engine off rather than letting it idle.

He twisted his torso towards me and opened his mouth to speak.

"Don't," I said, cutting him off.

I didn't want to hear it. I gave him a cold glare.

"This…" I pointed between us, "you and me…*we* are already a thing, no matter how much you deny it. I'm under your skin. I'm weaved into your soul. And you are part of me."

Diarmuid sank back into his seat. For the first time since I'd met him, he seemed like such a boy.

I did not want a boy. I needed a man.

I lifted my chin. "Call me when you get over yourself."

I pushed open the truck door and slammed it shut behind me. Then I walked, head held high, all the way up my path, his eyes burning into my back.

I did not look back. Not once.

If he wanted me, he'd have to grow up and come chase me.

57

Saoirse

The week went by and I didn't hear from Diarmuid.

I distracted myself by focusing on the new installations and preparations at my father's lab. The voice inside me that sounded like Diarmuid's and told me *don't do this* grew quieter and quieter.

Until Friday morning.

Diarmuid: Are you coming to the gym today?

My guts twisted as a jumble of emotions tangled around inside me.

Me: Are we still pretending that we don't want

each other?

Diarmuid: Saoirse...

Me: Diarmuid...

Diarmuid: You know how I feel.

Saoirse: And you know how I feel. Yet again we are at an impasse.

Diarmuid: I hate this.

My heart squeezed. I hated it too. But I was not backing down. I would not let him do this push-pull with me anymore. It hurt too much.

Me: I don't want to talk about this anymore.

Diarmuid: Then tell me something.

Me: Like what?

Diarmuid: Anything. How's work at the café going?

Guilt stabbed at my gut.

Me: Fine. Boring.

I hated lying to him. But telling him that I'd been fired from the café would just lead to too many questions.

Diarmuid: Wow. What a detailed answer.

Me: Don't be sarcastic. You don't wear it well.

Diarmuid: Well then tell me something else.

Me: It's my 18th birthday in a few months.

Diarmuid: Don't get arrested before then. You'll spoil my reoffender record.

Me: Diarmuid!

Diarmuid: Joking ;)

Me: I'll be 18…

Diarmuid: I'll make sure to wish you happy birthday.

Me: …

Diarmuid: Maybe your bracelet will get another charm.

Me: Better but not quite what I was thinking…

There was a long pause before his reply came back in.

Diarmuid: We should not be talking about this.

I rolled my eyes at my screen.

Me: Fine. We can wait until I turn eighteen to "talk" about it.

Diarmuid: Saoirse...

"Saoirse." My name barked out snapped my attention away from my phone.

I flinched, almost dropping my phone. I hurried to turn the screen off so Diarmuid's last message wouldn't give me away.

I was sitting in the corner of the lab, waiting on my da to finish up for the day. I'd come here with him to oversee the installation of the exhausts. So far so good. My da had spared no expense.

My father stormed towards me, murder in his eyes.

Guilt and panic flooded my body. Did he *know* who I was texting? I slid my phone down into the bottom of my bag.

"Da, what's wrong?"

He stopped before me. "I just spoke to Malachi. What the fock happened on fight night?"

I cursed internally. Malachi had finally told on me. Or perhaps my da had weaseled the truth out of him.

"What do you mean?" I asked, trying to play

innocent.

"Malachi said you left with your JLO instead of him."

I shrugged, trying to play it cool. "Diarmuid saw me there. After a brawl broke out, he came and pulled me out of the crowd because Malachi was too chicken-shit to do anything."

The frown on my da's face deepened.

I continued, feeling like I was rambling. "He just took me home because he doesn't trust motorcycles. He was there with another woman, Da. A date. It's not like we were alone or anything." *Liar.*

My da's eyes narrowed at me. "You and this Garda seem friendly."

I swallowed down a knot in my throat. "That's ridiculous. I just tolerate him when I have to see him. I don't tell him anything, Da, you taught me better than that."

Guilt threaded through me.

I was lying to my father. My own flesh and blood. The man who was taking care of me.

If he knew I was disrespecting him by falling for an officer, his heart would break.

"He seems interested in you. A little too interested." My da's jaw tightened. "I might have to pay him a little visit. Have a little talk with him…"

The violence in his tone was clear.

"No!" I cried just a little too quickly, then forced myself to stay casual. "It's honestly nothing, Da. He's just overeager, overprotective of all his assignments. If you threaten him, you'll make it worse."

My da studied me, mistrust seeping into the creases around his eyes. "I don't like you spending time with him."

I swallowed. "I don't spend time with him. It's just the bare minimum JLO stuff."

Liar. Liar. Liar.

"Yeah, well, you tell me when you have to go see the prick. I'll send someone with you."

My guts swilled as if poison had been injected into them. The attraction between Diarmuid and me was too potent, too fiery, too obvious. I couldn't let anyone see us together.

If my da ever found out about Diarmuid and me, he'd kill him.

58

Diarmuid

A knock sounded on my door as I was getting ready to head to work.

I threw on a shirt and strode to the door, my nerves jangling because I thought—hoped—it might be Saoirse. She was the only one who knocked on my door these days.

It was not Saoirse.

Liam Byrne stood on my porch.

I tensed, immediately glancing around him for signs of more of his men. A black sedan with dark windows sat on the street. I couldn't see who else was in the car.

"Mr Brennan," Liam said, his voice every bit as slimy

as his gelled-back hair.

I placed my forearm against the doorframe, blocking the entrance, making it clear that he was not welcome inside.

"Mr Byrne," I mimicked his pretense of politeness. "How can I help you?"

His eyes slid up and down over me, studying me, probably assessing me for any weaknesses.

"I heard that you...took my daughter home after last Friday's fight night."

My blood turned cold.

Of all the reasons to stay away from Saoirse, Liam Byrne had been the last thing on my mind.

If Liam thought even for a second that there was anything going on between Saoirse and me...

He'd kill her.

I shrugged, trying to play it cool. "She needed a ride. I was there on a date. She and I took Saoirse home."

"Next time, you leave her to me."

I bristled. "If I see Saoirse in trouble, I'm going to help."

"And what? You want to gain her trust? Turn her against her old man? It won't happen."

"Mr Byrne—"

"I won't tell you twice, Brennan." He leaned right in, his sour breath making the bile rise up in the back of my throat. "Stay away from her or else."

"Are you threatening an officer of the law, Mr Byrne?"

He smiled. "Of course not. I'm just a concerned

440

father trying to protect his only daughter."

He held my gaze for another tense moment, then strode towards his sedan and got into the back seat. I tensed, waiting for the windows to roll down and guns to appear. But they didn't. The car drove off. I could feel eyes watching me.

Saoirse didn't show up to our Friday evening appointment. Not that day, nor the following Friday. Or the one after that. Although I always made sure I was there at the gym, just in case. I found myself watching the door regardless of what I was doing, hoping to see her walk through it.

I wanted to call her. To go to her house. But I feared her father might be monitoring her movements.

Besides, there was too much between us.

Her age.

My job.

The kisses that burned through me like a fever at night as I twisted in my sheets.

Better to let things lie.

Months went by.

Her eighteenth birthday grew nearer.

Nearer.

Nearer.

Until it was only days away.

I couldn't fucking take it anymore.

Despite everything telling me not to, I texted Saoirse as I sat in my truck outside the gym after another missed session.

Me: Hey stranger.

My phone pinged with a message almost straight away.

Saoirse: Hey…

Me: How are you? You alright?

Saoirse: Good. You?

I'm shit because you aren't around to make me smile. I fucking miss you.

Me: Good, yeah.

Saoirse: What do you want?

She was pissed at me. Probably because it'd taken me months to contact her since we last kissed. She didn't know I'd been staying away from her *for* her.

Me: Just wanted to check in on you. It's been a while since I saw you.

Saoirse: Taken you long enough to notice I wasn't coming to our JLO sessions.

Me: I noticed.

I'd *felt* every day without her around like it was scraping pieces out of my chest.

Saoirse: What are you telling your boss?

Me: About what?

Saoirse: About why we haven't been meeting up every week as per the program?

Me: Oh.

Saoirse: Oh, what?

Me: ... There's something I have to confess.

Saoirse: ...

Me: The program doesn't require us to meet once a week.

There was a long pause before her next message came through.

Saoirse: You made that up?

Me: I exaggerated a little.

Saoirse: You made it up!

Me: Embellished.

Saoirse: I'm never trusting you again.

Me: *sad face*

Saoirse: Serves you right.

Me: Would it help if I said I only lied because I wanted to spend more time with you?

Saoirse: Diarmuid…

Me: You forgive me? :)

Saoirse: You can't say things like that to me.

Me: Things like what?

Saoirse: You can't say sweet things like that and kiss me the way you do then tell me we're not meant to be together.

Me: I'm sorry. I don't mean to hurt you.

Saoirse: I know you don't. But it doesn't stop it from hurting.

Me: I wish I could kiss away all your tears.

Saoirse: *cries* There you go again!

Me: *sighs* I'm sorry.

It seemed all that I did was hurt her.

Saoirse: I know. I wish things were different.

I sat in my truck outside the gym, gripping my phone, wanting her so badly it felt like a vice around my chest. I wasn't a religious man but I prayed to God, begged him, to help me do the right thing and to walk away from her.

Despite my prayers, my fingers flew across the keys, the truth of my heart pouring out.

I miss you, selkie. I miss talking to you. I miss having you next to me in my truck. I miss you even though I shouldn't miss you. I need to see you.

I flung my phone aside, disgusted at myself, the last message unsent.

I slammed my truck into gear and just drove. Selfish man. Why would you want to see her if it would only lead to destruction? Why do you still want her if it would only lead to her ruin?

When I got home later that evening, I got out of my truck, mind numb, mentally exhausted from running around and around in circles in my head.

I thought I saw movement through the frosted glass of my door. I frowned.

There it was again. My senses flicked back to life.

There was someone in my house.

Liam Byrne had seen my messages to Saoirse.

He'd come back to finish the job.

I grabbed a golf club out of the back of my car before approaching the front door, club raised behind me.

I neared the door and heard the sound of someone's voice inside. A man's voice. But it was too muffled to distinguish what he was saying. I heard another voice, also male.

There must be two of them.

Two of them I could take on.

I reached my front step. The door swung open and I prepared to swing.

There stood Danny and Declan.

"Jesus fucking Christ," I yelled, dropping the club by my side, "you two scared the shite out of me."

"What's the criac?" Danny asked. His six-foot-two frame was covered in his usual ripped black denim, dark hair wild like it'd been windswept, leather cuff around his wrist, grey shirt sticking out of the bottom of his black sweater giving his rock look a polished edge.

"Welcome home, asshole." Declan grinned from behind Danny's shoulder. He was the shortest of us at six foot but by far the stockiest, his muscles bulging out from his long-sleeved grey Everlast hoodie, designer sneakers on his feet that probably cost more than my weekly salary.

"How long were you two dicks sitting in the dark like

creepers waiting for me?" I asked.

"Too long," Danny said. "Get inside, you're letting the cold in."

They moved aside so I could get inside, flicking the lights on and leaning the golf club in the coat stand.

I shrugged my coat off and dropped my keys into the bowl near the door. "How the fuck did you two get in here?"

Declan pointed at Danny as he strode through my living room and disappeared into my kitchen. Danny tried for an innocent grin.

I shook my head. "You breaking and entering into places again?"

"No, officer." Danny raised his hands up in the air, then smirked. "Only in case of emergencies."

"Oh yeah? What's the fucking emergency that you had to break into my house?"

Danny raised an eyebrow. "Are you serious, bro?"

"He's only got piss-weak pale ale here, that's the fuckin' emergency," Declan called from my kitchen, undoubtedly from my fridge.

I threw my hands up. "If I'd have known you two freaks were coming I'd have bought something stronger. Or installed an alarm system."

I glared at Danny then Declan, now strolling out of my kitchen with three bottles of a local IPA and a bottle opener in his other hand. "You still haven't told me why you're here?"

Declan snorted as he handed me an open beer. "Nice to see you too, asshole. Thanks for rearranging your fight tour so you could come see me, buttwipe."

I was being such a shit. My shoulders sagged. "Sorry. I am being a grumpy fuck."

"Even more of a grumpy fuck than I am," Danny said, clinking his beer against mine. "And that's saying something."

"But we still love ya, Diar," Dex said.

"Otherwise we wouldn't be here," Danny said.

"It's a nice surprise," I muttered, uneasy with sentimentality. "Thanks for coming. Although some notice would have been nice."

Dex snorted. "You would have found some excuse not to have us here if we gave you any notice."

Dex took the armchair in my living room, his huge frame taking up the whole seat, leaving Danny and me to flop down onto the two ends of the couch.

I fought the uneasy feeling. I downed half my beer bottle and smacked my lips. "Why are you here again?"

"We're concerned about you," Danny said.

"Yeah, concerned," Dex echoed.

"This is an intervention of sorts."

"We thought you needed a boy's night to sort ye shit out." Declan finished his beer and made a face. "We definitely need something stronger than that piss if we're going to go all night." He grinned, pulling out a bottle of aged whiskey from his side. "Good thing I brought this along with me."

I rolled my eyes. "There's nothing to be concerned about."

Danny snorted. "Please, out of the three of us, I'm

448

supposed to be the morose one. And lately you've out-morosed me."

"Who's broken your heart?" Dex asked, leaning forward with his hands on his knees. "Is it that Ava again? God," he smacked his fist into his palm, "if she was a dude I'd go down there and break her balls."

"It's *not* Ava," I said.

"Then who is it? What's the problem, dude?" Dex said.

Danny caught my eye. He tilted his head towards Declan as if to say, *go on. Tell him.*

Declan noticed the look we exchanged. He pointed at Danny. "You fucking know." Declan turned to me. "He fucking knows, doesn't he? Motherfucker why am I the last to know about shit? Tell me. Right fucking now."

I let out a groan and rubbed my face. "It's nothing."

"Fuck off, it's nothing."

"Go on, Diarmuid," Danny said, "out of the three of us, he's the person least to judge."

"Yeah," Declan said, nodding, "no Judge-y Mcjudge here."

Danny let out a snort. "Because you've probably *done* worse."

"Hey, I haven't—" Declan grinned. "Yeah, you're probably right."

Danny rolled his eyes. Then threw a bottle cap at me. "Tell him, ye pussy."

Alright, dammit. I could have gone without saying it out loud.

Just say it. Like a Band-Aid.

449

"There's a…" *girl,* "woman…she just gets me. She sees me. And…she's smart as hell, funny, sexy as sin…" I let out a groan as images of Saoirse slammed through my body.

"Damn," Dex said, "give *me* her number."

I growled, my hands flexing into fists.

Danny whacked me on my shoulder. "He's joking, fool."

I forced myself to relax, but the urge to smack one of my best friends in the face for even suggesting he'd hit on Saoirse still clung to me.

"Oh shit," Dex said, his eyes widening at me. "You're in love with her."

Love.

God, I wasn't ready for that word yet.

"I like her. A lot. Okay, it's more than like," I admitted.

"And…?" Declan asked. "She doesn't like you?"

"No. She does." *Fuck me, she does.* "That's the problem."

Declan blinked at me. "I don't get it. You like her. She likes you. Wham, bam, babies."

"She's seventeen," I blurted out.

Declan frowned. Then he raised an eyebrow. "You've got your knickers in a twist about *that?* Seventeen's legal here, you dope."

"She's one of my JLO kids."

Declan's eyes popped open. "Oh."

"Yeah. Oh."

"Damn." Declan shook his head. "You're even more

depraved than I am. I need to step up my game."

Danny let out a laugh.

I let out a groan. "This isn't funny."

"It's pretty funny. How the mighty moral Diarmuid has fallen. Taken down by a pretty little jailbait."

"Come here and say that again, Mr World Title," I growled. "I might not be able to win against you but I'd fucking make it hurt like hell on the way down."

"Diar," Danny said, looking like he was getting ready to jump in between the two of us, "Dex is only joking around. You know it's the only way this unsophisticated fool can communicate." He shot Declan a dirty look as if to say *quit it, idiot.*

"Honestly, Diarmuid," Declan said, his palms raised in surrender, "you're making a bigger deal out of this than it is."

"I could lose my job."

Declan tilted his head. "True. But would that really be the end of the world? I mean, you hate the bureaucracy of the place. And you've been saying for years you've been wanting to start your own gym. Maybe this is your chance?"

I rolled my eyes. "I could go to jail, fool."

"Only if you get caught," Declan pointed a finger at me and winked.

I groaned. "It's not just about me. God, imagine what everyone would say about *her.* You know how conservative it is here. She's already fighting enough prejudice without my ancient ass adding another one."

"Fuck everyone," Dex said. "People are fucking

sheep. If she makes you happy, then fucking go for it."

I glanced at Danny, wondering if this advice was soaking into him, too.

"Don't," Dex pointed a finger at me, "end your life with more regrets than chances taken."

Danny raised his bottle. "Life advice from the Philosophy of Dex."

Declan winked at Danny and he raised his own bottle.

"I don't know…" I said.

"I do," Declan said, turning to me. "I haven't seen you talk about anyone like this before. Not even when you met Ava." He leaned forward. "She could be The One, couldn't she?"

I sank my face into my hands because I couldn't stand to look at either of them. Then I nodded.

"Then fucking go for it."

I rubbed my face, then sagged back into the couch.

Danny let out a whistle. "Who knew?"

"Who knew what?" I asked.

"That Dex-y was such a bleeding-heart romantic."

"Fuck off," Dex said, chucking a pillow at Danny and missing. "You are the fucking hopeless romantic, Mr Writer of Sad Love Songs."

Danny snorted.

"Hey. Hey," Dex said, bouncing in his chair. "What's better than banging a seventeen year old?" He looked expectantly between Danny and me.

I let out a groan. "Please, don't."

"Give up?"

"I will give up on life if you finish that joke."

"Party pooper." Dex threw a pillow at me. "Danny?"

Danny scratched his chin. "Go on, then. What's better than banging a seventeen year old?"

I smothered my own face with the pillow but it wasn't enough to filter out Declan's answer.

"Banging seven ten year olds!"

Danny made a face.

I shook my head at Dex. "You are truly disgusting."

He grinned. "Why, thank you."

Later that night, after I sent a roaring drunk Declan back to his hotel via cab, I set Danny up with blankets and pillows for a night on the couch. Danny settled onto the couch, the ends of his legs hanging off the end.

"Thanks for coming, Danny."

"No bother. You'd do the same for me."

"How is your thing going?" I asked. "With that girl?"

He just shook his head. *I don't want to talk about it*, written all over his face.

I understood. Danny would talk about it when he was ready.

I lay in my bed, my head spinning from too many beers and later, shots of whiskey. I was still churning over Declan and Danny's advice to get over myself and give it a go with Saoirse.

In a few days she would no longer underage.

But I was still married. She was still a decade younger than me. And it was forbidden for me to get involved with anyone from the JLO program.

My wants twisted with my morals, like Daniel

fighting with the devil, long into my dreams.

59

Saoirse

"You didn't have to do this, Da," I said, smoothing down my skirt as my da drove his car through the bumpy dirt road that led to the farmhouse on the back of his property.

"Why wouldn't I want to throw my little girl a birthday party? It's not every day she turns eighteen." He patted my knee and shot me a grin.

I forced a smile back. Actually, I didn't turn eighteen until tomorrow, which was a few hours away still.

Truthfully, I wasn't even sure I wanted to come. But I couldn't miss my own party. I wouldn't know anyone at this party. Sure, a few of them I knew from working at the lab. But they were all my da's friends. I knew Malachi.

But he'd stayed clear of me since Diarmuid scared him off at the fight night.

I couldn't invite any of the friends I'd made at the café I'd been fired from, not that I wanted to anyway, they proved themselves to be fair-weather friends.

Moina couldn't come from Dublin because she had to work.

And the only other person I cared about, I hadn't heard from in months except for one brief texting session that he ended abruptly.

My da pulled up in front of a grey stone, two-level building, the surrounding field grown wild with grass and weeds. There were already dozens of cars and bikes parked haphazardly across the front lawn, now brown and dry.

I slid out of the car, fussing with my black strapless dress. I'd bought it with the money my da had given me this morning as a birthday present, a huge stack of fifty-euro bills counting up to a thousand euro. I knew better than to leave that much money lying around so I cashed it as soon as I could into my bank account—the one I'd gotten as soon as I turned sixteen.

The living room was spilling out with bodies. The air was thick with the smell of pot and I wrinkled my nose at it. On the glass table was a bowl full of blue pills, several bongs and a pile of white powder. Empty beer bottles and shot glasses littered the carpet around the table.

"Look alive, you fuckers," my da said, stepping into the room with his arms out wide, "the boss is back."

A cheer went up throughout the room. My da walked

through the living room, getting back slaps and cheek kisses from the girls, leaving me standing at the edge.

"That's my baby girl, Saoirse," he yelled, pointing at me, "make her feel welcome."

Everyone yelled out hello, one of the girls sending me a wave, a few of the men giving me appreciative looks. Suddenly my dress felt too clingy, like every curve of mine was being shown off and I wasn't sure I liked who was looking at it.

"Let's get you a drink, honey," one of them said, wrapping an arm around my shoulders. "Or would you rather something...stronger?"

He was at least my da's age, his eyes glazed, his pupils dilated. Kinda cute I guess, if you ignored his crooked teeth.

I looked around for my da. But I couldn't see him. He must have gone out the back garden where I could see through the open back door that more people stood around a bonfire.

I was feeling less and less like this was a birthday party he'd organised just for me.

"What'll it be?" Crooked Teeth asked. "Coke? Meth? H?"

"Um, just a drink, please."

He dragged me into the tiny kitchen, overloaded with more bottles than a liquor store.

"You're a very pretty lady," he said, his eyes on my cleavage so that he managed to spill half of the rum and Coke he was pouring for me.

"I'm seventeen," I snapped. At least until midnight,

which was only a few hours away.

His grin widened as he handed me my drink. "Oh, you are fresh, aren't you?"

I snatched my drink away from his hand, my palm sticky from where the drink had spilled down the sides. "I need to find my da."

He grabbed my arm. "I can be your daddy, girl."

Ew, gross. I wanted to barf. "Let go of me."

I shoved him back and he let go of me, laughing. "I was only joking. Come back."

I turned and ran through the living room, looking for a friendly face. A loud sniff went through the air as one of the girls sitting around the living room table snorted a huge line of white powder.

She held her nose pinched with one hand and waved at me with the other. Her voice came out nasally. "Liam's girl. Come here and have some."

"Er, maybe later."

I spotted a couple in the far armchair I hadn't noticed before, her top around her waist and his mouth around her tit, her grinding on his lap. His eyes opened and locked onto mine. Holy shit. I ducked out of the living room before he could ask me to "come here and have some" too.

I stumbled out into the back garden, the heat from the bonfire blasting against my cheeks. Where the hell was my da?

I spotted him standing with a few other men, Jase and Malachi included, all of them sharing a glass pipe, taking turns burning down the crystal in the bulb and blowing out the thick white sour-smelling smoke.

My stomach churned.

This was what I was contributing to with my work in his lab. This debauchery and waste of lives.

My da spotted me and waved for me to come over. He should have been furious that all these people were doing all these horrible illegal things in front of his seventeen-year-old daughter. But he wasn't. "Saoirse. Come here, baby girl."

My eyes watered. I could have lied and said that it was from the bonfire smoke. But then again, who would I be lying to?

I dropped the sticky plastic cup of bubbly amber liquid, turned and ran, ignoring the calls behind me. I ran through the house, out the front and down the road, my bag slapping against my thighs. I ran even though I was wearing high-heel shoes and could trip at any minute, twisting my ankle or breaking my neck.

I ran until I was on the road. Until I realised I had no place to run to.

"Whatever happens between us, I want you to know you can always call me if you get stuck without a ride. No matter what time. Even if I'm not your JLO anymore."

Nowhere except...one.

Twenty minutes later Diarmuid pulled up beside me on this dirt road. I almost cried with relief when I saw the familiar truck.

I slid in, sucking in a breath to see him again. He was

wearing sweatpants, his t-shirt on inside out, his shoulder-length hair tucked under a cap. He must have raced out as he was when I called him.

His eyes raced over me. "Are you okay?"

"Yeah." I was now.

He didn't tear his eyes away, his eyebrows dipping over his eyes as if he wasn't convinced. "When you called you sounded upset."

"I'm fine now."

His lip lifted in a snarl. "Saoirse, what happened."

I shook my head. "Nothing, I swear. I was just upset because I thought it was a party for me, but it wasn't. There were people there I didn't know and they were doing...doing—"

Diarmuid shook his head, raising his hand to stop me. "I don't need you to explain the details, selkie. I'm just glad that you're okay. And that you called me."

I sank back in my seat and tried my best to hide the tears forming in my eyes.

"Thank you for picking me up."

He glanced over and shot me a smile. "Anything for you."

He drove us to his house instead of mine. I sat up in my seat when I realised where he was taking me.

"I, er..." he cleared his throat, "don't feel comfortable with you in that house of yours alone."

I didn't have the heart to explain that I was mostly alone anyway.

My heart began to pound in my chest as he pulled up in his driveway. When he turned off his engine, I swear it was so loud he could hear it.

Diarmuid and I would be in his house when I turned eighteen.

Alone.

"Stay there," he said, getting out of his truck.

Diarmuid came around to my side, opened the door for me and held out a hand. I was about to chastise him—I wasn't thirteen anymore and could get out my-damn-self, when he spoke, sounding bashful.

"Saw you were wearing heels. Didn't want you to trip getting out."

God, why did he have to be so fucking perfect?

I slid my hand into his, electricity crackling up my arm and down my body, as he helped me down.

For a brief second, we just stood there, holding hands. Facing each other. Studying each other in the glow of his porch light, trying to see if the months apart had changed each other.

His eyes traced the lines of my body, heat flaring in them. With that one look, he stripped me.

Diarmuid pulled his hand from mine and locked up the truck. I followed him, my legs shaking up the short path to his door.

"You...okay?" he called back to me. It was like he could sense I was near to passing out.

"Fine," I lied.

We entered his house and I wiped my sweaty palms on my dress. I jolted when he locked the door behind me. Oh God. Was this really happening? Was I really here?

I turned to face him. His eyes locked onto mine and

he chewed on his bottom lip.

Alone.

We were alone.

"What were you doing when I called?" I blurted out. "You weren't sleeping, were you?"

"Just watching TV. About to have a shower."

I nodded. "You do stink."

"Hey," Diarmuid cried out, then took a sniff of his armpit. "I don't smell that bad."

I let out a small smile. "No, not that bad."

He could never smell bad. Even sweaty and dirty he still smelled amazing to me.

"You want a shower first?" he asked.

I nodded. I wanted to get out of this dress and to wash off the splashes of rum now sticky on my legs.

"Let's get you set up."

I followed him through his house to his bathroom; he left and came back with a towel, a set of sweatpants and a shirt.

"These are the smallest things I own. They're not going to fit you at all," he said apologetically.

"That's okay. Anything is better than sleeping in this dress," I said, waving down at myself.

I looked up in time to catch his eyes roaming over me again. He quickly looked away when he found I'd caught him.

"I'll leave you to it."

He brushed past me in the tiny bathroom. The touch of his warm skin made my head spin. I squeezed my eyes shut to stop myself from passing out.

"Hey, so," he tapped on the door frame, making me turn to face him. "You look," he swallowed hard, "incredible, by the way." He looked almost bashful as he spoke. "Just thought you should know that."

"Like a woman?" I asked, my voice a near whisper.

He sucked in a breath. Nodded. "The most beautiful woman I've ever seen."

I could have died happy right there.

The smile that broke out on my face hurt my cheeks.

A woman.

Finally.

Diarmuid Brennan saw me as a woman.

60

Diarmuid

What the hell was I doing?

I should have just dropped her off at home.

I shouldn't have made that dumb excuse about her not being home alone.

I just wanted her in my bed again. Was that so bad? I'd missed her so much these last few months, I just wanted her near me.

I didn't even have to touch her. I just wanted to feel her warmth beside me. To know that she was safe, right next to me. That the world could no longer hurt her as it wished, it would have to go through me first.

I swear. I wanted nothing else. Just to *be* near her.

I glanced at the clock. Just past ten p.m. In less than

two hours, my little selkie would be eighteen.

She would be eighteen and...

Even if I *did* touch her as she lay in my bed, it would be okay.

Right?

If she leaned into my touch, if she spread her legs and opened her mouth for me, that would be okay.

Right?

And if I gave her body every single pleasure it deserved, that would be okay.

Right?

I rubbed my face. No. No no no. Can't think like that. No.

She was still ten years younger than me. She was still one of my kids.

How could I return to work and look at my supervisor if I touched her? If I...?

"I'm finished." Saoirse's soft voice floated to me from the corridor that led into the living room.

I turned my head, ready to tease her. "Leave any hot water for—"

My mind blanked.

She was wearing my Nirvana shirt. It was huge on her, falling to the top of her thighs. But it was *all* she was wearing.

"W-what are you wearing?" I stuttered.

She looked confused, then looked down at herself.

"It looks like your old Nirvana t-shirt." She stretched the hem of the shirt, making the material tighten across her breasts.

Holy shit. She had no bra on under that shirt.

She looked up and caught me ogling her. My cheeks burned. But I couldn't tear my eyes away.

I was going to hell for this.

"B-but…p-pants…" I muttered.

"Oh. I'm not wearing your sweatpants. They were wayyy too big for me. Even with the drawstring at its tightest they just fell right off me." She made a motion with her hands indicating pants falling off her. The movement caught my eye, drawing them to her creamy trim legs.

Legs that only a few weeks ago were wrapped around my waist as I kissed her on the bonnet of my car.

Legs that I'd love to wrap around my neck as I kissed her sweet little—

Holy shit.

Shower.

A cold shower.

A motherfucking cold shower right now.

Right now. Before she realised that bulge down there was my raging hard on. Before I pushed her up against a wall and found out if she was wearing *anything* under my shirt.

I pushed past her, mumbling something, incoherent probably, and practically ran into the shower, slamming the door and locking it behind me. I sagged against the door. That was fucking close.

A knock sounded from the other side, making me jolt.

"Diarmuid? Are you okay?"

"Fine. Yes, fine. Just...having a shower." I tore off my clothes and jumped into the shower, turning it on, yelping when the cold water froze me.

"Diarmuid?"

"Fine. All fine," I lied.

A cold shower. That was what I needed to calm the fuck down. To get my willpower under control. Right?

61

Saoirse

I must have nodded off sitting on the couch because when I came to the shower had been turned off. I loved Diarmuid's home, his couch covered in a sheepskin rug, a single side lamp on giving the living room a warm glow.

I stood up, listening out for Diarmuid. I walked softly down the short corridor towards his room, pausing as I reached the slightly open door.

He was in there. He must have just gotten out of the shower because he stood there, hair tied back into a bun, dampness touching the edges of his hairline, the only thing on was a pair of grey briefs that clung to his round ass.

I remembered standing just like this three years ago

watching him undress. He looked as he did then. Except he had more ink now, my eyes tracing the additional dark art spreading across his body.

He picked up a pair of grey sweatpants and tugged them on, turning his body so I could see his front.

Oh God. I stared at that bulge in his briefs before it was covered up by his pants as he straightened.

Now he was just shirtless. His firm muscular chest and ripped abs on display. Familiar ink across his arms and shoulders and—

There was a tattoo on his chest.

It hadn't been there before.

He was saving that spot. He hadn't found anything that meant enough to him to ink over his heart.

Jealousy surged through me. Who was it for? What was it?

I only realised I'd stepped into his room, drawn in by my raging curiosity, when he looked up.

"Saoirse," he exclaimed, then took a step back as if he were scared of me. "What are you doing?"

"I just…" I edged closer and closer. Just one more step and I could make out the tattoo.

My breath caught in my throat.

It was half seal, half woman done in black ink.

A selkie.

My eyes traced the delicate lines, the long wavy hair trailing over the selkie's shoulder.

"You got a heart piece," I said, my words shaking out through my teeth.

He blinked, then slammed a hand over his heart,

hiding her.

I stared at him, my head spinning, my heart swelling at the meaning of this revelation. "That's me. You put me over your heart."

"That's...ridiculous."

I took hold of his hand and pulled it from his chest. He let me, a large breath releasing from his lungs as if he'd just taken a heavy burden off his shoulders. Our fingers twisted together as they hung from our sides. My breath turned to lead lumps in my lungs.

I lifted my free hand and placed my fingertips on the selkie's face. He sucked in a breath and his chest tensed under my touch, wincing as if it pained him. But he didn't move to stop me. I traced the selkie from her head down to her tail.

"She's beautiful."

"You're beautiful," he whispered.

It all became clear now. Diarmuid's sturdy resistance. He wasn't worried that he was still technically married. It wasn't about my age. Or my being one of his assignments. Not really.

He had placed me over his heart. But he was terrified to let me in.

Once I got in I could never be torn out.

Once he let me in he'd never be free of me.

I'd be part of his lungs, using me to breathe. I'd be part of his heart, needing me to keep it pumping.

Like everyone he'd ever loved in his life, I could be torn away.

I've always been yours. And I will never leave you. I am as permanent as the ink over your heart, as the blood in your veins.

As I gazed into his eyes—his beautiful soft eyes, eyes that studied me like I was a constellation among the stars, eyes that placed me in the centre like the sun—I whispered these things.

I saw his eyes rim with love, watched as his walls began to crumble. And like two stars in the same orbit, we crashed together.

Our lips collided. Melding. Melting. Tongues meshing. Dancing. Playing. Our bodies pressed up together as if we were one, the heat of his bare chest radiating through my thin cotton shirt, crushing my breasts between us in the most erotic way, making my body feel like a jar full of fireflies.

His arms wrapped around my back, holding me there against his heart. My fingers tugged the band out of his small bun so I could tangle my fingers in his silky locks.

It felt like breathing after being held down underwater. My heart pounded against the cage of my ribs as if trying to get to his. I knew then that everything that made up *me* would be a traitor if it could find a way to leave my body and join his.

I needed to get closer.

As if he heard me, his hands slid down my back, cupping over my ass. Not close enough. I leapt up, wrapping my legs around him. I must have surprised him because he took a step back and fell, his bed catching him so he was sitting on the edge, me straddled across his strong thighs.

Still… I needed to be closer.

I tore my lips off him, avoiding him as he chased me with his mouth.

"Wait," I said, "let me…" I pulled away just enough so I could tug the shirt over my head, so I was straddled across his lap just in my white cotton panties. I pressed my bare torso against his.

We groaned in unison, our mouths finding each other, pouring our moans onto each other's tongue like wine.

He trailed his hands up and down my body sending heat waves through me, his thumbs brushing the swell of my breasts, the curve of my ass, wrapping around my neck to grip my head to him.

I wanted to know what every inch of him felt like. I wanted to *own* his skin.

My hands adventured across his muscles, across the artwork inked onto him. But it seemed no matter how much I touched him, it only fed my hunger instead of satiating it.

I rocked my hips against him, feeling the hardness waiting for me, and shivered.

He let out a groan, then his hands went to my hips.

For a second I thought he was going to stop me, to push me off. But then his fingers dug into my skin and pulled me hard against him.

He tilted his head, demanding more of me. All of me. All that I was prepared to give. All that I was aching to give.

I slid my hand between us to find his hardness, his sign of wanting me. Years I'd wanted him to want me like this, like a woman. Now he did. Now he was truly mine.

God, I could cry with the sweet agony of relief.

He pulled my hand from him.

Shit. Too much, too fast. I scared him off.

"Wait…" he breathed, placing his forehead on mine.

I gritted my teeth. "If you tell me we have to stop, I will kill you."

He chuckled, his fingers tracing my sides. "Impatient girl. I didn't say stop, I said wait." His features turned serious as he glanced at the clock. "It's only just eleven o'clock. You're still…"

Seventeen.

I brushed his hair out of his face. "I don't care." I've never cared. But now I understood why *he* did. "But we can wait an hour if *you* want to. Until I turn eighteen, if that makes you feel better."

He chewed his lip. God, I wanted to taste his mouth again.

Then he shook his head and said the words I was praying for. "What difference will one hour make?"

Thank God.

An hour was eternity. I'd been waiting for him for five years. I couldn't wait any longer.

His lip lifted up in a half-smirk as his fingers ran over the chaste trim of white lace on the leg of my panties. "Damn. This makes me feel really bad."

"I don't think you're being bad enough," I dared to say.

Our eyes locked. Hunger flared in his, dilating his pupils so they were black pools. Black pools I was falling

474

into.

"How bad do you want me to be?" His voice was the low rumble of thunder on the horizon, warning of a storm coming. I say, let it fucking rain. I wanted to dance in it.

"Do your worst."

His thumb brushed over the front of my panties, causing me to suck in breath.

He hissed. "You're soaking."

I was wet from the moment I laid eyes on his beautiful strong body. Soaked from the second he kissed me. *His* from the moment we met.

He traced his thumb on the edge of my panties, his other hand caressing my breast, brushing my nipple, teasing me, torturing me. God, he was cruel.

"Badder," I begged.

His thumb slid under the panties and found my clit.

"Oh," I gasped.

I'd never been touched there before. Not there. I mean, I had sex, technically, for less than a minute, but Kian had never put his hands on me.

It hadn't felt like this with Kian. It hadn't felt like this at all. I hadn't ached for him. Burned for him.

Not like I burned now.

Diarmuid began to rub the sensitive nub in tiny circles with the rough pad of his thumb, kneading my nipple between his other thumb and finger, everywhere he touched me radiating with waves of pleasure.

My head knocked back and I let out soft cries. I found my hips bucking towards him, trying to give him more access. I had to grip onto his muscular shoulders so I didn't collapse back.

He groaned as he watched me, his gaze burning across my bare skin. "I'm barely touching you and... God, you are so sensitive. So uninhibited. So fucking fresh."

With one hand around my ribs, he pulled me up along his torso so I was kneeling. Before I could ask what he was doing, he latched his mouth around my nipple. The thumb of his other hand slid farther back, finding my entrance, playing with me. The ache in me intensified.

He rolled my nipple between his teeth and his tongue and I let out a long moan.

My nipple slipped from his mouth with a pop. "Selkie, I regret so much that day I found you with that boy."

Oh God.

I regretted it too. I burned at the shame of the memory. Even as my body shook for more as his thumb ran up and down the wet length of me.

"Have you...? Since then...?"

I forced my eyes open to look at him. He was asking me if I'd had sex since Kian.

I shook my head.

"Fuck," he muttered, "you're practically a virgin."

I chewed my lip. Shit. Did he think me a girl again? Had I stopped being a woman in his eyes?

He slid one hand around my back and up to grip the back of my neck. "As much as I want to get real savage on you, let's go slow, okay?"

I didn't want to go slow. We'd been going slow for five years. I wanted him to go savage on me, to fill me, to tear me apart. To fuck me hard and deep and to make me moan like they did in porn videos. But I nodded anyway. I didn't want to scare him off.

He tilted up his chin and pulled me down onto his mouth. He kissed me long and deep, had me squirming against his thumb.

He pulled away from me with a chuckle. "You're impatient."

"I've been patient for five years."

His features turned serious, the dueling flames of hunger and tenderness warring in his eyes. He glanced down. "Let's get rid of these."

He lifted me up even higher, his hands on my hips, like I weighed nothing, until I was standing on the bed, my feet on either side of his thighs, his breath heating up the front of my panties.

He let out a sigh. "White cotton panties. Fuck, you're going to be the ruin of me."

He tugged them down, down, down my thighs, his fingers leaving a trail of fire down my legs as he went, helping me pull them out from my feet, one by one.

I was naked.

Naked in front of him.

And oh God. His face was right *there*. If he let go of me I swear I'd collapse, my knees were weak from need.

He gripped the backs of my thighs and pressed his nose into my soft curls and inhaled. "Sweet girl."

I squirmed. Not because I didn't like it. But because

it was something I didn't know how to react to. I should have practiced with other boys. But I didn't want to. I didn't want anyone but him. Had never wanted anyone *but* him.

"What's wrong?" he asked, his voice so sweet I could have cried.

I shook my head. I was embarrassed.

Diarmuid tilted his head as he looked at me. "Selkie, it's me. You can tell me anything, remember?"

I remembered. He was my Diarmuid, my hero. My Irish giant. Who fought off evil men and nightmares for me.

"No one's ever had their face down there."

His eyes widened. "No one?"

I shook my head, cheeks flaming at my inexperience.

"I would be honoured to be the first."

Before I could say yes or no or something, he leaned in again, holding me still with one hand and pressing apart my lips with the other, licking along my sensitive nub.

"Oh, fuck," I cried out.

His tongue was like fire and ice, sending electricity through me with one swipe.

"You taste like fucking heaven," he murmured against me before moving his tongue against me again. And again.

I fisted my hands in his hair, back arching, legs trembling, mumbling in tongues as I lifted my face to the heavens.

"My sweet selkie," he murmured into the centre of

me. "I can't..." *lick*, "fucking..." *lick*, "get..." *lick*, "enough."

He pushed my leg up, hooking it over his shoulder, opening me further to him, then he grabbed my other leg and hooked it over his other. I squealed from having my legs taken out from under me.

But I didn't fall. He was strong enough for both of us. He gripped my ass against his face with one hand and my waist with the other as I tangled my fingers into his hair.

I forgot about falling over—I forgot about *everything* else—when his mouth clamped down on the centre of me, his tongue flicking side to side, then up and down.

I was on fire. Delirious from fever. I ached for him. Burned for him. With every stroke of his talented tongue, I shook like I was infected with sickness. And yet, I knew I would die if he stopped.

I hardly knew what was happening when my orgasm overtook me, shaking through my body as if I had been taken over by a spirit.

Here, now, I was no longer the daughter of a criminal, the child of a whore.

I was absolved.

I was free.

When I floated back down to earth I was lying curled against Diarmuid's side, his sweatpants and briefs discarded so that he was naked before me.

I sat up.

"Selkie?"

I shook my head. Nothing was wrong. I just wanted

to look at him, lying out here before me. Naked.

I had never seen anything as beautiful. His long, thick body, coiled with muscle, inked like a painting. And me—his selkie—right there across his heart.

"I love you," I said. No shame to my words.

I loved him when I was thirteen. But that was the adoration of a child. The immature longing of a girl who wanted nothing more than to grow up. To take control of her own life.

I told him I loved him when I was thirteen but I didn't *know* how deeply I could love him until now. Until I was grown up.

It was in that moment that I finally forgave him for rejecting me at fourteen. For leaving. Because he had to.

Even though he left, he took me with him.

He placed me over his heart.

And he waited.

He waited for me.

Until I grew up.

Because I needed to grow up before I could be with him.

He brushed my cheek with his finger, pulling away a tear I hadn't realised I'd shed. Then he sucked it off his finger.

"Touch me," he said, a mere whisper, a plea.

"Where?"

"Everywhere. Anywhere. Wherever you like."

I traced his tattoos up his arms like I had done once before, revelling at the way his skin pebbled at my touch. I affected him.

I brushed my hand across the selkie on his chest, then feeling brave, I ran my fingertips across his small dark nipple.

It hardened underneath my touch. His breath caught.

Oh God. I affected him the way he affected me.

I had his skin. And he had mine.

The power surged through my veins and the need to touch him became like a drug.

I moved my hand lower and lower until I rested in the patch of his thick dark hair.

Holy shit.

His cock was long, thick and veined, the end like a swollen red mushroom.

That was a fucking weapon.

And there was no fucking way it was going to fit in me.

I felt his eyes on me, watching me, waiting. His pupils were glossy with desperation, with need, but he was holding himself back just in case I didn't want to continue. He'd sacrifice his needs for me. Given up his wants for me. He always had. I saw that now.

I licked the centre of my hand and curled it around his length, a rush of satisfaction going through me at the surprise in his eyes. I slid my hand up and down his length, just like I'd seen in pornos or had caught my ma doing to the men she brought home.

His leg twitched and he let out a moan.

A moan was good.

I kept going, urged on by his muttering, making sure to capture the precum beading at the end of him and spreading that over him too.

"Selkie. Your hands are like fucking silk. God, I love when you touch me."

He needed more. I needed more.

I got onto my knees so I could use both hands, my ass rising in the air.

I felt his fingers at my pussy and I let out a cry.

"Oh, sweet girl," he murmured. "I am going to fuck this tight little hole." He slid a finger inside me and I jolted, losing my mind completely as he found the deepest of me.

I was lost as he slid his digit out of me, then back in.

When he added a second finger I bucked, crying out his name. How could something both satisfy me and make me hungrier at the same time?

"Don't stop touching me," he begged, breaking through my reverie.

His cock. My hands had stopped moving. Right.

It took a few moments for us to get the rhythm right, but when it did, God did we move like liquid.

As I pumped his length and his hips thrust up, his fingers pushed into me as I rocked my hips back. Back and forth. Like a desperate dance. We were fucking without fucking. The sweet tension began to build in me again.

His fingers left me and I let out a cry from the loss. I grabbed for him. But he brushed my hands out of the way, grabbing onto my hips and pulling me over him so I was seated on him.

We both moaned as my slick heat met his hard

length. Without thinking, I rocked forward along him, letting my juices coat his erection, the head of him separating my lips when I slid forward enough. I could just rock myself into oblivion.

"Jesus, fuck, selkie, enough," he growled.

Enough? A stab of rejection went through me.

He sat up, lifting me up with one hand on my waist again. But he didn't push me off him. He just held me there.

"I can't wait any fucking more," he growled. "You're going to make me lose my damn mind."

With his other hand, he leaned over to his bedside table, pulling out a condom from his drawer and tearing it open with his teeth. In a second he'd rolled it down over him as I hovered there, waiting, my nerves tingling with anticipation.

His hand went back to my waist as he palmed his cock, directing the tip of it to my entrance.

I let out a whimper. Not because I was scared. But because I couldn't believe this was finally happening.

A flash of concern went across his face.

I wanted to reassure him, but I'd lost the ability to speak, utter need choking me. I just arched my back and rocked my hips so my pussy slid over the tip of him, wetting him with my soaking lips.

He hissed and all concern dissipated, replaced by a hunger, tenderness and love underneath it, the way it'd always been.

"I need you to slide down onto my cock. Slowly," he said through gritted teeth. The veins stood out on his neck as if he was holding himself back. "Get used to me. I'm going to stretch your sweet little pussy. But I don't want it to hurt."

I did. I wanted it to hurt so fucking bad.

But he'd never forgive me if I just impaled myself on him.

I had waited five years. What was a few more minutes?

I did as he asked. For him. Always for him.

With every millimetre that I slid down, I felt him pushing into me, stretching me apart. My walls resisted at first, a hint of burning waving at the edge of my need for more. But that sting soon ebbed away, pleasure swelling until it was all that I was. I slid down right to the base of him, fuller than I'd ever been in my entire life.

Our groans echoed throughout his room.

He was inside me. Where part of him had always been.

"Selkie…" he begged, his fingers gripping at my hips. "Please. Move."

"I…" I didn't know what to do, struck motionless with inexperience. Watching two people having sex and *having* sex were two different things.

How could I even admit this to him?

But he seemed to understand what I needed. The way he always understood.

He rolled me onto my back so he was on top of me. I groaned, the weight of him pressing apart my hips, spearing into the centre of me like the sweetest prison.

"Fuck me, like I've always wanted you to fuck me," I

whispered.

"Dirty girl," he hissed.

He slid out and thrust in smoothly, not slow but not fast. Perfect. Just like he was. Just like this moment was. He thrust again and pleasure swelled in me, as did my heart in the cavity of my lungs.

"*This* is your first time," he growled.

"Yes."

"There's been no one else. *Will* be no one else."

"No one," I cried, my hips raising up to meet his.

There was no self-consciousness anymore. No thought that he had a decade more experience than me. He moved and my body reacted. He demanded and I obeyed. He took and I gave. Like an ancient song of the ocean. The steady crash of waves. The ebb and flow of the tide. The rise and fall of the moon over the sea.

"Oh, God, Diarmuid." I was pushed to the edge of my second orgasm, my pussy clenching so hard around him I thought I'd break him.

His control over himself gave way. The humanity in his eyes fled. He fisted his hand in the hair at the back of my neck, tugging my lips against his mouth.

He got savage with me. Real savage. His tongue warring with mine, his hips slamming against mine like he was trying to break my back.

Pleasure thundered through me and I screamed. He cried out my name as he found his release.

He collapsed, spent, holding part of himself up on his elbows so he didn't crush me. Even though he was probably numb from his orgasm, he was thinking of me.

Like he always had.

Our breaths mingled, like two sea currents swirling against each other.

This was contentment. Here was peace. Love.

I had waited for it and now I had it.

Diarmuid was mine. And I, his.

Diarmuid rolled off me, disposed of the condom in his wastebasket. Then he tucked against his warm, hard body, my head on his chest.

I sighed, my fingers tracing my keepsake over his heart.

He glanced at something over my shoulder, then smiled at me.

"What is it?" I asked.

"It's just ticked past midnight. Happy birthday, selkie."

I grinned through the curtain of sleep over my eyes. "Best present ever."

It was.

I'd gotten *him*.

And yet, a part of me, deep down inside, was just waiting for it to fall apart, breaking me with it.

62

Saoirse

When I woke, the first thing I felt was warmth and love. I lay on my side facing out and Diarmuid was against my back, an arm slung over me, tucking me against him.

God, I could stay here forever.

I turned slightly so I could look at him. My beautiful giant carried so much weight about with him during the day, so much heaviness. Asleep he was still as handsome as awake, but his features softened, making him look more at peace. I tucked this secret about him away under my skin.

But like all wonderful things, it had to end. Fear wormed its way into my warm nest.

What if he woke up and regretted us?

What if he woke up and hated himself for what we did?

What if he hated me for seducing him?

I couldn't bear it.

His lashes fluttered and I held my breath.

His beautiful sleepy eyes searched and found mine. A smile spread across his face.

"Hey there, selkie." His voice was even more gravelly in the morning.

I let out a sigh of relief. "Hey."

"Fuck, you're beautiful."

I giggled. "Even with messy bed hair and pillow creases on my face?"

He traced a line down my cheek, his eyes glistening as they roamed over my face. "They're the sexiest pillow creases, and I love that I can witness your bed hair because it means you slept with me in my bed."

He yanked me closer against him, so that our naked fronts were pressed together. My softness against his hardness. I let out a low groan as heat and need flooded my body, nipples aching as they pressed against his chest.

I wasn't the only one who was getting turned on. I could feel his erection against my belly.

Need filled his eyes. He looked almost in pain as he leaned forward to claim my mouth. Our lips meshed and he rolled over me, covering me like a blanket, pressing my thighs open exquisitely with his hips, settling against where I ached for him. His hips rocked, his hardness sliding against my wetness.

The doorbell rang.

We groaned in unison.

"Ignore it," he said, dipping his head down my body to suck one of my nipples into his mouth.

I moaned and arched my back.

The doorbell rang again.

Diarmuid sighed. "It's probably a package or something. I'll be right back."

He rolled out of bed, tugging his sweatpants on. I gathered the blankets up against the chill in the air. He caught my eye and grinned.

"You look damn good in my bed." His eyes flicked to the bedroom door. "Maybe they've given up—"

The doorbell rang again, this time three times in a row. Whoever it was, they were not going away.

Diarmuid disappeared to deal with the postman or whoever it was.

Perhaps twenty seconds went by and he still didn't return.

I frowned, listening out for any type of sounds.

Could I hear voices?

I slid out of bed and pulled his large t-shirt on before creeping out of the bedroom and down the hallway. I heard Diarmuid's voice, harsh like he was angry and slightly raised but spoken in a kind of whisper, as if he didn't want the noise to travel down to me.

"—to do, Ava?"

Ava? That cursed name conjured up the image of the raven-haired beauty, and a rush of hatred burned through my veins. The woman with the wide hips and the big breasts. The woman who had Diarmuid under her spell. The one who took him away from me.

Diarmuid's *wife*.

She was here.

I slid as far as I could down the corridor without being seen, pressing my hands to the wallpaper.

"I know you're still angry with me." Her voice was soft, sweet sounding.

"Damn right I'm still angry."

"But that's good, don't you see? If you're angry it means that you still care underneath it all."

I squeezed my eyes shut. No. She could not want him back. Not now. Not ever.

Tell her to go away, Diarmuid. Tell her you're with someone else. Tell her you love *me*.

But Diarmuid said nothing. Denied nothing.

A stab of pain entered my heart. Diarmuid and Ava had history. They had a marriage. How could I compete?

"Diarmuid," Ava said, her voice softening, pleading, "I made a mistake and I'm sorry. But I'm still your wife. You made vows to me, didn't you? For better or for worse."

I heard Diarmuid sighing. "I did."

"Then you owe it to me—to *us*—to try to work this out."

I backed up, having heard enough, trying not to stumble as my eyes blurred from tears.

Once again, Ava was coming between us. And like last time, I knew Diarmuid would give in to her. His morals were too strong. They were married. He owed nothing to me. I was just…just a one-night stand. A fling.

He didn't say he loved me back last night.

My heart tore into pieces as I ran silently back into the bedroom, searching for my clothes, tugging them on. Finding my shoes. My bag.

I had to get out of here. I couldn't be here when Diarmuid came back in the room and told me that he was getting back together with his wife.

His fucking wife, Saoirse. He has a wife. What did you think was going to happen?

That he and I would be together? That'd we'd get a Happily Ever After?

I should have known better. Should have known that Happily Ever Afters were not for the daughters of criminals and whores.

I pushed open the window, a blast of cold air wafting in, and froze.

Stop, I told myself. *Give him a chance to explain.*

Running away was for children. Tantrums were for children. I was a woman. I would act like one.

I shut the window and lowered my bag down to the bed. I wasn't going anywhere. I wasn't running.

I would stay. And I would fight for him if I had to.

I was sitting on the bed when Diarmuid finally opened the door.

"Sorry I took so long." He could barely look at me.

I looked past him expecting a sullen Ava at his heels, but he was alone.

He spotted the bag next to me, my shoes on and realisation came over his eyes as they finally snapped to mine. "Do you know who was at the door?"

I nodded.

"Did you hear us?"

I twisted my fingers together in my lap. I would *not* cry.

I nodded again.

Diarmuid let out a long breath, stepped fully into the room and closed the door behind him.

"I'm sorry, selkie."

He was sorry.

I was sorry too.

I told myself that I wouldn't cry, that I would be strong, but my heart was breaking. Shattering. Again. I was just as unprepared for it the second time as the first.

But this time it was worse. This time I knew exactly how well Diarmuid and I fit. I knew how he felt underneath my hands, how he felt inside me. In his arms I knew love, I felt peace. I would never feel that again. I'd loved him since I was thirteen. I'd love him until I died.

Once the first tear rolled over the rim of my lashes, the rest followed, like a dam bursting.

"Saoirse!" He started towards me. "What's wrong?"

"I *know* you're still married," I began to blubber, "and I know she wants you back; who wouldn't? And I know how you feel about doing the right things and your morals. But she doesn't deserve you. And—"

"I want you."

I sucked in a breath, trying to blink my vision back to

clear. "What?"

Diarmuid sank to his knees in front of me.

"I want to be with you." His hands cupped around my face, and they brushed aside the wetness on my cheeks. "Only you."

My head spun. I couldn't believe what he was saying to me.

"I know I'm still married," he said quietly. "And it is *such* a process to get divorced here. Ava and I have to be separated for four years before I can start the proceedings."

"Which means she's your *wife*," my voice cracked on the word, my guts twisted with jealousy, "for now."

He nodded. "And in the eyes of society..."

"...this, *us*, we are wrong," I finished for him.

He nodded. "I don't care anymore."

"You...don't?"

"I've tried to do what's right for most of my life. Most of my life I feel like I just keep fucking up instead. Being with you is the most *right* I've ever felt." His face screwed up with pain. "I just don't think it's fair to ask you to bear the brunt of society's judgement if we were together. You don't deserve it."

"I don't care."

"Saoirse."

"Diarmuid." I flung myself down to the carpet so we were both on our knees. I wrapped my hands around his neck so he could do nothing but look right into my eyes. "I. Don't. Care."

He let out a long breath, like he was relieved. Did he

493

come in here thinking that I could have walked away from him?

"I want you. Have always wanted you." I ran my fingers through his hair. "You have my skin, remember?"

Diarmuid gave me a half-smile. "Your father won't like it."

My stomach turned cold.

My father.

"He can't know." He could *never* know. I chewed my lip. "Your work. They won't like it either."

His face became serious. "If my supervisor found out about last night, I'd lose my job. Probably do jail time."

"So, we're hiding this...us?"

"I don't want to hide you, you know that, don't you?" he asked, his brows furrowed in concern. "I want to scream your name from the very top of the Carrauntoohil mountain."

"As long as we're together. I don't care that we have to keep us a secret."

My insides melted as he wrapped me up in his strong, sure embrace. I would be happy being tucked away here in his arms forever. My harbour. My home. My family.

"We'll figure it out, selkie," his voice rumbled against my cheek. "Together."

He claimed my mouth firmly, a promise sealed in a kiss.

My body lit up like a flash fire, as it had done earlier, before we were interrupted. All other thoughts floated away as he lowered me to the carpet.

For a moment, before he stripped me of my clothes,

a stark feeling of dread came over me. Diarmuid and I might be together, but it was a thread made of thin silk. We had to be careful.

There were so many things—so many people— waiting to tear us apart.

Diarmuid and I spent a glorious Saturday in bed. That night we watched *The Dark Knight* on his couch, eating takeaway pizza. Well, we watched *part* of the movie, the other part we spent making out—and more, oh God, so much *more*—on his couch.

Sunday morning Diarmuid dropped me off a few blocks from home. I was supposed to go into the lab today. I told Diarmuid I had to work. Technically, I didn't lie. He just assumed that I was working at the café. I didn't correct him. And hated myself for it.

My da was sitting at the breakfast table with a black coffee and a cigarette in his hand when I walked in. I wished he would at least open a window when he smoked in here.

"Hey, Da…"

My voice was shaking, as were my hands. Why was I nervous?

He looked up from his paper with a smile, fag hanging from his lip.

"Hey, baby girl. Where you been all weekend?"

I forced a smile. I had texted him on the evening of the party letting him know I was staying with a friend. I didn't specify who. He replied, reminding me that I was working Sunday. He didn't ask who the friend was.

"Just with a friend, Da. I told you."

I hoped that he didn't notice I was wearing the same dress from Friday night's party. Washed, of course.

I shouldn't have been worried. My father was already distracted by something in the paper.

"Damn Garda." He flicked his fingers at the grey sheet. "They seized another fucking batch last night. Just outside of Dublin."

I froze. "Oh."

"Sons of bitches. I'd fucking love to give them all a good—" He made a stabbing motion.

My guts twisted as if he'd stabbed me. I swallowed down the lump in my throat. "I was thinking, Da, I'm not sure I should work for you anymore."

My father's face snapped to mine, a glint of something dark flashing in his eyes before it disappeared so fast I may have been dreaming it.

"Baby girl…what are you talking about?"

I smoothed down my dress. "I just… I think that what I'm doing is…well, wrong."

My father's eyes narrowed. "You like living here?"

"What? Yes, of course."

"You like eating the food I stock the fridge with?"

"Yes, but—"

"You want to go to university?"

"Yes—"

"This work you think is 'wrong'," he marked the word with finger quotes, "is paying for all this stuff. *For you.*"

"But—"

Bang! His fist came down on the table. "I don't want to hear any more of this fucking quitting bullshit," he roared.

I gasped, tears rimming my eyes. My first thought was to run. To *run*. From my own father.

He stood and grabbed me, wrapping me into a suffocating hug. I wanted to push him away. Instead I just stood there, frozen.

"I'm sorry, baby girl." He kissed my head, his breath stinking of smoke. "You have no idea how much is riding on our new investment."

He never called it drugs or meth. He only ever called it an investment. *Our* investment.

"I didn't mean to yell," he said into my hair, his voice taking on a softer tone. "You just made me so scared, I got mad. You see, I already made promises to some…important people. Some important people who will not take too kindly to me, *and my family*, if I don't deliver."

I understood exactly what he was doing.

He was threatening me.

Threatening me with injury to him and me if I didn't do what he told me to.

Oh God. Why did I say yes in the first place? Why did I agree to get involved?

My father pulled back and cupped my cheeks, his cigarette still trapped between two of his fingers, the smoke stinging my eyes.

"You'll keep with the agreement, okay, baby girl." It

wasn't a question. "One year, you work for me."

I nodded, because there was nothing else I could do.

One year.

How the fuck was I going to keep working in my father's lab for one year without Diarmuid finding out?

63

Diarmuid

"See ya, Nina," I called to the office girl as I made my way out of the station that Monday evening.

Nina shot up from behind her desk. "Holy shit."

I spun towards her. "What?"

Nina pointed a purple-painted finger at me. "You're…" she leaned in, peering at me. "Holy shit, you are! You're *actually* smiling."

Damn. So I was.

It had everything to do with the blonde angel who I was going to see later tonight.

She'd worked late last night. When I called her during her break, she refused to let me pick her up from work, telling me she would be too tired and that she'd see me tonight instead. I told her that I'd just pick her up and drop her off, making sure she got home safe. But she claimed she already had a ride. I'd almost ignored her wishes and driven over to the café to pick her up anyway, I missed her so fucking much. That was before I slapped myself internally and told myself not to scare her off.

Saoirse and I were going to make dinner together. I had a few hours to kill so I was going to grab my gym stuff, swing by the boxing gym, then shower before it was time to pick her up.

I shrugged at Nina. "It's a good day."

Nina's eyes widened, her glittery purple eyeshadow catching the light. "Who the hell are you and what have you done with Diarmuid Brennan?"

I chuckled. "Can't a guy smile once in a while?"

"Guys, yes. *You*, never." She narrowed her eyes at me. "Did you hit your head or something?"

I raised an eyebrow.

"Get replaced by a robot?"

"Have a nice evening."

"*Have a nice evening?*" Nina's eyes bugged out of her head.

I waved at her and strode down the hallway.

"You're freakin' me out, Diarmuid," she called after me.

I stuck up my middle finger at her over my shoulder.

"That's better," she yelled.

This late in the year the sunset was creeping earlier and earlier. It was already dusk by the time I pulled up into my driveway after the gym. I peered through the

500

windscreen wipers and the drizzle of rain.

There was a figure standing huddled at my door, her arms wrapped around her body, wet hair plastered to her head. I'd recognise her anywhere.

Saoirse.

Why the hell was she here? A shot of fear went through me.

Something was wrong.

I slammed my truck into park and yanked up the brake. I didn't even turn off the engine as I pushed my way out of the cabin. All I could see was her.

"Saoirse!" I ran towards her, cutting across the grass, ignoring the wet earth squishing under my feet. My only concern was getting to her.

As I neared, I could see the smudge of mascara under her pale green eyes. Was that the rain or had she been crying?

I grabbed her and pulled her against me.

She let out a low cry. "I'm wet."

Wet was an understatement. She was soaking. She must have been standing here for fucking ages. Fuck, why didn't I take my phone with me?

"I don't care," I said. I pulled back to look at her. The pain etched in her eyes cut me to the core. "What's wrong?"

"I tried to call you," she said, her lip trembling, accusation in her tone.

"I was at the gym. I left my phone. *What's wrong?*"

"My ma…" her face screwed up, "she's dead."

64

Saoirse

Moina called me.

And told me.

It had been an overdose. I shouldn't have been surprised.

I *was* surprised at how I reacted. By breaking down. With huge gulping sobs like I was drowning, clutching at my kitchen counter like it was my lifeline.

Then somehow through blurred vision, I was calling Diarmuid. My world was cracking up underneath my feet, and he was the first and only person I wanted to be with.

And with every missed call, my heart began to tremble.

So I ran. Through the rain, like a ship returning to its

safe harbour, until I reached his porch.

Where I waited—always waiting—for him.

Diarmuid took me inside the house. He stripped my wet clothes off me, dried my body, my hair, brought out clothes for me to wear. Then he pulled his armchair in front of the fire, sat me in his lap and pulled the largest, softest blanket that he had around us.

There I stayed, wrapped in his warmth.

He called his work and told them he was taking the next few days off. Then he called the coroner back in Dublin and arranged the funeral by phone. I sat, mute, numb, beside him, always clutching to a part of him as if he were the only thing tethering me to this earth.

The next morning, he packed me into his car and we drove to Dublin to attend my ma's funeral.

I didn't have a dress to wear or anything else with me for that matter. We stopped off at a shopping centre on the way and Diarmuid picked out a few things for me to try on, led me to the dressing room and practically changed me himself. And he paid for everything we bought.

He was my rock. He kept my world turning. While I remained still. While I was numb.

Diarmuid and I stood at the foot of my mother's grave, his arm around my shoulders the only thing keeping me steady. The pastor's voice droning on.

No one else came.

Moina had to work so she wasn't here. My da didn't

want to come. He had work, too. Also, quite frankly, he stopped caring about my mother a long time ago. None of her "men" bothered to come either.

"She had no one else, Diarmuid," I said, a near whisper, when the pastor had left us. "She had no one else except me and *I* left her. Sh-she died alone."

"Hey," he said turning me to face him, his strong hands on my shoulders, "this is not on you. She had her own stuff that she couldn't deal with."

"I should have tried harder. Made her get help. I should have—"

"*She* should have been a better parent. She could have asked for help, wanted to get help, but she didn't. Don't you dare blame yourself."

"W-why does it hurt so much? I-I didn't even like her," I choked on a laugh.

"Because she was your mother, and despite her many flaws, you loved her."

"I don't want to *be* her, Diarmuid," I choked out.

There it was, my deepest fear laid bare.

The irony was, by weaving myself into my da's business, I was following my ma's dark path. I was becoming the very woman I feared becoming. All it would take was for me to lose Diarmuid and I'd sink into a hole I could never crawl out of.

A sob ripped from my cramping, aching lungs. "I d-don't want to die alone like she did, with no one."

Without you.

"You won't," he said fiercely, tucking me into the safety of his arms. "I swear to you, you won't."

505

I wanted so much to believe him.

Diarmuid and I stayed in a boutique hotel in Dublin, south of the river in the beautiful Rathmines neighbourhood of Georgian houses and tree-lined sidewalks. We stayed there for several days, just walking under the willows along the swan-filled canal, holding hands, having a drink in a dark corner of the local wood-panelled "old man's" pub.

Slowly I was able to untangle this messy jumble of feelings, this ball of guilt and regret over the broken woman who gave birth to me.

But there were pieces I could not let go of.

Diarmuid pushed open the front door of his home in Limerick for me. I had to brush past him as I walked in, my body tingling from that mere casual touch. Even through all my grief, he could set me on fire with one look, one touch.

I walked straight into Diarmuid's bedroom and dropped my bag on the bed without even thinking about it.

This place was already feeling like home. He'd already made space for me to leave clothes in his drawers. He bought me a red toothbrush, which sat next to his blue one, and stocked his shower with my exact brand of girlie body wash.

"I don't know when I'll be able to pay you back for these last few days," I said as I began to unpack the bag full of clothes Diarmuid had bought me. We hadn't stopped at my house on the way to Dublin.

Diarmuid slid his arms around my waist. "You don't have to pay me back."

"Diarmuid."

"Saoirse." He turned me in his arms so I was facing him. "You are *not* paying me back."

I pouted.

He kissed my nose.

I pouted even more.

He smiled and kissed my lips. That was all it took for me to melt. To give in.

"You didn't have to do all that for me, you know?" I said when I pulled back, my breath a little heavier, my body a little warmer.

"I know. I wanted to." His pulled away and walked over to his dresser. "I have something for you."

"Diarmuid!"

What? More? He'd already spent too much.

He turned towards me, hiding something behind his back, a sly grin on his face. "I was gonna give this to you on Monday night, but…"

I shook my head even though I was smiling. "What have you done, Diarmuid?"

"Hold your hands out."

I did. Into my palms he dropped a small velvet jewelry box.

Oh shit.

"What have you done?" I asked again, this time my voice a mere squeak.

"I didn't give you a birthday present this year yet."

507

I blinked at him. "You…"

"I know I didn't have to," he said, taking the words out of my mouth, somehow knowing what I was about to say before I said it.

It was another charm. It had to be.

I cracked open the box.

But it wasn't a charm.

There, nestled in the navy velvet cushion, was a key.

I pulled it out, frowning.

"It's…a bit big for my charm bracelet," I said, immediately regretting it because it made me sound so damn ungrateful.

He laughed. "Silly selkie. It doesn't go on your charm."

"Then where does it—"

I knew where this key belonged. Which door it fit.

My eyes widened. "Is this a key to your house?"

He nodded, his features serious. "I never want you to have to wait on my porch again. Besides, you already have the key to my heart. I thought you'd like this one to match it."

He winked at me.

I laughed and threw my arms around his neck. I whispered, "Best present ever."

65

Diarmuid

Weeks went by. Saoirse and I fell into a routine. On the days she worked, she stayed at her house. On the other days, she stayed with me. I'd pick her up from a few blocks over from her house so her neighbours didn't get suspicious and tell her da.

At my house, we'd cook dinner together, watch movies, play board games. It was perfect bliss in our own little bubble, far removed from the rest of the world. The rest of the world who wouldn't think twice about judging us without knowing us.

We made love—God, did we make love—all over the kitchen, the couch, the shower, the bed, basically anywhere I could lay her or press her up against.

509

It was only when we had to leave the bubble—and each other—that things grew tense.

Niall fucking Lynch kept the pressure on at work for me to find something on Liam by squeezing Saoirse. This secret I was keeping from Saoirse started off as a splinter and it grew until it felt like an abscess, ready to burst.

I could not keep going like this.

I had to tell Saoirse.

But she'd never forgive me if I helped put her father away.

66

Saoirse

I stood at the end of a table of trays, the bottoms lined with white crystals.

The first batch was done. Perfected, actually. This meth was as pure as it could get.

But the surge of satisfaction of a job well done was hampered by a growing unease.

This drug had killed my mother. It had ruined her life well before she'd died. Now I was about to send more of it out into the world.

I was suddenly overcome with the urge to throw all the trays aside.

"I'm proud of you, baby girl." My da grabbed my shoulder and squeezed.

Not even the warmth of his pride could fully overcome this sickening feeling I had.

"Thanks," I said limply.

I couldn't keep doing this. I couldn't.

During the manufacturing process I was able to switch off, pretend it was something else I was cooking, follow the process like an unemotional detached machine. But now...

My father spoke about distribution and his investors, things I had no desire to hear.

"...and check out the cool packaging I came up with."

He pulled something from his back pocket, a flat, clear plastic sealable bag—a baggie—about the size of a playing card, and held it up to me, a logo branding one side in shimmering blue ink.

I snatched it out of his hand, the blood draining from my face.

There on the baggie was Diarmuid's selkie tattoo.

"W-What? How?" I gripped the edge of the plastic, my hands shaking.

"I saw the drawing of the selkie you'd doodled on a bit of paper at home. I liked the design and thought it represented you and your product perfectly."

Oh my God. I was going to be sick.

I was going to be fucking sick.

All of this meth was going to be distributed throughout Ireland carrying Diarmuid's selkie tattoo that he'd gotten for me.

"D-do you have to use that design?"

My da frowned. "What's wrong with it?"

Everything.

But he couldn't know the reason. I couldn't tell him.

"I just…feel weird having something I drew on your packaging."

My da tucked his hand around the back of my neck and pressed a kiss to my forehead. "Don't worry, no one will be able to trace it back to you."

Except *somebody* could.

What the hell was I going to do?

"You okay, baby girl?" my da asked.

I had to pretend everything was okay.

I forced a smile, trying to shove my panic down.

"Yeah fine. Just…tired." I shoved the baggie into the back pocket of my jeans and grabbed my bag. "I'm ready to go home."

"Yeah sure, baby girl. Just ten more minutes while I check on some stuff. Go raid the fridge."

Fuck. I didn't want to stay here, not for another second. I hated not having my own car. I still had a few more months where my licence was suspended. But I didn't care. I *needed* a way to leave this place when I wanted to. Otherwise I was trapped.

"I'll wait here," I said. "But I *need* my own car, Da, if I'm going to keep working out here in the middle of nowhere."

"Anything for my baby girl," my da called out over his shoulder.

Only when I was alone did I press my face into my hands and squeeze my eyes shut. I had to tell Diarmuid. I had to tell him before he found out.

How could I tell him?

The next day I waited on a predetermined corner as Diarmuid's truck pulled up. He jumped out and pressed me into the door of the truck, roping his fingers into my hair and kissing me as if it'd been years since he'd seen me. He kissed me as if I was everything.

As if I was perfect.

I wasn't.

As if I wasn't guilty.

I was.

I pushed him away and ducked my head aside. "Someone might see."

"Let them see."

He leaned in for another kiss, which I avoided.

He frowned. "What's wrong?"

You're going to realise how much of a liar I am. How bad I am. I'm going to lose you.

I opened my mouth to confess…

I couldn't do it. I couldn't lose that tender look in his hazel eyes. I couldn't lose his kisses.

"Nothing," I lied.

"Okay…" He opened the door for me, watching me warily.

I jumped into his truck and closed the door before he could ask me again. Before my horrible secret tumbled from my mouth. There had to be a way for me to tell Diarmuid and for me not to lose him. Maybe… Maybe he'd never find out?

Diarmuid walked around to the driver's side. I realised I was half sitting on a stack of papers. I pulled out the stack of papers from underneath me. They looked like three or four thin brochures amongst papers.

I frowned when I caught my name on the salutation on the top paper. I flicked through them. They were all addressed to me.

"What's this?" I demanded, turning to Diarmuid as soon as he slid into his seat.

A wave of guilt crossed his face. "I forgot I'd left them there. I was going to show you…"

"Show me what?"

"They're brochures from various universities that are open for scholarship applications. If you applied, they'd be mad not to take you. You wouldn't have to wait a whole year to start studying." He started the truck and pulled us out of the parking lot onto the road.

I leafed through the papers and brochures, my eyes bulging. "This university's in *Canada*. This one is in *Australia*."

"All the universities in Ireland are closed for applications until next year. You said so yourself."

My gaze snapped to his, a sudden realisation clawing at my chest making it hard to breathe. "You're trying to get rid of me."

"What? No!" he protested.

Tears rimmed my eyes. I tried to blink away the sting, but it didn't work. "You want me but you're embarrassed about me. I'm a nuisance to you. It'd be better for you if I just went away.

"Don't be ridiculous."

"Why are you sending me away?"

"I'm not sending you away. Saoirse, I just want you to know what else is out there. You don't want to stay in Limerick your whole life, do you?"

That's when I realised that Diarmuid didn't see a future between us. Whatever it was that we were doing together in secret, it would one day end. And soon, if I did go to university overseas.

"I thought we…" My voice broke. I sucked in a breath, steeled myself and tried again. "I thought you and I had a connection."

"We do."

"Why are you trying to break it?"

"Even if we have a connection, you're so young."

"I fucking hate it when everyone says that."

"It's true. You might hate it but it's true. I don't want you saddled with an old man like me."

"You're not old."

He snorted. "No, I'm not old. But I'm old enough to know better."

I squeezed my eyes shut, my nerves twanging.

"What if…" I began. "What if *this* is the life that I want? To stay here in Limerick and *be* with…someone?" I didn't have the nerve to say his name. I opened my eyes, searching his face for his reaction. "There's nothing wrong with wanting to stay in Limerick and be someone's wife."

His jaw ticked. "There *is* something wrong with it if

the only reason you're choosing that life is because you don't know anything different. Jesus," Diarmuid let out an exasperated sigh, "just *look* at the brochures, just *think* about it."

"Why do you care whether I go to college or not?"

"Because," he yelled, "you have more potential in your middle finger than all the teenagers I've mentored in my whole life. You have a chance to get out of here, to make something of yourself. I will not let you destroy it."

I sank back into my seat, the air inside the truck reverberating at the fury in his voice, my heart silently breaking.

"How will you know for sure if you don't see what else is out there? Don't choose me—" he halted. "Don't choose *this life* because you are ignorant of the other possibilities. You could *do* anything, Saoirse, *be* anyone."

"Except be yours." I whispered. "I'll never really be yours."

518

67

Diarmuid

"Take me home," Saoirse said.

I flinched. I hadn't been sure how Saoirse was gonna take these college brochures. I didn't think she would react this badly.

"Saoirse," I tried.

"Just take me home. Please."

Her jaw was clenched, her lips pressed together in a line. Arms crossed over her chest, eyes looking everywhere except at me.

I knew better than to push things when Saoirse was in this mood. I knew better than to try and explain. My best bet was to give her some space and wait until she calmed down. Then I'd have a chance of talking to her.

Knowing this, I did what she asked. I dropped her off near her house.

She jumped out before I could kiss her goodbye, slamming the door and running away from me without a word.

By the next afternoon she still hadn't responded to any of my texts. I sat at my desk at work unable to concentrate, tearing at my hair. I thought getting those college brochures for her was the right thing to do. Apparently not.

I hated that she was mad at me. I hated that she didn't want to talk. Not knowing how she was feeling, what she was thinking, was like an itch under my skin that I couldn't scratch.

I glanced at the clock. She had mentioned previously that she was working today. She should still be in the middle of her shift at the café. She'd be mad if I just showed up, but I couldn't take any more of this radio silence.

I got into my truck and slammed the door shut, sticking the key in the ignition. The passenger seat to my left was empty. Empty of Saoirse. Of the brochures that she'd taken with her, despite her anger at me. That was what had given me hope that she might come around. My heart felt like it was ripping apart when I thought of her leaving me, but I could not hold her back. I *would* not hold her back.

She had the most beautiful wings I'd ever seen.

She had to fly.

My eye caught on a small piece of plastic on her seat.

I grabbed it, about to crumple it up and chuck it in the small trash compartment when I realised what it was.

A small baggie.

The kind that drugs came in.

What the fuck? This wasn't mine. Someone must've dropped it in here.

And there had only been one person who I'd let into that passenger seat in the last few weeks.

Then I turned it over and saw the logo on it.

It was the selkie, the exact selkie I had tattooed over my heart.

I barrelled into the café that Saoirse worked at, almost knocking a customer over. I muttered my apologies and scanned the place for the familiar blonde head, but I couldn't see her.

"Can I help you?" A short dark-haired waitress walked up to me, weariness in her eyes.

"Where's Saoirse? I need to talk to her."

The waitress frowned. "Oh, Saoirse hasn't worked here for weeks."

She...

Why would she lie to me?

Where was she working if not here?

The blood drained from my limbs as an awful thought filtered through my head.

Apples don't fall far from the tree.

I sat down the block from Saoirse's house in a dark sedan, one of the unmarked vehicles from work because my truck was too familiar. I watched as Saoirse got into the driver's seat of a new Audi. Flashy car. Was that hers? Or her da's? And why the hell was she driving? She hadn't gotten her licence back yet.

She pulled out into the street and I followed her, making sure to remain far enough in the distance so as not to be made. I trailed her out of the city limits of Limerick into the countryside.

If that was Liam or any of his men, they might have picked me following them on these remote roads. They might have doubled back or taken a different route. But Saoirse was too young, too innocent. She didn't know how to avoid being followed.

Twenty minutes later on a deserted single-lane country road, she took a right turn into a driveway up ahead.

I slowed down as I passed. Her car was disappearing through an open gate, two men with guns manning it. *Guns*, for fuck's sake.

I kept driving. I drove and I drove, my head spinning.

Surely this was some mistake. Why was Saoirse entering a farmhouse guarded by men with guns?

Later that night, when everyone had gone home, I sat at my work desk, the Garda property database open on my computer. Based on the GPS in my car I worked out the coordinates of the farmhouse, and subsequently, the address.

I pulled up the ownership details on my computer screen. The property was held by an Irish shell company with very little information on it.

I dug further. The paper trail led to a parent company based out of Switzerland, one of Europe's tax havens. It took a couple of phone calls and threats to uncover the details. It was co-owned by none other than Liam Byrne.

I found it. Liam's place of operation. And by the look of the baggie Saoirse had somehow dropped in my car, it wasn't just weed they were producing now.

She was producing.

I couldn't believe that Saoirse had anything to do with her father's business.

But then again, maybe I could. Hadn't I done bad things too? Hadn't I crossed that line as a teenager?

A daughter with such a brilliant understanding of chemistry must have been an incredible discovery for an opportunist like Liam.

How dare he use his own fucking daughter.

How did he convince her? What did he offer her? What did he tempt her with? His love? His affection? Or maybe it was more insidious. Maybe he threatened her?

Saoirse was a good person. She didn't deserve to go to jail.

But I was sitting on information, information I was duty-bound to do something with.

The question was, what?

68

Saoirse

Diarmuid: I need to see you tonight. Please.

Diarmuid's text burned a hole in my phone. It'd been days since I'd seen him and I missed him like a hole in my soul, like a hunger that would not go away. But I couldn't bring myself to see him right now.

It wasn't just about the college brochures. It was my guilt over hiding what I had been doing for my father.

After I ran from Diarmuid's car, I called my da, crying. I'd managed to convince him to let me out of his business once I'd set up the manufacturing process and trained his staff. It could be taken over by almost anyone once they were trained properly.

I just had a few more days to go before I was free of any obligations to my da. I'd stashed away the money he'd paid me, almost ten grand. It was less than what I'd make for the year, but it was enough. Enough for me to move out of my da's home. To figure out what was next.

Then maybe Diarmuid wouldn't be so hesitant to be with me. *Really* be with me.

I could stop lying to him.

I just needed a few more days.

I texted Diarmuid back.

Me: I might have to work.

Diarmuid: I'm coming over there right now to get you. I'm not taking no for an answer.

I let out a huff. When Diarmuid got like this—all alpha and controlling—there was no denying him.

I guess I didn't *have* to be at the lab right this second. I could go later now that my da had bought me a car.

Me: Fine.

In less than ten minutes, Diarmuid texted to let me know he was waiting at our usual corner. Jesus, he must have been speeding or something to get here so fast. He must be excited to see me.

But when I climbed into the passenger seat of his truck and closed the door behind me, Diarmuid said nothing. He didn't even look at me, his dark brows pulled down over his eyes.

"Hey," I said, all shy.

It'd been five days since we'd seen each other. He was even more beautiful than I remembered, his shoulder-length hair pulled back in a disheveled ponytail. Even with those dark circles under his eyes as if he'd not been sleeping well. His knuckles on the hand that held the wheel were white, his shoulders pinched up around his ears.

He accelerated down the street as if we were being chased.

I slammed back into my seat. *Okaaaay.*

He still hadn't said anything by the time he marched me down his driveway and into his house.

I dropped onto his living room couch expecting him to do the same. But he didn't. He paced across the carpet, running his hand through his hair, causing pieces of his locks to fall out of the ponytail.

I frowned. "What the hell is up with you?"

He stopped pacing and stared at me as if he didn't know who I was.

I let out a huff. "If you're going to not speak to at all you can send me back home."

"You dropped this in my truck." He threw a crumpled ball of plastic at me.

I picked it out of my lap and uncrumpled it.

My heart stopped—literally fucking stopped—in my chest.

It was the baggie with Diarmuid's selkie tattoo on it. The one my father gave me. The one I'd lost.

"I can explain," tumbled out from my mouth.

"You better fucking explain."

I sucked in air. *Never talk to the cops.*

Diarmuid was a cop.

How the hell could I explain this without giving everything away?

I looked up at him, my mind whirring. Shining in his eyes was fury, underneath was bitter disappointment.

He knew.

He knew everything anyway.

"I'm sorry," I said.

"You're sorry."

"I was going to tell you…"

He let out a long breath that sounded like a hiss. "Tell me now. I want to hear it from your fucking mouth."

I swallowed. He never swore around me unless he was pissed. Diarmuid was extremely pissed.

"I was helping him. Using my chemistry knowledge to…" I couldn't say it.

"Say it."

I shook my head.

"Own what you did, Saoirse."

"I helped him cook meth. But just once."

Diarmuid let out a pained cry and fisted his hands into his hair.

My breath went all short, like I was drowning. This was it. This was when I lost Diarmuid forever.

"And the selkie?"

"He saw my doodle on a piece of paper of your selkie

tattoo." My voice became quieter and quieter. "He thought it would make a great logo…"

Something broke inside of Diarmuid, I saw it in his eyes.

My father had taken something special between Diarmuid and me and he'd tainted it. And it was my fault.

My own heart shattered and tears welled up in my eyes. "I'm sorry. I'm so sorry. I was going to quit. End of this week, I swear."

I pressed my face into my hands. I fucked this up. I fucked up so bad.

I felt Diarmuid's presence as he bent down to kneel before me. I wanted to cry out when he slid his hands onto me.

"Saoirse," his voice was soft, softer than I deserved, "everyone deserves a second chance. *You* deserve a second chance."

I sniffed and lifted my face to look at Diarmuid. "You really believe that?"

He brushed my cheeks with his thumb. "Yes."

My hopes began to lift. Maybe there was still room in Diarmuid's heart to forgive me. Maybe in time he could forgive me enough for us to be together?

"Even if it means making a sacrifice. A…difficult choice."

I sniffed. "What does that mean?"

Diarmuid's face turned hard, cold. And my hope turned to wood and splintered in my chest.

"You deserve a second chance," he repeated. "But your father has run out of chances. I'm sorry, Saoirse. But it's over for him."

My blood froze in my veins, turned brittle and snapped. "What are you talking about?"

"At this very moment, the Garda are converging on the farm where his operations are being run. He's being arrested, taken to prison for a very, very long time."

No.

My da.

My only family left.

I shoved Diarmuid back, scrambling away from him and over the back of the couch. "What have you done?"

"I did this *for you*," Diarmuid said. "I won't let him take you down with him."

I shook my head over and over. No. Not my da. I just got him back. He was a bad man but he was *my da*.

I spun and raced out the front door, grabbing Diarmuid's truck keys on the side table as I went. I ignored his yelling behind me as I tumbled out the front door.

I wrenched open the driver's side door of the truck, slid inside and slammed it shut, locking it behind me. Diarmuid slammed up against the vehicle, banging on the window and demanding I open it.

Right now, I could barely hear him. I could barely think of anything else other than getting to the station.

My da.

He needed me.

I yanked the seat forward so I could reach the pedals and reversed out of Diarmuid's driveway, narrowly missing a car that swerved and beeped at me. I jammed it into drive and hit the accelerator. As I drove down the familiar street, I adjusted my rearview mirror so I could see out the back properly. In it I saw Diarmuid running after me, getting smaller and smaller.

My heart let out a whine. But I kept driving.

I was breathing heavily, my mind racing as I drove to the station where Diarmuid worked.

I parked illegally on the footpath and tumbled out of the truck.

It was a fucking zoo. There were photographers and reporters everywhere, all clamoring to get a piece of my father, who was being led from an armoured van into the station by a group of Gards.

"Da," I screamed through the crowd, trying to get to the only family I had left.

He didn't hear me.

He couldn't hear me over the crowd of animals, all yelling at him, all wanting their pound of flesh. *Shut up, shut up everyone.*

"Da," I screamed again.

I tried to push my way through the crowd. But it was too thick and too deep. They were vicious animals who pushed back. I got an elbow into the side of my ribs, and I let out a cry as pain throbbed through me.

My da disappeared inside the station, a man in a suit striding out to address the crowd. He waved his hands for silence.

"My name is Niall Lynch, and I'm the head of the drug squad here in Limerick."

Lights from photographers' cameras flashed as the

crowd pressed in as if to hear him better.

"I confirm that we have raided a large property twenty minutes north of here that was being used as a drug manufacturing plant. We have arrested Liam Byrne, notorious head of one of the largest drug syndicates in West Ireland."

"Mr Lynch. Mr Lynch," reporters began to yell out. "What gave you the tipoff? What was the value of the drugs that you found? How big was the operation?"

Mr Lynch waved at the crowd to be silent again.

"I'll answer your questions one by one. I'll start by saying that this win for the people of Ireland is due to the tireless efforts of the drug squad and especially to the information gathered by one of our top people, Garda Diarmuid Brennan, who was doing some recon work for us."

No.

It couldn't be.

Diarmuid was working for the drug squad?

He… He used me.

He betrayed me.

"Saoirse!"

Someone grabbed me from behind and spun me.

Diarmuid was standing there, holding me. How the hell did he get here so fast? He must have flagged down a vehicle or something.

"Saoirse, let's get out of here."

"Let go of me." I tried to yank my arm out of his.

"Saoirse, dammit." He grabbed me around the waist, hauling me out of the crowd. "Not here where the reporters can hear you."

I let him drag me to his truck, parked up on the sidewalk halfway down the block.

He pressed me up against the passenger door, his fingers on my face, pushing back my hair, begging with me, pleading with me. "Saoirse listen—"

"I'm not listening to you. You *used* me. Everything you said to me was a *lie*."

"You don't really believe that." He grabbed my chin, forcing me to look at him. "Look at me. Tell me you don't think what I feel for you is the realest fucking thing on this planet."

I saw the pain there in his eyes, the anguish and the love.

I tore my eyes away, not wanting to believe, not wanting to let him in again where he could hurt me.

"Liar! You're working for the drug squad, that man just fucking said so. Was that why you slept with me? Because you wanted info about my father?"

"No, Saoirse. Let me explain."

"Leave me alone," I screamed, shoving him back. "I hate you, I fucking hate you."

I ran from him, ignoring his calls for me to stop.

And my heart broke. Not just for my da, who I'd lost, but for the man I thought I loved who had turned on me.

69

Saoirse

I ran until I was exhausted and collapsed, scraping my knees on the ground. I had no idea where I was, lying on the sidewalk, gravel biting at my skin.

I felt a strong pair of arms lifting me, then carrying me like a baby. Diarmuid's scent covered me like a blanket. I wanted to melt into him and yet I wanted to shove him away. I had energy for neither.

He must have been following me in his truck as I ran myself to exhaustion. The bastard. Why couldn't he just leave me alone?

And yet, a deep part of me sagged with relief at the safety I felt in his arms.

He placed me gently into the passenger seat of his

truck, and he buckled me in with care. I slumped in my seat, no energy left, as he drove me back to my house.

At my house, he tucked me into bed and kissed my forehead. "I'm not leaving."

"Well you're not sleeping in my bed," I hissed.

He flinched and nodded. "I'll take the couch."

He turned the light off and paused at the door, looking like he wanted to say something. He closed the door behind him and my soul cried for him to return, the spot beside me feeling cold and empty.

I didn't think I'd ever get to sleep. But somehow, I did.

The next morning the house was searched thoroughly by a team of Garda. I sat wrapped in my blanket in the living room, Diarmuid standing by watching me like a bodyguard. I couldn't bring myself to say anything to him. I couldn't even look at him.

I found out that my father had been charged with drug possession, manufacturing with intent to distribute.

I expected to be arrested with every breath. But it never happened.

The Garda didn't find anything incriminating at the house. As I knew they wouldn't. My da made sure he never brought anything back here.

"What happens now?" I asked one of the Gards, a middle-aged woman with blonde hair tied back in a ponytail. Out of all the guards she was the only woman, and for some reason I felt she mightn't be as bad as the others.

"Well, you're eighteen so you can stay here for now

without a guardian. Your father's lawyer should be by soon to advise you of your rights to the property."

"Is this my house?"

"For all intents and purposes…yes."

I pointed to Diarmuid, still standing silently in the corner. "Then get him the fuck out of here. I don't want him here."

Diarmuid straightened, took a step towards me. "Saoirse."

"Don't fucking let him near me," I screamed, my voice and body shaking. "Traitor. Betrayer."

The lady Garda placed a firm hand on Diarmuid's shoulder. Diarmuid didn't argue anymore as he left with them.

And I was left alone.

Over the next few days, Diarmuid came by several times a day, knocking on my door, begging me to open it, asking if I'd eaten. If I was warm enough.

I refused to let him in. I refused even to talk back.

I was a jumble of conflicting pieces, of warring sides, of clashing loyalties.

The man I loved had let my father get arrested. Now my da was going away for a long time.

If your father hadn't been doing the wrong thing…another voice argued.

Still, logic seems like a distant island when you're drowning in a sea of pain.

Today the knock on my door came again as I sat wrapped in that same blanket on the couch, staring at the fireplace.

Again, I ignored it. It usually took about twenty minutes for Diarmuid to give up.

"Saoirse?" a male voice called through the door. It wasn't Diarmuid's voice. "Open up, honey."

I sat up. "Who is it?"

"Brian O'Leary."

Diarmuid's old JLO officer. I walked slowly to the door, frowning. Did Diarmuid bring Brian this time to help convince me to open up?

"Diarmuid's not with me," Brian said as if he'd read my mind.

I opened the door. Indeed, it was only Brian who stood on my front step.

"If you are here to try to convince me——"

"I'm just here to see how you are," Brian said, lifting his palms up as if in surrender. "I'm not here for Diarmuid. He doesn't know I'm here."

I eyed Brian suspiciously for a second before I stepped aside and let him in.

Out of instinct, because it has been bred into every single Irish person, I went straight to the kitchen and put on the kettle to make us tea. I placed the Barry's teabags in the cups, a timeworn tradition, and poured in the water just off the boil, letting it brew before throwing away the bags.

I carried a small tray holding our cups, a small pitcher of milk and a bowl of sugar to the living room because everybody was fussy about how they took their tea.

Brian and I sat opposite each other. I spooned two lumps of sugar into my tea and stirred before pouring in half a finger of milk. I liked my tea sweet and milky.

"So…" I said.

Brian took a sip of his tea, a dash of milk with no sugar. "So, how are you?"

"Grand, yeah."

Brian nodded slowly. "How are you really?"

My shoulders sagged. "I'm angry. I can't believe he would screw over my father like that."

"Your father was doing some illegal things, wasn't he?"

I didn't answer, reality a knot in my throat that I couldn't swallow.

"From what I hear the drug squad was moving in on his operation anyway. His arrest would have come sooner or later."

I fidgeted with my hands on my lap.

Sooner or later, the devil catches up with you.

I thought about my mum and my da, and realised how true this was.

I owed the devil, too.

"I keep waiting for the Garda to knock down my door, to arrest me for my part in my father's business," I said. "I know I deserve it. I just feel like such an idiot."

Brian's eyes widened. "You don't know, do you, girl?"

"Know what?"

Brian set down his tea and leaned forward with his elbows on his knees. "Diarmuid made a deal for you. All of your involvement has been wiped from the record in exchange for him handing over your father. No one is gonna to come and arrest you. You have full immunity. A second chance."

A second chance.

I squeezed my eyes shut as they began to burn with tears. This was what Diarmuid was talking about when he said a second chance. He was trying to tell me what he had done for me. Instead I had been too angry to listen to him. Too certain that he had betrayed me when in fact he had saved me. My father was going down, that much was certain. But Diarmuid made sure that I wasn't pulled down with him.

When I opened my eyes Brian was watching me, concern on his face.

"Oh, Brian, I've been so cruel to him. I shut him out."

Brian shot me a small smile. "You have, but it's fixable."

"What if it's too late?"

He shook his head. "I would have been furious at Diarmuid for getting involved with you if I hadn't seen you two together. If I didn't see the way you two looked at each other, so real and...pure. He loves you as much as a man could love a woman. He'd forgive you almost anything. If you'd just ask."

That's when I realised that Diarmuid was the only one who ever loved me truly, He put my needs, my wants over his own.

Something my father never did.

70

Diarmuid

It'd been five days since Saoirse told me to get the fuck out of her house.

Five days that have felt like five years.

I stood in the shower, my forehead leaning against the cold tiles basically holding me up, hot water beating down on my back, trying to wash away my sins. Hah. They were too ingrained for that.

I missed Saoirse.

Missed her sass.

Missed her cooking.

Missed her presence beside me in the truck. On my couch. In my bed.

Under me. Over me. Pressed between me and the

mattress. The counter. The wall.

Even missed her yelling at me. Because even when she was yelling at me, at least she was talking to me. At least I had hope of talking my way back into her good books.

Every day when I went over to her house she refused to even answer me even as I knocked for ages. So long that the neighbours started staring from their windows, glaring at me with eyes that said, *keep that up and we're calling the Gards.*

I didn't do it right, when her dad was arrested. I should have taken the time to explain it to her. I shouldn't have let her run off.

I knew she was going to be mad, but…

I had no choice.

That fucker of a father was going down. I was not going to let him take her down too. Even if it meant bending rules. Rules I thought I'd never break.

Until her.

She broke *all* my rules.

A knock banged through my house. I growled and turned off the shower. Can't a guy wallow in peace, for fuck's sake?

I wrapped a towel around my waist, my long hair dripping water onto my shoulders, and strode towards the front door as it banged again.

"I'm coming," I yelled. "Fucking calm down," I added in a mutter.

I undid the latch and yanked open the door.

Saoirse stood on my porch, the Irish drizzle sparkling

off her hair like snowflakes.

She was here.

She came back to me.

Her eyes flashed with anguish when they locked onto mine. She'd been in just as much pain as I had these five days apart. Five days too fucking long.

"Diarmuid, I'm—"

I grabbed her, not caring who might be watching, yanking her against me and crushing my lips to hers.

Suddenly I could breathe again.

She moaned into my mouth and wrapped her legs around my waist as I stepped us inside enough so I could kick the door shut behind her.

I drank all her apologies on her tongue. I didn't need to hear it. She had nothing to be sorry for.

Actually, she did have something to be sorry for.

I tore my mouth off hers and glared at her.

She whimpered even as she clung to me like a monkey, her fingers tangling in my wet hair. "Are you mad?"

I nodded.

"I'm sor—"

"I gave you a bloody key," I growled. "What the hell are you doing standing out there in the rain *waiting* for me to let you in?"

Her eyes widened. "That's what you're mad about?"

I nodded.

Her eyes softened. "I didn't feel right just coming in. We haven't spoken in days."

"I gave you a goddamn key. Which means you come

in whenever you want. No matter if we're fighting. Or if I'm mad at you. My house is open to *you*. Period."

Tears rimmed her lashes. Fuck, I've made her cry.

"What's wrong, selkie?" I whispered.

She shook her head. "I love you."

That was all I needed.

I took her lips once more, infusing my kiss with the claim over her I'd been so afraid of until now.

Saoirse had been right when she accused me of using the overseas scholarships to push her away. I had been. Just like I used her father's arrest to push her away. To sabotage us.

Because deep down I didn't believe she was mine.

But these five days without her—these five days thinking I'd lost her—made me realise this. Made me pray to fucking God that if he gave me one more goddamn chance, I would grab onto her and never fucking let go.

I'd prayed to God to bring her back. And here she was on my porch. He gave her back to me.

She was the sky my soul circled in. Without her, my world had no air.

She was *mine*.

Not caring that we were both wet, I carried her into my bedroom. I stripped her of all her clothes, kissing each inch of skin that it revealed, making her moan louder and louder.

"I'm going to make you scream until you're hoarse," I promised her. "Until the neighbours call the fucking Garda on us."

Oh, the irony.

I held her hips down and plunged my tongue into her wet sweet centre. She thrashed on the bed and cried out my name.

Just before she crested the wave, I pulled back.

"Asshole," she yelled at me, shooting me a glare that would make the balls of a lesser man shrivel.

"I want to *feel* you coming around my cock. Need to feel it."

She shuddered as she looked up at me through damp lashes. "Okay."

As I reached over to the nightstand to grab a condom, her soft little hands wrapped around my dick and stroked it, running her thumb over the tip to spread the wetness around the head of my cock.

A shiver racked through my spine. Fuck. I almost came right there.

"Love your hands on me. But I need to be inside you more. I need to put this on." I waved the condom packet. "Five days is too long, selkie."

"I'm clean and I'm on the pill," she blurted out.

Bareback.

Oh fuck me.

My pretty little selkie wanted me to ride her bareback. I might have died and gone to Heaven.

She chewed her lip. "But if you don't want to—"

"I do." I threw the condom aside. "I'm clean. Got tested right after Ava. Haven't been with anyone else since."

She opened her thighs for me as I settled between them. I twisted my fingers into her hair, pulling it firmly so she was forced to look at me.

"Everything in my life has been preparing me for you. Here. Now," I muttered, my voice as soft as my hands were rough. "Couldn't love anyone else 'cause I was waiting for you."

I thrust inside her.

Claiming her.

Marking her soul with mine.

She let out a cry which I drank. I drank all her moans as I slammed into her, her body taking me, feeling like a piece of wet heaven, my soul drunk, my body burning as if soaked in whiskey and set alight.

It must have been all too much. The time apart. Her desperation after the wave I'd not allowed her to crest before.

She began to shake underneath me, thighs trembling, her hips bucking up to greet mine.

I watched her face as she came, the most beautiful fucking thing I'd ever seen. No inhibitions, no masks, just her pleasure open like a rose just for me.

My beautiful selkie.

But it wasn't enough.

I pulled out of her. Grabbed her hips and flipped her around, lifting her ass so she was on all fours.

"Diarmuid, what—?"

I slammed back into her, aiming right for that g-spot on the front wall of her pussy.

I knew I'd hit it when she let out an "oh my God" in a high-pitched voice, her surprised voice.

Yes, beautiful girl. You're going to come twice.

My thrusts turned into a relentless pounding. I reached around her and vibrated the pad of my fingers against her clit.

"Again," I demanded.

She screamed. Her body wracking and shaking. Her pussy clenching around my cock so hard I thought she might break me.

I couldn't hold on. My orgasm flashed through me like lightning and I let out a roar as I came inside her.

I clutched at her and collapsed, rolling to the side so I didn't crush her.

One day, I was going to come inside her when she wasn't on the pill.

One day. When she was ready.

I let out a sigh. So contented. So sated with my beautiful girl right here where she belonged.

I softened and felt myself slipping out of her.

Saoirse turned over to look at me, her cheek resting on my arm. "I'm all wet."

I smirked. "You're always wet around me."

She rolled her eyes. "No, silly. *More* wet than usual."

She reached down between her legs, then held up a dab of my come glistening on the end of her finger. Her eyes burned into mine as she stuck it into her mouth and sucked it right off, moaning under her breath.

Dear fucking God.

"That was so fucking hot."

It was her turn to smirk.

I rolled us so I was on my back and she was straddled over me. I lay there my eyes greedy for her, memorising her every curve, each freckle on her creamy skin, the exact shade of pink of her nipples. She rocked her hips back and forth along my length that was growing again.

I would never get sick of this woman.

I would never get sick of her, but...

I paused, my fingers stilling her hips.

She gave me a questioning look.

"So," I said, clearing my voice, "you still wanna stay here in Limerick? Be...someone's?"

Mine?

But I was too chicken shit to say it out loud.

She shook her head.

My heart dropped, cracking against the floor.

"I don't want to be *someone's*. I want to be *yours*."

The grin that burst from me hurt my cheeks.

"You are mine." I grabbed her hand and placed it on my selkie tattoo, right over my heart, right where she'd burrowed her way in and would never get out.

"You have my skin," she said as she slid down on me again.

"And you have mine."

The next morning, I woke up before my selkie. I slipped out to the kitchen to make her breakfast.

I scrambled up the eggs just like my girl taught me, seasoned them, kept the heat on low so they'd get nice and fluffy. I put the toast on at the last minute so it would be done just as the eggs were done.

I plated them up and placed the plates on a tray with

napkins.

Perfect.

I strode into the bedroom, a shit-eating grin on my face and froze.

Saoirse was awake, sitting on the edge of the bed, playing with something tiny in her fingers. The bedside drawer was still open from last night when I grabbed the condom that I never used. She must have spotted the damn thing in there…

I slid the tray to the bedside table and sat down beside her.

She lifted the thin gold band to the light. "I forget that you're married to someone else."

The sadness in her voice broke my fucking heart. I would give anything—*anything*—to take it away.

"She and I are over. We're so over I forgot I even had this stupid thing." I took the ring off her and tossed it in the trash.

"Diarmuid!"

I grabbed her hands and kneeled in front of her. "I want to be with you. I'm yours, selkie."

"Not completely."

I squeezed my eyes shut. I was still a married man. I was a selfish fucking bastard for wanting her to stay with me even before my divorce was final.

I opened my eyes to face her. "If you'd rather wait until I get divorced—"

"No!" Her eyes widened. "Diarmuid, no. I…forget I said anything. Forget that I even found the ring…" her voice trailed off.

I knew she wouldn't forget it.

If only I could go back in time, reverse the day I wed Ava out of a sense of duty. If only I could go into the future where I could put a ring on Saoirse's finger and one on mine claiming me as hers.

Saoirse and I got into bed and ate our now cold breakfast. As always, the room soon filled with laughter and smiles. But that ring was like a splinter in both our hearts. One that both of us tried to ignore, digging in every time one of us smiled.

On the first day I could, I vowed, I would apply for that divorce. The next day, I'd have a ring on Saoirse's finger.

Until then, I had to hold on to my girl as best as I could and hope life didn't find some reason to tear us apart.

71

Saoirse

Life was perfect.

I had Diarmuid and he was mine, truly mine this time.

Except we still snuck around like teenagers. We still barely went out in public together. If we did, we never touched in case someone was looking. We mostly stayed at his place, cooking dinner, watching movies, reading old Irish stories and legends to each other from a book he'd been given by Brian.

Diarmuid got me a part-time job at O'Malley's gym doing the accounts. I was able to keep padding out the money in my accounts, aiming for university.

Until *that letter* came in the mail.

The letter postmarked from Australia.

I was home alone, Diarmuid having dropped me off before he went to work. I tore it open, my heart beating in my throat, knowing full well where it came from.

Congratulations, Miss Quinn. We are pleased to offer you a full science scholarship to the University of Queensland, one of the top universities in Australia...

I'd gotten in.

I'd forgotten that I'd applied to all those college scholarships in a rage after Diarmuid and I had that fight.

They'd awarded me—*me*—a full scholarship. That meant I didn't have to wait to study. I didn't have to pay for tuition, for books. They were even offering housing for the full three years.

Oh my God.

Here was my chance to get out of Ireland. To see the world. To see what else was out there...

Diarmuid. I had to tell Diarmuid.

Except... My heart twisted. He'd make me accept it. How could I pass up this opportunity? He'd make me take it. He'd never forgive me if I didn't.

But he'd never leave Ireland. His job was here, his passion, his life's purpose. He'd be here and I'd be there and... Australia was so far away. Literally the other side of the world.

My heart cried out, tearing in two. The degree was three years. Could I stand being apart from— No, I

552

couldn't. I couldn't be apart from him for even three *days*...

Three years.

We'd already spent three years apart.

I wasn't doing that again.

No. I was staying in Ireland with Diarmuid and that was that.

I couldn't tell Diarmuid about this letter.

I wouldn't.

I didn't need this offer.

I was happy. Right here. With him.

I reread the letter, allowing myself a moment to dream.

Of Australia. Land of sandy beaches, palm trees, koalas. Of beautiful weather and vast sunburned horizons and the bluest sky you'd ever seen. At least, that's what I'd read.

I had four weeks to accept or decline their offer via a link to their website.

I should log onto that link and decline it. Right now.

Except something made me fold up the acceptance letter and slip it into the bottom of a bag in my closet.

Where it would burn a hole. For the next few days, at least...

72

Diarmuid

Days later I'd almost forgotten about the ring incident.

I'd certainly forgotten about it when I got this text from my girl as I was sitting at my desk at work.

Saoirse: Guess what's for dessert tonight?

Me: You. Naked.

Saoirse: Diarmuid…

Me: Saoirse…

A media message came through. It was a picture of an unbaked apple pie. I let out a laugh.

Me: We never did get to get that apple pie four years ago, did we?

Saoirse: Better late than never!

Me: Then I'm eating your pie

Saoirse: Diarmuid!

Me: ;)

I placed down my phone onto my desk piled with papers and files. My girl—my fucking girl—was in my house cooking our dinner. I couldn't wait to see her.

I didn't think I'd ever been so happy. I didn't think I *could* be this happy.

It might just have been a perfect day.

Of course, something had to come and fuck it up.

It came walking right up to my desk wearing a pair of red shiny stilettos.

"Mr Brennan."

I looked up at the devil wearing tight skinny jeans and an even tighter white jumper that showed off her cleavage.

Fuck my life.

"Who the hell let you in, Ava?" I growled.

The front desk knew not to let her in. She must have

556

sweet-talked a newbie or slithered her way in somehow.

"Why wouldn't they let me in? I'm *still* Mrs Brennan." Ava pouted and tapped her lacquered nails on my desk as she bent over, showing off her cleavage.

I merely sneered at her attempts to ensnare me. They wouldn't work.

Not now.

Not ever.

"Not for long," I said, slapping a finger to the calendar on my desk, to a date I'd marked in a red circle a few months away.

Ava flinched. "What's that?"

"The day I serve divorce papers on your sorry fucking ass."

"Diarmuid!"

"Go away, Ava. You're wasting your fucking time here."

Her eyes softened and she looked about to cry. I was not falling for her crocodile tears.

"There's someone else, isn't there?"

"Jesus, Ava—"

"Are you seeing someone else? Tell me, I have a right to know."

I slammed my fist on my desk, making a loud bang. I sensed my colleagues' heads snap towards us, but I ignored them, focusing instead on the face of the woman who I almost had a family with. I hardly recognised her.

"You," I pointed a finger at her, "have no fucking right. You moved in with that asswipe *two weeks* after we separated. You lost your fucking rights long ago. Now, get out of here, before I have you escorted out."

Her lip trembled. Ah fuck. She was going to cry. Liquid manipulation. Boy, had I fallen for it too many times. I would not hang around long enough this time to allow her to manipulate me. Not again.

I snatched the closest file from my desk. "Excuse me. Some of us have work to do. See yourself out."

I strode away down the hall until I found an empty interrogation room, slamming the door behind me and leaning my forehead against the door.

The only thing that could calm me down was knowing that my woman—my selkie—was at home waiting for me. And there was nothing—*nothing*—Ava could do about it.

73

Saoirse

I was making Dublin Cobble and apple pie for tonight's dinner, a mirror of our last dinner together four years ago.

The pie was in the oven and the cobble was almost done. It just needed ten more minutes on the stove.

The doorbell rang.

I gasped as a thrill rushed through me, causing my heart to beat faster. Would it ever get old having Diarmuid come home to me?

Never.

I untied my apron and slid my feet into a pair of nude stilettos.

Here was the second part of my surprise for him.

Me.

Wrapped in sexy white lacy underwear and stockings underneath my silk gown. It was cold outside, so I had to turn up the heating in the house so as not to freeze my butt off.

The doorbell rang again.

"Coming, baby," I yelled out as I tottered towards the door.

I felt so sexy, like a woman. I couldn't wait for him to see me.

I flung open the door, already pouting.

It wasn't Diarmuid at the door.

It was Ava.

Diarmuid's *wife*.

As beautiful as the last time I saw her. Standing there in tight skinny jeans and a white jumper that showed off her boobs, boobs that were still bigger than mine.

Of course, why would Diarmuid ring the doorbell? He had a key. I was so stupid.

I stiffened as her eyes rolled over me.

"Can I help you?" I said, tucking my robe further across my body. I told myself it was against the chill coming in from outside, not from the chill that radiated off her.

"You must be Saoirse." Her voice coiled around me like a snake. "You've certainly grown up since the last time we saw each other."

"Again," I said, through gritted teeth, "how can I help you?"

"We need to talk."

She shoved her way inside before I could stop her.

"I hope you're enjoying playing house," she sniped. "It won't last long."

I slammed the door shut to keep out the cold and spun. "You are not wanted here. Leave before Diarmuid gets home. Or I'll call the Garda."

She placed her scarlet-painted fingernails on her wide hips. "If you don't want Diarmuid to be arrested because of you, you'll listen to me, you little homewrecker."

Arrested?

"I know who you are. And what you've done." Ava pulled out a slim black mobile and waved it. "I've read all your dirty little text messages, including the ones from when you were *underage*."

Oh my God.

That was Diarmuid's phone.

How the fuck did she get a hold of it?

"The truth is, Saoirse," Ava strolled towards me, "Diarmuid is *my* husband. Mine. We deserve a chance to make it work."

"Those text messages…" I didn't think for a second they'd be used against him. "They're just words. He never touched me until I was eighteen."

I was lying.

He did touch me.

I let him.

Seventeen was legal in Ireland.

But what had Diarmuid said? I had to be eighteen to be legal for him because he was in a position of authority.

Ava put on a face of mock sympathy. "I don't think

the judge will see it that way, nor will his supervisor. The Garda can't be seen to be employing *pedophiles*, can they?"

Pedophile?

I choked on the disgusting word.

Diarmuid wasn't a pedophile. I was an adult. He loved me. He was the only person who truly cared about me. How could she taint the purity of what we had by even using that word?

But reality was a cold wind blowing through my heart. The sexy text messages on Diarmuid's phone were enough to incriminate him. To mark him. Brand him. People already wanted to think the worst of the long-haired, inked-up, gruff Irish giant.

The truth didn't matter.

"W-what do you want?" I asked, my chin still lifted as Ava came to stand right in front of me, so close I could smell the stench of her thick sickly-sweet perfume.

"Leave him."

"What?"

"Leave my husband. Go far away if you have to."

I shook my head. "He won't let me go."

She sneered. "Make up some excuse. You're a clever girl, you'll figure out what to say. Otherwise I take these messages to his boss. He'll be fired and arrested for statutory rape of a minor."

No!

Her words were like splinters digging into my skin. I could barely breathe, my chest was so tight.

Ava smiled, and it felt like poison. Then she drove the knife in deeper. "You don't tell him where you're going or give him any way to contact you. You leave Diarmuid and me to work things out. If you contact him, I'll call the Gards. If you see him again, I'll call the Gards. Understand?"

I was numb.

What choice did I have?

I would not be Diarmuid's ruin.

I could not destroy him and everything he held dear.

Somehow, I managed to nod.

Ava grinned, a painted pink smear that split open her face. "Good girl."

She patted my cheek and strode past me, bashing my shoulder as she went. I didn't have the strength to cry out. I just swayed like a tree about to be toppled.

Only with the slamming of the door did I come back to life.

The first sob tore out of my lungs.

I clutched at the back of the armchair so that I didn't fall. I wailed and cried like my world was ending. In some ways, it was. In other ways, it was already over.

I remembered the story of the selkie that Diarmuid told me when I was younger. How the selkie woman shifted to her seal form to save Kagan, her true love, but in doing so she could never return back to him.

This is what I had to do.

If I stayed, I'd ruin him.

And I couldn't be his ruin. I loved him too much.

To save him, I had to give up my life with him.

74

Diarmuid

"Selkie, I'm home." I pushed open my front door, expecting a smiling bundle of joy to run into my arms.

The lights were off. I heard no movement. But I could smell something amazing coming from the kitchen.

Strange.

I walked through the silent living room and into the kitchen. There was a baked pie in the oven and what looked like Dublin Cobble in the pot, but all the appliances were off.

Even stranger.

"Saoirse?"

I walked into the bedroom next. Rose petals were strewn over the bed. On the back of a chair was a silk gown and an underwear set I'd not seen before.

Where was she?

I called out her name again as I entered the bathroom.

My eyes flashed to the sink.

Her toothbrush was gone.

Her toiletries in the shower…also gone.

I walked back into the bedroom and flung open the cupboard. The few clothes hanging on her side were gone. What the hell was going on?

Where was my damn phone?

Fuck. I must have left it at work.

I strode into the living room and grabbed my house phone off the kitchen bench, thankful that I still hadn't gotten rid of this relic as did most of the people I knew. I punched in Saoirse's number and ran my hands through my hair as the call tone sounded in my ear.

A shrill ringtone sounded out from the bedroom.

Holding the cordless phone in my hand, still ringing, I hurried back into the bedroom.

Saoirse's phone was on the dresser.

"Fuck," I yelled out and threw the cordless phone against the wall with a crash.

Where the hell was she? Why did she leave without her phone? Where did she go?

Relax, Diarmuid. She must have popped down the road to the shops.

Taking her toothbrush?

I spotted a piece of paper underneath her phone. I pushed the phone out of the way and grabbed the paper.

It was a letter, tear-stained and partly crumpled. I could almost see her writing it out, tears falling, her fingers clutching at the page.

I'm so sorry to have to tell you this… Believe me, I never wanted to cause you any pain. I hope one day you'll forgive me.

You see, I've realised that you were right. I don't want to be young and stuck in this shitty town with a boring old husband. I don't want to be an eighteen-year-old wife.

I want more from this life.

*I want more than…*you.

I'm leaving. And I'm not coming back.

I'm sorry.

I am a selkie and you need to set me free.

Please don't come looking for me.

Please be happy.

S

I dropped the letter, my head spinning.

This was not happening. This wasn't real.

Saoirse loved me.

I didn't fucking believe for a second she would come to this decision on her own.

Was this her father who had somehow managed to get one of his men on the outside to take her?

Did they threaten her? Was that why she fled?

I grabbed Saoirse's cell phone, jammed it into my pocket and strode through the house to the front door, swiping my car keys as I went.

I would not stop looking until I found her.

I yanked open the door only to find someone standing on my step, hand lifted to knock.

"Not now, Ava," I growled, pushing past her. Right now, you were either Saoirse or in my way of finding Saoirse.

"Diarmuid," she chased me down the path as I aimed for my truck, "where are you going?"

"To find something I've lost," I muttered.

"Stop. Will you just listen to me?" She grabbed my arm as I unlocked the driver's door.

I spun, glaring at her. "You don't fucking get it, do you? I don't want you anymore. Not even if there was nobody else. Not even if you were the last fucking woman on this planet."

She gasped.

I yanked my arm out of her grasp, slid into the driver's seat and slammed the door in her face.

That brought her back to life.

"You're going to regret this, Diarmuid," she yelled, her voice muffled through the door.

I rolled my eyes, reversing the truck onto the street.

I already regretted her. How could I possibly regret her any more? I shoved Ava out of my thoughts. The only thing I cared about right now was finding Saoirse.

On the way to Saoirse's house, I rang Brian. He picked up on the third ring.

"Have you seen Saoirse this evening?" I demanded before he even got a word in.

"What? No. Why are you calling from her phone?"

Fuck.

"Ring me on this number if you see her. She's missing. I think it might be her da."

I caught the beginning of a curse before I hung up.

Minutes and several speeding limits broken later, I skidded up onto the sidewalk in front of Saoirse's house. All the lights were off. I ran up to the door and banged on it anyway, calling out her name over and over.

"No one's home, lad," a male voice called to my left.

I turned my head to find the neighbour sticking his head out the next door.

"You sure?"

"Sure as night follows day."

I nodded thanks to him and ran back to the truck. If she didn't come home, where else would she go?

I thought over her note. The clothes and toiletries missing.

Fuck.

I slammed my foot on the accelerator and headed for the train station.

I parked illegally and ran into the station, my Garda badge out as well as a photo of Saoirse I'd found on her phone ready on the screen.

I ran up to the front of the queue at the nearest ticket booth. "Excuse me, Garda business," I muttered, ignoring the muffled protests of the travelers waiting in line.

"Have you seen this girl tonight?"

The lady behind the counter shook her red hair, her eyes looking like owls from behind her thick frames.

"Look closer. Please. Did she come in, buy a ticket?"

The lady leaned in to the phone screen, then shook her head again.

I went to the next counter. Asked the same question. Got the same response.

I pushed to the front of the last counter.

"Please," I begged, "tell me you've seen her."

"Have, actually."

My eyes snapped up. The man behind the counter was a latte-skinned gentleman, dark hair, Mediterranean I guessed, probably in his early twenties.

"Are you pulling my leg?"

"No, sir." He grabbed the phone and moved it up to his face. "Yeah, I remember her 'cause she was crying, her eyes all red and puffy." His eyes narrowed at me. "You ain't the one who made her cry, no?"

"Fuck no," I growled. "I'm trying to find her."

"She in trouble?"

Truth was, I had no fucking clue what was going on.

I ignored his question. "Do you remember what ticket she bought?"

He nodded slowly, suspicion still clouding his eyes. "Can I see that badge again, please?"

Oh, for fuck's sake.

I pushed the badge at him; he peered at it. Then glanced at me. "How do I know it's not fake?"

I was going to kill this man.

"It's not fucking fake. Just tell me where the girl went." I let out a long breath, trying to calm myself down. "Please," I said in a softer voice. "She could be in danger."

The ticket man slid my badge back towards me and sniffed. "She bought a one-way ticket to Dublin. Train she was on left about ten minutes ago."

I sagged with relief. Finally, I knew where she was going.

"Just one more question, please? Did she come with anyone? Was anyone forcing her to go with him?"

"No, she looked alone."

Alone?

Why would Saoirse flee to Dublin alone?

I would ask her. If I sped, then I could make it to Dublin Heuston Station before her train pulled in.

I ran back into my truck, calling my thanks to the ticket seller. I already had my foot on the accelerator before my door was shut properly. I headed towards the highway which would take me all the way across the country to Dublin.

Her train left about ten minutes ago which meant I had just over two hours to get from here to there.

I could make it. If I toed the speed limit all the way.

I yanked the wheel of the car onto the M7, gunning it into the fast lane, praying that there would be no roadworks or accidents along the way to slow me down.

Five minutes on the highway and the blue lights of the Garda flashed behind me.

Fuck. I checked my speedometer.

I had been going about ten kilometres over, but not too much that I couldn't plead my case, flash my badge and be on my way in less than five minutes.

I flicked on my indicator and pulled over, the patrol

car pulling up behind me.

The officer strolled up to my window that I'd opened.

I didn't recognise him, a short, ruddy-faced man with sideburns. He leaned into my window.

"Do you know how fast you were going there?"

"Sorry, officer. Trust me when I say it's an emergency." I flashed him my badge which he squinted at.

"A fellow Garda," he said, his voice languid and slow. "You weren't setting a right example there, lad. Licence and registration, please."

I handed him my papers. He eyed over them as I fidgeted in my seat.

"We're just going to run this through the system. Standard procedure. Sit tight now."

I let out a long breath. So much for a quick getaway.

I drummed my fingers on the wheel, praying that they'd hurry the hell up. There'd be no problems with my papers. My registration was current, I had no outstanding fines or speeding tickets.

A few seconds later the officer returned to my window. I should have known something was wrong when I caught sight of the other officer behind him.

"Step out of the car."

"What? Can you tell me what's the problem, officer? I really have to be somewhere."

"Step out of the car," he simply repeated.

Fuck me.

Better get this over with.

I stepped out of the truck. In a flash the officer had spun me around, my arm around my back, and pushed me up against my truck.

What the fuck?

"Diarmuid Brennan, you're under arrest for statutory rape of a minor."

75

Saoirse

Dublin.

A place I didn't think I'd be returning to any time soon. It seemed to me a grotty hole, filled with every sad memory of mine.

Every time I'd arrived here I'd been crying. Where we moved after my da was arrested. When my ma died. When I left Diarmuid.

Moina nudged my cup of tea closer to me and wrapped her arms around my shoulders. I'd just finished telling her all about what'd happened, tears spilling out from my lids like they were connected to my words.

"I'm sure you'll figure out—"

"There was no other way, Moina. Ava is such a bitch.

She would go straight to the Garda if she didn't get her way. The only way I could save him was to leave him." My voice cracked.

Not even Moina's shushing or arms could comfort me. The only thing that could—that ever really could—was a certain pair of warm, strong arms covered in beautiful ink.

Arms I'd never feel again.

Just when I didn't think my heart could shatter any further, it did. I pressed my face into my hands as another wave of tears stung my lids, my future stretching like a lonely and broken road.

It took days for me to get enough energy to shower. The hot water beating some element of life into my body.

What the hell was I going to do now? I needed a job, or to study or…a distraction. I couldn't stay at Moina's forever.

Wrapped in a towel, I stood in Moina's bedroom, my bag still on the chair, unpacked. Moina was at work so I was here alone. I pawed through my meagre belongings. A crumple of paper at the bottom of my bag caught my attention.

I pulled it out.

It was my scholarship to University of Queensland in Australia.

The deadline hadn't passed.

I could still accept.

For the first time in days a tiny ray of light peeked through the bleak landscape of my heart.

After I changed I borrowed Moina's laptop and

logged into the university website using the passcode they'd given me.

Welcome, Saoirse Quinn.
Congratulations on being awarded a full scholarship with us. We hope you accept.
Please choose below.

My mouse hovered over the Accept button. Once I accepted there was no going back. I would be moving to the other side of the world where I knew no one. Where no one knew me as the daughter of a criminal.

It would be a fresh start.

A new beginning.

My chest filled with resolve.

Without Diarmuid I needed a new beginning. Outside of Ireland, because everything here and everywhere here just reminded me of him.

I clicked Accept.

76

Diarmuid

I never thought I'd be looking out from this side of the bars.

As I sat in my own cell in Limerick jail, awaiting the arrival of my lawyer, I spotted a lot of my old colleagues peering at me from the entrance to the holding cells, accusing eyes, hateful stares.

I didn't care what they thought.

There was only one person I cared about. And she was getting farther and farther away from me.

It turned out that Ava had stolen my phone from my desk that day she'd confronted me at work. After I rejected her, she'd hand-delivered the phone with Saoirse and my text messages to the nearest Garda station. A warrant was immediately issued for my arrest.

When the highway Gards had run my licence through the database, the outstanding warrant pinged. Hence, my arrest.

My lawyer, Gerard Boland, finally arrived. He was an old friend of Brian's, probably the only reason why he took me on as a client. He sat opposite me in the visitor's room, a damp grey box with no windows, dressed in dark jeans but with a sports jacket on over a white button-up shirt.

For the longest time he just sat there looking at me.

"The charges are bogus," I finally said.

Gerard folded his fingers together calmly, too fucking calmly. "You tried to resist arrest."

I let out a sigh of frustration. "I wasn't resisting arrest. I had something important and time sensitive to do."

"What?"

I remained quiet. There was no way I could admit to chasing after Saoirse, not with this charge over my fucking head. "That's not important anymore."

Any chance I had of intercepting Saoirse at the train station in Dublin was long gone.

The lawyer sighed. "I can't help you if you won't help me."

I leaned in, the cold metal cuffs around my wrists clanking against the edge of the table.

"Find Saoirse," I begged. "She'll testify on my behalf."

But more importantly, *find her.*

77

Saoirse

I clambered out of Moina's car just outside of Terminal 1 at Dublin airport. I pulled my new suitcase only half full out of her trunk and adjusted the carry-on backpack on my back.

"Thanks for dropping me off," I said.

"Of course. Oh, I'm going to miss you, girl," Moina said, her eyes filling with tears.

"I'm going to miss you too." I clasped her in a hug.

She clung to me as if I were a life raft. "You better not forget me. Keep me updated with how you're going."

"I'm going to Skype you so often you'll be sick of me."

"You better."

I pulled away and shot her one last nervous grin before I turned to the terminal.

"I'm so proud of you, Saoirse," Moina called to me as I walked away. "You go kick some Aussie science butt."

I laughed, even though my stomach was twisting in my body.

I checked in.

Then made my way towards the security clearance. Before I passed through, I looked back, expecting to see a certain Irish giant running after me to stop me.

But he wasn't there.

This isn't a cliched movie, stupid girl.

It hurt that he hadn't even bothered to come and find me.

It was what I had intended with my cruel goodbye letter. But deep down I thought he would still come looking anyway.

And now I was leaving to go where he'd never find me.

78

Diarmuid

This last two months had been a fucking headache.

I rubbed my forehead with my fingers, trying to ease the growing headache as I sat in my armchair, my lawyer sitting opposite me on my couch. I'd been released under house arrest, a tag locked around my ankle. It still sat there, beeping every so often to remind me that I was effectively a prisoner.

"I was able to get the text messages thrown out as evidence," Gerard said. "Without the text messages and without Saoirse's testimony they have insufficient evidence."

Neither my lawyer nor the Garda had been able to locate Saoirse. Her bank records showed that she withdrew all of her money five weeks ago, making it impossible to track her.

She could be anywhere.

She might not even be in Ireland anymore. If she were here, she would have stepped forward to clear me. Surely.

"Did the Gards check the passenger manifests of all outgoing flights these last six weeks?" I asked.

Gerard pursed his lips. He was a good enough guy and did his job well, but he was still weary of me.

"The Garda are understaffed, you know this. They're not going to spend manpower chasing after a girl who doesn't want to be found. Besides, they've dropped the criminal case against you for insufficient evidence."

My shoulders sagged.

If I still had my work log-ins, I could walk right into the station and look this information up myself. It would take a while, and my eyes would probably bleed from my head, but I wouldn't stop until I knew where she'd gone.

But there was no way in hell they were going to let me past the front desk.

"You should be happy about this," Gerard said.

"Yeah, I am. You did a good job, thanks."

The damage was done, though. My reputation was ruined.

The Garda had tried to keep my arrest quiet while I was being investigated. It didn't look good for them to hold me up as a public hero one minute for helping with the arrest of Ireland's most notorious drug lord, then demonise me the next for allegedly having a sexual relationship with the said drug lord's daughter.

The story had been leaked anyway. No prizes for guessing who leaked it.

Once the story broke, there was no way the Garda couldn't react.

I was suspended without pay from my JLO position. I'd received hate mail from several parents of kids I'd previously worked with. Someone had spray-painted *pedophile* across the side of my truck.

All these things I could handle.

I'd been hated before when I was a juvenile delinquent and causing trouble. I was judged because of my size, my tats and my gruff demeanour.

This wasn't what cut me.

What cut me was I hadn't been able to go after *her*.

My lead was cold. She could be anywhere by now.

"The Garda should be round soon to take off that cuff." Gerard pointed at my electronic shackle.

I let out a gruff noise. "So, it's over. I can go where I want?"

My lawyer leaned forward, letting out a sigh. "I'm afraid not."

What now?

"It appears Ava is suing you under civil law. She wants to take your house and most of the cash you have saved up because you cheated on her with a minor. In a civil case, unfortunately, the text messages *are* admissible."

"I didn't fucking cheat on Ava. We'd been separated for almost four fucking years."

Gerard shifted in his chair. He always got

uncomfortable when I swore. "Technically you are still married to her."

"She cheated on *me*."

"Do you have proof?"

I spluttered. "Half the fucking city knows. She moved in with the guy."

Gerard tilted his head. "She's claiming that they were just housemates."

I snorted. "She's a fucking liar."

"Unfortunately, unless you have proof, she'll have the upper hand in your divorce proceedings."

I sank my face back into my hands. I was out of a job. This house and my life savings was all that I had. Ava was going to take it from me.

I was so fucked.

79

Saoirse

Sunny Queensland, beautiful one day. Perfect the next.

That's what their slogan was. And it was true. I'd never seen such blue skies in my life. Never felt the heat like I felt here.

The university had set me up in an off-campus student accommodation, a building made up of three- and four-bed apartments filled with only students, only a fifteen-minute walk from campus.

I got along with all three of my female housemates, all of them also doing a science major. Two of them were from Australia, the other an Asian student with perfect English.

I loved my new life: studying, learning and the occasional party (hey, I was a college student after all).

I loved my classes. Loved this sprawling campus with its rows of purple jacaranda trees and beautiful old sandstone buildings curling around open courtyards.

I loved being away from Ireland and no longer being the girl whose ma was a whore or the daughter of a criminal.

But something was missing.

Diarmuid.

For three months I'd missed him so much it felt like I carried a knife around in my guts. I walked around only partly alive, a hollow space sitting in my chest.

I hoped Diarmuid was okay.

I prayed that he didn't hate me too much.

Would this aching ever fade?

Perhaps. Given enough time the wind could brush away a mountain. But by then my body would have long turned to dust and ash.

I emailed Moina often, sometimes daring to ask if she'd heard from him. Her answer, like always, was *no*.

Diarmuid hadn't even come looking for me, it seemed.

This thought always brought a sharp pain to my guts. I shoved it aside. I had been the one who broke his heart. I worded my Dear John letter so that he'd hate me. So it'd be easier to let me go.

Even though I didn't want him to let me go.

Stupid.

"Is this seat taken?"

I shook myself out of my reverie and looked up. Standing by my desk was a boy about my age, blue eyes and a shock of dirty blonde hair cut short. He was the opposite of Diarmuid Brennan if I'd ever seen one.

"No. Go for it."

"I'm Tim," he said as he sat down. He had a cute drawling Australian accent.

"Saoirse," I said as we shook hands.

His hands were soft, unlike Diarmuid's rough ones.

He tilted his head and I noticed how clear his blue eyes were. "Sorry, how do you say your name again?"

"Sier-sha," I pronounced. "It's Irish."

He smiled. "I thought you had a cute accent."

I blinked. He was flirting with me.

"Um, thanks."

"What brings you to Australia?"

I hesitated just for a moment before smiling. "Just needed a change. To see what's out there."

He nodded. "I get you."

He thought he did. But he didn't really.

No one did.

Except for Diarmuid.

A flash of pain went through me at the thought of him. Would there ever be a day when I wasn't reminded of him?

Tim and I chatted while we waited for the lecture to start. He was from a farm in the countryside and he'd moved to Brisbane to study agricultural science. He laughed at my jokes that weren't that funny. And he smiled at me the whole time we were talking.

I couldn't say it wasn't nice to be the centre of someone's attention.

But still, I felt like there was a chasm between us. Like maybe he might not be so friendly if he knew where I'd come from.

"Hey, so... I wasn't here at last week's lecture. I was hoping you'd let me buy you a coffee after class. To pick your brain about what I missed, of course." He smiled at me.

I wasn't so ignorant that I couldn't read between the lines. He was asking me out.

I waited for the flip in my stomach, the kind of flip I got when Diarmuid was around.

It never came.

But Tim was here. And Diarmuid was not. He would never be.

Once again, the pain punched me in the stomach, and I felt for a second like I might pass out.

"You okay?"

I waved off his sweet concerns.

I had to move on. Right? At least, I had to try.

I forced a smile even though I felt like I was betraying Diarmuid. "Sure. Let's have coffee."

80

Diarmuid

I knocked on my supervisor's door.

Coilin's head lifted and his eyes widened for a split second before he waved me in.

I walked into this familiar office for the last time. Sank into the chair in front of him for the last time.

"You look like shit, Diarmuid."

I snorted. "That's what happens when the world turns against you."

Coilin had the decency to look uncomfortable. "The charges against you have been dropped but we—"

I waved my arm at him, cutting him off. "Save it, Coilin. I quit."

Coilin opened his mouth, then shut it. Then he

nodded. "It's for the best, Diarmuid."

Fuck him.

Fuck them all.

I gave the Irish Garda eight years of loyal service and they couldn't even have my back when shit went south.

I would still keep making a difference with troubled teens. That was my life's passion. But I'd just have to find a different way of doing it.

Once I fought my way out of this divorce case with Ava.

I picked up the few personal items at my desk. I could feel everyone's eyes on me, which I ignored. I waved goodbye to Nina, the office girl, probably the only one in here who I actually didn't mind.

"We'll miss you around here, Brennan," she said.

I gave her a half-smile. "No, you won't because I'm a pain in the ass. But thanks for saying so."

No one else spoke to me, no one else came to say goodbye.

Except...

"Brennan!"

Niall Lynch called out to me as I strode down the hallway. I gritted my teeth. He was already in my bad books for letting it slip publicly that *I* had been the one to give him the tip-off about the location of Liam Byrne's drug manufacturing plant. He'd promised me he'd keep me out of it. Fucking liar.

"What the fuck do you want now, Niall?"

"Why are you such a cunt, Brennan? I was coming to wish you well. You could have ended up with a promotion if you hadn't done anything as stupid as fuck your assignment."

I bristled as I turned to face Niall. If he spoke about Saoirse in that way one more fucking time...

"I was *not* fucking my assignment."

Niall let out a snort. He leaned in, voice low. "I know you were sleeping with her, Diarmuid. I *saw you* with her the night I searched her house."

He searched her house.

A puzzle piece clicked into place.

He was the one who had broken into Saoirse's house. He was the guy that knocked her over.

"Hold that." I shoved my box of personal items into the arms of a passing junior.

Crack.

My fist connected with Niall's nose. He sprawled back, landing on his ass on the carpet.

I stood over him and pointed a stern finger at him. "*That's* for hurting her when you knocked her over, asshole."

Then I grabbed my box and stormed out the building, never to return again.

81

Saoirse

I stopped at my door and paused. A hand slid onto my waist and I turned to face him. I looked up into clear blue eyes.

"Thanks for another lovely evening, Tim," I said.

He grinned. "You are very welcome."

He leaned in and pressed his lips to mine. I kissed him back, wrapping my arms around his neck, ignoring the rush of guilt. He was always sweet and soft when I wanted it to be hard and fierce. I wanted to lose myself. I wanted him to make me forget.

Instead, the face of a certain dark-haired giant rose up in my mind as clear as if he were here. I broke off the kiss.

"Good night."

"Hey." Tim kept his arms around me, pressing a kiss to my forehead. "When are you going to be mine, huh?"

I frowned. I hated when he brought this up.

"Tim, we've only been seeing each other for a few weeks."

He let out a groan. "Plenty of time for you to figure out if you want to be with me. I know I want to be with you."

I squeezed my eyes and hid my face in his chest.

Here was a guy who would be good for me. My age, studying the same kind of degree as me, and came from a decent family. The kind of wholesome, sweet guy that a girl like me would be lucky to be attached to.

Why couldn't I just say yes to being his girlfriend?

Diarmuid's face flashed in my mind. And the memory of his hands on me made me shiver even as my insides burned.

I didn't feel this way when Tim touched me or kissed me. We'd done little more than that. I always pulled back and he never pushed although I knew he wanted more, physically and emotionally. I felt like I didn't have much to give and the guilt ate at me. Tim deserved better. I wasn't ready to give up on trying to move on. I had to move on. Right?

I let out a sigh. "I need more time, Tim."

He frowned as he cupped my cheek, pulling my face up to meet his gaze. "Man, that guy really did a number on you, didn't he?"

I stiffened. "What guy?"

"The one who broke your heart so badly that you can't let me in."

I sagged, unshed guilt brimming my eyes, shame burning my cheeks. "How did you know?"

He chuckled, but it wasn't unkind. "I may just be a farmer's boy, but I'm not so naïve, Saoirse. You're holding yourself from me. There has to be a reason." He shrugged. "I guessed at the reason. But you just confirmed it by your response."

I lowered my head, unable to keep looking into his eyes. "I'm sorry."

He pulled me against his body and kissed my forehead again. "It's okay. I can wait."

I squeezed my eyes shut and swore to myself that I'd try—really try to get over Diarmuid.

82

Diarmuid

Four months later... I was still trying to fight Ava in the divorce courts.

All I wanted to do was go after Saoirse. The need to get her back was a like a demon clawing under my skin, every day passing made these devils howl louder.

But I couldn't.

Not now while my life was a fucking mess.

Even if I found Saoirse, begged her to come back to me, how could I expect her to take me back if I was still married to that bitch? What could I offer her, jobless and facing bankruptcy?

Saoirse already wanted *more*, deserved *more*. How could I expect her to take me when I had nothing?

I dragged my sorry ass to my fridge. There was nothing in here but two bottles of pale lager. Declan was right. I needed something stronger than this shit.

It was only eleven a.m. but I'd stopped caring. I grabbed both beer bottles and took the caps off them, settling into my armchair and guzzling one of them down.

A knock sounded at my door. I groaned.

I didn't want to speak or talk to anyone right now.

Declan and Danny had both come to visit me while I was in jail even though I told them not to. Now they were taking turns calling me every other day like I was a kid on suicide watch. I'd been ignoring their calls lately.

That was probably one of them. Or both. No one else except Brian wanted anything to do with me these days.

Perhaps if I ignored them they'd go away?

The knock sounded again.

Ah, fuck.

I got up, grumbling. The poor fucker on the other side of that door was going to hear enough cussing to send him running like the devil was after him.

I yanked open the door, ready to growl at the offending person.

But it wasn't Danny or Declan.

On my step was Maeve, one of Ava's old school friends. The one who became a nurse. She was the most decent of the snippy, bitchy lot. I never did understand why she and Ava were friends.

What the hell did she want?

"Hi, Diarmuid," she said, seeming nervous.

"Let me fucking guess. You're here to deliver a message from the bitch."

Maeve shook her head. "Ava doesn't know I'm here." She glanced around as if checking to see if anyone was watching. "Can I come in?"

I narrowed my eyes at her. I wanted to kick her off my property, to get back to wallowing in peace. But something in her tone made me pause.

Ava didn't know she was here.

Now I was curious. We all know what curiosity did.

I stepped aside and let her in.

Maeve walked a few steps into my living room, then spun to face me. I didn't offer her a seat. Didn't take one myself.

"Talk."

Maeve jolted at my harsh tone. "I...I think what Ava's doing to you is wrong."

Not that Maeve's opinion mattered. But it was still nice to hear, I guess.

"Tell her that."

Maeve shook her head. "Ava won't listen to reason. I couldn't stand by again..." She paused. Swallowed.

Again?

"Maeve," I said slowly, "what do you mean...*again?*"

"I've been so racked with guilt all these years. That's why...that's why I have to tell you... Ava lied to you."

I let out a snort. "Tell me something I don't know."

Maeve shook her head. "No, you don't know *this*. But if you do, perhaps you can use it against her. For the case, I mean. I know she's suing you."

A trickle of hope broke through my grey din. I narrowed my eyes at Maeve. She could be lying. Ava could have sent her over to feed me bullshit to fuck up my case against her.

"How do I know this isn't a trick? Some kind of scheme Ava's cooked up to fuck me up even more."

Maeve's eyes widened. She shook her head vehemently. "I wouldn't. I'm not. She and I aren't even friends anymore."

Strangely I believed her.

"Let's say I believe you. What could you possibly know about Ava that could help me?"

"Four years ago… She was never pregnant."

Everything in my world froze.

The clock ticked.

One second.

Two.

"*What?*"

Maeve shook her head, her eyes growing wide with apprehension. "She was worried you were going to leave her. Said you were spending too much time with this…girl."

Fuck.

"She decided to fake a pregnancy. She knew you'd 'do the right thing'," Maeve marked these bitter words with finger quotes, "you'd marry her, move back here with her."

The fucking bitch.

Anger boiled inside me so hot it felt like it was blistering on my skin.

But on the outside, I was frozen in disbelief that a woman I once shared a bed with could *do such a thing*.

"She asked me to fake the doctor's pregnancy test. Here's the proof." She handed out two slips of paper to me that she pulled from her jacket pocket.

I unfolded them and stared at each one.

On the first paper was a pregnancy test result for someone named Emer Ellis.

"I'm sorry," Maeve said, dipping her chin. "I know I should have told you earlier. I wanted to."

This whole fucking marriage was a sham.

All these years I'd suffered her making a fool out of me while she ran around with my last name and with other men.

I held myself back because I thought to be married to Ava *meant* something.

Half of me wanted to punch a hole in the closest wall. The other part wanted to grab Maeve and shake her. But I forced myself to remain calm, at least on the outside.

Four years ago, I would have blown up, completely lost the plot at this revelation. But now, now just I wanted to be done with Ava.

I wanted it to be done. Out. Over.

Then I could go after what was really important. Or who...

A small, maniacal part of me began to laugh as a plan began to form.

Ava yanked open her apartment door at my banging. "What do ye—? Diarmuid?"

Her hand went to brush back her bedhead, her lids batting at me, her chest pushing out towards me so her robe split apart.

Unbelievable.

I knew she had a guy in there with her. I could fucking smell him on her.

I didn't care one fucking bit.

I pointed my finger in her face. "I know how much of a liar you've been, Ava."

Ava's face changed from sultry to pissed. "If you're not here to play nice, you can speak to my fucking lawyer."

I shoved a copy of the two pregnancy tests in her face. "My lawyer has the originals."

She grabbed the paper, her hands shaking, her mouth dropping open. "Where'd you—?"

"Doesn't matter. I found it."

She looked up at me, fear in her eyes. "I can explain."

"Save it. I didn't come here for an explanation."

Ava swallowed. "What do ye want, Diarmuid? You want me to say I'm sorry?"

"No." I leaned in. "Drop the fucking case, give me a fucking divorce and don't ever EVER darken my door again."

I banged on Moina's door, hoping to hell that she still lived here. Otherwise I was plum out of leads to follow in hunting Saoirse down in Dublin.

I heard footsteps inside and moments later the door opened.

Moina stood in the doorway, barely changed since I saw her last, four years ago.

She jammed her arms across her chest. "It's about bloody time you came looking for her." Moina raised an eyebrow. "What kept ye?"

I snorted. "You haven't seen the news?" I asked in disbelief.

She shook her head. "Don't watch or read that poison. The media is full of shit."

Well, that explained a lot.

"Trust me," I said, "I came as soon as I could."

Moina didn't probe any further, merely stepped aside to let me in.

Her apartment hadn't changed, still neat and cozy. Perhaps a few more used books with well-worn spines crammed into her shelf.

Moina closed the door and I spun to face her.

"So…where is she?"

Moina pursed her lips. "Unfortunately, I've been sworn to secrecy. I can't *tell* you where Saoirse's gone."

"What? Tell me why she left me, then."

Moina pressed her lips together and gave me a look. "I can't *tell* you anything."

"What was the point of letting me in, then?" I spluttered with frustration.

Moina narrowed her eyes at me, then walked over to the bookshelf. "Saoirse was really upset when she arrived

605

here. I can't tell you why, but let's just say, it was not her choice to leave you."

Not her choice…

She was forced? By who?

Ava.

The realisation dawned on me as soon as I asked the question. I'd been so dumb. Of course Saoirse wouldn't leave unless she thought she had to.

Hope rose in me. Maybe there was a chance she'd take me back.

"Like I said," Moina continued, "I can't *tell* you where she's gone. But I can't be responsible if you draw your own conclusions."

She pulled out a piece of paper from the bookcase and gave me a look before she walked over to her tiny dining room table and placed the piece of paper onto the empty tabletop.

What was that piece of paper?

Moina walked up to me and grabbed my arm, squeezing it. "She loves you so much. Do you love her?"

"With everything I am."

Moina's eyes grew wet. "Then go get her."

Moina took a step back and cleared her throat. "I'm going to the bathroom. Which means I'll have to leave you here alone." She gave me a pointed look as if to say, *you get it?*

I nodded slightly, my eyes darting over her shoulder to that piece of paper on the table.

Moina walked out of the room and I pounced on the paper.

It was an acceptance letter addressed to Saoirse Quinn.

From the University of Queensland for a full science scholarship.

My heart warmed.

She did apply for the scholarships. And she got one.

My smart, beautiful girl. You make me so proud.

"You got everything you need?" Moina asked, stepping back into the room.

I kissed her cheek and waved the paper. "Thank you. Hang on, selkie, I'm coming to get you."

I called Declan on my hands-free as soon as I got in the car.

"What's the craic, asshole?" Declan said when he answered the phone.

"Mate, I'm going after Saoirse."

"Fucking finally." I could practically hear Declan fist pumping in the background. The brute was a closet romantic. "You found her, then? Where is she?"

"Australia."

"What? Hang on, we need Danny here, too."

I heard a hold tone. Twenty seconds later two excited voices came over the phone, Declan and Danny.

"Shit, are you really going to go get her?" Danny asked. Declan must have caught him up to speed already.

"Yes," I said.

"Even though you're shit-scared of planes."

I gritted my teeth, already breaking out into a cold fucking sweat at the idea of getting on one of those flying death traps. "Yes."

"Road trip!" Declan called.

"What? The two of you eejits are not coming."

Declan snorted. "We are if you want to use my jet."

His jet?

"Since when do you have a fucking jet?" Danny asked.

"Just bought it," Declan said. "Hawker Beechwood, interior's just been updated."

Danny let out a whistle.

"I *do not* need to use your private jet," I said. "You two *are not* coming."

That was final.

"This is one sweet plane," Danny said as he dropped into the leather seat in front of me.

Declan had just finished taking us on a tour through his new indulgent purchase, a private jet with five cabin areas done up in black leather and wood. Bold and masculine, just like its owner.

"Got a pretty good deal for it too." Declan eased himself onto the couch that ran along one wall. His eyes flicked to me. "You okay, Diarmuid?"

"Fine," I said through my clenched jaw.

He raised his eyebrow. "Really?"

"Really."

"'Cause you look like you're about to rip my armrest to shreds."

I glanced down. My knuckles were white, nails digging into the leather armrest. I forced my fingers open like rusty hinges.

"Well, it's a twenty-four-hour flight including layover in Abu Dhabi. What d'ye say we play a game." Declan pulled out a deck of cards with one hand and a bottle of Macallan aged whiskey with the other.

Danny straightened up. "Hell yeah."

I let out a groan. "Hell no. The last time we played, *someone* lost their eyebrows."

Danny snorted.

Declan chuckled and threw a wadded-up napkin at me. "Don't fall asleep early on us like a fuckin' grandma."

"It's nine in the morning."

"It's six o'clock where we're headed." Declan began to pour healthy fingers of amber liquid into three glasses.

I crossed my arms over my chest. "Not playing. Not drinking."

"You just don't want to get your ass whooped again."

"You have never whooped my ass in poker."

Declan raised an eyebrow.

"Chicken," coughed Danny.

"I think you still owe me fifty quid from the last game," Declan said as he shuffled the deck.

I snorted. "I owe you nothing, cheater."

I knew what they were doing. Trying to distract me. And it was working.

Half an hour later we were crowded around the table, on our third drink and several hands in, using onion and cheese Tayto crisps as our poker "chips". I barely registered it as the plane taxied onto the runway.

Declan leaned over and grabbed one of Danny's

crisps, stuffing it into his mouth.

"Hey, eat your own damn crisps," Danny said, swatting at him.

Declan grinned. "Crisps always taste nicer when they're someone else's."

Danny caught my eye and grinned. He and I both snatched a handful of Declan's crisps, fitting as many of them as possible in our respective mouths.

"Hey!" Declan cried.

"Hmmm, you're totally right, Dex," I said through a mouthful of stolen crisps.

"Tastes so much better," mumbled Danny.

"Bullies," Declan muttered, but he had a smile on his face.

I flinched as the plane's engine roared. As we took off down the runway, I tightened my belt as much as it would go, my heart feeling like it was going to bang out of my fucking chest.

"Your turn, Diarmuid," I heard Danny say.

I squeezed my eyes shut as the point of the plane lifted off and my stomach dropped. Saoirse's face flashed in my head and I felt her all around me.

I'm coming, selkie. I'd cross the fucking world for you.

I don't believe in the paranormal or any of that shit. But in that plane, I swear, I felt her presence like a calming warmth around my shoulders. And I relaxed just a little.

The plane leveled off in the air and my shoulders relaxed completely.

I opened my eyes to see Danny and Declan watching

me.

I shot them both a smirk and dropped a handful of crisps into the pot. "Ready to have your asses handed to ye?"

83

Diarmuid

Australia.

Fucking hot as shite.

Sweat was pooling down the small of my back as Declan, Danny and I strode through the University of Queensland campus.

Danny, sweet-talker that he was, was able to get Saoirse's details off the very smitten college housing administrator. Moody bastard as he was, that boy could sweet-talk the pants off a nun if he wanted to. A handy skill to have when writing love song lyrics.

I was planning on waiting until she'd finished class. Until she'd come home and I could surprise her on her doorstep, when we'd have plenty of time to catch up.

But I just wanted to see her first. To make sure she was okay. Before I crashed back into her life.

My heart hammered as the clock struck on the hour and the students began to pour out of the lecture hall that Saoirse was scheduled to be in. Any second now and I'd see her again.

It'd been almost seven long months since she left me. Seven months that had felt like seven years.

It felt a little like déjà vu as the crowd of students exiting the lecture hall parted and Saoirse stepped out into the open.

Fuck me. She was more stunning than all of my memories of her. Her blonde hair had gotten even longer and the sun had kissed it with even more golden highlights. She was showing of her long legs, now a golden brown, in a pair of denim shorts, a black Nirvana t-shirt tucked into her shorts.

I remembered her wearing my Nirvana shirt all those months ago…and nothing else.

She must have bought her own.

She missed me just as much as I missed her.

I couldn't wait until this evening.

I strode forward from my hiding place in the shadows of a neighbouring building, ready to break into a run towards her.

A boy slung his arm around her shoulder and spun her. I hadn't even noticed him next to her until he touched her.

My blood simmered. If that asshole didn't take his hands off her—

She smiled up at him.

I halted.

She *smiled* up at him.

He leaned down and kissed her.

The sight of it sucker-punched me in the throat. But it didn't prepare me for what came next.

She slid her hand on his cheek and kissed him back.

Danny cussed from my side, confirming that I wasn't dreaming this sight.

Seven months and she'd moved on. With someone her age.

She was happy without me.

She might have not chosen to leave. But she'd found a better life anyway. One I had no business ruining.

My spirit crumpled right then and there. I staggered back, wanting to run away, to scrub my eyes of the sight of Saoirse with someone else, another part of me unable to look away.

They broke apart and walked side by side, his arm still around her shoulders. They looked good together.

Wholesome. Clean. The kind of couple people smiled at when they walked past instead of sneered at.

I'd only ever wanted what was best for her. I only wanted what would make her happy.

I watched them until I couldn't see them anymore, disappeared into another building.

"Let's go," I said, finally getting the strength to turn away.

"You're not going after her?" Declan yelled.

I lowered my chin and shook my head.

Declan grabbed the material of my shirt in his fists. "You," he growled in my face, "are not flying halfway round the fucking world just to give up now."

"But she's with a—"

"Fuck the other guy." Declan's eyes blazed. "She belongs with *you*. Go remind her of that."

84

Saoirse

"Come on, Saoirse," Tim said, "my parents are only up for the weekend and they want to meet you."

"We're not even official," I cried, panic gripping me. "I can't meet your parents."

Tim rolled his eyes. "Saoirse, we've been dating for weeks."

And for weeks we'd been doing this dance. He'd push, I'd pull back.

I tried to move on. I did. But...

"I'm still not ready for anything."

Truthfully, I might never be. Diarmuid still haunted my dreams, still ghosted my heart.

Tim let out an exasperated noise. He'd been so

patient. But he was getting tired of my refusal to let him in. How could I when someone already took up all the space in my heart?

"Maybe we should take a break this weekend," he said quietly. "Have some space from each other. Maybe then you'll figure out what you want."

It was a veiled ultimatum. Either I'd decide to be with him or I would lose him. I should be panicked at this thought.

Why did I feel relief?

After I said goodbye to Tim I went home to a quiet apartment.

"Hello?" I called out as I locked the apartment door behind me, kicking my shoes off at the door.

No answer.

This was weird. There was usually at least one housemate here in the evenings.

I noticed a light coming from the kitchen, heard the hum of one of the appliances. Dammit, someone must have left something on.

I walked in to turn it off, my bare feet cold on the tiles. The light was coming from the oven. Inside was an apple pie.

Who the hell was baking one now? It looked almost done, too.

"Anyone home?" I yelled.

Hearing nothing, I turned off the oven and opened the door to let out the heat.

The smell of apple pie hit me right in the heart. Memories slammed into me so hard that I stumbled back.

Diarmuid and I never got that apple pie.

What I wouldn't give to share a slice of apple pie and vanilla ice cream with Diarmuid.

I sighed. And knew right then that I could not say yes to Tim. He deserved someone who wasn't so broken, someone who could love him back, really love him back.

I walked down the hallway to my bedroom, a cosy room which let in the morning sun. I dropped my school bag on the bed and went to drop my keys and handbag on the dresser when something caught my eye.

A tiny blue velvet box.

What was this?

I dropped my keys and bag beside the box and picked it up, turning it over in my hands. Did one of the girls leave it here by mistake?

Or was this for me?

There was no note. It wasn't my birthday or anything.

I cracked the box open.

Sitting in the centre of the velvet cushion was a tiny silver airplane.

A charm.

Just like the ones on the charm bracelet that I wore all the time.

"Hey, selkie," a voice came from behind me.

Oh my God.

I dropped the box on the dresser, my hands flying to my mouth.

I thought I heard his voice.

I missed him so much I was going mad, hearing his voice when he couldn't possibly be here.

I didn't dare turn around.

It would break my heart to see that he wasn't really there.

"Why won't you look at me?" the voice came again.

This time a sob left my mouth.

It couldn't be. It couldn't be. I was going mad with grief.

Two warm hands slipped onto my arms. The scent of Diarmuid's cologne and man washed over me. This time the sobs could not be contained.

He gently turned me to look at him. He looked so damn good. I wanted to run my fingers through his beard, through his hair now pulled back into a ponytail, trace the ink showing from his sleeve.

All I could do was shake my head.

"What? How are you here?"

He smiled, that perfect gorgeous smile that was only for me. "I flew here, silly."

"But you're scared of planes. Terrified of them."

He shrugged. "I guess I just never had a good enough reason to fly halfway round the world. Until you."

Everything in me melted.

I reached for him but the frown marring his beautiful face stopped me.

"Who is he?" Diarmuid asked, his voice cracking. "Your new boyfriend."

Oh God. He must have seen Tim and me.

I shook my head, all the words, the explanations getting caught around the fist of guilt around my throat. How could he forgive me after seeing me with someone else? How could I have done that to him?

"I'm sorry, Diarmuid," I choked out, unable to look straight at him. "I'm so sorry."

I felt the life drain out of his hands still holding onto my arms. They slid off me and he took a step back from me. The distance ached. It felt like a thousand oceans all over again.

"Just tell me...do you love him?" he whispered. "Does he...make you happy?"

What?

My face snapped up. The pain etched in Diarmuid's face almost broke me. He thought I'd moved on?

I reached for him again. This time nothing would stop me. I touched his face, clasped my hands around his head, tangled my fingers in his hair.

"I tried to move on. I tried. But... I am yours. You have my skin."

"But you looked—"

"We went on some dates. He's a nice boy. But I'm in love with someone else."

His eyes jumped up to meet mine. Hope surged in them.

"You," I said. "I love you. Will love you until my dying breath."

He crushed his mouth onto mine, his arms folding around me. Our heads tilted so we could get closer, tongues warring and dancing with each other.

My head spun, and I felt like I was flying, weightless over the ocean.

He was here.

Diarmuid was here.

He found me.

Even though I left him. Even though I said all those horrible things in that cursed letter.

I pulled away, eyes scanning over his face, greedy for each inch of him. He looked so damn good, better than any of the memories I'd been carrying around for him. "How did you—? And Ava—?"

He shushed me with a finger against my lips. "We have all the time in the world to talk. Later. Right now, I need you, need to feel you. All of you."

He stripped me of all my clothes and I stripped him of his. He lowered me to my bed and climbed in between my legs. I moaned long and loud as he thrust into me in one smooth movement.

He made love to me.

Then he fucked me so hard that I screamed.

Good thing no one else was home.

Epilogue

Saoirse

Three years later…

"Please welcome to the stage, our very own valedictorian of this year's graduating class…Saoirse Quinn."

I grinned as I made my way up to the front of the stage, my navy robes swishing around my feet, golden tassel bobbing off my cap on one side of my vision.

These last three years of college in Australia had been the best of my life.

Diarmuid and I moved in together in the first year we'd lived here, a cute one-bedroom apartment only a ten-minute bus ride from college.

Diarmuid, Danny and Declan had gone thirds in a boxing gym. Diarmuid ran the place but Danny and Declan were silent partners. Made sense as they were both still living elsewhere.

Selkie's Gym in Indooroopilly, Brisbane was doing well. Really well.

Diarmuid had linked up with the local youth groups, and the youth rehab centre had organised training programs to help troubled youths. Boxing gave them focus, purpose and taught them discipline. Boxing helped to channel their anger and rage.

I got to know and love both Declan and Danny, both of them making sure to visit whenever they were touring down under.

The kids at Selkie's Gym especially loved it when the world title holding MMA fighter, Declan Gallagher, came to help train them.

Diarmuid was living his dream, being his own boss and working to make a difference in the lives of teens and kids, just as he was born to do.

I was living mine.

"Dear graduating class," I began. I'd worked all week on this speech, but it'd taken me a lifetime to work on the message. "Back in Ireland everyone thought they knew who I was. My mother was a whore and I was the daughter of a criminal…" I revealed my very personal story to the listening crowd.

I'd gone back and forth about how much to reveal of my past. I was afraid I'd be judged yet again, I'd be scorned or rejected.

It was Diarmuid who'd convinced me otherwise.

"The only way others learn from us is not by our perfections," he had said while we'd been cuddling in bed, "but by our mistakes, our failings, our vulnerabilities. Be bravely you, selkie. Those who deserve you, won't judge you."

That's when I understood why Diarmuid kept his hair long, his scruffy beard and marked his arms and back with his life story.

He was brave. Braver than anyone I'd ever known. He made sure only those who didn't judge him were the only ones who deserved him.

I spotted Diarmuid's face in the crowd. Watching me. Here for me. Smiling for me. My heart felt so full I could have burst.

Beside him were Declan, Danny and Danny's new girlfriend, who I'd not met yet.

I raised my eyebrow at Diarmuid. I'd have to ask him about that later. Danny *never* brought girls around.

I focused back on my speech, not needing to read my notes because I'd memorised them.

"What I have learned most in my time here is that you don't have to accept the life you were given. Make your own. Choose your own. Your own path. Your own future." I caught Diarmuid's eyes and smiled. "Your own family."

I'm so proud of you, he mouthed and grinned back at me.

Tears rimmed my eyes, but I forced myself to go on, despite my wobbly voice.

"Move towards your future with the knowledge that this life is *yours* as you want it to be. Congratulations, class. We are graduated! Here's to *our* future."

I threw my cap in the air amidst cheers and clapping, a sea of blue blurring in front of me.

When the ceremony was over, I was swarmed by the friends I'd made the last few years, all wanting hugs, congratulations and promises to meet at the graduation party someone was having. Including Tim.

After Diarmuid found me, I'd sat down with Tim and explained everything to him. He'd been shocked and upset, but he'd understood. We'd stayed friends. A few months later he found his own happily ever after in the form of an exchange student who was now his long-term girlfriend.

Once I broke free of my fellow students, I rushed through the crowd to find Diarmuid. I didn't have to look very hard. The three Irish boys were all over six two, Diarmuid the tallest at six five.

I ran towards him, a grin on my face. As I reached him, he dropped to one knee and produced a box. I tripped over my robe and almost fell on my face.

He caught my arm and steadied me.

"Hey," he said almost shyly.

"Hey." I'm not sure how my voice was working, my throat was so dry, but it did. Barely.

He let go of me when I was steady and opened the box, looking at me with the most tender look in his eyes. I could hear the hush of the people around us, watching us.

In the centre of the velvet box was a diamond ring, the band decorated with tiny lines.

"W-What is this?" I asked. A stupid question. An excuse to give me time to get over my shock.

"A hint," he said, his voice croaky. He cleared his voice. "It's not for your charm bracelet."

This box.

This ring.

He was asking me to be his wife. I peered closer at the lines, their shape catching my attention.

"Is that...the serotonin molecule engraved along the band?"

He nodded. "The happiness molecule. You make me so happy, Saoirse. Be mine. Be my wife."

I threw myself into his arms and kissed him, amidst the cheers of our friends around us.

"Silly fisherman," I whispered. "I've always been yours. You have my skin, remember?"

He grinned.

"And you have mine."

The End

Dear Readers,

I arrived in Ireland three years ago without a clear sense of "home", thinking I'd move on soon, just as I had done for the previous four countries before that. But this beautiful country and its kind, warm-hearted people have embraced me. I understand what home means and now that I've found it, I don't want to ever leave.

You can't understand how honoured I am to showcase this beautiful adopted country of mine in this new series. I've tried to stay true to Irish-isms, annoying my Irish friends with all manner of questions about Irish life and culture. Any mistakes are all mine and not meant with any offense.

I hope you enjoyed Irish Kiss! Declan and Danny's stories are in the works.

xoxo Sienna

Beautiful Revenge

A Good Wife Novel
Sienna Blake

My name is...*was* Alena Ivanova.

Five years ago, I made a mistake. A big one. One that cost me the only man I will ever love.

Now, in the lonely moors of north England, I live with my cold, cruel husband. My only friend is his daughter from a previous marriage. At least I didn't starve to death during the bitter Russian winter.

When my husband arranges for a potential investor to stay with us, a mysterious self-made millionaire by the name of Mr Wolf, imagine my shock when *he* walks in...

My name is...*was* Dimitri Volkov.

Until she broke me.
Five years I've worked for this moment.
Five years I've dreamed of revenge.
Bit by bit, she will watch her charmed life crumble to the ground.

Then when she needs me the most, when she is desperate, scared and alone like I was all those years ago…

I will destroy her.

Although this book is part of a series, it is a standalone novel.

Out Now

Love Sprung From Hate

Dark Romeo 1
Sienna Blake

I didn't know she was a detective, the only daughter of the Chief of Police.

I didn't know he was a mafia Prince, heir to the Tyrell's bloody empire.

It was only supposed to be one night.

God help me, I can't stop thinking about that night.

So when she walked into the interrogation room, my heart almost stopped.

I can't believe he might have tortured and killed someone.

I have to avoid her at all costs.

I will be his downfall.

So begins a deadly game of cat and mouse, of blood and lust, of love and duty, and of an attraction so fierce the consequences are inevitable...

Inspired by Shakespeare's Romeo and Juliet, this is a retelling for mature audiences. Don't enter the Underworld if you're scared of the dark.

Out now

Get your FREE ecopy of Paper Dolls!

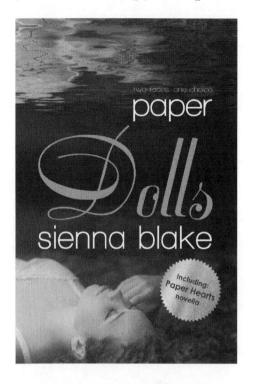

Join my Reader Group

for your free ecopy of my full-length, standalone romantic suspense, Paper Dolls. You'll also get access to exclusive giveaways, a sneak peek into what's coming up next, vote on covers and blurbs, and interact with me personally.

http://bit.ly/SiennasDarkAngels

Or sign up for my Newsletter

for new release, sales & giveaways alerts:

www.siennablake.com

Did you enjoy Irish Kiss?

The best way you can show me some love is by posting a review at your retailer! Don't tell me, tell the world what you think. (Then message me so I can thank you personally.) It really helps other readers to decide whether my books are for them. And the number of reviews I get is really important. Thank you!

If you're a Blogger,

please signup to my VIP Bloggers List for ARC opportunity alerts:
http://bit.ly/SiennaVIPBloggers
Blogs will be verified.

Stay sexy,
Sienna
xoxo

Stalk me! I like it

www.siennablake.com
www.facebook.com/SiennaBlakeAuthor
www.instagram.com/SiennaBlakeAuthor

Books by Sienna Blake

Bound Duet
Bound by Lies (#1)
Bound Forever (#2)

Paper Dolls

Dark Romeo Trilogy
Love Sprung From Hate (#1)
The Scent of Roses (#2)
Hanging in the Stars (#3)

A Good Wife (Standalone Series)
Beautiful Revenge
Mr. Blackwell's Bride
The (Fake) Princess Bride ~ *coming Fall 2018*

Irish Kiss (Standalone Series)
Irish Kiss
Teacher's Kiss ~ *coming in 2018*

Acknowledgements

Firstly, thank you to my FlexHuddlers who helped make this book what it is. For answering the zillion questions I had on Irish-isms. Thank you for being like family to me. Especially to Sinead who brought me into her family and home when I needed help.

Special thanks to the real Diarmuid for letting me use his name.

To Kathy of Book Detailing, and Christie and Anita of Proof Positive. Thank you for being part of my editing team. My book is in the best hands with you all.

Thank you lovely Julia Lis for your priceless feedback on an early version. Love you!

To Terrie of Just Let Me Read. Thank you for everything you do. I could not do this without you.

To my Facebook Reader Group. Thank you for your input on my title, cover and blurb. Love you all. Thank you all for being a tiny safe haven online when I was going through a rough time.

To my fabulous early reviewers and book bloggers. You guys. I'm touched that any of you want to read and review anything I write. Thank you, endlessly!

Thank you Giorgia for that hot af cover. We had to go through about a million drafts, but we got there and it's stunning!

If I've forgotten anyone, it's because of a lack of memory not a lack of care.

Finally, to you, my dearest readers. For your messages of support, for every book you purchase and every time you recommend me to a friend. Thank you for making this little girl's dreams come true.

About Sienna

Sienna Blake is a storyteller. An inksinger of Happily Ever Afters with grit, and alter ego of a *USA Today* Bestselling Author.

She loves all things that make her heart race—rollercoasters, thrillers and rowdy unrestrained sex.

If she told you who she really was, she'd have to kill you. Because of her passion for crime and forensics, she'd totally get away with your murder. *wink*